DARK TIDE RISING

ANNE PERRY

DARK TIDE RISING

A William Monk Novel

BALLANTINE BOOKS • NEW YORK

Published in the United States by Ballantine Books, an imprint of Random House, a division of Penguin Random House LLC, New York.

BALLANTINE and the HOUSE colophon are registered trademarks of Penguin Random House LLC.

Originally published in the United Kingdom by Headline Publishing Group, London.

ISBN 9780399179914
Ebook ISBN 9780399179921

Printed in the United States of America on acid-free paper

randomhousebooks.com

2 4 6 8 9 7 5 3 1

FIRST U.S. EDITION

Book design by Karin Batten

To Clay Bunker and Christina Hogue Bunker
for their friendship

DARK TIDE RISING

1

MONK SAT BESIDE THE fire and felt the heat seep through him. Outside was the kind of clinging silence that only fog brings. The river was shrouded, and dusk came early this time of the year. Monk was unusually conscious of being happy. This deep sense of peace was not a casual thing. He looked at Hester in the chair opposite him and found himself smiling.

He was not aware of the first knock on the door. It was only when Hester stood up that he realized what the sound had been. He rose quickly. "No, I'll go." Reluctantly, he went into the hall and unlocked the front door.

Sir Oliver Rathbone stood on the step, the porch light glistening on droplets of fog that covered his gray hat and the shoulders of his coat. His lean face was without its usual aura of wit.

There was no wind at all, and yet a breath of chill accompanied him.

"Come in," Monk said quickly, stepping back to allow him room.

Rathbone obeyed and pulled the door closed behind him. He shivered, as if suddenly aware of how cold he was. He took off his hat and coat and hung them on the hall stand, stuffing his gloves in his pockets.

"It must be bad," Monk said. They had known each other for years—in fact, for nearly all of the fifteen years since the Crimean War had ended in 1856. There was no need for social niceties.

"It is," Rathbone replied. He both worked and lived on the north side of the Thames, so for him to have crossed the river to visit Monk at home meant the issue could not wait, even just until morning.

Monk led the way to the sitting room and opened the door into the warmth.

"I'm sorry," Rathbone said to Hester. They, too, had known each other long and well. Rathbone had met her when she was a nurse, newly home from the Crimea and still believing she could change the world of medical treatment and its attitude toward nursing, and women in medicine in general. That seemed like a long time ago now. But the cause, even now, was hardly begun.

"You look frozen," she said with understanding. "Tea?" Then she reconsidered. "Whisky?"

Rathbone smiled very slightly. "No, thank you. I need to keep a clear head." He turned to Monk. "I know I'm intruding, but it can't wait . . ." He sat down in one of the chairs next to the fire.

Hester said nothing, but she prepared to listen intently.

Monk merely nodded and took the seat opposite Rathbone.

"A man came to me an hour or two ago in a state of extreme distress." Rathbone's expression reflected his own understanding of pain. "His wife has been kidnapped. Her life is forfeit if he does not pay a ransom, which is a fortune. He is a wealthy man, and has succeeded in raising the amount—"

"When was she taken?" Monk interrupted.

"I know what you must be thinking," Rathbone replied with a bleak smile. "How did he raise the money so quickly? Unless he had it in a safe somewhere, this would not have been possible. She was taken yesterday, which, if you remember, was actually a beautiful day for this time of year. He was given until tomorrow, at about this time. The exchange is to take place—"

"Why the devil didn't he report it immediately?" Monk interrupted him.

"He intends to pay. What he wants of us is—"

"Us?" Monk cut across him again. "If he wants the police, he should have gone to the regular London police, and yesterday, for heaven's sake, when the trail was hot!"

Rathbone shook his head. "He doesn't. She was taken from the riverbank, which makes it your area. And the ransom is to be paid on Jacob's Island, which—"

"I know what it is!" Even though several years had passed since that bleak case, Monk shivered involuntarily at the memories the name "Jacob's Island" conjured in his imagination. He could still see the fat man sinking slowly into the tidal ooze, his mouth open, screaming, until the mud cut him off, and inch by inch he disappeared from sight. His body had never been found.

Monk came back to the moment: to the firelight, to Hester, now sitting and leaning toward him, concern in her face; to the lamplight on Rathbone's hair, which had more silver in it than before. Jacob's Island was one of the worst slums in London. On the river's edge, it was not literally an island, but a region of interconnecting waterways with old offices and wharfs. The warehouses built upon them were sinking slowly into their foundations as they rotted away and collapsed one on top of another. Jacob's Island could be reached by land across one bridge, and by water through several landing piers.

"He wants the River Police to go with him to the exchange, the payment for his wife's—Kate Exeter's—life," Rathbone said quietly. "That's all he came about. He doesn't expect you to catch the kidnappers, or to save the money, just to see that the exchange is made, and he and Kate leave there safely."

"Kate Exeter?" Monk turned the name over in his mind. There was something familiar about it, but he could not place it.

"Harry Exeter," Rathbone said. "His first wife died. Kate is his second. About twenty years younger than he. He's devoted to her."

Compassion showed in Rathbone's face. He himself had married a second time, only recently. He had a happiness he had never believed possible, after the disappointment of his first marriage, followed by bitter loneliness. Rathbone knew how exquisitely precious happiness was, and how fragile. He tried not to think of the possibility of losing it again, but it was clear in his eyes, in the strain of his position, that his empathy with Harry Exeter was based in his own emotions, not imagination.

Monk did not need explanations. "So, he spent yesterday and today getting the money," he concluded.

"Yes. He has nearly all of it, and his assurance of the rest tomorrow. It's the price of five good-sized London family houses, in a decent area," Rathbone replied. "I came to you tonight because Exeter's in my chambers now. I want you to meet him. Get all the information you can. You'll need tomorrow to plan. He has to hand over the money himself. It's part of the bargain."

"And bringing the police into it?" The consequences of even one slip were appalling.

"Doesn't matter," Rathbone said gravely. "He's allowed to have at least one man go with him. He insisted on that. He doesn't know the place, and he pointed out that alone in an area like that, carrying a bag full of money, he'd be lucky if he made it as far as the agreed rendezvous spot."

"Why wouldn't they pick some reasonable place?" Monk asked, but already he knew the answer. Jacob's Island was a warren that the ordinary Londoner would be utterly lost in, frightened, disoriented, always afraid of the rising tide. "I'll come and meet him," he said before Rathbone could answer him. He stood up. "Get all the information I can. Tomorrow I'll choose my men and speak to them. Some of them know Jacob's Island fairly well. Although the damn place is changing all the time."

Rathbone stood as well. "Thank you." He turned to Hester. "I apologize," he said, "but it should all be over after tomorrow night. Exeter will be considerably poorer, but his wife will be safe, even if she does have nightmares for a while."

"They pass," Hester said ruefully.

Monk looked at her, concerned. She had been kidnapped not so long ago. He could recall her waking in the night, gasping, fighting the blankets, once even weeping uncontrollably. He had held her close, assuring her. And now she was thinking of this woman who had been kidnapped and was waiting, terrified, perhaps on Jacob's Island, trusting her husband could and would pay the ransom.

"We'll get her back safely," Monk promised. "It's the money they want. And thank God Exeter seems to have it, and is willing to pay." He glanced out the window. It was dark outside now. The fog smothered everything.

Hester smiled. "If she's as lucky as I was, the kidnappers will be caught as well. Go now! Poor Exeter will be frantic with worry. Assure him, as much as you can."

He smiled and leaned forward to kiss her quickly on the cheek. Her skin was warm, soft as always, and he inhaled the fragrance of her hair.

Rathbone was already waiting at the front door, his hat and coat on. He undid the latch, grimaced as he saw the fog was thicker than before, and stepped out into it. Monk followed after him, his coat on, too, though he still felt the damp cling to him immediately. He closed the door behind him and heard Hester lock it. He followed Rathbone down the familiar path to the street. By the time he reached it and looked back, the house was already swallowed up in the thick darkness.

From somewhere down the river a foghorn gave its long, mournful cry. There was no other sound. Even their footfalls were muffled on the pavement.

"There'll be no ferries over the river," Monk remarked. "We'll have to see if we can find a hansom on Union Street. The Rotherhithe road is right on the water, and it'll be even thicker there."

Rathbone fell in step with him without commenting. The nearest bridge was a stiff walk from where they were, and Lincoln's Inn, where Rathbone's chambers were, was a good deal farther than that.

It was half an hour before they found a cab, almost on the bridge.

They heard the horse's hoofs on the cobbles, muffled by the distorted echoes. It was almost upon them before they saw its lamps approaching. Monk stepped into the street and caught the horse's bridle, bringing it to a stop.

"Hey!" the driver shouted, fear sharpening his voice as he raised his whip.

Monk saw the shadow of the whip before it could strike him. "Police!" He moved forward, allowing his face to be seen, if dimly, in the small circle of light. "We need a ride to Lincoln's Inn, please. Double fare."

The driver grunted. "Up front?" he asked.

Monk fished in his pocket, and Rathbone did the same. They handed over the coins gratefully and climbed inside.

It still took them nearly three-quarters of an hour. Rathbone's chambers were all lit, and his clerk opened the door before Rathbone had time to ring the bell.

"I'll get you tea, sir," the clerk said. "And a couple of sandwiches. Would cold beef be satisfactory?"

"It'll be perfect," Rathbone said warmly.

"I already took the liberty of serving Mr. Exeter, sir. He doesn't look well, poor man."

Rathbone thanked him and led the way to his own suite of rooms. He opened the door, Monk on his heels.

Immediately a man standing at the hearth turned to face them. He was above average height. His thick, fair hair was liberally sprinkled with gray, visible mostly at the temples. Monk guessed he would have been good-looking, were he not frantically worried, his skin slick with sweat.

"Monk?" he asked, stepping forward. "Are you the commander of the Thames River Police?" Without waiting for an answer, he grasped Monk's hand. "Thank you for coming. It's a filthy night, I know. But this can't wait. I am Harry Exeter . . ."

"Yes, I'm Monk." He took the man's hand briefly. "Rathbone told me about your situation."

Exeter was shaking, in spite of the warmth of the room. "I've got almost all the money. I'm picking up the rest tomorrow. I have to be the one to hand it over. Don't argue with me about that. They insisted. Kate . . ."

"I won't argue with you, Mr. Exeter," Monk assured him. "I'd like to know as much as you can tell me. That's the best we can do tonight. Tell me what you know, and what you suspect. If you have ideas of who could be behind this. And, for heaven's sake, sit down, man! Clear your head as much as you can. I have some idea how you feel."

"How can you?" Exeter asked, his voice raised as if a sudden fury moved him. "How can you possibly know?"

"Because my wife was kidnapped a little while ago. I was lucky, I got her back. And we'll do everything possible to get your wife back," Monk replied.

"Oh . . ." Exeter looked at the floor. "I'm sorry. I . . . didn't think. When something like this happens, you feel so helpless . . . so alone. Everyone else looks safe, and you . . . you don't think anyone else can know how you feel."

"I know. I felt desperate, too. But we got her back safely."

Exeter searched his face, as if trying to judge how much of what Monk said was true, how much an attempt to calm him.

Monk gave him a brief, tight smile. "Don't worry, Mr. Exeter, your wife will be returned to you before we do anything to catch the kidnappers. Have you any idea who they are or why it was she who was taken? Any enemies?"

"Kate? Never!" he said vehemently.

"I meant you . . . your enemies."

"Oh! Yes, I suppose so. Every successful man makes enemies. I'm good at what I do. When I win a contract, it necessarily means that someone else loses. But that's business. I lose, sometimes. I don't hate the man who wins. I learn from it!"

"If anything comes to your mind, do let me know," Monk dismissed the subject. "Now tell me what happened."

"Kate had luncheon with her cousin, Celia Darwin. They are quite close. It was a lovely day, if you remember, nothing like today. They walked along the riverbank in the afternoon."

"Where, exactly?"

"Over Chelsea Bridge, and then along Battersea Park—"

"Were there many people about?"

"I suppose so. I really don't know. Celia was distraught! Poor woman felt as if it were somehow her fault. I couldn't get a lot of sense out of her. I'm sorry."

"It doesn't matter. We can ask your wife when we get her back. What did Celia say?"

"That a young man came up and asked the way, then started some sort of conversation. Celia's attention was diverted, and the next moment a group of people came by and Celia and Kate were separated, and when the newcomers were gone, Kate was, too . . . and so was the young man. She thought at first it was nothing, just silliness, but then when Kate didn't come back, she grew frightened and called for help. The police came, but there was no sign of Kate."

"The police looked for her?"

Exeter's expression filled with a mixture of anger and desperation. He seemed to be trying everything he could to keep his voice steady. "One pretty young woman, one plain one. A young man who apparently was handsome." He spread his hands helplessly. "They drew their own conclusions. Celia told them Kate was married, and would never do such a thing. Celia was so upset. She is plain and older, and she has a pronounced limp. They thought she was feeling alone, unwanted, and they didn't believe her. They intended to reassure her, but they only ended up insulting her."

"And then?" Monk prompted.

"She couldn't tell them anything more. They sent her home."

Monk nodded and returned to the subject of the kidnappers and the demand for ransom.

"And then they sent me a lock of Kate's hair, and a piece of her dress, and a demand for money. They were all in an envelope that was pushed through my letter box." For a moment, Exeter lost control of his emotions and buried his face in his hands.

Monk was not sure whether to stop, or if that would only draw attention to Exeter's momentary breakdown. He decided to continue. "Did you answer them? Was it required?" he asked.

"No," Exeter replied after a moment. "There was no way to answer them. They told me how much money they wanted, or they would . . . kill her. And how and when I was to meet them and make the exchange." He lifted his face up. "Jacob's Island, for God's sake! It's a hellhole!"

"Do you know it?" Monk was surprised. As far as he knew, Exeter developed expensive land, and built even more expensive houses on it.

"By repute. I haven't been there. Why on earth would I? That's another reason I need help. I imagine you have to know it?"

Monk gritted his teeth. "Yes. What instructions did they give you? Any particular time?"

"They drew a sort of map. I gather there are tunnels and passages when you get across the bridge and into the worst part of it."

"Do you have the map with you?"

"Yes," said Exeter. He fished in his inside jacket pocket and passed Monk an extremely scruffy piece of paper. It was dog-eared, partly torn, but when it was opened out, it was drawn clearly enough to show directions for access by way of the river, through a couple of very old, collapsing houses, and into a tunnel that divided. An arrow was drawn one way. There was some wreckage to be climbed over and around, and more cellars, stairs, and tunnels.

"What time?" Monk asked, his stomach knotting up because he was already certain of the answer.

"What?" Exeter looked at him.

"Let me guess . . . about half-past three . . . four . . . ?"

"Four o'clock. How did you know?" Exeter was incredulous. He glanced at Rathbone, who also looked startled.

"Dusk at this time of year," Monk answered. "And low tide. By five the tide will already be rising again, cutting off some of these tunnels." He took a long, deep breath. "We'll do it, Mr. Exeter. But there is no room for error. None at all."

"Oh God!" Exeter buried his face in his hands.

Monk waited a few moments for Exeter to recover himself, then continued, "I will speak to my men, choose which to bring, and we will meet at the Wapping Police Station at quarter-past three—"

"That's early," Exeter interrupted.

"We have to go by water to get to the place marked on your . . . map. If we are early we can stand off, a hundred yards away. We can't afford to be late."

"No . . . no, of course not. I'm sorry."

"So meet us at the station. You know where it is?"

"Yes."

"At quarter-past three. With the money . . . or as much as you have."

"I'll have it all." Exeter said it without hesitation, but his voice was hoarse.

"Good. We'll get her back." Monk held out his hand, and Exeter grasped it.

2

Monk was up well before dawn the following morning, and by daylight he was already on the water. It was going to be a long day, and he had to get all other business out of the way, plus make plans about meeting the kidnappers, long before three o'clock. The wind had risen in the night and the fog was almost gone. Just a few gray veils of it hung over the center of the river, and even those shredded when the slack tide turned and came back up on the flood. The swell of the water carried the ferry Monk was on, and he felt it with misgiving. In a few hours they would be on Jacob's Island, aware that time was short, the water deepening, making the mud softer, hungrier, moving the planks and loosening the rotting boards. Half an hour, and it would be enough to knock a man off balance. An hour, and it would suck him down and drown him.

He shivered as the ferry passed in the shadow of the huge boats anchored in the Pool of London, awaiting their turns to unload. Forty more yards and he would be at the Wapping Stairs and the Thames

River Police Station. The night watch would have kept the potbellied stove alight, and inside it would be warm.

The last few yards of the water were choppy. The ferry swung alongside the stairs. Monk paid the fare with a word of thanks and stepped out of the boat, about the same size as the police rowing boats he was used to. Still, it took balance and care. Anyone who slipped on the wet stone would be in the water in seconds, drenched to the skin.

He ascended slowly, even though he knew every inch of the steps. When he came to the top he felt the wind catch him again. He was glad of his thick peacoat and the muffler round his neck. He walked quickly across the open dock and through the police station door.

"Morning, sir," Bathurst said cheerfully. He was young and keen, although after all-night duty he had to be tired. "You're early, sir." His face shadowed with a flicker of anxiety. He started to speak, and then changed his mind.

"You're right," Monk said bleakly. "There's a reason I'm here this early, and without breakfast. Anything to report for the night?"

"No, sir. Marbury and Walcott aren't back yet, but it's been a quiet night. I think the fog kept everybody in. No point in stealing if you can't see what you've got."

"Then write it up and go home and get a good day's sleep. I want you bright and full of energy back here at three o'clock this afternoon."

"Sir?" That was well before his next shift began, and Bathurst's uncertainty about whether to point that out showed clearly on his face. He was twenty-six, but sometimes to Monk he looked about nineteen.

"We've got an operation later today, at turn of the tide. I want all my best men on it. Is there any tea left?"

Bathurst turned away, but not before Monk had seen the flush of pleasure in his face. "Yes, sir. I'll fetch you a mug. There's bread I could toast, if you like?"

"Yes," Monk accepted. "Thank you." Poor devil. Bathurst would be a good deal less pleased when he knew they had to go to Jacob's Island. He hated the place as much as everyone else.

Monk had eaten two slices of toast and drunk a large enamel mug full of hot, slightly bitter tea by the time the other two men came back. Hooper arrived, and Bathurst eventually left.

"He looks cheerful," Hooper remarked, taking his heavy seaman's coat off. He had been in the Merchant Navy before joining the River Police, and he knew how to dress for all weathers. He hung it up and turned to look at Monk. He had a comfortable face, strong features, and steady blue eyes, often narrowed against the wind or the light off the water. He was a big man, with a rare, sweet smile. "You're in early," he remarked. "Something happened?"

Monk signaled him to close the office door. Other men would arrive in a moment or two, and he wanted to keep the Exeter case private, until he could decide who else to use on it.

Hooper closed the door silently and then, without asking, sat in the chair opposite Monk's desk. They had worked many years together, since Devon had died and Monk had replaced him as commander. When Orme was killed, Hooper had taken over his position as Monk's second. There had never been any formal decision. The whole battle, with the gunrunners and the fire, had demanded the utmost from every man. Their grief afterward had prevented any celebration of a promotion. No one felt any pleasure in filling a dead man's place.

Hooper seemed to know something was troubling Monk, and he was waiting to learn what it was.

"We have a big task later today," Monk answered the unasked question. "I told Bathurst to come back, but I haven't decided who else to use, or how many men we'll need." He looked at Hooper's face. He was a hard man to read. There was strength in him, and beneath it an unusual gentleness, but scars of hardship and bad weather at sea, experiences that he told no one, made his expression more opaque the longer you looked at him.

"Oliver Rathbone came to my house last night," Monk went on. "He represents a man whose wife was kidnapped on Saturday afternoon. The kidnappers want a lot of money, but he can raise it. He wants us to go with him to make certain the exchange takes place without any trouble."

"Us? You mean the Thames River Police?" Hooper's eyebrows rose. "Why?"

Monk breathed out slowly. "Partly because she was taken off the riverbank at Battersea."

Hooper stiffened.

"But mostly because the exchange is to take place at low water this afternoon, which is just before dusk," Monk finished.

He saw Hooper's face change. There was no perceptible movement, but it was as if somewhere inside him a light had gone out. Perhaps Monk saw it because it reflected perfectly how he felt himself.

Hooper took a breath and asked the practical questions. "The husband told you? How does he know she was taken from the river walk? Did anybody see it happen? Who is he? How did they get in touch with him?"

"Yes, he told me. He doesn't want to fight over it. He's more than willing to pay. He just wants his wife back, and safe. His name is Harry Exeter. Big property developer. Got a project going in Lambeth. He's done quite a few things."

"Rich? Or pretending to be?"

"He says he's going to get the last of the money today. He doesn't seem concerned about it." Monk remembered Exeter's dismissal of the amount, which was more than even most professional men would earn in a decade. And he spoke of it as if it was only an idea in his head, not a reality. Monk wondered what he had sold, or pledged, to come up with so much in so short a time.

Hooper frowned. "You didn't say how they got in touch with him."

"A note was pushed through the letter box."

"Was that the first he knew of it?"

"No, she was out walking with a cousin, a Celia Darwin, when she was taken. But apparently Miss Darwin is somehow disabled, and couldn't do much about it. She called for the police, but of course the kidnappers and Mrs. Exeter were long gone by the time the police got there. I would guess almost certainly in a rowing boat, for them to disappear so completely and so quickly."

"Does that make it our case?" Hooper asked.

"Not specifically, but they want the exchange at Jacob's Island." He saw Hooper's mouth tighten. "Exeter asked Rathbone for help, and Rathbone came to me. I think that was Exeter's hope, God help him." He meant it. What was getting to Monk more than his dislike of any of the waterside slums, the alleys, the slack-water refuse on the tide, the rotting wood, the stench was putting himself in Exeter's place, and imagining how he would feel if it was Hester, or anyone he knew. This was the price of caring, and caring is a driving force of life. He had discovered that slowly, step by step, in the years since his life had begun for a second time, when he had awoken from an accident without a past, except in other people's memories. He seemed to have no family or friends who wanted to claim him. Day by day he had learned why, at least in part. He had lost none of his skills, physical or mental. He was still the best detective in the Metropolitan Police. But he was also a man with enemies, many of them perhaps deserved. He did not like much of what he had learned about himself.

Finally, the police had dismissed him. He had worked as an independent inquiry agent for a while, but it had been an erratic living. Then he had had a case that led him to the Thames River Police and, at the end of that affair, he had joined them.

Now he knew the pleasure and the pain of friendship, of love, of belonging. Without knowing anything of Harry Exeter, he imagined being in his place.

Many years ago, Hester had been a nurse with Florence Nightingale in the Crimean War. She was stubborn, brave, quick-tempered, and loyal. She had a fierce tongue that had got her into all kinds of trouble. She always kept her promises, however wild, and she cared about all sorts of people, mostly those the rest of society preferred to ignore.

If Kate Exeter was anything like Hester, her loss would leave an emptiness that nothing else would fill. If Monk was alone, he would hear nothing but silence, forever—and having known love, the loneliness would be vast enough to consume him.

"Sir . . ." Hooper broke into his thoughts. "Has anyone spoken to this cousin?"

Monk smiled bleakly. "Not yet. It's a little early to call. Apparently, she was upset yesterday and the police didn't think she'd be of much use. They hardly even believed her account at first."

"Is there anything else to try?"

"No. Exeter only wants us to assist him in paying the money and getting his wife back. And on Jacob's Island, that's no foregone conclusion."

Hooper's face showed his disgust. It was only the slightest change from his normal expression, but the alteration was clear to anyone who knew him as well as Monk did. He was certain he understood what was in Hooper's mind.

"I don't know if she's still alive," Monk said. "The thought occurred to me, too, and I daresay it has to Exeter."

Hooper looked at him quickly.

"Of course," Monk went on, "they may have no intention of handing her over. She could already be dead. But they want the money, so it's not likely. If she's not alive, we'll have to take the kidnappers, whatever Exeter says. But if she is, getting her back is our priority. It's what we're there for." He said the words slowly, as if he thought Hooper might misunderstand, though he knew better. He was repeating them to himself. He was afraid that his own emotions might override his judgment, and he would make choices he would regret. "But once Kate is safe . . ." He did not need to finish.

"Jacob's Island," Hooper said. "There is a score of ways in and out of that place, 'specially at low tide. We're taking no risks." It was not a question but a reminder that they would easily lose their own men if they were trapped in the low-lying passages as the incoming tide swirled through the ruins, eddying in places, carrying away more timber, shifting mud, and debris.

"I know!" Monk said sharply. He did not need reminding. He was not the only man to have nightmares about being trapped by a newly fallen timber below the high tide just as the filthy water rose.

"Who are we taking?" Hooper included himself without question.

Monk had been considering it since Rathbone had left the previous evening. Each time he had woken in the night, the question had come back. "You, me, Bathurst," he began. "Laker . . ."

Hooper looked at him steadily. Laker was young, cocky, ambitious, far too often flippant when he should have been serious. On the surface, he seemed pretty full of his own opinions. But ever since Monk had seen his courage in the gunfight on the smugglers' ship three years ago, and his loyalty and grief over Orme's death, he had not doubted Laker's worth. None of which stopped him from criticizing him, or slapping back his occasional insolence, but the trust was there, and Laker knew it. And, of course, Hooper knew it, too. He had been as much a part of that dreadful night as Monk himself.

"We'll need more than that," Hooper reminded him. "Even if we knew where we're going to meet them, there are at least six ways out of any part of the place. And I don't suppose we know how many kidnappers there are?"

"No idea," Monk replied. "We could manage four or five of them."

"I'd say we need as many as . . . six. Judiciously placed, they should be able to stop any escape," Hooper said thoughtfully. "Two more."

"Marbury . . . ?" Monk made it more of a question. Hooper had worked with Marbury more than he had. Marbury was a lean, quiet man from the Kent coast. He had worked the marshes of the estuary and was used to the vast skies and tangled waterways, with their interconnecting rivers. The flight paths of birds fascinated him.

Hooper smiled. "Yes, sir. He watches things. Good at observing the smallest differences. Good on tides, too."

"Jones?"

Hooper hesitated.

"What?" Monk asked.

"Not yet," Hooper replied. "He'll be good in a couple of years. Too green now."

"He's one to watch," Monk said. "He's good with oars. Guide a boat anywhere."

"Too quick," Hooper said. "Needs to take a second look before he acts."

Monk was unconvinced. He was interested to see if Hooper would stick with his view. "Sometimes you need quick action, or the chance is lost. We'll be fighting the darkness and the rising tide, as well as the kidnappers. We can't afford to wait while someone makes up his mind."

"What none of us can afford is a man who jumps before he looks," Hooper argued. "You asked me, sir. I say take Walcott. He's a stubborn little bastard. Snappy, like a terrier. Got no fear, once he's on the scent."

Monk smiled in spite of himself. The description was a good one. "Right! Then Marbury and Walcott it is, with Bathurst, Laker, and you and me. We should be on the water by half-past three, and at Jacob's Island before four." He took a chart out of the wide drawer that held them and spread it over his desk. It showed the part of the river where Jacob's Island was, with mud-banks and tidal ebb and flow marked very clearly. Made that spring, it was the most up-to-date chart available.

Hooper studied it wordlessly and Monk followed his gaze, noting the half-sunken slipways, the mooring posts that emerged from the mud like rotting teeth, the channels where the water was deeper and the current correspondingly swifter, the wharfs that were still usable.

Of course, one extra-high tide could alter them considerably. The late September neap tide this year had been very high indeed.

"No time to check it," Hooper said, thinning his lips as he spoke. "And we can't afford to ask now. Word would get around. Did they ask Exeter to go alone? Make any threats about bringing in police?" He looked troubled.

"No. Exeter said as long as they got the money, that was it. He begged me to come, with men. All he cares about is getting his wife back. He's afraid they'll double-cross him at the last moment."

"The kidnappers may kill her anyway, if they see us," Hooper pointed out. "Has he really thought this through?"

"I don't know. He's just terrified of going in there alone and not being able to get out again. I'll go in with him, up to just short of the meeting place, and then they can make the exchange. Six of us armed and dressed like off-duty merchant sailors or dockers should be enough," Monk continued.

"More like river pirates or beggars," Hooper replied. "Seamen can do better than Jacob's Island. If I was sleeping rough, I'd rather be somewhere the tide doesn't reach."

Monk was annoyed with himself. He knew the river well enough to have thought of this. Not that the outward appearance would be so different, but the way of moving or holding one's head, sheltering from the wind or hiding from sight, would. Think like a thief and you would have the best chance of looking like one.

He stood up. "Right. We'll tell the men and decide where they'll go in. We'll have to do some careful positioning to block every way out. You go and see if you can find Celia Darwin. I'll give you her address. She may have noticed something. It's not much of a chance, from what Exeter said of her, but we'd be stupid to overlook it. Whatever happens, be back here at three." He wrote down the address Exeter had given him and handed it to Hooper.

Hooper looked at it. "Ceylon Street. Where's that?"

"Just off the Battersea dock road. Not so far from where Kate Exeter was taken, but nothing like Southwark Park, where the Exeters live, even though it's close. Exeter said Celia was the cousin from the side of the family that married down. He didn't say his side married up, but the fact that he said anything at all suggests he's . . ." He looked for the word.

"Jumped-up," Hooper supplied for him.

"Yes," Monk agreed. "Doesn't make him any less a victim. Or his wife. Apparently, she liked the cousin enough to be close to her. They were friends. Be patient with her, Hooper. She may be . . ."

"Upset. She's not worth much if she isn't, sir."

Monk smiled again. "Yes. Doesn't mean she won't remember something."

CELIA DARWIN HAD BEEN at home in her very modest house on Ceylon Street when Harry Exeter had called upon her. The previous day had been the worst of her life. All past pain or disappointment was swallowed up by the loss of Kate, the cousin who was like a younger sister to her.

She ran to the door to answer it herself, not giving her one maid the chance. She flung the door open and saw Exeter on the step. For a moment hope surged up in her; then she saw his face, and it died.

He came in, almost pushing her out of the way.

"What is it?" she asked. "What has happened? You've heard something?" She followed him into her small parlor and closed the door behind them.

He turned to face her immediately. He looked terrified. His skin was drained of all color.

"They want money," he said. "More than everything I have . . . or they'll kill her."

He already knew that she had nothing, not even anything to sell. The few pieces of jewelry her mother had left her were worthless. He had pointed that out, in one of their more unpleasant exchanges.

"What can I—" she started.

"I know you loved her . . ." he began.

"I still do!" She would never have dared raise her voice to him before, but now nothing else mattered.

"I know," he said quickly. "And Kate knew—knows it, too. I know how to raise the money, but I . . . I should ask your permission, even if it is actually Maurice who has the power. Celia . . . please?"

She did not hesitate. He was referring to Kate's inheritance from her maternal grandmother, which she would come into when she was thirty-three, just over a year from now. If she died before that time, the money would go to Celia and her cousin Maurice Latham. He was a lawyer, and naturally the trustee. One did not give such responsibility to a woman.

"Of course," she said instantly. "Will it be enough?"

He relaxed. His whole body eased as if the pain had left him. He smiled at her through sudden tears in his eyes. "Yes. Yes it will just do it, with what else I have. Thank you, Celia. I . . . I knew you would agree . . . but I still had to ask you."

"And Maurice?" she pressed. She had little affection for him, although she had known him on and off for most of her life. He had always seemed condescending, as if he regarded her as something of a failure, having neither a useful occupation nor a husband and children to care for. And she owned that he was probably in some senses right. She had not these things. She was of a class too high to be a servant and not high enough to have inherited anything but the smallest means. Nor was she pretty, with that slight limp.

Exeter was slow to answer. "Oh, Maurice will be all right, I'm sure. I had to ask you first. Thank you, Celia. I know you love Kate, and would do anything . . . you'll be on my side, if I have to argue with Maurice . . . won't you?"

Was that why he had come to her first? Maurice was a pompous man at times, but he would never refuse to save Kate's life! It was her money, after all . . . unless she died before she could inherit it. But that was a vile thought. Celia could feel her face heat up at even allowing it into her mind. "But it won't be necessary," she said.

"No," Exeter agreed. "I didn't mean to . . . Celia, I'm . . ."

"I know," she said quickly. "We all are. There's no need to explain yourself. None at all. Go and speak to Maurice, and get this done. Don't waste time with explanations. Just get her back!"

"I will," he said with a bleak smile. "Thank you."

He had turned and found his own way to the front door, and she had heard it close behind him.

It was going to be all right! They were going to get Kate back. The nightmare would be over. Thank God.

HOOPER TURNED MONK'S REMARKS about the cousin, Celia Darwin, over and over in his mind, as he made his way upriver from Wapping to the pier just south of Chelsea Bridge, and then walked the mile or so to Ceylon Street. If Celia was out, he would have to wait for her return. Tomorrow would be too late to be of any use.

Hooper did not know women well. He had joined the Merchant Navy as a young man. His home was unsettled, his father rough-tongued, a man more used to expressing himself with his hands than with words. When his mother died, Hooper had been happy enough to escape.

He had come ashore after twenty years of sea and did not look back. Those times were better passed over. The Thames River Police seemed a natural place for him, and he was at ease with it, surprised to find himself good at the work. And he liked Monk. Of course, in many ways the commander was a difficult man, but he was honest, in his actions as well as his words, and Hooper was not afraid of him.

Hester Monk was the only woman Hooper was comfortable with, too plain in her speech for most men who liked a little coquetry in a woman. And Hester did not even know how to behave that way, much less wish to.

What would Celia Darwin be like? From what Exeter had told Monk, not much use, but he had to try.

It was a pleasant neighborhood. Not prosperous, as he had imagined Exeter's to be on the north side of the river. Did Exeter have to pledge his house to raise the ransom?

He came to Ceylon Street and turned the corner. It was quiet in the clear, sharp winter sun. He stopped at number twenty-six and knocked on the door, then stood back so as not to crowd whoever opened it.

It was a very young girl, perhaps fourteen. She was dressed in a plain dark-brown dress and white apron. "Yes, sir?" Her eyes were wide with alarm at finding a large man she had never seen before on the doorstep.

"Good morning," Hooper said quietly. "Is Miss Darwin at home?"

She clearly did not know how to answer, which meant that Celia Darwin was in, but very possibly not willing to see him.

"I am from the River Police," he continued. "It is about her cousin, Mrs. Exeter. Miss Darwin may be able to help us."

"I'll ask if she's . . . well enough . . . to see you," the girl answered, then was clearly unsure whether to close the door on him or not.

He stepped back, to help her decision.

She gave him the ghost of a smile and closed the door.

Then, in a few minutes, she returned and let him in.

Celia Darwin received him in the parlor. It was a small room, very tidy, but somehow it looked lived in. The cushions on the settee, arranged for comfort, were well-worn, the colors faded. The fire was already lit, although it was banked low and with much coal dust to close it off from burning too quickly. There were ornaments on the mantelshelf that had no relationship to each other, except in the mind of the person who had collected them: a single candlestick from what had once probably been a pair, an old pewter salt dish with a matching spoon, a crystal vase such as might have held a single bud, a china frog with a pleasantly ugly face.

Celia Darwin stood in the center of the softly patterned carpet, whose colors were wilted by time and wear. She was taller than he had expected. Her face was very pale, her features stronger and blunter than was fashionable, but he saw a sincerity in her that pleased him.

"I'm John Hooper," he introduced himself. "I'm here to find out what you remember of Saturday's events. I'm sorry to ask you to go over it again, but anything you can tell us might matter." He was careful not to suggest any answer to her. He had made that mistake before and learned how easy it was to skew someone's thoughts.

"Of course," she answered. Her voice was soft and unusually pleasing. "I understand that it is necessary. Please sit down, Mr. Hooper." She sat herself, in the middle of the sofa.

He took the armchair opposite her, a little closer to the fire. After the cold wind on the river, it was welcome. "Thank you. You were walking together along the path a few yards from the riverbank?"

"Yes."

"Do you often do that?"

"You mean, might someone know to expect us? Yes, I think so. Usually, if the weather is fine, about once a week."

"At the same time of day?"

"Usually."

He noticed that she answered with as few words as possible. He did not find it terse. On the contrary, it felt relaxing to him. He avoided asking if she and Kate had been close. If they had, it would stir her emotions, perhaps too much to control. He would rather judge by the tone of what she said, the pitch of her voice. "You were walking together, talking?"

"Yes, but we were silent now and then. As we were at the time the man spoke to her. He behaved as if he knew her. He was respectful, but not . . . timid." She looked up at him for an instant, and he saw how distressed she was. Then she looked down and continued speaking. "I thought they were acquainted, and I did not wish to intrude . . . to be part of a meeting that did not really include me. I wish now that I had!" Suddenly she was angry with herself, and it was sharp in her tone.

"Then you might have been taken, too," Hooper said quickly.

Celia looked up at him. "Then she would not have been alone!" Her eyes filled with tears and she blinked them away angrily, yet un-ashamed.

"But you are here to tell us anything you noticed about him."

"He was about two or three inches taller than Kate," she began. "And Kate is tall—as tall as I am. He was dark-haired, but he did not have dark brows. I noticed it, because it was unusual. His face was long—long nose, long chin—but altogether not ill-looking. And he moved easily, even gracefully."

"Thank you. That is very individual."

"He was slender," she went on, "and dressed in dark clothes. Very ordinary. I could not describe them usefully, I'm sorry."

"What direction did he come from?"

"Up the bank. From the water."

"So, you looked away. To allow them privacy?"

She looked down at her hands, motionless in her lap. At a glance they seemed at ease, until he noticed the pale knuckles. "I wish I had stayed. I moved quite a few yards away, so I didn't look as if I were overhearing them. I looked the other way. A group of people passed me. I would say six or seven. And . . . when I looked back, they were gone! It was only a few moments . . . or perhaps a little more."

"But you didn't hear her cry out?"

"No. If I had, I would have gone to her, fought with him, if necessary. I had an umbrella: I could have struck him with it."

"Was there anyone else near you? Say, within fifty yards?"

"Only the group I mentioned, moving away quite quickly. I looked around to see if she had gone in any other direction, or if there was someone I could ask. There was no one."

"Then he chose his moment carefully," Hooper said softly. "There was nothing you could have done, except describe him, as you have."

She faced him squarely. "Please do not try to make me feel better. It is . . . condescending."

He should have been irritated, but instead he felt the heat rising up his face.

She saw it. "I'm sorry, Mr. Hooper. I am distressed and afraid. It seems not fair to you. You are trying to help me concentrate on facts that are painful. I would like to just sit here and weep, but I realize that would be embarrassing and quite useless."

"I am also trying not to distress you more than necessary."

For the first time, she smiled. It gave a great gentleness to her face. "I know. Are you going to try to get her back?"

"Yes. Mr. Exeter has managed to raise the money." Perhaps he should not have told her, but he did not regret it even so.

"Oh . . ."

"You did not expect him to?"

She looked away. "I don't know . . . I'm not sure."

Hooper opened his mouth to suggest what she might be thinking, then knew he should not.

She was silent for a moment.

"I do not care for him," she said very softly. "But I am glad he has. Please . . . please help him to make the exchange safely."

"We'll do anything we can. They want the money—he wants Mrs. Exeter back."

She watched him for several long seconds.

He would not promise her that all would be well. The words were on the edge of his tongue, but he had learned better.

Oddly, the silence was not uncomfortable. He knew she understood.

Finally, he stood up. "Thank you, Miss Darwin."

"Was it any use?" She rose also.

"It will be, when we have your cousin back and we can go after them without endangering her."

She gave a tiny nod. "Thank you, Mr. Hooper."

He took his leave and walked out into the clear, cold air blowing up from the river, but the warmth of the room stayed with him.

IT WAS LATER THAT same morning that Celia received her second visitor. She was having a cup of tea, trying to steady her racing imagination, wondering how Kate was, if they were being cruel to her, browbeating her—or worse.

"Miss Darwin," the maid began nervously.

Celia looked up. "Yes . . . ? I'm sorry. Did you speak to me and I didn't answer?"

"No, ma'am. Mr. Latham is here, he says it's important. I wasn't sure whether you wished to see him." The girl looked nervous. She adored Celia and knew that Maurice would upset her.

"It's all right. Ask him to come in. I suppose you had better bring a second cup. The tea is still hot."

"Yes, ma'am." She went out, almost brushing past him in the doorway as Maurice came in. He was no taller than average, but very robust, and had put on a little weight in recent years. He was about the same age as Celia. Kate had been the youngest of the three cousins, and an only child.

Maurice closed the door behind him, perhaps imagining the maid might listen in to the conversation. He was always suspicious where Celia thought he had no need to be. She would not say so, but she thought he was judging other people by his own standards.

Today Maurice looked very grim, as she would have expected. How could anyone smile in the face of current events?

"Good morning, Maurice," she said quietly. "I have sent for another cup, if you would like tea. It is fresh."

"How can you be worried about such trivialities at a time like this?" he said tartly. "Really, Celia, there is no use hiding from the truth. You can deny it as much as you like! It will change nothing. We are facing tragedy, and the most appalling crime. No doubt the newspapers will plaster it all over their front pages." His mouth was tight, unusually bleak, even for him. He might have been quite good-looking if years of uncertain temper had not marked the lines of it downward.

Celia felt the warmth drain from her. She tried to keep it from showing but knew he read it in her. "If we get her back it will not be a story the newspapers will be interested in," she replied. "And good manners are a habit. It is natural to ask you if you wish for anything." She meant it as a rebuke.

He ignored it. "Harry has asked me, as trustee of Katherine's funds, for permission to withdraw them entirely from Nicholson's Bank, and hand them over as ransom payment. It is a major responsibility, but I feel I have no alternative. Obviously, it is what she would wish." He gave the ghost of a smile. "It is of no use to her if she is . . . not alive."

"Of course not," Celia agreed sharply. "There is no question. You must do so immediately."

"It is only right that I tell you!" he replied, equally sharply. "Should Katherine die before she inherits the money, it is split between the surviving cousins—which, as you are aware, are you and me. If she dies, it is yours and my future that is being paid . . ."

Celia could hardly believe her ears. Surely, he was just being pedantic? "Maurice, it is her money! It is inconceivable that either of us should refuse to save her life with it."

"Of course it is. I still should tell you. After all, should she die, for some reason, you would come into an enormous amount. It would alter your life entirely. You would be a rich woman—even with your half of it. It would alter your prospects even more than mine. I have my own profession. To you . . . for a start, it would make you marriageable. Even a man of a background suitable for you to accept would not turn his nose up at that kind of a fortune."

She felt the color flame up her face. The remark was true, and it hurt. She wanted to tell him that no fortune on earth would make him marriageable to a woman of any taste, but it was not true. More to the point, it would only show how deep the knife had cut.

"I am more than willing to give it up for Kate's safety," she said coldly. "It was never mine, nor did I ever think it so. I thank you for the courtesy of informing me. Harry has already done so."

"He is not trustee of it," Maurice said with a tight smile. "I am. Grandmama ensured that he had no access to it whatever. That was her intention. I grant this because I have no moral choice, and because the police are handling the affair."

"Precisely. Then if you do not wish for tea, I won't keep you. Thank you for your . . . courtesy."

He gave her a cold look, suspicious of sarcasm, but took his leave all the same, saying he had much to do.

When he had gone, she stood alone in the room, suddenly aware of being colder, as if the fire had gone out. She had not expected or wanted the money, but it made her aware of how alone she was. She would miss Kate unbearably. All the money Celia would ever have would be a small price to pay for Kate's release.

3

WHEN HOOPER ARRIVED BACK at the station, Monk went over the plans again with all the men concerned, apart from Bathurst, who had not yet arrived.

With difficulty, Monk refrained from second-guessing himself. He knew from experience that altering plans in the last hours could lead to mistakes, especially when the pressure was intense. Obedience must be instinctive. There might not be time for consideration, weighing, and judging.

Bathurst came at last. He had the scrubbed look of a schoolboy woken too early in the day: bright-eyed, but not quite awake; still slightly bemused, but ready for anything. Monk saw Hooper take him aside and tell him his part in the plan. Even from across the room he could see the moment Hooper mentioned Jacob's Island. The smile died from Bathurst's face, and his body stiffened, but he nodded.

Monk wondered if he had ever been that young, and keen. He had no idea, that time lost along with all his other memories. He would like to think he had, but he doubted it. Bathurst had been born in the south, and had known the river all his life. Monk knew that he himself had been born in Northumberland, almost on the Scottish border. He had no accent. He must have worked hard to get rid of it, lose the lilt in his voice. How badly he must have wanted to belong!

Exeter came five minutes earlier than they had agreed the day before. He was wearing old clothes and a heavy jacket, such as dockworkers wore to keep out the cold. He was carrying a very battered-looking Gladstone bag. Seeing Monk glance at it, he nodded, his brow puckered.

"I've got it all," he said. "You ready?" His voice was unsteady, and his face was pale. Even the bitter wind off the water hadn't whipped color into it.

"Yes, sir," Monk replied. He didn't know why he added the "sir." He did not usually, but he felt a profound sympathy for Exeter. No degree of regard was adequate to assure him of Monk's dedication, professional and personal, to recovering Mrs. Exeter alive. "We will leave in half an hour, perhaps a few minutes less. The tide is with us, although it will be low water at about four."

"And dark," Exeter added, then looked as if there was something else he wanted to say, but he could not think of the right words for it.

Laker walked over to them. "Excuse me, sir, would you like a cup of tea? It's pretty strong, perhaps not what you're used to, but it's hot." He was looking at Exeter.

"No, thank you," Exeter said a little sharply.

"Sir?" Laker turned to Monk.

"Yes, please," Monk accepted. There was all the difference in the world between strong, stewed tea on the potbellied stove, too sweet, and often with no milk, and the tea at home, fresh, fragrant, subtle-flavored, and definitely without sugar. But this served its purpose.

Laker went off and returned a moment later with two mugs, giving one to Monk, and offering the other to Exeter.

"Thank you," Exeter answered, and took it. He smiled bleakly over the rim of the enameled mug. "Is he always so persistent?"

"I daresay he's been along the river on a winter dusk more often than you have," Monk replied.

"On kidnaps?" Exeter asked.

"No, thank God. But on other cases."

Exeter took a sip of the tea and tried not to grimace, but failed. "How often do you drink this stuff?"

Monk smiled at him. "You get used to it."

Exeter gazed back, quite openly searching Monk's face. What was he looking for? Assurance? Courage? A promise?

Monk could not give him that. He turned aside and offered instead a rough plan of Jacob's Island, and the ways they intended to enter so as to reach the spot indicated on the piece of paper Exeter had shown him.

"Is that what it looks like?" Exeter asked. "I can see why they chose it." He looked back up at Monk. "You're not going to try to catch them first, are you?" His voice wavered between certainty and doubt.

Monk had already given his word. "No. But if the chance arises after we have Mrs. Exeter safely out of there, then we'll take it. We don't want them to take the money before we've got her back."

Exeter breathed out slowly, and something like a smile returned to his face. "I'm sorry. I shouldn't have doubted you. I apologize."

"In your place, I would have, too," Monk replied.

They drank the tea slowly, watching the hands of the clock move round its face. Marbury arrived, and three minutes after him, Walcott. Quick words were exchanged.

Exeter did not move at all, except to take the mug to his lips. His knuckles were white.

At twenty-five minutes past three, Monk gave the signal to leave and they went out without speaking again. The wind was rising in the open space across the dock, and the last of the sun stained the sky to the west with color, lending the scene an unnatural beauty. The tide was nearly at its lowest. Stretches of mud glistened smooth, almost like flesh in the brief, lurid glow. To the east, where they were headed, a pall of darkness was rising swiftly.

They climbed down the steps to the boats, three to one, four to the other, leaving one behind in case there should be an emergency elsewhere. One other boat was already on patrol. There was no sound but the scrape of boots on the stone and the slurp of the water against the dock.

Hooper went ahead with Marbury and Walcott. Monk took Laker and Bathurst and directed Exeter to sit beside him in the stern.

They pushed out into the current, following after the others, rowing in long, even strokes, each man holding his single oar. They could go on like that for hours, and frequently did.

Monk tried to think of something to say to Exeter that would reassure him, but nothing came. Conversation seemed artificial, as if he did not understand the fear and apprehension Exeter must feel. What had been the last thing he had said to her? Something trivial? If it was something critical, what would he pay now to take it back? Had he ever told her all that she meant to him?

The light was already graying, losing color. There was no wind, but the cold was penetrating. Monk's face felt stiff with it, and he missed being able to pull on the oar and warm himself with the effort. There were times when he felt his whole body ache with it, but he also found a comfort on the river.

They moved swiftly. There was no resistance from the tide. The water was already slack. Not much light was left, but he could still see the other boat ahead of them quite clearly. The bigger ships at anchor had their riding lights lit. It was strangely still, almost as if they were painted onto the darkness, with the skyline of the city drawn behind them. Lights along the shore blinked on, chains of them where there were roads on the bank. A few moved: carriage lamps; on the water, ferries. It was quarter to four in the afternoon, but too late to work, as it was too easy to make a mistake because you couldn't see.

Ahead of them, Monk saw Hooper's boat turn toward the bank. Laker rested on his oar, and Bathurst rowed harder, bringing the bow round.

"Aren't we going the other direction? Downriver?" Exeter spoke for the first time. "The other way in? That's what they're expecting." He turned sideways in the seat. "We've got to stick to the plan!"

"We are doing," Monk assured him. "We've got to stop in the lee to light the lamp."

"Oh. Of course. I'm sorry."

"We're going to do exactly what they told us. The other men are going in upriver of us, as we planned." He put out a hand on Exeter's arm, and felt it rigid beneath his fingers.

"Are we late?" Exeter demanded.

"No, nor are we early. If they're any good at this, they will have been here long before us."

"Kate will be frozen . . . and terrified."

Monk tightened his grip on Exeter's arm. "If we rush, we may make a mistake."

Exeter looked down at the lamps, although he could barely have seen them. "I'm sorry. I . . . this is hard. I . . ."

"I know," Monk said quietly. "Not much longer now. Help me light these. We won't see a damn thing without them."

"I imagine you don't see much in a place like this, even in daylight," Exeter observed bitterly.

They were entering the waterways around Jacob's Island, and the other boat had gone out of sight, upriver. The houses reared up out of the water on either side of what was a short canal. They balanced on rotted stilts, leaning this direction and that, according to what had given way first. The river water barely covered the thick, viscous mud that sucked anything of weight into itself, like quicksand.

Monk had seen men fall into it. Their bodies were never found. God alone knew what lay beneath its stinking surface. It barely moved. There were no eddies or swirls here, nothing to cleanse either at low tide or high.

"This place is like death," Exeter said hoarsely. "Perhaps hell is like this. Worse than burning!"

Monk looked at him. His face was starkly shown in the lights of the bull's-eye lanterns. The yellow glow caught and magnified every line, deepening the shadows. Monk thought he must look nearly as haggard as that himself. But the tension in Monk was far less. This was only his job, his professional success or failure. For Exeter, it was everything that mattered in his life.

"You have the money," Monk said. "All they asked? They must expect you to bring someone with you. You can only get to the site by water. You're going to give them the money when you've seen your wife and she's well."

"But if—" Exeter began.

Monk looked at him. "You want to change your mind?"

"No! No. Of course I don't. It's just . . . get this over with. It is the only thing I can do, and . . . second-guessing myself . . . there's no point. How much further until there's something we can land on? All I can see is mud and water and rotting wood that wouldn't take the weight of a seagull, never mind a man!"

"Not much further," Monk assured him. "There's a stone wall a dozen yards over there, but watch your feet. You don't want to step on a rat."

"Wouldn't the damn things get out of the way?"

"Not if they're dead."

Exeter swore under his breath.

Three minutes later, they arrived at an old mooring post by a flight of steps. The wood was rotten, but the iron core of it still held firm.

"Where are we going?" Exeter said, the note of panic rising high in his voice again. "There's nothing here!"

"Over there." Monk pointed. "There's a loading bay there, and beyond it the entrance to a cellar, and a tunnel."

"It's under the water!"

"Not now. It's low tide."

"The tide will turn any moment, and we'll be drowned!" There was an edge to Exeter's voice: Fear, a nerve struck? Memory of some other time?

"Then we'd better be quick!" Monk passed one of the bull's-eye lanterns to Exeter. "Come on." He stood up carefully, keeping his balance, and stepped up onto the shallow stone slab. He turned to offer his hand to Exeter.

Exeter rose also, but his balance seemed uneasy. He hesitated a moment, then took Monk's hand and leaned on it with more weight than expected. There was an instant adjustment, then Exeter moved and put his feet on the stone. Laker was a yard behind him; Bathurst was to stay and keep the boat ready for their return.

Monk waited only an instant, then faced forward, holding the light ahead of him, and very carefully moved along the stone slip and into the darkness of the tunnel mouth. It looked like an ordinary loading bay, except that the wood was wet up to head height. This would be an underground river at high tide. Even in a couple of hours it would be an ever-deepening morass.

When they had gone twenty feet from the entrance, the last of the daylight was swallowed up. Monk refused to look backward. He had memorized the passages and now concentrated on finding his way: how many steps, how many walls, broken or whole. He could hear the rats skittering along the wooden beams that still survived.

Was the water at his feet rising, or was it only his imagination?

Ahead of him, the way divided. A flight of stairs went upward and disappeared. Monk went straight past it. He knew that it led nowhere. The next floor had been carried away when the rafters fell in. The way from here, against all instinct, was down. Now the ground was open, but they must come back in less than an hour, or the current filling it with the weight of the incoming tide would carry them off their feet.

Exeter stopped.

Monk turned back. "There's no other way, come on."

A rat scuttled along a beam and fell off into the water with a heavy slop somewhere ahead of them.

Monk held the lantern up. The light shone on Exeter's white face.

"Let me go over it again," Exeter said hoarsely, clearing his throat for the umpteenth time. "We go together as far as what must be the next set of stairs. You wait there, I take the money up, and the very first turning to the right leads to another few steps down. A bigger room. They'll be there. I should give them the money, but make sure

Kate's there and all right. Hooper will be waiting to come from the other side, if . . . if . . . she's not."

"Right," Monk agreed. "Don't go anywhere else, or you'll get lost."

Exeter's face muscles tightened and he winced at the thought. "I know! I know. The tide is rising. Can we get on with it? I can't bear the waiting. I must see her! Hear her speak . . ."

Monk nodded. "Go!"

Exeter hesitated only an instant, then squared his shoulders. Without looking at Monk again, he moved forward into the darkness, the wavering lantern in one hand and the Gladstone bag in the other. He reached the steps and began to climb them slowly, making sure not to slip on the wet surface. They had been covered with water only an hour ago, and in another hour would be again. Then the light disappeared and Monk was left alone with the creaking wood, the dripping water. Something above him moved. Bats? They were al-most invisible. The air could be full of them.

He knew his men were not far away, and yet he felt utterly alone. The bone-aching cold settled in, the dampness on his skin as if noth-ing was dry, not his hands, not his face, not his body, at once sweating and chilling.

Minutes ticked by. The building settled as if it were surrendering to the tide and the mud. There was no wind down here, no rattling breath, but he imagined he could hear the tide creep higher.

How many men were involved in the kidnapping of Kate Exeter? There had to be at least three, more likely four, to be sure of guarding her all the time. They would keep it to a minimum. Fewer ways to split the money.

Monk shifted his weight to keep from cramping. What was hap-pening? If they were there, as they said they would be, Exeter must have reached them by now. Maybe they weren't! But only a fool would play games here. If they lost him, he could be anywhere. If he went the wrong way, slipped and fell, dropped the case with money, they might never find him. The tide would drown them just as easily as it would Exeter or Monk, and any or all of his men.

Why could he hear nothing? No, that was wrong. He could hear the rats, the water creeping. The tide would be well into the flow now! Rising inch by inch. More than two or three feet deep and it would be strong enough to pull a man off balance. Three feet and it would drag him along, or break a rotting log, blocking the way out, or carry him into the darkness, like being eaten. The stench was appalling. Who knew what dead creatures the mud contained, reduced to bones and stew? Something moved in the water.

There was a cry ahead of him, a hoarse, grating sound of surprise and pain.

Monk was galvanized into action. Holding the lantern high to light the way as much as possible, he ran forward and stumbled up the slippery steps. He fell on his knees and only just saved the lantern from smashing. He reached the top and an open space. It was the wreck of a room, one wall gone and looking out on the black water about ten feet below them and the tangle of wreckage breaking through the surface.

There was a sound behind him. He swiveled to face it, and the lantern was knocked out of his hand. A heavy blow struck him on the chest, and another on the jaw. He fell hard, splayed on the filthy floor. He avoided a third blow, but now without the lantern he could not see who had attacked him. He judged where the next blow might come and kicked hard. He judged right, and he felt his foot land on flesh. There was a cry and a curse. Another blow just missed his head, and the weight of a man's upper body fell across his chest. He struggled to free his other leg and kicked at air.

A blow landed on his shoulder. Now he had a better idea of how the man fought and was able to land a hard punch on the other's throat. He heard the satisfying groan, and the next moment the man's weight went slack. Monk rolled from beneath it and dived for the lantern, now covered with mud. He grasped it and set it upright. The other man was already moving. Monk could see him more clearly now. He was dressed in working clothes, such as any waterman might wear: thick, warm, browns and grays, a woolen hat pulled over his head and part of his face.

Before he could get his balance, Monk hit him with all his weight and he went down again, but one foot caught Monk on the shin. In trying to keep his balance, Monk dropped the lamp. There was the high, thin sound of breaking glass, and then complete darkness. Monk moved back and to the left, moments before the man passed where he had stood. There was no point in trying to find him. He must go forward and find Exeter, or at least some of his own men.

He pressed on in what he thought was the direction Exeter had gone. He could hear sounds ahead, but all he could see were shadows here and there, a break in the darkness as the outside light was reflected off water. Everywhere there was dripping. He stopped again, to see if he could hear movement. Nothing! He took a few more steps. Still nothing.

Then, ahead of him, the sound of someone limping. He moved as softly as he could toward it. Then a light, a bull's-eye lantern, and the dark form of a man carrying it. There was something familiar in his step.

"Laker!"

"Is that you, sir?" The figure lurched toward him eagerly, holding the bull's-eye up.

"Are you hurt?" Monk demanded.

"Not much. You, sir?"

"No. Any idea how many there are of them? Did you see Exeter?"

They were only a yard apart now. In the lantern light, Monk could see a bruise on Laker's face, rapidly darkening.

"Did they miss you, sir?" Laker asked.

"No. Exeter's ahead of me. Behind you!"

"Then he must have taken a wrong turn," Laker replied. "We'll have to go back for him." He sounded terrible.

"Can't have gone far." Monk forced himself to sound positive. "They want the money, and they know this place. They're only trying to not get caught!" This was far from what he felt, but he mustn't let Laker know that.

Together, they moved back over the ground Laker had covered, picking their way through the debris on the floor by the light of Laker's lamp. Something moved above them, flying in the dark.

There was no sign of Exeter.

The outside light was getting less. Twilight came slowly, but it was well after sunset and there would be little light in the winter sky.

Laker stopped suddenly, almost falling. "Damn!" he swore, his voice cracking with tension. He bent over and gently turned the body that had tripped him, then gasped.

Monk pressed forward, his throat so tight he could barely breathe.

Laker moved the lamp closer and then looked at Monk, his eyes wide and dark with fear. It was Hooper. His face was smeared with blood.

Monk felt as if it were he himself who had been struck. He was numb with the pain of it, and the immediate denial. "No! He can't . . ."

Laker moved the light even closer, as if seeing more clearly would make him realize it was not really Hooper, just someone in his clothes who looked like him.

Hooper stirred. "Take that out of my face," he said haltingly. "I can't see!"

Monk felt tears sting his eyes immediately.

Laker swung the lamp away.

Hooper blinked, then struggled to sit up. "Damn, my head hurts! Where's Exeter?" He tried to turn sideways, to climb to his feet.

Monk leaned forward and held him back. "You all right?"

"Yes! Just . . . hit me on the back of the head. Didn't even see the bastard. Where's Exeter? Damn you, let me stand up!"

Monk gave him his hand and pulled. Hooper was heavy and still dazed, but he made it upright. Without speaking, they all moved behind Laker, who had the only light, and followed him the way Hooper said he had come.

Monk had lost his bearings. He thought Exeter was only about twenty yards ahead of him, at the place he was supposed to meet the kidnappers. Exeter had insisted on going the last space alone, and repeated the directions over and over. Had he fought them over the money? They were obviously here! They had attacked Monk, Laker, and now Hooper as well. Were they making sure nobody followed them?

"Listen!" Monk said sharply to Laker.

Laker ignored him. He was already going as fast as he could in the poor light of one lamp and the little daylight that came through broken roofs and rafters and crumbling walls. The slurping was getting faster, and they must be as aware as Monk was of the water rising to the lower timbers, gathering force as the tide started to come in.

They found Marbury, dazed and limping. One side of his jaw was bruised, but it did not stop his grin of relief at seeing them. He dropped the piece of timber he had been holding as a weapon.

"Have you seen Exeter?" Monk asked him.

"He must be that way." Marbury turned. "It's the only way left."

Silently, they went where he pointed, Laker first with one lamp, and Marbury last with the other. No one spoke. It took intense concentration to avoid potholes, rotting timbers, fallen beams across the path. Everything was wet. They were well below the high-tide line, and no one forgot it. Soon this would be filled to the ceiling with filthy water, black, airless.

It was Laker's bull's-eye that shone on Exeter's terrified face, streaked with mud and blood and swollen, with one eye almost closed. "Have you got her?" Exeter shouted at him. His voice cracked and he drew a long shuddering breath. He looked at Monk, and Monk saw the hope die out of him, almost as if he had shrunk into a smaller man, beaten, all but lifeless.

Monk answered. "No. We all fought with them, and one is lying back behind us. She must be ahead. Did you give them the money? What did they say?"

Exeter looked stricken. It was difficult to tell how badly he was injured. There were quite a few dark stains on him that looked like blood, but it could have been his own or that of one of the kidnappers. If he could stand, that was all that mattered now.

"Yes . . . yes. I fought with some of them, several, I don't know. They took the money, but I don't know where Kate is. I've looked. They left her. Please . . ."

"Of course. Give me your lamp. I'll lead the way."

Wordlessly, Exeter handed him the lantern and fell in step, close behind Monk. Hooper, Marbury, and Laker all followed, stumbling in the dark, tripping over timbers, odd bits of rotted furniture, years old and sodden wet. When they reached the bottom of the stairs at the far side, the water was already ankle-deep. In half an hour, it would be over their knees, and the pull of it enough to knock them off balance and carry them away, battering them senseless against the pieces of wet, broken piling. If they caught a foot in refuse, they could drown. They all knew that, except possibly Exeter.

Monk lost track of time. Was it a quarter of an hour or only five minutes before he rounded a corner and came into a room that was almost dry? It was open to the weather completely on one side, but it was landward, and much of the wood was unbroken.

Monk stopped abruptly. He saw what they all would, as soon as he moved out of the way. The body of a woman was sprawled on the floor, over on the far side against the wall. There was blood every-where. And the dark outlines of rats were approaching her, curiously, scenting food.

Monk gagged, horror stopping his breath.

Behind him, Exeter let out a terrible cry and flung himself on the floor, touching her gently, sobbing her name over and over.

Hooper moved past Monk and went to Exeter. He did not try to lift him or move him away. A glance was enough to know that he could not help her now.

Monk walked toward her, his stomach churning, his mouth dry. He forced himself to look beyond Exeter, at what was left of his wife. The only good thing was that she must have died quickly. There would have been no time to feel the pain of the terrible wounds. Please God, not even enough to realize what had happened to her.

He turned away. "Laker, go and get the police surgeon. You'll have to head back through the tunnel and find Bathurst. Take Marbury. Don't try that tunnel alone. Be quick. The tide's coming in so you'll have to return at the landward side."

"Yes, sir. Shall I get some more men, sir?"

"There'll be nothing to find tonight. Get the police surgeon, and . . . someone to see to . . . us. I don't know who's hurt, or how badly. God knows how many kidnappers there are, or if they're still here."

"Yes, sir. I'll get as many as I can . . ." Laker wanted to say something more, but there was nothing. He turned and ran back, as fast as he could go, with Marbury on his heels.

Monk looked at Exeter, crouched on the floor, his body shaking, crippled with grief. How could he help the man? What was there to say? He was locked in his own world of grief, and nothing else would matter to him now.

The only thing was to get him out of here, physically safe and dry, and not cold to the bone with shock. There was no comfort to offer.

4

THE TIDE WAS STILL rising. There was nothing more Monk, or any of his men, could do on Jacob's Island. The police surgeon had taken Kate's body away. He would report to Monk sometime tomorrow, when he had something to say.

There was absolute darkness now. The tide had already risen high enough to fill the lower cellars and passages dangerously, and some of the men were hurt badly enough to need more than the temporary patching up that the police surgeon could do.

Monk himself ached in every bone, but how much was bruising and minor cuts and how much the torture of utter failure, he did not yet know. Fortunately, the men he had left guarding the boats, Bathurst and Walcott, were unhurt and could row them back up to Wapping.

They went in silence. There was no sound but the slapping of the water against the wooden sides of the boats and the rhythmic creak of the oars. Nobody spoke. Whatever their thoughts were, they were too raw and too complicated for them to find the words.

Monk sat in the stern while Bathurst rowed. It was a heavy task alone, and Bathurst was straining with the effort, but at least the flood tide was with him. Laker nursed his wounded arm and sat awkwardly with one bandaged leg straight out.

The other boat was ahead of them, its one riding light bobbing as they hit choppy water. Monk could see nothing more than that.

What had happened? They had followed the plan exactly, done everything the kidnappers had instructed, as to both time and place. Exeter might not know anything about Jacob's Island, but he had followed the directions, and the more often Monk went over it in his mind, the more certain he was that they all had done so exactly. They had not been a yard out of place. What had gone wrong?

Or had the kidnappers done something wrong? Quarreled among themselves, perhaps? Fallen out as to shares of the money? Certainly, they had not killed Kate by accident. Injuries like that could not happen by mistake. As he pictured her, trying to force the image out of his sight and failing, it came to him again that her feet were still tied together. So she had not tried to run away. The slaughter was deliberate! Why?

There was hatred in it: deep, almost insane. What could Kate Exeter possibly have done to awaken such a feeling in anyone? Monk had assumed it was about the money. Heaven knew there was enough of it to account for any depth of greed. But obviously it was something far more visceral than that.

Was it even about her at all?

Exeter himself seemed a far more believable target. She was just a means to hurt him. Did he actually know who was behind this? He had affected to have no idea, and believe the ransom was the point. Was he lying to hide a reason he was ashamed of? Or was hiding it part of the price?

In that case, the kidnappers had not believed he would remain silent after Kate was returned to him. It would not be the end, as he had said, but only a hiatus.

That was pretense, too. He would hunt them now, until either he was dead, or they were.

There must be a very terrible story behind such a crime. Tomorrow, Exeter might tell them himself. If not, Monk would have to press him further.

He realized again how cold he was. Not only his face, exposed to the damp river air, but his body, deep inside his layers of clothing. His feet were numb. His hands ached, and he could not even feel the scraped skin on his knuckles where he had struck the man who attacked him.

Some of the others must feel worse. He had seen the ragged slash on Marbury's shoulder and arm. Hooper's face was dark with bruising. They were all splashed with mud and some were wet through.

The air was clear. He could see riding lights from anchored ships all around him, and lights on both shores. The patterns were long familiar. That must be Wapping ahead of them now.

Half an hour later they were in the station. The potbellied stove had been refueled, and heat spread throughout the open room. Hot tea was made for everyone, the wettest clothes changed. It was just after seven, and pitch-dark outside. It had all happened in less than four hours, and yet instead of being the end, they had barely passed the beginning.

Monk looked around the other men, filthy, exhausted, four of them injured to some degree or another. Now began the dissection, piece by piece.

"Walcott?"

"Yes, sir?"

"Did anyone pass you at the river going toward Jacob's Island? Anyone at all?"

"No, sir. The water was flat and I would have seen all of it. Not a soul." His voice was firm, without hesitation, and he looked Monk straight in the eye.

"Bathurst?"

"No, sir. A boat passed within about thirty feet, but kept right on going. They must have seen me, unless they were half asleep, but no one came back. And I watched for it."

"Then either they got there before us and were waiting, or they came in from the landward side," Monk concluded. "How many do you reckon there were? Start with you, Laker."

"Just one man, sir, but he took me by surprise. He came out of the darkness and I didn't hear him above the general creaking and dripping. He hit me pretty hard from behind, and I went down, but I managed to get up when he came closer, and we fought, but he got away."

"Which direction?" Monk asked. He was not sure if the answer would be of any use, but he must give them the feeling that he had ideas, even solutions. They all looked utterly defeated. And that was how Monk felt. "Marbury?"

"I saw only one man, sir. We had a stiff battle, but when I hit him with a really good blow, he went down. I think it was after he had attacked Laker, sir, because he was already filthy and battered-looking, mud on his clothes as if he had lain on his back in it. And it was near dark by then."

"Thank you. Hooper?"

"Came from a side passage, sir. Hit me with a plank of wood. It was rotten, but it was very heavy, because it was wet. Broke across my back. I went down sideways, but I got up again. Sort of rolled over. We fought hard and I was pretty well beaten. Couldn't get my breath."

Monk nodded and looked around at each man. "Same thing happened to me. They ambushed us. Which means they were expecting us."

"They got four of us, sir, and Exeter, and they had someone to hold Kate—" Laker began.

"Unless she was already dead," Monk cut across him. It had to be said. "And they never intended to hand her over." It still suggested three men, at the very least. "And they had come from the landward side, or escaped that way anyway. Walcott? Bathurst? You sure you saw nobody?" he asked again.

Both men thought for a moment, then shook their heads. "No, sir," they said almost together. "And one of us had to have seen anyone leaving by the river. You can't miss a boat in the water, even at dusk. Your eyes get used to the shadows," Bathurst added.

"So, they left by land. With the money."

"Could have left it there," Laker argued. "Go back for it later."

"And expect to find it?" Monk asked incredulously. "The damn place is moving, sinking, rearranging itself every ten minutes. Not to mention the tides rising and falling twice every day."

"Then they took it," Walcott said flatly. "And left us nothing but the body of that poor woman."

That was greeted with silence.

It was Hooper who broke it. He looked up, his face a confused mask of pain. "Why did they do that? They didn't even do it . . . quickly! You don't slaughter an animal like that." His voice cracked and he struggled to control it. It was Monk he was looking at.

Monk felt it acutely. It had seemed a good plan, as good as could be involving so much uncertainty. He had told Exeter it would be all right, and Exeter had done exactly as he was told, and lost everything.

Monk looked from one man to another. They looked like a bunch of stray, whipped dogs, bruised, bloody, most of them wet through with the pungent river mud. But above all, they looked beaten. They had trusted his plan, and it had failed in every way.

Bathurst blinked. "But he was going to give them the money!" he exclaimed, his face tight with anger. "Why kill her?"

"Perhaps she recognized them," Walcott said, with a cadence in his voice that implied it was an obvious answer.

"Then why wouldn't Exeter know them, too?" Bathurst shot back. "He said he didn't."

"Maybe he lied?" Marbury suggested. "Perhaps he knew perfectly well who they were, and he felt guilty. Or perhaps saying he didn't know them was part of the price?"

"For what?" Hooper asked. "Getting her back alive? Then why keep silent now? He didn't get her back, and he lost all the money as well. If he knows who they are, he should be the first to say."

No one argued with him.

Monk thought about it. He forced himself to remember Exeter's face, his voice, and the agony in it. And the horror when he saw

Kate! That cry would stay in Monk's ears forever, as if the silence had only just closed over it.

Hooper was looking at him. Was that pity in his face? They had really failed this time and, as the leader, it was Monk's failure. It could not be put right now. Even if by some fluke of luck they got the money back, it was Kate Exeter they wanted. Harry Exeter was willing to pay—that much and anything else—to get his wife back. Monk would have felt the same. Had that made him timid? Robbed him of decisiveness?

But what could they have done differently? They had done exactly what the kidnappers had asked, to the letter: time, place, amount of money, sending Exeter in with it alone.

"Someone hated Exeter enough to rob him of everything," Monk said slowly. "They had the money. We were no threat to them if they simply took it and went. It was nearly dark, and the tide was rising. It was the perfect situation for them. They had every advantage."

"Why didn't he tell us that there are people who hate him to this degree?" Hooper wondered. "There's more story to this."

"Doesn't matter now," Laker said bitterly. "The poor woman's dead, and they have got the money. But on the other hand, since they've got all he cares about, there's nothing left to lose in going after them. And when he's absorbed what's happened, and got over the first shock a little, he'll be furious, and take the edge off his grief with anger. A lot of people do."

The rest of them turned and looked at him. Their faces reflected a range of emotions: agreement, pity, suspense, even fear of what that anger might bring. No one disbelieved it.

Monk had been too immersed in his own reactions to think about that. He did not want to imagine how Exeter felt. It was too painful, too all-encompassing to face. But Laker was right.

What he had not said, and what weighed on Monk's mind with further pain, was the thought that the kidnappers had known so much about their plans. There were five or six different ways the River Police could have got in, but the kidnappers had known precisely which ones they were going to use, how many men, and where they were along those tunnels and passages. What he forced himself to wonder was, who had told them?

It hurt even to think the words, and yet they were there, whether he said them or not. Some changes had been made to their plans at the last minute. One had even been made as they reached Jacob's Island in the fading light. It could only have been passed along at that time. So the traitor had to be one of his own men. The knowledge closed around him like a thick mist, blinding, close as the air he breathed, and knotting inside him with a rising nausea.

He could not face it tonight. He had other, wretched things he had to do, starting with telling Rathbone what had happened.

Then he should go to Exeter, but with some sort of plan. At the moment, he had nothing in mind. He could not tell him anything that would help, and yet he could not blame the men, as if he were not the cause of it all. He could not let Exeter think he did not care, or did not realize that it was his fault. And it was. One of the men Monk had chosen, and trusted, had betrayed them.

He looked at them all, sitting and standing awkwardly, aware of at least some of the depth of the disaster. They were cold and filthy and, above all, hurt. The physical pain was there; some of the emotions were beginning to show. They were all looking at him, not at each other. The suspicion was taking hold.

"All right," Monk said quietly. "There's nothing more we can do. Go home. Get as much sleep as you can. Look after yourselves. Unfortunately, those that are fit are going to have to start again tomorrow. Good night."

MONK TOOK A HANSOM to Rathbone's house. It was late enough that Rathbone was likely to be home. Since his remarriage, he did not go out to social events unless required. He was happy in Beata's company. They often found much to talk about, but silence was also companionable. So many of life's necessities could be conveyed by a glance, a smile, or even a touch. Heaven knew, Rathbone had waited long enough for that kind of happiness. Monk knew it himself. He had imagined Rathbone would find it with his first wife, never fore-seeing the tragedy ahead. He also knew that Rathbone had found it in the very beginning, when he had been in love with Hester, but she had chosen Monk.

It was not particularly cold in the hansom, and yet Monk was knotted up inside, clenched too tight, as if he were frozen.

They arrived and Monk got out of the hansom awkwardly, his foot sliding a little on the black ice of the pavement. He paid the driver and walked up to the front door. He pulled the bell rope and stepped back.

The door was answered almost immediately by Rathbone himself. He took one look at Monk and his face tightened. There was no need to speak. He stepped back to allow Monk inside.

Monk followed him, engulfed immediately by the warmth. Some-how, the sheer comfort made him feel worse.

"You look perished," Rathbone said quietly. "You need some dry clothes. Come in to the fireside. I'll get you a whisky." He turned and led the way into the withdrawing room.

Beata was already standing. She was a beautiful woman, in a quiet, serene way. Her hair was so fair as to be nearly silver, but it was the calm within her that overrode everything else. It was not the absence of pain that filled her, but the overcoming of it. Rathbone never told Monk what was behind her brave serenity, except that it was rooted in her first marriage to a powerful and vindictive man.

Now she came forward. "Oh, William, you look frozen, and . . . and wounded! What would you like? Hot soup? A brandy? To speak privately with Oliver?" She looked him up and down. "Dry clothes? I am sure I can find something of Oliver's that would fit you, at least well enough for now."

It was instinctive to decline, to avoid putting her to trouble, and perhaps even more to avoid admitting needing help. That was fool-ish. It must be perfectly obvious to her that he ached for help of every sort. "Thank you. And soup would be excellent. I am tempted by the brandy, but I have more to do tonight, and a clear head is needed."

"I'll be back in about fifteen minutes. Give me that wet coat and I'll set it by the fire," she instructed.

He obeyed, and when she was gone he stood by the fire. He realized he was too wet and too muddy to spoil the armchair by sitting in it.

Rathbone remained standing also, a tacit mark of companionship. "What happened?" he asked. He knew this was what Monk had come to tell him.

"We planned it down to the last detail," Monk replied, staring into the flames. "We even altered a couple of things at the last moment, just as we landed. I hate that place." His voice grated with emotion. "It's cold and wet, everything sour and rotting as it slowly sinks into the slime."

Rathbone's face grew paler and the lines around his mouth clearer as he realized the depth of Monk's defeat, if not its entire nature.

"No doubt they chose it for that reason," said Rathbone. "And because Exeter would be utterly lost in it, and unable to fight back or follow them. But I hadn't thought he cared about keeping the money, and still less about their being arrested!"

"I don't think that he did," Monk said flatly. Now that it came to saying the actual words, it was even harder than he had expected. "But he did care about getting Kate back." He watched Rathbone's face as he slowly guessed what may have happened.

"You mean . . . they took the money, but kept her? What do they want? More money? I don't think he has it! I think it took an extraordinary effort to raise this much."

"No." Monk forced himself to say it. "They killed her—horribly. Slashed her to bits . . ." He choked to a stop.

Rathbone went ash pale. "Oh God!" He seemed about to say something more, and then realized the futility of it. Monk would not have said such a thing were it not the complete and unarguable truth. "He knows . . . ?" Rathbone began.

"Yes. He was one of the first into the place where it happened. He saw her." Monk would never forget that cry.

"Did you get any of them?" Rathbone asked.

"No. We hurt a few quite badly, and most of my men were hurt, some more than others. They knew where we were." That was the hardest thing to say. It was the one thing he still had to deal with, and he didn't know where to begin. How could he have been so wrong about one of his men? And it was like a drop of ink in a glass of water. It stained everything. Who would do such a thing? And why? Greed? Fear? Hatred? Some kind of hideous error?

Rathbone shook his head. "I suppose you don't know how . . . or from who?"

"Not yet."

Beata came back into the room with an armful of clothes. She spoke to Monk. "Go and try these on. See if something fits. If you want a hot bath, please have one. The soup will be another ten minutes at least, and I'll not serve it until you are ready."

He hesitated. It seemed an unnecessary self-indulgence.

"If you succumb to pneumonia, you are no use to anyone," she said firmly. "From the look on your face, you're going to have a lot to do in the next little while. You'll need to be at your best."

He looked at her calm, clear eyes and read in them compassion, but not an ounce of yielding. He smiled and took the clothes.

Twenty minutes later he was back by the fire in the sitting room, tasting a dish of hot soup. He felt a lot better physically, and he certainly looked it in some of Rathbone's older clothes, which came close to fitting him, though he was taller and broader in the chest and shoulders. Beata had taken his clothes and promised to return them when they had been dealt with. She had said it with a twisted little smile and sadness in her eyes. The coat, she had said, would probably be a week, at least.

Rathbone waited until the soup was finished and then looked straight at Monk. "Tell me what happened. I don't know whether I need to know, but I might."

Monk recited everything as well as he could, both his own memory and the accounts of his men.

"I see," Rathbone said at last. "Is it possible that the kidnappers also took another hostage?"

Monk was confused. "What do you mean?"

"Someone else," Rathbone explained patiently. "Perhaps someone belonging to one of your men? To assure his cooperation?"

Monk let his breath out slowly. The thought had not occurred to him. How stupid! How obvious, now that he saw it. It was the one thing that would explain such a betrayal. "I don't know," he said slowly. "But I shall find out. Poor devil! That I could understand. But it doesn't explain why they killed Kate, and so savagely. We are looking for an enemy, either of hers or of Exeter's. You would think that anyone so bestial would stand out, wouldn't you? They ought to have red eyes, or huge canine teeth, or some other feature that would mark them as different."

Rathbone smiled uneasily, but his eyes held no criticism. "Monk, you know as well as I do that the face of evil is not so easily recognizable. The worst people I've ever known look pretty much like anyone else. And they didn't think they were evil. They had done a thorough job of convincing themselves that they were justified, even that they were the victims of some persecution or other. The raving madman is perfectly easy to recognize. It's the one who believes he's good, that all he does is justified, who is hard to see. The one who is in the center of his own universe is the real danger." He sighed. "Poor Exeter. He must be devastated."

"He was. I've got to go and see him, see if he has any idea who is behind Kate's murder, if he can scrape his brain together enough to think at all, that is. I wouldn't blame him if he drank himself into oblivion."

"You have to see him tonight?" Beata asked. "You're exhausted."

"Tomorrow I shall have to start searching for any evidence there is, find out if anybody along the river heard anything, knew anything. And more than that, which of my men betrayed us . . . whatever his reason. I hate this more than . . ." He did not finish the sentence; it was irrelevant anyway.

Half an hour later he forced himself to stand up and take his leave. He went out to look for a cab to take him to Exeter's house, having got the address from Rathbone. The street was quiet. A hansom passed him at a brisk trot. A carriage turned down a mews entrance toward its own stables, home for the night. He envied them.

He started to walk, mainly to keep warm. In the main thoroughfare, with more traffic, it would be easier.

It did not take him long after that to find a hansom, and far too soon he arrived at Exeter's door. He told the cabby to wait, in case there was no answer. It would not have surprised him, and he certainly would not blame Exeter if he refused to see anyone at all, least of all Monk.

But a manservant answered the door and let him in as soon as he gave his name. He paid the cabby and went inside. He dreaded this. He had no answers. It had happened to him before, this feeling of not knowing desperately important things, crucial things that people were going to ask him to explain. He was very aware of wearing clothes that did not fit him, the trousers coming to his ankles, not to his boots, the jacket slightly tight across his shoulders. But at least he did not carry the stench of the river with him.

He was shown into a study where a fire was roaring in the grate. Exeter stood in front of it, slightly to the side, leaning against the mantel as if unaware of its heat. Perhaps he would never feel warm right through again. He might burn his skin and not warm the bone. His face was gray, and the glass of whisky half drunk in his hand did not seem to have brought any blood to his veins. He attempted to smile and failed. It was like a leer on a death mask. It made Monk feel worse.

"Have you news?" Exeter asked, clearing his throat before he spoke.

"No," Monk admitted. "Except that there is no other conclusion than that one of my own men betrayed us. Even if someone knew beforehand, we made last-minute changes. They knew exactly where to expect us."

Exeter nodded slowly, as if it was only just making sense to him.

"I have no idea who, or why," Monk went on. "Unless the man

also had someone being held hostage, and they would kill them if he did not betray us." It made sense, but it was no excuse.

Exeter's eyes widened a fraction. "I can't imagine anything that would make me consent to that," he said hoarsely.

Monk thought he could. If it had been Hester, would he have gone ahead? He could not bear even to think of it. "One life for another?"

Exeter shuddered. "I suppose I can't blame him," he said quietly. "If they had said to me, 'Kate's life if you do your duty,' I might have betrayed anyone at all—but not her. Let it be, Monk. If that's what it is, the poor devil will suffer enough. Perhaps it was somebody's child? Could you deliberately let your child die, to save some woman you did not even know?"

Monk knew that he could not answer that. He knew all the men had families of some sort, except Hooper. There was no one mentioned in his papers and he had never spoken of anyone. Monk identified with that, both the freedom and the loneliness.

There was a heavy silence in the room for several seconds.

"Somebody might know something that will help," Monk said. "There'll be word on the river. People might have friends, and more importantly to us, they'll have enemies. I'll find them. Not that it's much comfort to you. I'm not pretending it is."

Exeter gave something like a sob. "No," he whispered. "Right now, I don't give a damn if you find him or not. Later I will. Later, I'll put the rope around his neck and pull the trapdoor myself."

Monk could only agree.

Slowly Exeter looked up. "Talk to me about something—anything. Do you like working on the water? Do you like being a policeman? If you like the challenge, I can understand that . . ."

Monk sensed Exeter's intense loneliness. He would be torn between wanting privacy, not to be questioned or probed in his grief, and yet needing human contact as well.

"Yes, I like working on the river," he answered. "I find that now I'm used to it, I like the effort of rowing. I like the moods of the river and sense of space."

Exeter looked as if he were, at least for the moment, actually listening. "Ever been to sea?" he asked.

Monk answered without hesitation. "Yes." It was something he knew from evidence in a case not long ago, and from flashes of memory: bright, hard sunlight and the heave of the deck beneath him as the ship fought the open water.

Exeter's face quickened with interest. "Where?"

"Barbary Coast," Monk smiled. "Gold Rush days, '48, '49."

"Round the Horn," Exeter said, as if the words were an incantation.

Monk could only remember a few glimpses of that: the storm, the immense seas like rolling mountains, the vast rock face of Tierra del Fuego rising in the distance. The endless violence of the wind and water. Pitting yourself against an elemental force no man had ever conquered, only survived, and then not all.

"Me, too," Exeter said softly. "If you've sailed round the Horn, you are a man—whatever you were before." He put out his hand and Monk took it and gripped it hard. He did not add words. They only weakened a meaning that was beyond the reach of those who had not experienced it. He met Exeter's eyes, and nodded.

5

Hooper woke up the next morning, stiff and still tired. His head ached and felt heavy. It was an effort to move his legs, and both shoulders were stiff, the right more than the left. His fingers would hardly move, they were so swollen. Memory of the previous day returned with a chill he felt through his entire body. His bare feet were ice cold even on the rag rug as he swung them out of bed and stood up. He was used to physical discomfort. Long years at sea had taught him to disregard it. He knew today that part of it was due to his reluctance to face the tragedy of this case and begin the long task of trying to untangle it. He washed and shaved in cold water and dressed in his regular, nondescript working clothes, both warm and comfortable.

He ate his usual breakfast of thick, hot porridge and drank two mugs of tea as he pondered.

Kidnapping seemed to be increasing lately. This was the third one this year, but both the others had involved men. The money had been paid and the hostages recovered. One of the victims had been badly beaten, but he would heal. This case was infinitely worse. Compared with Kate's death, the money, although a huge amount, was almost trivial.

Who had betrayed them? Hooper had fought with that half the night. He had considered every man, and at first cast them all aside. But dreams came even through the exhaustion of sleep, dreams of shifting faces, people not being who they seemed, altering all the time. Even as he pursued and fought them, they changed into someone else, strangers he thought he knew but didn't. That was why he woke so cold; the feeling was inside him.

Hooper knew that he himself was not who he seemed. He had faced that fact all of the twenty years since the mutiny that had caused him to leave the Merchant Navy, to seek a new career and a new identity ashore. He had told no one. He had almost told Monk, on occasions when they had been close. There was a rare bond between them, and he admired and trusted Monk. He did not want to break that trust by telling him the truth about himself. He would never break Monk's trust by telling anyone of Monk's secret vulnerability and the past he could not remember, yet Hooper could not trust Monk with his own past, which he could remember only too well.

Why not? Did he think Monk would betray him? Not unless Hester's life depended on it. It was because Monk would think so much less of him, and that would cut more deeply than he could overcome. Hooper had very few people in his life whose opinions could wound him. In fact, Monk's was the only one.

He cleared away his breakfast dish and put the porridge pan to soak, then collected his coat and went out. He lived not far from the Wapping Police Station. It was easier to walk than to look for a hansom, and it was always cheaper. He turned up his collar and walked briskly. The light on the water was glittering. The wind had drawn all the staleness from it and the water was choppy, a touch of white foam curling here and there. It would be hard work rowing against it. The gulls were crying, searching for food. They were noisy, greedy beggars, but he loved to see the light on their wings and the easy, seemingly careless way they rode the currents. At first, he had liked being at sea;

there was a freedom to it, always moving, the sense of infinite possibilities.

But you were also marooned with the men of your crew. Fate chose your companions for you. You had no say in that at all. Your needs and your safety depended upon them, and theirs upon you. There was no escaping that. Even now when he closed his eyes, he could see the white faces of the other men, the fear they could not find words for. The sea was capricious, beautiful, merciless like some primitive god that was never appeased. You could make no bargains with the sea. It was all-powerful. And yet from it came the breath of the world. He was born to an island race. It was in his blood.

He was almost at Wapping. It was time to put past loyalties out of his mind and face new tests. One of the more bitter ones was starting today, in a matter of minutes. Who had betrayed them? Why? It was going to be painful; it always was. But was it going to be a surprise, or something they always should have seen?

Hooper reached the Wapping dock, crossed over the open space to the police station door, and went inside. He hung up his coat and immediately knocked on Monk's office door.

"Come in," Monk called from inside.

Hooper pushed the door open. "Good morning, sir." He entered and closed the door behind him. One glance at Monk's lean face, the lines of tiredness, the strain about his stance, and Hooper understood exactly how he felt.

"Not very," Monk said in a flat voice. "It's in the press. They got on to Exeter first thing this morning, and there are flyers out already. I expect the midday editions will have all the details. At the moment, it's just kidnap and murder, but the rest will come."

Hooper gritted his teeth. He thought of suggesting that the papers might help them, but even if not until the evening editions, blame would be placed on the River Police quickly enough, and they would be accused of incompetence. Then the betrayal would be exposed, even if no particular man was blamed. It was only a matter of time. "We better start looking into what happened."

"If you're going to tell me it was one of our own men who betrayed us, I know. For God's sake why, Hooper? Why would any of us do that?" He looked dazed, as if getting up slowly after a bad fall, still uncertain of his balance. "Is any man that desperate for money? How much? Half the ransom? More?" He shook his head. "Or is it a threat? Next time you are alone on the river at night, you'd better watch every shadow, listen for each footfall? Have we come to that: We're more afraid of them than they are of us?"

"No, sir," Hooper replied, although it was not so difficult to imagine. "But there have been one or two kidnappings lately. What would you have paid for Mrs. Monk?" It was a harsh thing to ask, but appropriate.

"I've no money to pay . . ." Monk began, but then, as the realization came to him, he stopped. It didn't have to be money; the motivation could be anything. "God, Hooper, where does it end? The only man who's safe is the man who has nobody he cares for. And who wants such a man on the force? Who would want to be such a person?"

Then an even bleaker look came into his face, a pain Hooper had not seen in him before.

"I don't know enough about my own men," Monk began. "Just facts, details, things one says lightly. Not the depth behind it."

So, it was regret. Perhaps even shame. "You're the commander, sir," Hooper said. "There's a distance—"

Monk gave him a glare. Hooper stopped. It was true, even if Monk did not want to hear it. He was in command. It was necessary a captain's men did not see him as an equal. It may be painful to be alone, but to a degree it was necessary. Hooper remembered his own captain that last voyage. Ledburn had certainly been alone, unapproachable, unreachable. Hooper had wiped from his mind the last time he had seen him. He did not want to face it at all, and certainly not now.

Monk seemed frozen.

"I can tell you a little about them," Hooper said, his own voice sounding strange in his ears. He knew the men were shy in front of Monk, afraid their personal remarks would leave them vulnerable.

Monk was waiting. Perhaps it was time for a measure of truth.

"Laker has a brother," Hooper began. "Don't know whether he's older or younger, but they're not close. Yet a bit of a rivalry there. I think the brother's more . . . orthodox. Never considered Laker quite good enough. Don't think they keep in touch, but he's always there in the background."

"Does Laker need his approval?" Monk said with surprise.

"Probably. Although he'd never admit it." Hooper smiled very slightly. "And he'd certainly not make the changes in his own way of living that would earn it. But family loyalty is a hard thing to deny, when it comes to the point."

"You mean that if the brother was in trouble, Laker wouldn't let him down?"

"I think if his brother was in trouble, Laker would be the last person he would ask for help," Hooper said, remembering the expression on Laker's face when mentioning his brother's name, the mixture of anger and pain in it. "Which is a pity," he went on, "because Laker would be the best person to help him—in most things anyway—maybe the only person who would be brave enough, and imaginative enough."

Monk winced.

"Bathurst comes from a big family," Hooper said. "Lost his father a while back."

"And if the kidnappers took one of his family?" Monk asked. His whole body was awkward when he spoke, his muscles aching.

"He'd have come to you," Hooper replied simply. "He thinks very highly of you. He'd expect you to understand . . . and help. God knows how!" Monk looked as if Hooper had just placed a lead weight on his shoulders. Hooper felt as if he could see right into his head.

"Walcott has a wife and son," Hooper went on. "Don't know much about them. Don't know much about Walcott himself, for that matter."

Monk's curiosity showed. He did not bother to put the question into words.

"There's nothing really wrong with him," Hooper answered. "Doesn't fit in yet. Too soon. He's a man who takes his time."

"And Marbury? He hasn't been long with us either," Monk said.

"He's good on the water," Hooper replied. He was surprised at that. For a man not born to the water, Marbury was unusually at ease. "Quiet. Nothing wrong with that."

"No family?"

"Yes. Wife and daughter. Lost a son a while back. Don't know how. He doesn't talk about it, and I didn't ask."

Monk thought for a moment.

Hooper waited.

Monk raised his head. "Who don't we know about? Who's in debt? Who's courting someone, and vulnerable? Who's got God knows what secret, and is terrified of being exposed?" A shadow crossed his eyes, of memories lost, or imagined. "Maybe terrified of having someone they love cut to pieces by the bastards who did this? We've got to get them, Hooper, or this is never ending!"

"I know that, sir. And we've got to keep the river safe as well. This could be meant to rock us so badly that we forget everything else. There could be something else planned, and we're so full of doubt about ourselves, and each other, that we miss it." He met Monk's eyes squarely and saw a sudden flare of gratitude in them. It was there and then gone again, but he recognized it. He smiled very sadly. "We're still on for the raid tonight on the warehouse? There have been two others there recently, but this time we know, and there'll be no excuse if we fail."

"I know. And yes, we are," Monk said firmly. "Can't let everything else slide because of this. What did we do wrong, Hooper? Why did they kill Kate?"

"I don't know. I might go and see the cousin again. See what else she knows about Kate . . . or Exeter." He felt a faint heat rising up in his face. "This feels personal. He's done a lot of business. Made a lot of money."

Monk's answer was very quiet. "Yes, it does. Seems like a deep and terrible hatred to me. Frightening thought—to have an enemy like that."

"Does Exeter have any suggestions?" Hooper asked.

"Not that he's telling us."

"Can't blame him. I wouldn't want to think that anyone hated me that much. Or even more, that in some way, however obliquely, her death was my fault."

HOOPER COLLECTED CLACTON AND explained their task as he had decided he would, walking along dockside, close together so they would not have to raise their voices to be heard.

"All of them, sir?" Clacton was clearly extremely uncomfortable. He was about fifty, a very ordinary-looking man, until you noticed his mouth. Even in repose he almost smiled. There was an ease about him usually, but now that Hooper had just told him they were to investigate the five men who had been on last night's rescue attempt, he was uncomfortable.

"Yes," Hooper said firmly. "If you leave someone out, then they are unprotected . . ."

"Unprotected!" Clacton stopped and turned to face Hooper. "You're saying one of them betrayed you—more important, betrayed that poor woman to her death. And I'm supposed to investigate all of them to see if . . . if they did it?"

"What would you do, Clacton, if they took the person most important to you, and said you betray your mates or I'll kill her—or him—slowly? Pull them apart like a cooked chicken."

"Stop it!" Clacton raised his voice angrily. "I'd tell Mr. Monk and—"

"Would you? Are you sure?" Hooper asked. "Believe me, you're not . . . not if it happens to you. I don't know what I'd do . . . if I had someone I loved."

Clacton was about to speak; then he seemed to see the second meaning behind what Hooper was saying. That he had no one.

Hooper could see the moment of compassion in Clacton's eyes. And he liked him for it.

"Yes, sir," Clacton said. "I'll make sure they're all safe and accounted for. I may not get it all done today, if they aren't exactly where they ought to be."

"Just be thorough. I'll see Mrs. Monk's all right, and Scuff . . . sorry, Will." He could not help a bleak smile at his own correction. Scuff was a mudlark, a child who survived by scavenging in the tidal mud at the Thames bank—at least he used to be. He did not know exactly how old he'd been at the time Monk first met him, but he claimed to be eleven, which made him about twelve when Monk had adopted him. Actually, he had adopted Monk. He had been street-smart, and river-wise. At eleven, he had known about the tricks of the eddies and tides, of the sudden weather changes, and certainly more of the various kinds of people who survived on the river's margins than Monk did. He had also known that Monk was a soft touch for a ham sandwich and a hot cup of tea. Hooper thought Scuff must have been closer to nine than eleven. But that was years ago . . . what did it matter now?

Scuff had gone reluctantly to live in Monk's house, at first very nervous of Hester. Women were an unknown quantity, and he was afraid of her gentleness. He would not expose his vulnerability by needing anyone. Over the years he had adapted, even gone to school. Monk had expected he might become a River Policeman like himself. Instead, Scuff had chosen very firmly to be a doctor, or at least as far along that way as he could . . . like Hester. After her experience as a nurse with Florence Nightingale in the Crimean War, she knew as much as many doctors. Scuff was now apprenticed to a man named Crow who had practiced unlicensed medicine among the poor for years. Recently, he had qualified officially with Hester's help and on her insistence. Scuff, who had no idea what his real name was, had decided that "Scuff" was not a name for a doctor. He would not be William, like Monk, but he would be Will.

Clacton had learned all this by listening. He would begin the task Hooper had given him. Anyone who cared was vulnerable. He said very little, but it was there in his face. He would understand what torn loyalties were about. "Yes, sir," he said to Hooper.

Hooper smiled, satisfied, as much as was possible in the circumstances.

It took Hooper most of the morning to make sure Hester was safe. He ascertained that she was at the clinic she ran in Portpool Lane, and left it at that. It took him longer to find Scuff . . . Will, but he, too, seemed safe.

He found him assisting Crow, the doctor who was training him, with a street accident.

Hooper was pleased, but not without a twinge of envy. There was no one he had influenced so well, no one who trusted him, no . . . "love" was the word. No one who loved him as completely as this young man loved Monk. What opportunities had Hooper wasted by being so self-contained? Had he allowed the past to close him off? He knew the answer even as he framed the question. Monk's past was a shut book. He himself had no idea what ghosts, good or bad, it might hold. But he had not denied the present.

Hooper had. Perhaps it was time he changed that.

Except that the past lay across him like a shadow, and he was afraid that it heralded the coming of the night. He had escaped the mutiny so thoroughly he had almost forgotten it. Now, with Monk needing to know about the vulnerabilities of all his men, it loomed large again, filling the horizon. Hooper had kept his silence for so long it amounted to a lie. It was a burden that would prevent him from getting any job at all, let alone as a River Policeman, which he loved and was good at. One reason he had not sought promotion was to avoid the attention and the exhumation of the past that it would bring.

So why was he going even now to see Celia Darwin for information about the Exeters? Because she was the only source they had on a personal level? Or because he wanted to see that strange, gentle, quiet woman who seemed to have so much more to say, if only she was asked? And because he found himself smiling at the thought of seeing her again?

It was a painful conflict of feelings inside him, high up in his chest, where it choked his throat, but he went anyway. His feet seemed to take him there, without his conscious direction. He was still turning over the weight of it when he stood at the door and she answered it.

"Good afternoon, Mr. Hooper," she said in surprise. "Have you some news already?"

"No, ma'am, I'm afraid not." He felt guilty for raising her hopes falsely. It occurred to him only now to wonder if Exeter had even told her of Kate's death. Damn! He should have thought of that. She did not look as grieved as she surely would had he done so. There was no choice open to him but to be honest. "Has Mr. Exeter not spoken to you today?"

She stared at him, and the color drained from her face. Her eyes were clear, gray, like the evening sky, and filled now with tears.

"I'm sorry," he said in little more than a whisper. It was not the time to express the fury he felt that Exeter had not told her himself. She should not hear of Kate's death from a stranger.

She shook her head slowly, not denying what he implied, but perhaps denying the hope inside her.

"Would you like to go inside and sit down?" he suggested. "If you have no maid present, I can make you a cup of tea. Tell me where the kitchen is."

"No . . . I . . . I can . . . Mary is out on an errand. She'll be back soon." She was fumbling for words. "If you didn't mean to tell me about Kate, then you came for some other reason." She backed away from the front door and found her way to the parlor, accidentally catching her elbow on the corner of the doorframe. She winced, but said nothing, as if she barely felt it.

Hooper closed the front door.

Celia went into the parlor and sank into one of the chairs.

"Kitchen?" he asked.

She looked up at him, puzzled. "I beg your pardon?"

"I'll find it," he replied, and turned away. Poor woman. She looked devastated. Was it for Exeter, or Kate, or because she had lost perhaps the only family and the best friend she had?

He found the kitchen quite easily, and there was a teapot on the table. He pulled the kettle over onto the hob and made sure there was water in it. He had lived alone all his adult life and was used to such things. Like many men in the Merchant Navy, he could cook a little, sew, and generally look after himself.

Ten minutes later he carried the tray of tea into the parlor. His intention had served not only to bring her tea, but to give her a little time to compose herself. She sat upright now, her hands folded in her lap and her face so white she looked as if there were no blood in her.

"Mr. Hooper, will you tell me what happened, please? Was Mr. Exeter hurt? I don't think I want the details. He may not find me of any use at all, but I must be aware. Kate would have wished it."

Her choice of words gave away perhaps more than she thought.

He poured the tea and passed her a cup, offering the milk jug at the same time. She poured in milk, then took the cup and set it down on the table between them, her hands shaking a little.

"We did exactly as we were told," he began. He would tell her the truth but without the details. "At Jacob's Island, which is a terrible place, full of old houses settling into the mud and passageways so old and so rotten that portions are under the high-water mark. We followed their directions. Mr. Monk and Mr. Exeter went ahead with a case full of money."

She blinked. "Just the two of them?"

"That was the instruction. The rest of us stayed well back, in the various passages. We were all attacked, as if they knew where we were." He wanted to be careful not to give details that would distress her even more. He hurried on. "No one was badly injured. Just bruised and filthy. Then Mr. Exeter completed the last bit alone, as he had been instructed. They attacked him, too, and took the money." How could he say this so it would be the truth, but not as brutal as it had been? It should have been someone she knew who told her, someone she loved and trusted, someone who could hold her in his arms and let her weep.

She was waiting, watching him.

"I'm sorry," he said softly. "They killed her anyway."

She sat motionless, staring at him.

"Perhaps Mr. Exeter's trying to think how to tell you, a gentler way . . ."

She blinked and the tears slid down her cheeks.

"Would you like me to leave you?" he asked awkwardly.

"If you would prefer."

"I wouldn't! I . . . I just thought you might . . . you don't know me," he said awkwardly.

She made a visible effort to regain her self-control. She reached for her tea and found it unexpectedly cool enough to sip. She looked at him questioningly.

"I made it with boiling water," he answered. "I just put a drop of cold in afterward."

"Oh. Thank you. Tea should always be made with water on the boil."

"Yes, I know."

"Did she suffer?"

"No," he lied.

"It must have been very quick. Thank you." She sipped the tea again. "I know that may not be the truth, but I would prefer to accept it. And I will find it easier now, when Mr. Exeter chooses to come and tell me."

"Surely he will? When he has composed himself. He was desperately upset."

"Of course." There was little emotion in her voice, or her face. Perhaps she was controlling her own feelings too tightly. Or maybe she felt something for Harry Exeter that was not appropriate at this time of bereavement.

"Or he may write," she went on. "Sometimes writing is easier. You can read it over and over, to make sure it is what you really want to say. And of course you don't have to be present when it is read."

"You don't care for him very much, do you?" Hooper asked bluntly.

"How careless of me to have made it so obvious. I shall miss Kate all the rest of my life. She was the sister I did not have."

"I'm sorry," he said. "Time may heal the wound, at least on the outside, if not deeper. But even on the outside, the scar doesn't always go."

She smiled. "One sees such wounds in the eyes, and hears them in the silences, don't you think?"

He did not answer. She had seen them in his eyes, or he chose to think she had. He sipped his tea instead. There were lots of questions he wanted to ask her, and a good detective would have found a way. He did not want to. It seemed intrusive, not what he wished to be here for. But he must at least try.

"If I ask Mr. Exeter, in time, if he has any enemies who might have done this for some kind of revenge, do you think he would tell me anything helpful? I hate to disturb him so soon, but we must catch these people, if there is any way."

She looked surprised. "You think it was personal?"

"It's possible. He isn't the only wealthy man in London."

She considered it for several moments. "It would be about money, I expect, and land. He's developing a big area somewhere on the south bank, I think. People can be jealous."

"I'll look into it. What about Kate? Was there anyone who envied him because of her?"

"Possibly. But how could anyone who loved her have killed her?" She drew in her breath quickly. "Oh, you don't mean love, do you? You mean a kind of possession. 'My wife is more beautiful, more dazzling than yours.' Like owning a fine horse, an Arabian instead of a plain pony. I don't know. She never mentioned anyone else . . . in that way. I think . . ." She did not finish.

"What?" he asked.

"I think she was very lonely," she finished quietly.

The back door closed with a sharp click and there were quick footsteps along the passage. Next moment, the maid knocked and then put her head around the door. "Oh, miss, are you all right?"

Hooper rose to his feet. "Thank you, Miss Darwin, I'm sorry I had to come with such news." He looked at the maid to make sure she understood that there was a tragedy. "And thank you for the tea."

Celia met his eyes for a moment and he was satisfied.

"Not at all, Mr. Hooper," Celia said. "I think it is not so hard this way. Thank you."

6

Monk went home in the mid-afternoon after spending the morning with the Metropolitan Police, learning what he could elicit about other kidnappings. The lights were on at the house in Paradise Place, which meant that Hester was at home. Whether he told her about the case or not, the sense of isolation, and above all of futility, would be eased a little by her presence.

She must have heard the door, maybe even been half listening for it, because she came from the kitchen immediately. She was not wearing an apron. Perhaps she had been working on the clinic papers, as she often did, spreading them all over the kitchen table.

She did not ask how he was. Instead, she looked at him gravely, at his clothes, the angles and the lack of energy in his body, then straight at his face. She understood, and made no comment on it.

"You have to go out again . . ."

"Yes."

"Can't they do it alone?"

"Yes. I'm not going because they need me . . ."

"Loyalty?" she asked.

"No." He followed her down the hall into the kitchen and sat down on one of the hard-backed chairs while she cleared her papers away. "It's not out of loyalty. In fact, rather the opposite." It was hard to say, even to her, who uniquely understood duty and the importance of trust. And yet it would be a relief to tell her; he knew that, too.

She was waiting, seeing the struggle in him.

"Hester, one of them betrayed us, and Kate Exeter was slashed to death. He is one of us, and yet that divides him from us forever. The kidnappers know he can be made to do that! They own him—he knows that and so do they. How can I not know who it is? Yet I don't even sense it."

"Because you're not looking for it," she answered. "You have to take most of what you know about people at face value. They trust you. Whether they like you or not, they know you are brave, honest to a fault." She smiled very slightly. "Short-tempered and precise. But that you'd be loyal to them and to the job, whatever it costs. I know other things about you." Her face softened and her eyes were tender. "Things they'll never know: things you dream about, things that recall moments of pain, and happiness, things you regret, and things you'll always remember. They'll never know those things about you, nor will you know those things about them."

He found himself coloring faintly, but it was from pleasure. He had trusted her with everything of himself, even if he had not entirely meant to.

"I need to know them better," he said aloud. "One of them is carrying an intolerable burden. After what happened to Kate, the guilt must be like an open blade inside him. What can't I see?"

Her face tightened. "Be careful, William. Whoever it is has already gone far past the point of returning! He'll—"

"I know," he said quickly. "I'll be careful."

She watched him silently for a few seconds, then turned and paid attention to getting his food.

WHEN MONK LEFT, HESTER stood alone for several minutes absorbing the emotions that almost overwhelmed her. She had been careful not to show how deeply she felt his pain while he was still there.

Perhaps he thought he was concealing it. For all their intimacy on so many levels—the laughter, the pain, the tenderness, even the need—he was still a proud man, and in some areas, very private. He still did not trust anyone, even her, with the raw edges of his own doubt, the pain that hurt him more than he could bear with grace.

She had seen it in his face, even if he thought he was hiding it. She could feel the urge inside herself to protect him, but she had no idea how. If any one of them, especially Hooper, had betrayed them inadvertently, or was placed under some unbearable pressure, it would destroy something inside Monk that he did not know how to repair.

There must be something she could do! Arguments of words, all the tenderness of touch, would not heal him. They might show him how much she loved him, how deeply she felt his pain, but that was not enough. It was putting a bandage on the wound. And wounds of the heart sometimes needed scouring of the infected part, just as those of the flesh needed removal of the bullet or broken knife tip.

She decided to go tell Scuff—Will now. She need not tell Monk she was doing so; he still thought of Will as a child, to be protected from certain realities. She knew better. He was learning to be a doctor. If he was going to follow in the footsteps of the duties she had learned in the army, he would have to face the rigors of amputation and other invasive surgeries. They always hurt. Sometimes the patient died from the shock to the body, but they would otherwise die for certain from their untreated wounds.

Will would understand the need for the truth, whatever it turned out to be.

Hester put on her coat and left the house immediately. She walked down the hill to the Greenwich ferry and took the first boat across. She did not know where Will would be, but she knew where to begin looking. The place to start was always at the free clinic run by Crow, the onetime street doctor, skilled but unqualified, whom she had known for years. She had finally persuaded him to take his exams. Terrified, he had done so and passed. Not perhaps with the highest of marks, but enough to qualify, and to do the work to which he had dedicated his life, and at which he had abilities that could not be quantified on paper.

He had now agreed to teach Will, in a practical way, all he could. He understood Will's dream to be a doctor and the limits of his schooling, which made it difficult to gain a place in a university. So far, it was working very well. When it was time to take surgery to a higher level, they would have to think again.

She reached Crow's clinic and found him in. As usual, he was delighted to see her and flashed his luminous smile. And as usual he was dressed all in black and busy with patients. Nevertheless, he stopped long enough to tell her that Will would be back in ten or fifteen minutes.

"Can I help?" he asked after a moment's hesitation. "It's bad?" It was half a question, half a judgment made from her expression. He had always been able to read her emotions. It was part of his nature, and a large part of his skill.

She did not evade the truth. "I want to borrow Will for . . . maybe a day or two. It's . . ."

"The kidnapping," Crow finished for her. "If he could help, he'd be no use to me or to anyone if I tried to stop him. If I can do anything, you'll tell me?" That really was a question.

"Yes," she said immediately. She did not know whether she would or not, but it would hurt him deeply if she said no.

Will came in shortly after that, and one glance at her face was enough to alarm him. He hardly resembled the eleven-year-old mudlark they had first met. He was now twenty and several inches taller than Hester. He was confident, filled out, and strong. But she could still see the vulnerable, street-smart survivor in him, the child nobody wanted, who had found Monk when he was new to the riverbank.

"What is it?" Will demanded immediately. He looked anxiously at Hester.

They were alone in one of the rooms in which Crow kept stores. They would not be interrupted. Briefly she told him what had happened, and why it mattered so much.

He stood perfectly still. He was used to dealing with sickness and injury, being cold, hungry, alone, but being in a close group, apart from Monk and Hester, was new to him. Disillusion and betrayal were things he had not had to face before. When you trust no one and believe in nothing, you are vulnerable to anything, and yet in some ways also to nothing. He was still learning what it was to belong irrevocably, not to be able to walk away because the ties are too deep, too woven into who you are, who you want and need to be, where all that is comfortable and precious resides.

"Well, it couldn't be Hooper." He made it a statement, but his eyes pleaded for her to assure him of that.

Should she? She had never lied to him, even in the hardest of times.

"We've got to prove that it isn't." She chose her words carefully. She had first known Will when he was a slender-necked, narrow-shouldered little boy, but fully independent, trusting no one, and with a deep suspicion of all women. His own mother had turned him out for the new man in her life, who protected her and the younger children. It had taken Scuff a long time to allow himself to care for Hester. He had loved Monk easily, because he had been able to teach Monk much about the river he had known since birth.

And yet it was Hester's career he had chosen to follow, not Monk's.

"And the others, too," Hester went on. "I'll check on Hooper. Will you look at Bathurst for me? And when we know about them, we can tell William."

Will nodded. "Tell me all you know about Bathurst. I know people. I can find out."

"Thank you. And . . ."

"What?"

"Be careful. It was a terrible thing they did to . . ."

His face looked pinched. The secure, loved young man disappeared and the frightened child, trying so hard to prove he needed no one, yet so desperately wanting someone, was clear in his eyes. "I will," he said firmly. "Don't worry."

WHEN MONK LEFT HESTER at home, he returned to Wapping and found Hooper and the rest of the men waiting for him, prepared to go catch the group of men who had successfully carried out two warehouse robberies and escaped both times. The River Police could not afford to let them slip away again.

"Ready?" Monk asked quietly.

Hooper looked at him steadily. "They're as ready as they're going to be. None of their families is missing, but you can't escape the fact that someone told the kidnappers which way we were coming in."

Ten minutes later, they were in the boats and pulling away from the Wapping steps. The wind was cold and the tide was well past low water and coming in fast. It would be a hard pull on the oars against the current. Monk threw his weight into it.

He wondered if he should try to say anything to the men to build spirit. He was in a boat with Walcott and Marbury. Hooper, Laker, and Bathurst were in the other, just a few yards away, their black bows cutting across the silver dappled water. The moon was higher now, and there were very few clouds; not the best night to catch people off guard. To anyone used to the river, they looked like exactly what they were: a police river boat, two rowing, a third man in the stern. No ferry rowed in that arrangement, and they had no platform on which to carry cargo. They were obviously moving swiftly, and with purpose.

For several minutes they rowed in silence, except for the creak of the rowlocks and the swish of the water. Careful planning had gone into the raid, and everything indicated they would be successful. And yet since the kidnapping, they no longer trusted each other. Monk could feel it in each of them. They pulled the oars steadily against the weight of water, against the incoming tide, but with anger rather than exhilaration.

Monk could see that in the set of Marbury's shoulders, and on Walcott's face, toward the bow. He avoided Monk's gaze. They were all anticipating the same thing, working toward it, but separately. He knew their skills, certainly, and there were many. Their weaknesses were few, but he was mindful of them. For example, Laker sometimes thought he knew far more than he did. He was irreverent, but it hid the fact that he really did have considerable respect for both Monk and Hooper; he just didn't want them to know it.

Bathurst was keen to learn, hungry, and likeable. He was curious—a good quality in a policeman. Curious people looked for answers. It was Walcott and Marbury who were unknown, therefore suspect, whether that was fair or not.

Monk looked at Walcott sitting in the stern; a smaller man than Marbury, but pugnacious. Occasionally, when he thought no one was listening, he sang old bits of music-hall songs rather well. Once or twice, Monk had caught him, and he had immediately fallen silent. Pity. It was a pleasant sound. Why did he feel the need to conceal it?

They passed in the shadow of a big ship lying at anchor. It was suddenly too dark to see each other, or anyone else if there was another boat in the shadow. That was careless.

"Pull away!" Monk ordered sharply, throwing himself against the oar and digging deep into the swirl of the current.

Surprised, Marbury obeyed. He was stronger and heavier than Monk, if not as skilled. The boat went off course for a few yards. They shot out of the shadow into the moonlight again. There was no one else close to them.

Monk said nothing.

They still had a quarter of a mile to go. They rowed in silence, weaving past the huge shadows of moored ships, riding lights high above them and reflected yards away in the black surface of the water. Each man was silent with his own thoughts. When they reached the Bull Stairs, where they were going to go ashore, they pulled in, shipping the oars and tethering both the boats.

They went up the stone steps, one at a time, Hooper first.

Bathurst slipped and Walcott caught him.

"Watch what the hell you're doing!" Walcott said sharply. "You'll take us all down."

"Then get off my heels," Bathurst snapped back.

"Shut up, both of you," Laker hissed, his voice brittle.

Monk was the last, behind Marbury.

At the top of the steps, they separated, some to the right toward the loading dock and the cranes, some, including Monk, to the left, the warehouse entrance. They moved slowly, eyes sufficiently accustomed to the dark without lamps.

Ahead of them they could see figures moving. It was exactly what Monk had expected. The thieves were taking the cargo. He motioned his own men to stand back; if they moved before the men loaded the bales, the thieves could not be convicted of theft. At last, something was going exactly as planned.

There were two ships at the dockside—which one were they going to?

A man, bent double under the weight of the bale, passed within eight feet of Monk, who remained motionless. After several seconds, another man passed.

How many more? Monk inched sideways, as close to the warehouse wall as he could get. He saw Marbury to his left and made a gesture to him to move along toward the side door. He was aware of the tension. Did Marbury know Monk did not trust him? He must. He and Walcott were the new men.

Marbury obeyed. Then, a few moments later, they both slid silently round the gaping open door of the warehouse and inside. Over at the far end, there was one lantern on top of a pile of boxes. They could clearly see two figures moving more casks and bales, cooperating with signs and signals to each other. The soft sound of their footsteps, shuffling under the weight, was only just audible.

The men passed only nine or ten feet away from them, with the loads weighing them down. They were taking the whole shipment.

Monk rapidly adjusted his thinking. They must have a barge and would be going where there was a winch of some sort to help them unload, upriver or down.

No more men passed. It was time to go. Monk moved softly along the side of the warehouse, back to the edge of the water. The men were stowing the last of the load. Two more men stood ready. Monk knew, even in the dark, from the very grace of their steps that they were bargees. It was a highly skilled job to guide the flat-bottomed craft, squared off at bow and stern, to keep an easy pace, especially when carrying a full load. Were at least two of them bargees? Or were they additional thieves? That would make one more man than Monk had expected. Misinformation? Another error?

Monk moved nearer to make out in the dark what the thieves were doing. The barge was only a few feet from the shore, the loading almost finished. He was sure of that because the corner he could see, in the shift of moonlight through the cranes and the shadow of the ships along the shore, was so low in the water it would not take any more weight. Luck, or perfect judgment? It occurred to him that this was not the first time these men had done this.

The River Police boats were on the far side of the dock, at the opposite steps. Monk touched Marbury's arm and pointed away. Marbury followed him the twenty yards back to where they were moored and down to the water. They climbed into their boats quickly and Walcott, at the back oar, pulled away and round the corner to the open water. The current felt stronger.

They were pulling out into the river, into the main stream of the flood tide. They could see glimpses of the barge ahead of them. The other police boat was invisible.

Walcott was facing Monk, back to the prow, as all oarsmen were. Occasional lit windows and strings of lights along the street were visible where the alley ran down between warehouses to the shore.

"Want a hand?" Marbury offered.

"Think I can't manage on my own because I've not got arms a yard long?" Walcott replied.

Marbury ignored him.

Monk was searching the river ahead for the other boat, with Hooper, Bathurst, and Laker in it. He could not see them.

There was no sound but that of the oars and the rush of the water, and far away a man shouting. Where the hell were they?

Then Monk saw them twenty yards ahead, almost level with the barge. What the devil was Hooper doing so close? Then he realized: the current was growing stronger as they came to a tighter bend in the river. He was moving out to avoid the eddies between the piers of London Bridge. He was not paying attention, and they had come much further than he thought. What were they making for? Not a ship, but another warehouse.

The barge was passing right under the shadow of the bridge. It was already out of sight. What if it went right round, turned, and came back?

"Steady!" Monk commanded.

Walcott dug in more deeply. "We'll lose them," he said. "Sir, tide's helping." He dug in and pulled deeply again, ignoring the order.

Marbury half rose to his feet, as if to take the oars from him by force.

"You'll have us in the water, you fool!" Walcott said. "Or is that what you want?" He dug the left oar in deeply, and the right one came out of the water, slicing the wave and drenching Marbury with it.

Marbury swayed and fell over sideways, landing hard on the gunwale.

"Sit down!" Monk grated between his teeth. "Are you trying to draw the attention of everybody in the bloody river?" His mind was racing. Had that been deliberate? Whether they said it or not, all the regular men suspected Walcott or Marbury. Did Walcott and Marbury suspect each other? Or did one of them know because it was him? And he had to blame the other, for his own survival?

It was Monk's task to know which one—and save the other. That man's life was in his hands, depending on his skill and his judgment, which had become so flawed.

Marbury sat down and picked up the oar. He dug it into the water and pulled it hard enough to send the bow sharply to the port.

Monk swore under his breath, but said nothing more. They passed under the Queen Street bridge. Ahead of them, the barge was sliding into the shadow of Blackfriars Bridge, and the light of the streetlamps shone in bright patterns on the water. They were distorted near the piers, by the strength of the current eddying and pulling under. Monk knew only too well how powerful it was. Small boats could be caught and smashed against the pillars, then sucked down.

"Pull out!" he shouted. He could feel the boat slewing sideways out of control. He heard the fear in his own voice. There was nothing he could do. To take the oar from Walcott now would drive them straight into the whirlpool, spinning down under the surface, breaking the timbers against the stone.

Seconds passed. Walcott was grasping and slipping. Marbury let his oar slide and lifted it out for a second, and Walcott regained control. The next stroke was almost even, the one after straight again.

Monk could feel the sweat on his body and the icy air cold on his face.

They were past the eddies and back to the shadow of the bridge. The water was still running swiftly; there were cross-vortices where the currents met. Now Monk saw the other boat ahead, Hooper at the starboard oar, Laker at the port. Bathurst sat hunched forward in the stern. He probably held the grappling iron in his hands, ready to board the barge when they drew level with it. They were traveling smoothly, picking up speed.

There was a bargee standing in the prow of the boat, leaning on his pole, and another in the stern, his body angled to make it obvious he was watching the approaching boat. He would know by now it was not a ferry because of the speed of approach.

"Fast as you can!" Monk said above the rush of the water and the creak of the rowlocks.

Walcott and Marbury obeyed silently.

The moon was rising, shedding more light on the choppy water.

There were hardly any clouds in the sky, but the river before them was obscured by a huge bend.

Ahead, the barge was slowing as the five men prepared to defend their cargo. Monk saw one of them wield the long barge pole like an immense staff, sweeping it through the air. Anyone it struck would go into the water, possibly with his head split open. Truncheons and even cutlasses would be useless against it.

Hooper stood up, deliberately slowing his boat, letting the oars drag. Laker was standing, just out of reach of the barge pole. He looked easy on his feet, swaying with the movement. Bathurst was bent over, leaning forward.

"Other side?" Marbury questioned.

Monk made the decision instantly. "No. Same side."

"Sir? Don't you want them having to defend from both sides?" Walcott argued. There was fear in his voice. He had no confidence in Monk, and he did not care who knew it.

This was a fight Monk needed to win, more even for his men's morale than to get back the stolen goods and arrest the thieves. "Ballast," he said briefly, as if that were enough. Walcott would realize soon enough, when the barge began to tip.

Hooper brought the boat alongside and Laker leaped onto the barge. He attacked the second man wielding the barge pole, ducking beneath its swing and catching the man by the legs, sending him crashing into the boxes. They rolled over, arms flailing.

Hooper rose to his feet as Bathurst shipped the oars. The first bargee swung his pole. Monk could hear the sound of it as it slashed through the air, missing Hooper by inches.

The other thieves started to come over from the far side. One of them jumped from the barge onto the boat, sending it rocking wildly. Hooper lost his balance and fell, and Bathurst had to step sideways over the forward gunwale.

Laker was getting the better of his man, but there were now two more attacking him.

The barge rocked so hard, two of the bales shifted, sliding to the starboard and making the barge list badly.

One of the thieves yelled something, an order, a warning. Two of them tackling Laker left him immediately and started to heave at the boxes, to no effect. There was fear in their voices now. The current was fast and strong. It was slowly carrying them backward toward Blackfriars Bridge and the eddies beneath.

Monk smiled grimly, only too aware of the danger. He had not meant it to be this close. A man who went overboard in the Thames did not often survive. It was not such a big river, but it was full of powerful currents, bending back on each other as they found obstacles, filthy, strongly tidal, and, at certain times of the year, cold enough to rob you of breath.

Marbury understood now and was putting all his weight against the drag of the boat. They were nearly at the barge. Walcott was ready in the bow, grappling hook in his hands. Monk's decision to board on the same side as the first boat obliged all the thieves to spend as much time trying to stop the barge from capsizing as fighting the boarders.

Monk would have liked to keep all the cargo to return to its owners, but he was not going to risk a man's life to save it.

"Stay here!" he ordered Walcott. He and Marbury moved to the side, away from the others so as not to tip the boat, and then leaped onto the barge. Monk went for the nearest man, using the cudgel all police carried. It was heavy, easily adaptable, and silent. Unlike a gun, it could not run out of ammunition or misfire.

He fought hard, dangerously, with more violence than he had anticipated. But it gave him a deep, savage feeling of satisfaction to be able to strike at a thief, catch him in the arm that he had raised to hit Laker, and feel the bone break as he connected with it.

The man let out a howl of pain and lost his balance, landing hard on the edge of one of the crates. Laker slid away from him and grabbed one of the thief's legs in time to stop him from going overboard.

One of the men with barge poles was swinging it around his head like a long staff. It caught Monk on the shoulder, and he felt the jar of it right through his body. Marbury flung all his considerable weight on the man with the pole and sent him flying. But the man rolled over and stumbled to his feet again, coming back at Marbury.

Laker was on Monk's far side, jabbing with his fist at one of the thieves who doubled up. There was a scream and a loud splash as someone went into the water. The barge was drifting, still going up-river with the tide, but lying across the current and sliding further out into the mainstream of the river.

Both police boats were tied together, one onto the near end of the barge. There was a man, unconscious or dead, lying on top of one of the bales. Another slid down onto the deck between boxes. At least one was gone into the water.

Monk tried to make out silhouettes. He recognized Hooper from the outline of his head, Walcott from his stature and the tight, swift way he moved, like a bantamweight boxer. His blows, though, were those of a street fighter, kicking and gouging included. But the thieves would fight like that, too, with no rules, survival their only aim. Monk and his men also had to be aware they could be carrying knives. Most sailors did, although usually for practical use, not fighting.

Monk was struck from behind and pitched forward, turning as soon as he could. Some instinct remembered from his shattered past made him hunch hard and low, and then swing the cudgel again. He took a glancing blow on the side of the head and retaliated with his right knee to the groin, and then in the same movement, a blow to the throat. The man went down and stayed there.

Monk turned to see Marbury fighting with a bald-headed man. He could see that much in the light of the half-moon: the sheen on his skin, the dark patch of blood on his ear. His face was twisted with fear.

Monk looked at Marbury. He was not swinging wide, but hard and low, with his body weight behind it. Then he aimed at the man's head.

Monk leaped forward and knocked Marbury off balance, then hit him, not with all his weight, but enough to startle him and ruin his swing.

The man backed away, the terror still in his face.

"What in hell's the matter with you?" Monk shouted at Marbury.

Marbury stared at him for a moment as if he would strike back, such fury in his eyes that Monk felt a twinge of fear for himself. For a terrible moment his mind leaped to Kate Exeter. Had she seen the same look, just before she felt the blow that killed her?

Hooper was behind Marbury. He had two men manacled together. At the far end of the barge, Bathurst had two more.

Walcott seemed to be poling them very slowly toward the shore, anchor at the ready.

"Get in the boats and bring us all in," Monk said to Marbury, his voice thick in his throat. "Now!"

Slowly the rage eased out of Marbury's face and he obeyed. He was a good waterman and, with Hooper's help, they got the barges into sheltered water and cast anchor. Then they took the thieves back to the shore, minus the one who was dead and the one who had been lost in the river.

It took an hour to hand over the thieves and get the dead man ashore and to the police surgeon. Hooper attended to that before Monk faced Marbury, who was standing under a streetlamp on the dockside.

Marbury turned to leave.

"Marbury!" Monk called out sharply.

Marbury turned and looked at him. In the gaslight, his face was haggard, huge shadows around his eyes.

"What was that man to you?" Monk asked.

Marbury frowned.

"You'd have killed him if I hadn't stopped you. Don't lie. Who is he?"

"He lived down the street from me once," Marbury said, and his voice cracked. "We fought over some stupid thing, and I won. He beat my dog to death. And you're right. I would have killed him."

Monk looked at Marbury, who was standing with his shoulders bowed but his head up. He was wet, filthy, exhausted, and probably bruised all over, but it was the grief that consumed him. Monk could see that, almost feel it himself. "Then you'd better do it where I can't see you," he said quietly. "Don't want to have to take you in for it."

Marbury's face softened, his eyes shone with tears, and he turned and walked away, as if he needed to be alone.

Monk understood.

AT THE WAPPING POLICE Station they formally charged the thieves. Monk thought they were finished and could at last go home when Hooper came to him, his step brisk. He stopped in front of Monk's desk.

"Sir, one of those men has an interesting story . . . to trade."

"Trade?" Monk said with little interest. "For what? We have them."

"He knows something about the kidnapping of Mrs. Exeter. He says he actually took part in it."

"What?" Suddenly Monk was wide awake. "What part did he take? Are you sure?"

"He described Mrs. Exeter and Miss Darwin," Hooper replied. "He saw them, all right. He wasn't going to tell me anything apart from that. And none of it was in the newspapers. He was there."

Monk pushed his chair back and stood up, his joints and back stiff from the fight on Jacob's Island, and then this evening.

Hooper turned and Monk followed him to where one of the men from the barge was sitting. He looked up at Monk, ignoring Hooper.

Monk stopped in front of him. "All right. What have you got to offer, and what do you want for it?" he asked tersely.

The man studied Monk's face. He was perhaps thirty, fair-haired, quite pleasant-looking, if he was to smile. "I want to get out of here, with no charge," he answered.

"And what have you got, other than taking part in a kidnap and murder, for which you will be hanged?" Monk countered.

The man stiffened, but he did not yield. "I had no part in what 'appened to 'er," he said a little unsteadily. "I just rowed the boat. I took the one what took 'er in. I rowed 'im downriver to Jacob's Island, and that's where 'e took 'er, an' paid me. 'E told me it were a prank. Get even with 'er 'usband. She were alive when 'e went. And I ain't telling you no more till I get suffink from you. I row—that's all I do. Don't steal nothing, don't kill nobody."

Monk looked at the man steadily. Was it worth letting him go to get the name and description of the man who took Kate? What guarantee was there that it was the truth?

"Describe the woman," he said.

"Young one, tall, dark hair, very 'andsome, she was. Wearing a dress with flowers on, green, mostly. She had a little mark on 'er face, 'ere." He pointed to his cheek. Monk remembered it on what was left untouched of Kate's dead face.

"And the other woman?" Monk asked. The man could hardly have glimpsed Celia. What would he say?

"Older. She limped a bit. Never saw 'er face, but she was about the same height. Only saw 'er for a moment, but I'd say she older," the man replied.

"And you're just a man who rows people on the river," Monk stated.

"Yeah. That's right. Not really a crime. You can't prove I ever did, 'cos I didn't."

"Right," Monk agreed. "We won't charge you, this time. What was the name of the other man in the boat that took Mrs. Exeter from . . . where?"

"The Embankment, north side."

"His name?"

"Lister. Albert Lister."

"Describe him."

"Wiry. Quite tall. Long face. Long nose. Fancy dresser, when 'e can. Likes fancy jackets."

"Who was there when you dropped Mrs. Exeter off at Jacob's Island? Was she conscious then?"

"Yeah, I didn't see nobody else. But could've been any number o' people. You know Jacob's Island?"

"Yes."

"Then you know there could 'a been a hundred people 'ere, an' you wouldn't 'a seen them."

"Yes. Cut him loose, Hooper. But get all his details. We won't forget him."

"Yes, sir."

"Hooper!" Monk called as Hooper turned toward the thief.

"Yes, sir." Hooper faced Monk once again.

"Thank you," Monk said, with obvious sincerity in his voice.

WHILE MONK WAS ON the river, Celia Darwin was sitting beside the fire in her parlor feeling alone, too tired to weep. She missed Kate terribly. It was not that they went anywhere together that was so special; it was the pleasure of sharing it. They talked of everything and nothing, remembered things that were funny, or beautiful, or just unexpected. They thought of all the places it would be wonderful to visit, not with any expectation of actually going. It was the dreams shared that mattered.

It was everything shared that mattered. It was having someone with whom you could laugh at the small things, the dreams, and at times the fears or disappointments. To speak with somebody who never saw you unkindly, who laughed with you, not at you.

She realized that thinking this way of Kate was making the pain deeper, yet not thinking of her was more difficult and felt like a betrayal, as if she had not been so intensely important after all!

Celia was disturbed by the doorbell. She did not want to see anyone, certainly not some well-meaning friend who couldn't say anything meaningful. Because there wasn't anything to say. She hoped it was not the minister, come out of Christian duty. If it was, she would claim to be unwell.

There was a tap on the door and Mary came in. The poor girl did not know what to say either. Celia should really be kinder to her.

"It's Mr. Exeter, miss," Mary said. "I can't leave him on the step . . ."

"No, of course not." Celia stood up with an effort. The leg she limped on had never hurt before. It hurt now. Or perhaps it was just the consuming pain that was everywhere.

"Come in, Harry," she said when he stood in the hall. "Would you like tea? Or . . . something else?"

He shook his head and walked over to the chair on the other side of the hearth. He fell into it rather than sat down. He looked as if he had not slept since Kate was taken. His face was haggard and he was badly shaved, with little cuts in the skin here and there, as if he would not sit still for his valet to work. He was pale, and his dark clothes hung on him, robbing him of form and color.

"How are you?" he asked, his voice sounding unnatural. She was trying to remember the last time he was here, in fact if he had ever been here before. What should she say to such a question?

"The day has gone by heavy and slow as a steamroller," she replied to him.

He looked at her with surprise. "I didn't know you had such a turn of phrase. It has, hasn't it?" He gave the ghost of a smile. "I told myself I came to see how you were, as if I could do anything about what you must feel. But in truth I came because I can't stand being in the house anymore. Every room is filled with memories of Kate. I expect her to come in through the door any moment. And as each moment goes by, she doesn't. I had to get out, even if only to remind myself that the rest of the world is still there. Does everyone bereaved feel like this?"

"I expect so," she replied. "It seems just like that to me."

He leaned forward a little in the chair. "I knew it would," he said softly. "I came for my own sake. Does that sound brutal? I don't mean it to. I'm sorry."

"No," she said quickly. "There is no need to apologize. I feel . . . I feel the same. There is a great hole in the middle of everything. It's . . . it's good to speak to someone who feels the same. It's a terrible loneliness when you can't share it."

"You're very understanding, Celia. I can see why Kate loved you like a sister . . ." He stopped suddenly and bowed his head, as his voice choked with tears.

"I'll get us a cup of tea," she said, rising to her feet and leaving the room to offer him a little privacy until he could compose himself. This was a side of him she had never seen. It made it all better . . . and worse.

MONK SET OFF FOR home that night tired, filthy, and bruised. However, none of his men was seriously hurt, and they had captured the thieves and most of the stolen goods. Only one crate had been lost. It was no doubt deeply settled in the mud at the bottom of the river.

It was a good result, but not the one Monk had been looking for. He was no further along in discovering which of his men had betrayed them, was ultimately responsible for Kate Exeter's death. He definitely had seen a more emotional side of Marbury, who was clearly another lonely man, in spite of having a family. Perhaps they were not close? Or perhaps the loss of a son had driven them apart, exposed the gaps between them that had been carefully concealed before. It happened. People blamed each other out of anger and the belief that someone had to be at fault. Anger could be easier to bear than grief. Perhaps the dog had offered him trust and an unjudging love that he had badly needed.

It shed no light that Monk could see on the kidnapping.

How could he have worked with these men, some of them for years, and yet apparently known them so little that this could happen?

He was walking up the hill from the ferry, toward Paradise Place. It was one in the morning. He was tired and the road was steep and icy in places. His body ached. He was bruised from fighting, but the hurt inside him was more insistent. He liked Hooper. He had always liked him. Only now did he realize that the trust did not go as easily the other way. Hooper trusted him as an officer—he knew that—but not as a man. Monk knew very little about him. He seldom spoke of himself, and Monk was only just becoming aware of this. He vividly remembered sitting in one of the boats and talking to Hooper about his own amnesia, the utter silence in the stretch of years before waking in the hospital after the accident, as if he had been born that instant.

Bits of the past came floating back. The sudden flashes had stopped quite a while ago, but every so often events occurred, other people knew him, liked him or disliked him, and he had no idea why. He had discovered painfully why some people hated him. He had had to tell Hooper because one of those threats had been real, and very serious. He could remember every moment of that time: the light on the water, the gentle rocking of the boat in the current, the whisper of water around the hull, Hooper's face.

Hooper had understood and not blamed him, certain of his innocence, even when he was not himself. And yet, he knew nothing of Hooper. Monk felt bitterly alone as he leaned forward in the steepest and last few yards of the road. He did not know himself. How did Hester trust him? Or didn't she? Was she biting back suspicions now and then, and too gentle to tell him?

He reached the front door and took out his key. Hester would have locked the door at dusk but not yet shot the bolts, until he came home. He opened the door, closed it, bolted it, and stood in the hall. It was warm and smelled faintly of lemon and beeswax.

She must have heard him because she appeared at the top of the stairs in her dressing robe. Her eyes widened when she saw his appearance, and she came down the stairs quickly.

"William, are you all right?"

He wanted to say, *No, I'm not. I hurt inside so I can hardly bear it, and I don't know what to do to make it stop.* Instead he said, "Yes," far more calmly than he felt. "Just a bit bruised . . . and wet."

She walked up to him quietly and put her arms around him, disregarding the mud and water on his coat.

He hugged her hard, almost hard enough to hurt, he knew, but it didn't stop him. It was several moments before he let her go—too long to avoid having her feel his emotions.

"What is it?" she asked. "Is it Exeter? Have you found anything more?"

She did not ask if he knew who had betrayed them. Was she being tactful, or had he forgotten to tell her the full extent of it? Now he could not remember. She would be so disappointed in him. He searched her face and could read the concern, but not the reason.

She was always loyal, wasn't she? But what was she thinking? That he couldn't hold a command? That he was clever with facts, but he had learned nothing about people in all the years they had been together? He could not judge men, because he did not know himself, and they sensed that and did not trust him. Hooper was the perfect example.

He moved away from her and took his coat off. He hung it up. There was no point in cleaning it. The mud would come off better when it was dry anyway.

"A little," he answered the question. "We know how many men were involved, and we've got our eyes on one of them. Follow it tomorrow. This evening, we got half a dozen thieves for robbing a warehouse."

She looked at him for a moment or two, waiting for him to continue. Then, realizing he wasn't going to, she turned to go into the kitchen. "I've a hot lamb stew on, and mashed potatoes, if you're hungry?"

"Yes, please." He was hungry but, even more important than that, he was allowing her to do something to help him, which she wanted to, and he would not have to talk while he was eating. He followed her into the kitchen and into the scullery beyond that, to wash his hands and face, get rid of the taste and smell of the river, at least superficially.

He thought of Rathbone and Beata, eating in their elegant dining room. He had let them down. Exeter had trusted Rathbone, and Rathbone had trusted Monk.

And then he thought of Exeter, who was probably not eating at all. Was he sitting in his big house, alone, memories of Kate all around him, and a glass of whisky in his hand? And then another, and another, until at least for a while he could not feel the pain?

The stew was hot and, when he bothered to taste it, delicious. He ate carefully, in silence. He wished Hester would ask him, demand that he tell her what information he had about Kate Exeter. Monk and Hooper planned to begin looking for Lister in the morning. Perhaps it was the first real lead. It was a relief when at last she did, tentatively at first, as if she were afraid of the pain it would cause him. He wanted to share it, say it over again, and believe it would lead somewhere.

MONK LEFT EARLY FOR Wapping. The clean clothes and freshly shaved face and brushed hair only masked the tiredness he felt inside, as he walked stiffly up from the ferry and into the Wapping Police Station. Hooper was a little late in, and he looked no better than Monk felt. His face was pale and it cost him a visible effort to appear interested. Several other of the men were here already, noticeably Walcott, who looked cold, in spite of sitting the closest to the potbellied stove. His attention was entirely on the paper he was writing up at his desk.

Was this what it was going to be like until they found out who had betrayed them? What if they never did? Could they go on with suspicion and a sense of lost fellowship, no one daring to turn his back on the man who was supposed to guard their backs in trouble, catch the error they had missed, believe in them when the public saw only their choices and their omissions?

They could not function like that. Those who could would find other jobs; probably the best of them would go. What would that leave?

Hooper was a good man in every way. Would he be the first to go? Laker was young and ambitious. The Metropolitan Police would be lucky to have him.

Hooper was standing in front of Monk's desk.

Monk looked up.

"Got a bit of information, sir," Hooper said. "Could involve this Lister. Lot of money changing hands that can't easily be explained. Looks like they may be splitting up some of the ransom—people who are not usually in that type of good fortune. Not thieves or fences, or anything of that kind. Talking hundreds, not the odd fifty or so. Sort of proportion you'd expect from real violence. And cash, not sale of stolen goods, unless it was something big, and taken long enough ago for the fuss to have died down."

Monk's attention was complete. "Any name? Like Lister, for example?"

"Maybe. Jimmy Patch, one of my informers, says it's enough to rent a house for the rest of his life."

"If this is money from the people who took Kate Exeter, the rest of his life could be a couple of weeks," Monk said sourly. "Do you think it's a lead?" He wished it too much to trust his own judgment.

"It's the best lead we've got, sir. Questioned everybody up and down the river. Lots of people don't like Exeter, but can't find anyone with a real grudge. Most of it's just because he's richer than they are, and can make a better deal. He's failed sometimes, but so has everyone else. Nobody can tie him to anything crooked. Takes a few chances, but most people admire that."

"And Kate, his wife?"

"Apparently an heiress in her own right. Didn't marry him for his money. Can't find anything about her that's suspicious. And before you ask, she's not the sort of woman to have had an affair. Whatever she actually felt for Exeter."

Monk stiffened. "Whatever she felt for him?"

Hooper hesitated only a moment. "I spoke to Miss Darwin again. It's only an impression, but they were close, more like sisters, and maybe Kate wasn't as enamored of Exeter as he was of her."

"Could that just be Miss Darwin's emotions, projected on a woman who seemed to have everything? Didn't you say she was the poor cousin, and with a limp into the bargain?"

Hooper's expression hardened. "I didn't get that impression, sir. I thought her unusually honest. A practical sort of person."

Monk's attention tightened. He was used to Hooper's choice of words, and his certain way of understating his approval. "You thought well of her?"

There was a faint color in Hooper's cheeks. "That was my impression, sir."

"Then we'd better go and find Jimmy Patch." Monk rose to his feet. "See if he can lead us to Lister."

Hooper remained where he was in front of the desk.

"What's the matter?" Monk asked.

"It could be unpleasant, sir. If there's that much money involved, even if it isn't our murder, it could turn nasty."

"If there's that much money involved, it's already nasty," Monk answered. "And we damned well better be involved."

Hooper still did not move.

Monk stared at him. "Well?"

Hooper spoke very quietly. "One of us is in this, sir. None of us knows who we can trust, and who we can't. You should be asking that, sir, not out in the water where you can meet with an accident."

"I can meet with an accident in any dark alley, just as we all could," Monk replied between his teeth. "Or are you afraid for yourself on the water with me?"

Surprise, then anger, took the smile from Hooper's face. "No, sir. I reckon I'd be a match for you, if it came to that. And you don't like that dark water and the currents any more than I do."

Monk was too startled to reply for several seconds, and then he laughed. The black, bitter humor he felt was too close to pain, but it broke a certain tension inside him. "I'm coming at it from the other end," he said. "I don't know who the hell it is, from here. Maybe if we catch some of the kidnappers, they will show us who's the inside man, God help him. Come on." He moved away from the desk and this time Hooper followed him.

Out on the water they were busy with movement and surrounded by the sound of the river. Silence was easier, but the unanswered question was still there between them. Monk had trusted Hooper without ever having to think about it. He was straight about everything, even to the point of awkwardness. When he needed to be tactful, he resorted to silence. And yet he could be extremely gentle when he saw injury. He could convey understanding in the simplest language. What was it now that he could not trust Monk to know? The thought of how ugly it must be frightened Monk. A part of what he so liked in Hooper was his lack of complexity, of the kind of secrets that haunted Monk himself. He was not pleased to see himself so shallow.

They moved swiftly, still catching the low tide, but it was already past slack water and it became harder as they went down past Limehouse, along the stretch toward the Isle of Dogs.

Monk's thoughts grew darker as the morning light showed the wharfs and docksides more clearly. Some of them stretched far out into the river, the water swirling around the broken stakes and half timbers where the boards had rotted away in places. The mud-banks were clearly visible now, but at full tide they disappeared. A conjuring trick twice a day. Now you see them, now you don't. At high tide the dockside vista looked peaceful, even rich, while men were busy unloading the treasures of the earth, come in from every place you could think of, and many you couldn't.

If Hooper had betrayed them, what conceivable thing had made him do it? Perhaps someone he loved was a hostage as well? Yet he had never spoken of anyone at all. He seemed a man utterly alone. All his friendships were with the men he worked beside—Monk himself, most of all. Was that a sham?

Monk thought of himself before the accident, the self he saw only from the outside. He had apparently had no real friends; allies, colleagues—yes, but not anyone to whom anything of his dreams and his fears could be shown. Perhaps his accident had been the best thing that had ever happened to him, even with all the confusion that had followed it, and the overwhelming tension that he himself had committed the crime that he was sent to solve.

Monk and Hooper landed at King's Arms Stairs along Limehouse Reach and went ashore. They were both casually dressed, as if they were seamen paid off from some ship and ready to find another, but not in any great hurry. Monk altered the upright way he walked and mimicked Hooper's easy roll, as if on a gently pitching deck. He pulled his cap further forward on his head to shade his eyes, which were steady, steel-gray, with an intelligence most people remembered. They found several groups of men, and Monk let Hooper do the talking. As inconspicuously as possible, he watched the ones who were idling, overhearing, and also watching.

They spent quite a while in a busy public house with beer and sandwiches, talking, apparently casually. After they had finished and lingered a bit, Hooper stood up.

"Outside the Dancing Bear in twenty minutes," he said. "Better not be early. Looks too keen. And it's pretty obvious. Sitting ducks, if anyone's that way minded."

They arrived accordingly a few minutes before the time. Five minutes later, they saw a shadow move across the open space and disappear close beside them, in the darkness against the wall. They heard nothing.

"Got some news, Patch?" Hooper asked in a perfectly normal voice.

Patch squawked loudly and demanded to know if Hooper was trying to kill him. "Could've scared the life out of me!" he accused.

"Money?" Hooper replied.

"I ain't got no money. Leastways, none that I'm gonna give you. What do you want to know? I dunno who cut that woman up. Bloody barbarian, if you ask me."

"You know about spending money," Hooper replied. "Maybe you know where it came from? You know the fences around here. You know the pawn shops. And most of the time you know who's done a good job recently, and got a bit to spend. Now you tell me who's got money you don't know where it came from."

"What's it worth?"

It was Monk who replied. "It's worth a blind eye, next time you need me not to see something. This man's nasty, cut up a helpless woman and took the money anyway." The minute the words were out of his mouth, he knew it was a tactical error. Now Patch would be more afraid of the man than of Monk. How could he repair it? He deliberately softened his voice. "Someone paid him. That's the man we want."

"How the hell do I know?"

"You know someone's got a lot of money, and you don't know where from," Monk replied. "That'll do for a start."

"No, I don't! I just told Mr. Hooper I do 'cos I'm scared of him. And I owe him one, for letting me go sometime."

"That's right," Monk agreed. "It's comfortable to have Mr. Hooper on your side, isn't it?"

"Yeah . . . right! He's straight, Mr. Hooper is."

"It will be even nicer to have me on your side and to have me owe you one, believe me. And it would be very nasty at times to have the shoe on the other foot. I'm good at remembering. And I'm good at forgetting, when it suits me."

Patch hesitated.

There was silence but for the drips of water from the eaves and the distant murmur of the river. "And I can be discreet," Monk went on. "Or not . . ."

"It were Lister. Casual like. Does a job here and a job there. Bit of a dresser, he is. Likes nice coats. Don't know where you'll find him. Prob'ly down the river from here. Other side. Deptford way, maybe. I'm not going with you, and you can't make me."

"Need a bit more," Monk said, breathing easily, controlling his sudden, sharp interest.

"Like what?"

"Favorite pub? Habits? Something so we know it's him. There's more than one 'Lister.'"

"Pig 'n' Whistle. But he don't drink beer. Likes that Irish stuff—Guineas—or what you call it. And that's all!"

"That's enough," Monk replied. "Unless, of course, that's all fluff out of your head!"

"It ain't! You owe me, Mr. Monk. And it'll bite you in the end if you don't keep your word! I'll make sure o' that."

Monk and Hooper went back to the boat, rowed downstream and across, and moored at the nearest stairs to the public house. They had quite a long walk and knew that when they got there, they might have an even longer wait before they heard mention of or saw Lister, who had recently come into a sizeable amount of money.

It actually took them the rest of the afternoon and a lot of other gossip before they found him. Lister was a slender man of average height, but he seemed more than ordinarily spry, moving with the nimble elegance of a dancer or a fighter.

"Interesting," Hooper said quietly. "Seen him before?"

"No. Wonder where he's come from," Monk replied.

"Want to bet me that that coat's new?"

"No takers," Monk said. "Only the second or third time on, I'd say."

"Bought with blood money?" Hooper moved his weight as if to stand up.

Monk put a hand on his arm and pulled him back. "Let's watch him for a while, see who he knows, what he does."

Hooper sat back down. "Better we follow him than take him in here," he said almost under his breath. "We may not be able to make anything stick. If we follow him, we'll learn who his contacts are. Follow them to the power behind him. Maybe backtrack a little? See who he's been seeing over the last few days? It's the first promising lead we've had. Give me one of the other men who worked with us on the night."

Monk hesitated. If Hooper was the traitor, and Monk did not trust him and let him know that by refusing, then it would be obvious and Hooper would know. "Good idea," he said quietly. "I'll get as much background on Lister as I can and have him bring it to you. A couple of days should tell us if Lister could be our man. But who's behind him? And, Hooper . . ."

Hooper looked at him.

"They're dangerous. Be careful."

Hooper smiled.

Monk stood up and walked away to pay the bartender for his drink, and for Hooper's, too.

CELIA WAS AT HOME in the early evening when there was a knock on the front door, and a moment later Mary knocked on the sitting-room door, then came in looking startled.

"There's a Miss Bella Franken to see you, Miss Darwin. She says it's regarding a financial matter, and . . . and Miss Katherine."

"A financial matter? What on earth has it to do with me?" Celia was totally confused. "You had better ask her to come in."

Mary withdrew, and a moment later a young woman came into the parlor. She was small and neat, and dressed almost completely in black.

"I'm sorry to intrude at such a tragic time, Miss Darwin. I feel as though I should have come sooner. I am not certain if you will care, at this moment, but I should not decide for you."

"Decide about what, Miss Franken? Please do sit down and be comfortable. May I offer you something? At least tea? It is a bitter night outside."

"I feel guilty that I did not come before, but I was not certain. I was afraid it would be . . ."

"What is it, Miss Franken?" Celia wanted to be civil to this young woman, but this was trying her patience. Grief dwarfed everything else.

"I work for Mr. Doyle, at Nicholson's Bank."

For a moment Celia did not see the connection.

"Which has the money of Mrs. Exeter's trust . . ."

"It is not mine to give, or not to give, Miss Franken. I don't care in the slightest about it. The trustee, my cousin Maurice Latham, did consult me . . ." She was finding it hard to keep her composure. The whole tragedy was a fresh, deep wound. "I . . . I hardly care about the loss of the money. Perhaps you don't understand, but it was never mine."

"I know that, and I am more profoundly sorry than I can say," Bella answered softly. "But I have to tell you. I cannot keep it secret. I have reason to believe that there has been steady embezzlement from it, over a period of years. It is quite a large amount, if I am correct. I . . . I cannot disturb Mr. Exeter over this now."

"Then Mr. Latham . . ."

Bella Franken sat motionless, her back rigid, the small muscles in her neck tight. "Mr. Latham and Mr. Doyle, the bank manager, are the trustees."

"Oh . . ." Realization washed over Celia in waves. Maurice! A thief! Or Mr. Doyle, the manager? "Could . . . could either one of them do it without the other knowing?"

"Not if they were taking care," Bella Franken replied. "Of course, if they were not checking, it might not be noticed." She looked extremely uncomfortable. "I have to go to the police. I wished to tell you first. I'm sorry."

"I understand," Celia said quietly. "You must do so; it is only right. We cannot overlook theft. Or maybe we can clear it up, find that it is our mathematical error." She smiled a little weakly. "You must be cold. Will you take some tea? Or even cocoa?"

"Yes . . . thank you." Bella Franken glanced at the curtained window, and Celia was sharply aware of how dark and cold it was outside. It must have been a strong impulse that had brought her here.

"Excuse me." Celia rose to her feet again and left to go and ask Mary to bring two large mugs of hot cocoa. Perhaps tomorrow she should go to Mr. Hooper and tell him about this? Seeing him again was an oddly comforting thought. She found herself smiling when she took the tray from Mary and returned to the parlor.

But after she opened the front door to say goodbye to Bella Franken and felt the icy wind and watched the young woman leave, alone in the dark, she stood in the hall and thought again about going to see Hooper. What would he think of her? That when Kate was killed, all she could think of was the money she was not going to inherit, because it had been taken by Kate's killers? It was gone anyway. Did it matter? Not in the slightest to Celia. And yet it did matter to her what Hooper thought of her. Let Bella Franken tell the police. She understood it.

8

Hooper remained in the public house after Monk left, nursing a pint of ale and gazing around the room as if deep in thought. To an extent, that was true, but his eyes kept returning to the figure in the well-cut jacket with the fancy lapels. Was Lister one of the kidnappers? He was thin, narrow-boned with little visible muscle on him, which was why his coat hung so elegantly, but that did not mean he was weak. Hooper had known men like that at sea. They were far stronger than they looked, and they had the endurance that many a heavier man did not. Long-distance runners were made like that!

He did not want to be noticed staring at Lister. He shifted his apparent attention to a spot a couple of yards away, where he could still see him if he moved. On the surface, Lister was not a bad-looking man, but the longer Hooper saw him, the more he noticed a predatory air about him. It was temporarily disguised behind his wide, thin-lipped smile. There was little warmth in it. More like jubilation, as if he had won something.

Hooper remembered an officer like that whom he had known in

the Merchant Navy. Mellis was very seldom unfair. The rules were strict and he was very careful about breaking them only when he was certain he could get away with it. And he always did. The thing that first reminded Hooper of Mellis was the way Lister fingered the lapel of his jacket. Mellis had had a similar mannerism: a liking for the texture of fine material, and a certain vanity, a consciousness of how he looked. He was a very good judge of character, most of the time. The only big mistake he had made was in Hooper. And it had cost them all, in the end.

But Hooper did not want to remember that. He had put it so completely out of his mind that years had gone by without his thinking of it, except first thing in the morning, when he had woken from a bad dream. He still had them, saw some of it all over again. But until now, with the question of betrayal so sharp in the air and Monk wanting to know everything about men's pasts, it came back more often, more easily. He found himself guarding his tongue, keeping silent rather than risk a slip.

Was Lister anything like Mellis? Or was the resemblance coincidental, a trick of the light and a single mannerism, just another man who liked to dress well?

He wondered who Monk would send to take his place following Lister. He would have chosen Laker in other circumstances, but suspicion had rested on all of the men who had been on the kidnap raid. There had not been enough light for any of the kidnappers to recognize them, any more than they could recognize the kidnappers. All they'd been aware of had been shadows, movements, creaks, and splashes, which could easily have been a rat or simply the tide, until the blow came and it was too late. All Hooper knew about the man who had attacked him was that he was not as tall as Hooper, but then Hooper was tall, and the man was fast and strong and had taken Hooper completely by surprise. The other policemen had said the same.

Lister rose to his feet at last, settled what seemed to be a sizeable bill—he must have been buying drinks all round—and then went out a side door to an alley. Did he know he was being watched? Or was that just his habitual way of leaving? If it was nothing more than the closest entrance to the direction he was going, then Hooper would go out of the front door and round the side to the left, quickly, and catch him before he turned off and was lost.

Hooper caught up with him fifty yards later and stayed well back. If Lister was aware he was being followed, he gave no sign of it.

Fifteen minutes later, he stopped at a pawn shop. Hooper waited outside, across the street. After nearly half an hour, Lister came out, holding in his hand a very fine gold pocket watch. He admired it in the streetlight for several moments before slipping it into his inside pocket and attaching the long gold chain through his buttonhole. It would take a fast and very slick pickpocket to remove it, and Hooper imagined Lister would be prepared for that and deal with the man accordingly. He was obviously pleased with his new treasure. He walked down the street as if he owned that, too, a swing in his stride.

Hooper followed him until Lister went to his lodgings at about eleven o'clock that night. It was dark and cold. There was already a frost. Hooper went home, ready to be up at six to find Lister again. He doubted the man would be up early, after the amount he had drunk during the evening. A sharp headache was a possibility.

It took him a long time to fall asleep. His thoughts shifted to the anxiety never far from his mind. Which of his own men had betrayed them, and not only them, but Exeter, and the wife he had loved so deeply? And what other secrets would the search lay bare? Perhaps it was selfish in the face of such grief to think of personal fears, not yet realized, but he could not discard them. When he lay alone and silent in the dark, there was nothing to hold them at bay.

In the end he turned to pleasanter things to force the darkness out of his mind and let the peace of the night take over. He wondered about Celia Darwin. There was a grace, a calm dignity about her that even the grief of Kate's death could not take from her. She was a woman who could stand with peace of mind in the middle of other people's chaos. The more he thought of it, the more it seemed like a kind of beauty now complete, more lasting than perfection of face or charm of coloring.

The thought was gentle and only too easy to believe. He went to sleep with a smile on his face.

HE WOKE IN THE morning and made breakfast. He had no need of a landlady, and he was a very passable cook himself, although a woman came in to clean and do the laundry during the day. She had a key, and he seldom even saw her. The arrangement suited him well.

He had just begun to eat when there was a knock on the scullery door. He got up reluctantly and opened it, ready for a possible attack. He relaxed when he saw Laker in the light from the kitchen lamp. He stood back.

Laker was dressed in very ordinary working clothes, but he still managed to look neat. "Morning," he said casually, stepping in. "Sorry to interrupt your breakfast." He sniffed and looked at the kippers on the table.

Hooper closed and relocked the scullery door, then returned to the stove. "Want a cup of tea?"

"Please," Laker accepted. He sat down. "And a slice of toast, if you can spare it?"

"I suppose you want a kipper, too," Hooper observed. "What are you here for, apart from breakfast?"

"My landlady doesn't do breakfast at this hour," Laker said with a shake of his head. "And I'm here to watch Lister with you, of course. Couldn't catch up with you yesterday because I had no idea where you were. Thought it better to get a decent night's sleep and start when I knew you were here. Did he do anything interesting yesterday?"

"Spent a lot of money," Hooper replied, and told Laker what he had seen. While he was recounting the day, his mind was at least half occupied wondering why Monk had sent Laker in particular. Was it possible he had found something to prove Laker's innocence? If so, Laker would be watching Hooper as much as he was watching Lister.

He took another kipper out of the pantry and fried it for Laker. Then he gave it to him, along with a slice of toast and a cup of tea.

He considered asking Laker about what Monk had said to him, but there was no way he could word it so that he would not sound suspicious. He was not sure that being so open about it would help. Laker was just frank enough to challenge him on the past he never spoke about. It was so very easy to feel suspicion, and lose sight of all the times they had been there to help each other, to share a risk, a triumph, a disaster, a joke, even a single cup of tea. He decided to keep silent. If this turned dangerous, neither of them could afford open enmity, whether it was based on an actual betrayal or just the psychological betrayal of thinking the other capable of such a thing.

Did he think Laker capable? Not the man he thought he knew. But then, how many layers were there that he did not even imagine? There was so much in his own past that no one knew; not even Monk, and certainly not Laker.

They spent the early part of the morning waiting for Lister to come out of his house. He took until half-past ten to get over the amount he had drunk to celebrate the previous evening. But then he left the front door at a brisk pace and walked down the street to find a cab on the main road. Hooper and Laker were fortunate to find a vacant cab to follow him. Twice they nearly lost him in traffic, and were surprised when he got out in South Kensington. He walked three blocks before going into a very nice restaurant and immediately over to a corner table, which had apparently been reserved for him.

Hooper glanced at Laker. Of the two of them, he looked more likely to be at home in such a place.

Laker simply nodded and went in. Hooper crossed to the opposite side of the street and waited. Did Monk have some idea where Lister might go that he had chosen Laker, who of all of them could most easily pass for a gentleman? Excepting Monk himself.

It was only just over forty minutes later that Lister came out, accompanied by a balding man, of middle age, discreetly dressed and carrying an attaché case. He looked nervous. He glanced around, as if to see who else might be in the street, then spoke quickly to Lister and shook his head with something that looked like distaste.

Lister smiled and, turning cheerfully, walked away.

Laker came out of the restaurant, glanced across at Hooper. Then without making any sign, he followed after Lister.

Hooper went after the man with the case, who walked rapidly, crossed the next street in the same manner, and only just missed being struck by an omnibus. Hooper had to stop for the vehicle to pass and then run to catch up with his quarry.

Eventually, they came to a small private bank and the man went in at the side entrance. Hooper waited nearly half an hour, but the man did not appear again. Finally, Hooper went inside and picked up a book off one of the tables. It advertised the financial services available. He looked over the top of it at the tellers and clerks going about their business. None of them resembled the man he had followed, except in the sobriety of their dress.

Finally, he asked if he might see the manager.

"Mr. Doyle is extremely busy, sir," one of the clerks told him. "May I ask what it is concerning, and give him your name, sir?"

Banking was something Hooper knew very little about, and he did not wish to draw attention to himself and his ignorance. It might warn the man who had met with Lister, and who he now was almost certain was Roger Doyle, the manager. He noted the bank's name and address and would report it to Monk. Could it be the bank that had helped Exeter finance the ransom?

He had no idea where Laker had followed Lister, and no way of knowing. He decided to return to Wapping and report the connection between Lister and Doyle. He was halfway there when he realized he was reporting to Monk directly, because he didn't trust Laker to do it after they had met up again and reported to each other their findings. It was a sharp and painful thought. He had doubted some men's competence before, but never their honesty. He fought a hard knot of anger against the man who had betrayed them, not only for the act of betrayal and what it had cost Kate Exeter and those who had loved her, but what it had cost the men at Wapping regarding their trust in each other. He had taken it for granted for so long that he had not realized how much it made up his view of the world, and his part in it.

It was Monk's opinion that mattered to him the most. He had had to work to earn it. Monk had not doubted his abilities for long, as no man had before him, since Hooper was a young man. His trust came later and was much harder to earn, because Monk did not trust easily. Only when Hooper had learned of his accident, the loss of memory, and the whole reinvention of himself did he understand why. His isolation had been complete. He had had to build his relationships one at a time, trusting no one until tested and proven.

Hooper would not say that he knew Hester more than instinctively, but he would trust her with anything, more even than Monk. She was fierce at times, opinionated certainly, always loyal to the oddest people, but there was a gentleness in her, a willingness to forgive, to pick up the lost, to heal, that he would trust beyond the loyalty of any man. Would he lose that with the loss of Monk's trust?

He would like to think not, but he did not want to put it to the test. It would hurt too deeply if he was wrong. Was that cowardly? If it was, so be it. There were some wounds one knew would be too deep, because of all the other things they meant.

By late afternoon, Hooper, having left a message for Monk at the Wapping station, was catching up on sleep before searching the pubs to find Lister again, when he heard sharp knocking on the back door. He rolled out of bed and went downstairs to stop the racket before it disturbed his neighbors.

He found Laker on the step, looking dirty and exhausted.

"Who was the man you followed?" Laker asked immediately, rushing inside and sitting down on one of the two hard-backed kitchen chairs.

Hooper pushed the kettle over onto the hob, then bent down and restoked the stove. Finally, he turned to face Laker. He was probably twenty years older than him, and he felt every day of it, but he also was deeply aware of the fear in the younger man. Anxiety showed very plain in his features, now that he was too tired to guard it. The jokes and the banter were gone, all self-protection perhaps, but it was part of his nature. The man was ambitious, keen to prove himself. He had made the odd remark, lightly, about his brother, but Hooper had seen how deep the need was for Laker to prove that he could excel, even if it was in a very different field.

And there was more behind the need to succeed—something for Laker to prove to himself—but Hooper had no idea what it was, and no need to know.

"Laker," he said.

"What?"

"The other man was a bank manager, small bank, but very nice offices. Lots of money there, I think. Very quiet, well-dressed people inside."

Laker was paying attention now. "What was Lister doing with him?"

"I don't know if we can find out. Banking's very private."

"We better tell Monk. He might be able to."

"I did. At least, I left a message for him."

Laker's face shadowed for a moment, so fast it was almost invisible. "Didn't trust me to?"

"If you were following Lister, you didn't have time to."

Laker smiled. He did not believe him, but he chose not to pursue it. Perhaps he didn't trust Hooper either.

"Where did Lister go?" Hooper asked.

"All over the place," Laker replied ruefully. "I lost him for a while, but most of the time I was behind him he was just enjoying himself, dining exquisitely, indulging himself."

"How?"

"How do you think? He could afford the best." Laker's face showed a mixture of envy and disgust. "Then he went to a brothel down by the docks, and I lost him. I figured he probably was not going to do anything meaningful for the rest of the day. I've got to eat something and sleep. I feel like something a dog threw up!"

"I can see that," Hooper said drily. "Want some stew? Mutton, potatoes, turnips, carrots?"

"Those yellow ones?"

"Certainly not! White turnips with mutton."

For the first time, Laker laughed. "Right! Thank you."

———

THEY CAUGHT UP WITH Lister the following morning, after a long, cold wait outside his rooms. It seemed he was making the most out of his wealth, particularly the luxury it afforded him of lying in on a cold, wet morning with a mist coming in off the river and the distant call of the foghorns every few minutes.

"I hope we're not parked here all day," Laker said with a shudder. "He's in bed with some tart, while we're out here freezing our backsides off."

"He'll get hungry sooner or later," Hooper replied, hoping profoundly that it was true.

They did not have much longer to wait. Twenty minutes later, the woman came out, looking pleased with herself and clutching a good-quality coat around her shoulders as she passed down the street. Ten minutes after that, Lister came out himself, wearing his jacket collar turned up and his hat pulled down.

"Sure it's him?" Hooper asked softly.

"Oh, yes," Laker replied. "That's his stride; turns his left foot in."

"We'll have to stay close," Laker observed as they set out after Lister, who was already getting harder to distinguish in the mist. "Damn weather! If he gives us the slip for more than a few minutes, we could end up following someone else half the way to bloody Gravesend!"

Hooper agreed, but did not say so.

For over half an hour they followed Lister along narrow streets, occasionally cutting through alleys and then out again. Hooper wondered whether he was actually going somewhere, or if he knew he was being followed and was amusing himself. Were they being laughed at?

"Where the hell is he going?" Laker grumbled.

Then Hooper put his hand out and grasped Laker's arm, pulling him to a sudden stop. The figure ahead of them had stopped also. Just beyond them, in the gloom, Hooper could see two more figures, one large, one considerably shorter. They could hear voices now, but not distinguishable words. All around them every surface was wet: the pavement of the dockside, the warehouses to the left, the cranes standing idle, towering into invisibility above them. The gutters were spilling over from the night's rain; the unloaded kegs and bales piled to the right were waiting for cranes to lift them when the mist cleared; the rooftops disappeared into the fog. And everywhere were the sounds of the river water flowing past them, swirling in eddies where the current was broken by pier stakes or dock steps. And unlike darkness, fog distorted direction. Even the foghorns Hooper could place only because he knew where they were.

Suddenly, there was a scuffle ahead of them, a shout of pain, and then a string of curses. The figures bunched together, swayed, and then one of them slid to the ground and stayed there, motionless.

The two left standing lunged at each other. One swung his arm around, high over his head and then down again. There was a shout of fury and pain; then they locked together.

Hooper charged forward, Laker only a step behind him. They ran across the open space between them and the fighting men. Hooper had his cudgel out, ready to strike the attacker when the fellow was stunned and almost knocked off balance.

Laker was faster, lighter, and he caught up with Lister, who was climbing to his feet awkwardly. Before he was fully upright, another figure appeared out of the mist and struck the standing man with a short, sharp jab, and then another. The man doubled up, gasping as if he had been winded, choking for breath. He subsided slowly, helpless to fight back. The new figure moved swiftly toward Lister, who was still dazed.

Hooper realized what the man was going to do when he saw the flicker of light in his hand, only for a second. It was a large blade. Hooper kicked as hard as he could at the man's kneecap. It was not where the man was expecting the blow, and he fell back, sideways, with a gasp of pain. Laker swung his cudgel at the larger of the two remaining men and then turned to Lister. But Lister saw his chance and, quick as an eel, he shot between them and slipped into the shadows, instantly invisible.

Laker started after him but took only two steps. He was leaving

Hooper with three men. Admittedly two were weakened, but it was still too many. The man on the ground was getting up again.

"Come on!" Laker yelled. Lister had gone, and he was the only one they needed to catch.

The man with the knife hesitated. He was of average height at least and well built, although in the mist none of them could be easily recognized again. And this man would be impossible to identify, because the lower half of his face was muffled.

He stood still for an instant, then struck forward with the knife, missing Laker by a few inches. He turned on his heel and was gone into a deeper shadow cast by a stack of kegs. His footsteps sounded for a moment, then were gone. Fog swirled around him in a momentary drift and then closed again, thicker than before.

The two men who were left looked ready for a further fight. Was it just a dockside robbery gone wrong? Or the attempted murder of Lister? For what? Any number of things, most probably for some of the money he was flashing around. Did they know him?

"Arrest them," Hooper said, suiting his action to his words and grasping the bigger of the two men.

Laker manacled the other and they walked them to the nearest local police station. But even though they spent the rest of the afternoon questioning them, they learned nothing. Both men swore they followed Lister because of the money he had been spending, intending to rob him. They had not expected his strength or skill in defending himself.

So who was the third man who had turned up, apparently to rescue Lister? Or had he intended to rob him instead? They had no idea. Lister was not there to press charges on all his attackers, and these men under arrest had not had the chance to steal anything.

Hooper acquiesced to the local police, letting them go.

"What the hell happened to Lister?" Laker said as they left to go back to Wapping. The fog was still thick, and now the wind had risen slightly, drifting round them, one moment wrapping them in a thick blanket, the next opening up views a hundred feet long. Everything dripped. The icy air was heavy with unfallen rain.

"I don't know," Hooper admitted. "I don't know whether the third man was there to help him or hurt him."

"The more I learn about this, the less I think I know," Laker admitted.

"I know I wish Harry Exeter had never crossed our paths," Hooper said with intense feeling. He meant it with an all-pervasive sorrow. It had damaged his friendship with Monk, which mattered to him more and more as he realized the extent of it. It had robbed him of his trust in the men, all of whom but one were totally worthy of any loyalty he could give.

But it had also introduced him to a woman whose inner grace he could not entirely dismiss from his mind. And thinking of her made him realize how much was missing from his life, and would always be missing, because of one action on a merchant ship twenty years ago.

If he had it to do again, knowing what it would cost him, he might not. Yet he still felt it was the only thing he could have done and slept, at ease with himself, disturbed by fear but not by guilt.

Or, with some wisdom, more courage, would he have found another way?

"We all have secrets," Laker said suddenly. "A man has a right to them."

Hooper looked at him with a clearing of the fog and saw his face seeming older, without the usual humor. Perhaps he had been hurt, too, in ways he could not share.

He wanted to agree with Laker, but, unwilling to risk further conversation, he did not know how.

"It doesn't help much," Hooper said unhappily at Wapping the next day.

Monk seemed determined to be optimistic. "It's the first break we've had. And you said Lister got away?"

"Yes. But it may not have been more than a fight over money. He was throwing it around like he had lots more where that came from," Hooper pointed out. "He's . . . lightweight, behaving like a fool. He's slick enough and a good street fighter, but he's not got the brains to plan the Exeter kidnap."

"But he knows who has," Monk argued. "Which is almost certainly why someone tried to kill him. You're sure that was what the third man was trying to do? Not rob him?"

"Yes, he meant to kill him." The more Hooper played it over in his memory, the more certain he became. "Ask Laker," he added.

"You trust Laker?" Monk asked it with a twisted smile, little humor in it.

Hooper imagined he could hear the pain behind the question. He thought for a while. Did he trust Laker? He pictured Laker's face in the momentary light before the fog swirled back again. He had been remembering something, some incident, some loss, with shame, an awkwardness, as if it still hurt. But if there was guilt in it, Hooper had not seen it. He found himself defensive. Was that because he wished to defend not only Laker, but himself as well? "Yes. He's young, but not too young to have a wound or two."

"Twenty-eight," Monk told him.

"Well, he came to my aid yesterday afternoon, when he could've finished me if he'd wanted to. And if the third man was behind the kidnapping, and Laker betrayed us, that's what he would've done."

"And you think the third man was behind the kidnapping? Not just someone else who saw Lister flashing money around and decided to take some of it?" Monk asked.

"I don't know. It was just an impression. Why kill him if all he wanted was money?"

"And you're sure he meant to kill him?"

"I was then, but now I don't know," Hooper admitted. The impression remained, but was it fear? "He only attacked Lister, not either of the other two."

"Lister had the money," Monk said.

"I know that, because the other two hadn't had time to rob him, but did the third man know that?"

"I agree with you," Monk conceded. "We'll go with that. It's all we have. I'll tell Exeter."

"Want me to come with you?" Hooper offered. A part of him would have given a great deal to avoid encountering Exeter's grief again. He had no way of easing it at all. It was painful to see, and he felt guilty as well. They had failed in every way to keep their promises to the man. It was cowardly to refuse to look at your errors and allow someone else to suffer. But he also wanted to know if he could see the shadow that Celia Darwin saw in Exeter. Perhaps an arrogance? An insensitivity? Had he given Kate everything he thought she wanted, without ever asking her?

Why on earth did he need to know that? Because he wanted to

believe that Celia Darwin was not petty minded, denying what she could not have, needing to see a fault in it.

Ridiculous. And yet he stood up and went with Monk outside, into the fine rain, which seemed to have cleared the fog away, at least for a while.

They took a hansom ride and were at Harry Exeter's house by late morning. They expected to find him at home. He was too recently bereaved to be having any social life, and his businesses took care of themselves, at least for a while. His juniors would be expected to call on him, rather than he call upon them.

The house still had all the elements of mourning: the drawn curtains and the black wreath on the door, small and discreet. Inside, perhaps the mirrors were turned to the wall, even some clocks stopped, but there was no sawdust on the roadway to muffle the sound of horses' hoofs.

The butler opened the door to them, inquired how he might help, and then conducted them through to the withdrawing room, where a huge fire was burning. Harry Exeter sat in the armchair, staring into the flames. He rose as they came in and went straight to Monk, initially ignoring Hooper. He held out his hand.

Monk took it and Exeter grasped onto him. "Any news?" he asked. "I can see it in your face. What is it? What have you found? Have you some idea who it was? Tell me!"

Hooper knew Monk well enough to read the expression in his face, the sudden hardening of resolve, the effort to imagine what Exeter must be feeling and to meet it not with pity, but with measured honesty. He had seen it all before, if in more measured degree. This was the first case where they'd been involved before a violent tragedy occurred, believing they could avoid it. Monk was carrying it all himself. He would not expect Hooper to share it.

"We think we have identified one of the kidnappers," Monk said levelly. "He has certainly spent a great deal of money lately, and he never has before. He hires out his services on violent jobs, and we have an informant that placed him at Jacob's Island."

"An informant?" Exeter was clearly startled. "From other kidnappings?"

"There are always kidnappings," Monk replied, his voice gentle, as if he did not want to make Exeter's grief even worse. "Not like Mrs. Exeter's. Not as . . . brutal. Hers was unique in that. And usually we get the victims back. It is self-defeating not to return the victim, or next time no one will pay. They trade on hope." The contempt in his voice was lacerating.

Exeter must have heard it, too. "Then why Kate? Did they not believe I would pay? I had the money." His face was anguished. "I was there! With it all! Did they think I couldn't get it, do you think? I could! I did!" He seemed desperate that they should believe him.

"It was an enormous amount, Mr. Exeter, but I don't think they would have asked for more than they thought you could get. It would be pointless. Some men would not even try . . ."

"But I did!" Exeter protested again. "I did everything exactly as they asked. They could not expect me to come alone! I don't know the damned area! I could only get to it, where they asked, by river. I needed you to guide me, and they had to know that." He looked at Hooper for understanding, perhaps reassurance, that it was not his error that was responsible for the disaster.

Hooper tried to convey by his expression that nothing better or different could have been done.

"You had the money," Monk said quietly. "You gave it to them as they asked."

"But they did kill her . . . because I made some kind of mistake?" Exeter forced the words out, as if he had been trying to find the courage to ask himself that question since the night it had happened. He looked at Monk, pleading for the answer he needed.

"What could you have done differently?" Monk asked. "You followed their instructions to the letter. They must have intended to kill her all along. They did it as you got there. Nothing could have prevented it. They knew you would find the money and that you would come. Which means they knew you."

Exeter closed his eyes tightly, and shook his head. "That's too horrible to think of. Do you believe they knew Kate as well?" Suddenly his eyes were wide, searching Monk's face. "Did they? And could still do that to her?"

Monk put the thought they all had into words. "If they knew her, perhaps she knew them also, and they dared not let her go?" If that was so, Kate would surely have realized it, too! He could not imagine what terror or pain she had suffered.

"Tell me it wasn't someone I know!" Exeter said between his teeth. "Will the law blame me if I kill them?" He stared at Monk, as if seriously trying to judge if he could do it or not. It was possible he really was toying with the idea.

"Don't," Monk said quietly. "Please . . ."

Exeter's whole body was taut with knotted muscles, as if he would attack someone this moment, if only he knew whom.

"Have you ever seen a man hang?" Monk asked, his voice still soft.

"What?" Exeter was startled. "No, of course not. Why?"

"It's not a nice way to go," Monk answered him. "Especially if it's done judicially. It's quite barbaric, actually. You are probably awake all night. They'll send a priest or chaplain to you, for you to have the last rites, confess and all that. Maybe at that point you realize in a few hours you're going to cease to exist. Or worse, you are going to face judgment, everlasting punishment, from whatever deity there is. And you can sit and watch the hands go round on the clock, ticking your life away, and it won't be as if anyone believed you were going to heaven!"

Exeter shuddered. "What's your point?" He gave the ghost of a smile. "Although I realize hanging would be a very civilized refinement of torture that killing him myself would not be. A slow sort . . . of pavane of death. Right. I'll settle for that. You've convinced me. Is that what you were going to say?" He opened his eyes wide.

"No, I came to tell you we found a man behaving extravagantly and we think he could be connected with the other kidnappings."

"Why didn't you arrest him? Do you think he's going to lead you to the others?"

"We were going to arrest him," Hooper replied, before Monk could speak again. "We were following him. He encountered a couple of other men, who may have intended to rob him. Then someone else came and attacked them all, tried to kill one man . . ."

"They killed him? Now you'll never know."

"No, we rescued him. But while we were fighting off the others, he escaped," Hooper corrected him. "But we'll find him again. And next time, we'll arrest him."

"But he'll have the others after him," Exeter said. "Won't he be safer in custody? Oh! I see. Of course, if you try him and convict him, he'll hang, and he would probably rather be murdered on the dockside."

"Exactly," Monk agreed. "But we'll find him. We know the dockside, too, and we have informers."

"And you think he'll tell you who the others are?" Exeter asked eagerly. "Can you offer him any leniency to do that? God, I want to know! There's nothing left for me now, except justice. I want them to suffer as much as Kate did. And don't tell me that's wrong! It may be. I don't give a damn."

"I think most people would understand that," Monk nodded. "And as long as you don't kill them yourself, the law has no problem with you."

There was a moment's silence. A log settled in the fire with a shower of sparks.

Exeter looked up at Monk. "Thank you. If you . . . if you have the chance to speak to them, ask them why. Why did they do that to her? If it was someone who knew her, and not just the money, I want to know!"

"I don't think you do." Monk shook his head slowly. "But it was a hell of a lot of money, and if it was just about that, then I think you do want to know. That would mean it was not an enemy of yours, choosing that way to hurt you, and it was in no way your fault."

Exeter did not move, but he seemed to crumple; he looked smaller. "You're right," he said hoarsely. "I want to know that . . . I need to know. I think you know me as well as anyone could. You're a good man."

Outside in the street, Hooper and Monk did not speak for a long time. Hooper was filled with his own thoughts, and he guessed Monk was, too. There were many emotions stirred, memories of love and pain, regret, mistakes that could not now be undone, maybe never could have been.

FORESEEING LISTER'S ATTEMPT TO escape both the police and whoever it was that had attacked him the previous night, Monk organized a search party of six men, including himself, to apprehend him. He could not spare more. The fog had lifted and it was a much milder evening with a three-quarter moon. They began along the docks beside the Limehouse Reach, trying the public houses Lister was known to frequent. The streets were still damp and the tide was flowing upriver, carrying the smell of salt on the wind.

Monk and Hooper walked separately, so as not to appear to be together. Neither of them doubted that Lister would now be very wary indeed of police, or of anyone who seemed to be following him.

It took two long, tedious hours to find him, beyond Limehouse and into the Isle of Dogs, much further east than expected. He was enjoying himself greatly in one of the dockside public houses when Hooper went in, wandered around, and saw Lister with a full tankard of ale and a group of dockers and watermen around him, all with tankards in their hands. He looked set to stay for some time: not only enjoying himself, but safe. As long as he paid the bill and kept the company, no one was going to attack him—kidnapper, thief, or police.

Hooper went out again into the street and found Monk in the shadow of a wall, looking bored.

"He's inside," Hooper said quietly. "Just got a fresh pint of beer. He's treating half a dozen heavyweights. Didn't stay long, in case he recognized me, but I reckon we'll have to stay outside until he comes out, and then follow him until his 'escort' takes its own way. We'll not do any good in there. Didn't want a roughhouse we couldn't win. We could say we're police, and he'll say we've come to kill him. They'll attack first, and then if they realize we really are police, they'll have to get rid of us, or face the consequences. One guess what that'll be!"

"We'll move up the street a bit." Monk shifted his weight a little. "Out of the wind," he added. "Feel it in your bones when the tide turns!"

They walked slowly away from the public house and turned the corner into the next alley. They turned again along the back entrances of the houses opposite and passed backyards grimy with coal dust, fallen garbage, and here and there broken slates. It was some time before they discovered a passageway that looked out on the street almost opposite the public house, with a decent sideways view of the back door.

"Give me a leg up onto the roof of that shed, and I'll be able to see the back door," Monk said. "We'll be out of his line of sight, if he's looking."

Hooper obeyed and accepted Monk's arm to haul himself up. It was hardly comfortable, but it did afford an excellent vantage point from which to see the public house.

They remained silent, watching. Every now and then one of them changed position. Hooper's mind began to wander. Who was Lister waiting for? Was Kate's kidnap and murder done out of hatred of Exeter? If so, did Exeter really have no idea who it was? Were there so many possibilities?

And which of Monk's men had he corrupted, too? Hooper knew it was not himself. He had never suspected Monk. And for no concrete reason, he did not believe it was Laker. That left Marbury, Walcott, and Bathurst. Why? Money? Blackmail over some weakness? He shivered momentarily, as if a cold wind had arisen. There, but for the grace of God, went he! No one knew about his past to blackmail him. But if they did? Would he have the strength to say go to hell, and do your worst? Would he escape, make a run for it? Were his actions on the *Mary Grace* still a hanging offense, after all these years? Was there anyone left alive who knew the truth, the real truth, behind the apparent stories?

What would Monk make of that? Hester would understand—or would she? She was sort of an army person, in a way, an army nurse.

What about Celia Darwin?

Why was he thinking of her? He would probably never see her again. Were it not for the past and the *Mary Grace*, would he? Would he deliberately go and find her?

He was still thinking about that, how good it would be, when a hand reached up from the paved ground below and grabbed his ankle. He lost his balance and slid down, only just righting himself before he fell off the roof and landed awkwardly. He was immediately struck a hard blow across the face and fell sideways. A moment later, another man moved across in front of him and struck Monk, only Monk had already moved forward, and there was a grunt of pain and a curse. Hooper stumbled to his feet and struck the man with a short, hard punch to the gut. Almost immediately he himself was hit from the side, a hard blow to the head. He felt sick as the darkness opened up and smothered him. Then there was a stinging pain in his thigh.

Careless. He had been thinking when he should have been listening, watching, nerves stretched for anything out of the usual pattern.

He took a deep breath and then lashed out at the sound of a man stopping close to him. He had no idea who he was. But it was not Monk's elegant boots he kicked as hard as he could.

Someone gave a shrill cry and lost his balance, swearing savagely.

Then Monk was in front of him. "Come on!" he shouted. "Lister's gone. Come—" He broke off as the first man climbed to his feet, ready to fight again. There was no time to chase after Lister. Hooper and Monk needed to save themselves and get out of this without serious injury.

Ten minutes later, they were at the far end of the road looking into the main street and the public house.

"We've lost Lister," Monk said bitterly. "Our own fault. Weren't paying attention. We're slipping, Hooper. Where the hell did he go? And who were the other men?"

"More kidnappers?" Hooper suggested.

"If they were all together, why did Lister run off?" Monk asked. He swore, then turned around slowly. There was no way to tell in the darkness which direction Lister had gone, or might continue to go, or whether he might double back or even cross the river.

Hooper was suddenly aware of how cold he was, and how his bones ached and his flesh hurt where he had been struck. He would feel far worse tomorrow morning.

"Where did he go?" Monk asked. "It was only a few moments. He could still be around."

"So could the other men!" Hooper said sharply. "Come on!" He grabbed at Monk's arm and pulled hard. "If they're part of the kidnapping, they'll come after us."

Monk pulled away so sharply Hooper was almost knocked off balance. "We can't wait. There are only three of them, and this time we'll take them by surprise. It's our only chance to get them all!"

Hooper knew it was risky. These men might be armed with knives. In the night, by the docks, they wouldn't hesitate to kill a police officer, if they were cornered. And that was if they even knew Monk and Hooper were police.

Hooper hesitated only a moment. An elation was growing inside him. Monk may not realize it, but there was no greater trust in another man's loyalty than to go into such a fight beside him. It did not occur to him until later that Monk had not even for an instant questioned that Hooper might not trust him!

They went quickly and quietly, close together, down the main street, staying near to the curb. It made them visible, if anyone was looking, but staying close to the walls also made an ambush almost impossible.

In a hundred yards, they met a cross street. Right led to a dead end, left toward the river. A quick glance and they chose the left. They passed a timber yard and tried the gates, but they were locked and chained. There were stairs at the end, down into the water, and a narrow ledge leading around a corner and out of sight. The water swirled past them, gathering speed. One misstep would be fatal.

There was no way within sight down to the river.

Monk turned upriver and saw riding lights in the distance. "Too far away," he said, his voice tight with tension. "Couldn't have got all the way there in that time."

Hooper stared ahead across the river. There was a rowing boat a hundred feet away. Then he saw an oar, lying in the water only a few yards from the shore. "There's no one rowing!"

Monk swung around to look. "Damn! Do you think that's him in it? Lister?"

"With no oar?" Hooper asked. "If he dropped it, why didn't he pick it up? He didn't get far out with only one."

"Scull? From the stair?"

"In this tide?"

Monk squinted across the water. "Is that even moving?"

"You mean is he dead already?" Hooper asked, his voice grating with the misery of yet another defeat.

Monk turned away. "We'll have to get another boat and go out after him. Where do you think is the closest place to find one?"

Hooper looked round. He knew this part of the river moderately well. "Next warehouse after this might have one. There's a passageway over here." He pointed. It was invisible from where they were standing at the water's edge, but he knew that the gates into the alley hid a narrow slit between buildings. "Have to look out for an ambush." He nearly told Monk to keep his hand on his knife, then bit the words back. Monk already knew.

They went quickly and silently across the street, into the passage and along it to the far end. They found a boat, a fast, light shell of a thing, to take a man out to any of the ships at anchor. They unhitched it and Hooper took both oars. The boat was too narrow for two men side by side.

It took them nearly ten minutes to catch up with the drifting boat, now well into the current and being carried upriver on the flood tide. One glance inside, by the light of a bull's-eye lantern Hooper held high, showed them everything that was of immediate import. Lister was dead. His throat had been cut from side to side and his shoulders and chest were soaked with blood. It was not an injury a man could possibly have inflicted upon himself.

It took another two and a half hours to get the body and the boat ashore. They put Lister's boat in the custody of the Wapping Police Station and took the body to the police surgeon, although they doubted he would tell them anything that was not already obvious. Lister had been put in the boat alive, and then his throat had been cut with a large and very sharp knife, or possibly an open razor of the type known casually as a cutthroat, although nobody felt like making even a gallows-humor remark about that now. He would have died almost immediately, although from the frozen, almost gargoylelike horror on his face, he'd had time to see it coming and knew exactly what was going to happen.

It was well into the small hours of the morning when Hooper went home. He was cold, tired, and aching all over by the time he took off his clothes, washed until he was clean enough not to spoil his sheets, and finally went to bed.

Hooper slept fitfully and awoke late and heavy-headed, as if he might have been wearing a hat too tight for him. He washed, shaved, and dressed, then left immediately for Wapping, without even taking a cup of tea. It was his duty to be there, and his personal need. Had they heard anything more? He remembered looking at the body last night, searching the clothes, the pockets, the shoes, anything at all. Had fresh eyes this morning seen anything he or Monk had missed?

It was a sharp morning with clear skies, and the autumn sun was dazzling. It showed the world in too clean a light. The other men looked as exhausted as he did. Someone had brought a pile of ham sandwiches from one of the street peddlers, and there was fresh hot tea in the big enameled pot. Hooper felt a wave of emotion that the old warmth and camaraderie seemed to be there, but he soon realized it was an illusion. They were trying to make it look as if it was the same. It wasn't: it wouldn't be until they knew who it was who had betrayed them. And even when they knew, and had dealt with him, the knowledge that it had happened would mean it could always happen again. The safety of absolute loyalty had been a delusion.

Bathurst was busy making more tea, and they shared the sandwiches. Monk arrived a few minutes later, with the police surgeon. Laker and Marbury were sent to examine the rowing boat. Monk said he would go, at a decent hour, and tell Exeter the news. It might give him some small comfort.

"Do you think Lister was killed for the money?" Hooper asked. "And does that mean those who killed him were the other kidnappers? Or just that he was fool enough to show that he had money to spare?"

"I don't know," Monk replied, some of the light going out of his face. "As I said, I find it hard to believe he was the brains behind the kidnap. He was . . ." He did not bother to finish the sentence.

Hooper knew what he meant: Lister had shown a careless, impulsive, spur-of-the-moment reaction to having money, not that of someone who planned meticulously. The kidnapping was planned in advance, piece by piece.

"He might be the man who actually took Mrs. Exeter, sir," he said.

"Maybe," Monk agreed. "He could look respectable enough. We'll never know."

"Miss Darwin might recognize him," Hooper suggested.

Monk stared at him. "With his throat cut? You can't expect her to look at that, Hooper. Look at a dead man in the morgue, and say whether it was the man who kidnapped her friend and slaughtered her? According to Exeter, she's a quiet sort of woman, shy and not . . . not reliable. Why upset her for a testimony we couldn't rely on, even if it came to the worst?"

"It would be useful to us to know." Hooper found his reply a little sharper than he had intended. His resentment of the characterization was palpable.

Monk looked at him with more attention. "Is Exeter wrong about her?"

"Yes, sir," Hooper replied without hesitation. "She's quiet. That

doesn't mean she's unreliable, just . . . just a more serious person."
That sounded heavy, stolid, and she wasn't, just badly hurt. There
was light inside her, and delicacy . . .

Monk smiled very slightly. "Then go and see if she can tell you.
But be careful, Hooper. This man kidnapped her cousin and may be
the one who murdered her. And now he's been killed himself. They'll
make him look as decent as possible, but he's still a man who died
violently. She may never have seen a dead body before, let alone a
murdered one."

"Yes, sir. I will."

Hooper set out straightaway. He had no idea if Celia Darwin
would be at home. He had no idea of the pattern of her life at all. He
felt as if they knew each other, which was ridiculous. They had talked
like comfortable friends, but beyond her relationship with Kate Exeter, he knew nothing of her daily life, her wishes and dreams, what
she did that mattered to her. And she knew nothing of him at all,
except that he was with the River Police. She had probably not given
him a thought between the time he stepped out of the front door and
the time when he would knock on that door again.

He stood in the sunlit street and knocked. He would be almost
relieved if she did not answer.

It seemed like no time at all before the maid was there and he had
to explain himself.

"Oh, yes, sir. If you'll come in, sir?" She stepped back and invited
him inside.

He wondered for a moment if he had misrepresented himself as
more important than he was. This was going to be difficult.

Celia was in the sitting room at an old mahogany desk, writing
letters. She looked up as soon as he came in, and the maid announced
him.

Celia rose to her feet, looking a little flushed. Was she wondering
what had brought him back so soon? "Good morning, Mr. Hooper,"
she said quickly. "Do you have news?"

He had rehearsed, and yet the words seemed inadequate now, so
formal as to be a rebuff. "Yes, Miss Darwin, we have found a man we

believe to have been involved. Unfortunately, he was killed by two other men who may also have been involved. It looks likely it was over the money."

Her face was impossible to read. "The money might once have been important to Harry. I believe there was a great deal of it. Even so, I think he now hardly cares. And if, as you say, this man is dead, then he cannot tell us anything."

There was a downward fall of disappointment in her voice, and also in her face.

"We don't know for certain that he was involved." He sounded to himself as if he was making excuses, and he hated that. "But he could have been the man who actually took Kate from beside the river-bank." He realized he had used her name as if he had known her, and had a right to. It was too late to take it back now, and he would be drawing attention to it if he apologized.

She stared at him, her eyes very steady. "You want me to tell you if it is the same man, if I recognize him?" she asked.

"If you'd be willing to?"

"Yes." She drew in a deep breath. "Yes, of course I will. I don't know if I will be certain . . . but I shall try."

"Thank you, Miss Darwin." Now he had the responsibility of tak-ing her to look at Lister. It was even more his responsibility than she knew, as it was he who had suggested they ask her to do this, not Monk. The last thing he wanted was to cause her pain or embarrass-ment, if she were to faint. But she also knew a ghastly experience was coming, and she did not shrink from it. He wished there was some way he could protect her.

She collected a heavy cloak from the cupboard in the hall and went to the front door. She gave instructions to the maid and esti-mated what time she would return. She sounded so normal, as if she was taking a usual walk, maybe to post a letter, but Hooper could see the stiffness in her. He admired her composure. He thought again how graceful she was. Pleasing to look at, calm like a summer dawn, not all full of froth and need for attention, like the wind in daffodils.

Then he blocked out his own stupidity and followed her along the street, catching up in a few steps because his legs were so much longer than hers.

They walked toward the main road. He did not want to ask her to wait for an omnibus, and he did not know the routes in this area.

"Have you always lived here?" he asked, then thought how foolish that was. He was a policeman, taking her to see if she could recognize a corpse! This was not a social occasion.

"Here, or in Kent, much further to the south," she replied. "It's so rich, the countryside. I miss it sometimes." She glanced sideways at him. "But you're not Kentish, are you." It was a statement.

"No. Essex, further down the estuary toward the sea. Flat coast. Some people think that's boring." As he spoke, he thought of the wide skies he had loved as a boy. They had set him dreaming of horizons, and what marvels might lie beyond them.

She was looking at him. "You don't." She said it as if she knew. "Sometimes it's a shame to have everything known, every hillside, every cliff or beach, or even all of the trees. Then you don't have to build them in your own mind, because they're already built." She turned away. "I'm sorry. That's a bit fanciful. I'm trying not to think of this wretched man. Dreams are so much safer . . . sometimes."

He wanted to comfort her, just a hand on her arm. But it would be intrusive.

He stepped into the road and hailed a cab. When it stopped, he handed her up into it, then followed. He gave the driver instructions quietly: just a street name and number, not that it was the morgue.

"Do you want to be safe?" he asked. "Never surprised?"

"You make it sound so . . . dead! Oh. I'm sorry. That was an unfortunate thing to say—when we're going to such a place . . ." She trailed off, embarrassed.

He hid his smile. "I think that 'hibernating' would be a better word."

"How gentle you are," she said. "Going to sleep for a while is so different from never having woken up in the first place. But we can't pick and choose to sleep through the bad bits. And how would you know if you did, that you didn't dream them anyway?"

"You'd miss the cold," he pointed out.

"And the winter furrows can be so beautiful across the ploughed fields, and the new fallen snow, and . . . and . . ." Her voice choked off. "I miss her already, and it's only been a week. There are so many things you can't talk about to just . . . anybody."

"If you've ever had even one person you can speak to, you are fortunate," he replied. "And if you can share with one, perhaps you can share with another. Some people can't put a name or a word to anything and really mean it."

She lifted up her hand as if she would touch his arm.

He sat painfully still, hoping she would.

Then she realized what she was doing and withdrew it.

They sat in silence, but it was companionable. He thought about broad estuary skies and birds on the wild winds, white gulls, skeins of geese with their wings creaking. There was no other sound like it. One day, perhaps, he would tell her about it.

They arrived at the morgue and Hooper paid the driver, then stood to help Celia out, taking her hand. She did not seem to lean on him at all.

They went inside, and he took her to a room to wait while he went for the police surgeon. Then they accompanied him to look at the body of Lister.

He had been considerably tidied up; nearly all the blood had been removed. He looked ashen now. There was almost a bluish tint to his skin.

Celia looked at him quite steadily, but she stood very close to Hooper. He would like to have put his arm around her, if he had dared.

"Has he blue eyes?" she asked.

Hooper had no idea.

"Yes," the police surgeon told her.

"Then that is the man who took Kate. He . . . looked brighter-colored then. He moved gracefully."

"Are you sure?" Hooper asked.

"Oh, yes, he has that funny little mark on his nose. I thought it stopped his face from looking too exact. Poor man. It's too late to mend anything now, isn't it! May we leave, please? I don't like this. It's all so perfectly . . . pointless."

"Of course." This time Hooper did take her arm, whether she thought it forward of him or not. He wanted to steady her because she looked a little off balance. "We shall get a cup of tea—very hot."

"We?" She gave the ghost of a smile. "I am not your responsibility, Mr. Hooper."

"We," he repeated firmly.

10

Monk was still working at nearly half-past six, putting together the details of Lister, everything that was known of him, and the police surgeon's report of his death. There were a few marks on his body, as if he had very recently been involved in several fights. None of them had been serious, but they had left deep bruises, some of them very shortly before his death. His actual death looked to have been quick. A single knife stroke had severed his throat almost to the spine. There were no obvious wounds of self-defense.

Probably two men took him by surprise, Monk deduced. It fitted in with what both Hooper and Laker had told him. Then Hooper had brought in Kate Exeter's cousin, Celia Darwin, and she had identified Lister as the man who had taken Kate from the riverbank in the beginning. Monk was still weighing all the new evidence and trying to work out what it meant, if it added anything to what they already knew.

He felt a strong burst of cold air as the outside door opened and a young woman came in. She wore a long black coat and had the collar turned up to protect her face from the wind. She stopped just inside the door and stared at Monk.

"Can I help you?" he asked, getting up and walking slowly toward her.

She stopped and gulped. She was quite small, slender, and dressed almost entirely in black. She looked fragile, and at this moment, almost rigid with tension.

"Who are you?" Monk asked. "This is the Wapping station of the Thames River Police. I'm Commander Monk. Is this where you wish to be?"

"Yes. Yes, it is." She took a deep breath. "I'm Bella Franken. I'm a bookkeeper at Nicholson's Bank. I . . . think I might know about some money that was used for the ransom. I think . . ." She stopped and bit her lip, waiting for Monk's reaction.

Nicholson's was the name of the bank to which Hooper had followed Roger Doyle. Did this mean anything? Was the money the key to what had happened?

"Tell me about it, Miss Franken. Come into my office and sit down. It's warmer in there, and I'll make fresh tea."

She followed him obediently. When she had sat down in the chair opposite his desk, she pulled onto her lap a soft-sided bag and opened it. She took out a sheaf of papers and handed them across to him. At a glance, they looked to be dozens of loose sheets crowded with figures in columns, hundreds of them, all neatly set out in the same hand, and all in ink.

She pushed them across the table toward him. "I have made copies of the ledgers over the last several months. You may want to see all the numbers, but I have made small marks beside the ones that are of importance."

"This is your writing?" he asked.

"Yes."

He glanced down at them and, after a moment's study of the ones she had marked, he could see what appeared to be discrepancies. But they could easily have been accidental transpositions in the copying.

He looked up at her and saw her solemn expression awaiting his response.

"What are these numbers, Miss Franken? What do they represent?"

"Movements of money in and out of Mrs. Exeter's accounts," she answered.

"Mrs. Exeter?" he asked. "Mrs. Exeter has an account of her own?"

Bella Franken's expression was bleak. "It was a trust, Mr. Monk. She has no access to it, nor does Mr. Exeter. She will come into it on her thirty-third birthday, which is more than a year in the future. Until that time, it is in the stewardship of Mr. Doyle, the manager of the bank, and Mrs. Exeter's cousin, Mr. Maurice Latham. He is a civil lawyer." Her face was carefully empty of expression, and Monk imagined she did not like Maurice Latham.

Bella drew in her breath and continued, "At the time of her birthday, Mrs. Exeter was to have inherited the entire sum. If she should die before that time, it does not pass to her husband. The bequest is very specific. It is equally divided between the other two cousins, the sole children of Mrs. Exeter's mother's widowed sisters."

"Who are?"

"Mr. Maurice Latham and Miss Celia Darwin."

"And they are aware of this?"

"Of course."

"Is there . . . ?"

"No ill feeling," she answered before he could struggle for words to frame the question with delicacy. "And Mr. Exeter has no access to it at all."

"What are these figures, and why have you brought them to us?"

"Because someone has been very carefully removing small amounts, over three or four years, and concealing it with clever bookkeeping. I had to spend several hours going over and over the pages to find it."

"And the only people with access to it are Maurice Latham and your manager, Mr. Doyle? Are you sure?"

"Yes." There was no hesitation in her voice at all.

"It's all in your writing." He felt as if he were apologizing. "He can say it was not accurate, that you have transposed numbers and there is no error in the books. I'm sorry."

"Of course it is in my writing," she replied. "So is the original. I am the bookkeeper. All the ledgers are in my writing. But in the original, Mr. Doyle has signed off on each page. He checks them all, but of course he does not do all the writing. That takes hours, copying from one sheet of paper, receipts, count of money, and all the tasks that go into keeping an exact accounting. This is not meant as proof, Commander Monk; it is a means for you to find the pieces yourself and see how the money is where it should not be, with no explanation."

He looked down at the sheets again. Without her marking specific lines, he doubted he ever would have seen the pattern. "Have you shown this to the regular police? Or anyone else in the bank?"

"No. I . . ." She did not need to tell Monk that she was frightened. It was written in her face, the stiffness of her body beneath the black coat, and the white knuckles of her left hand clenched in her lap, while her right hand pushed more papers toward him.

He had no need to tell her she was endangering herself by bringing him this information. He wished he could tell her that she was protected, that he would see to it that she was safe, but he was filled with the dark weight of broken promises. He had promised Exeter they would follow the plan exactly and get Kate back, and he had lost both her and the money. He had found Lister, against remarkable odds. They had gone to arrest him and found his dead body. It was only because Celia Darwin had identified him that they knew for certain he was the kidnapper. But did they *really* know that? Would her evidence have stood up in court? She had seen him only for a few moments on the riverbank. She had been a startled and frightened woman. Later, she had been asked to look at a mutilated corpse, with a gaping wound where his throat should have been. She had said yes, that was the man, but would she have said yes whomever it had been, so wanting it to be him?

And Hooper had wanted it to be. How far had he influenced her?

Usually Monk would not have doubted Hooper, but he thought Hooper wanted so badly to achieve something, as much to discover who had betrayed them as to punish Kate's killer, perhaps he saw progress where there was none. And Monk was so keen to solve this, for exactly the same reasons, that he was slow to accept it.

"Miss Franken, have you seen or heard more than this? Any meetings you are aware of?"

"I have seen Mr. Exeter come in three or four times in the last few weeks. I have tried to remember which days exactly, but I can't. I'm sorry. I imagine Mr. Doyle could tell you but I do not have access to his diary. I am very seldom in his office. Sometimes I take him ledgers, if he asks for them."

"Have you worked for him a long time?"

"It seems like it. Eight years; as head bookkeeper for only three."

"There is another bookkeeper?" He wondered if that was where the errors had crept in.

"There used to be. Mr. Ernshaw left just over two years ago. We have not found a replacement for him yet. I can manage."

"It must stretch you considerably to do two jobs," Monk observed.

She smiled, charming and full of wry amusement. "I am not over-taxed, Mr. Monk. I do not sit up by candlelight straining my eyes over columns of figures. If I organize myself properly, I can quite easily manage. And do you think that had I made an error, it would result in exactly these figures? I have a feeling, to judge by your expression, that they may mean more to you than they do to me."

"You're very observant, Miss Franken. What was your impression of Mr. Exeter and his trust in Mr. Doyle?"

She was uncomfortable; she looked down. "It is hardly my place to have impressions of Mr. Doyle or his clients. I am desperately sorry for Mr. Exeter. Of course, I know only what is in the newspapers, but it is one of the most dreadful stories I have heard."

"Has Mr. Exeter visited the bank since then?"

"Yes, once. He looked like a ghost, poor man."

"You think he obtained the ransom money with the assistance of Mr. Doyle?"

"Yes."

"It would be natural, if Nicholson's is where Mr. Exeter banks. Why did you fear it might be breaking your confidentiality to bring this to me?" Monk felt hesitant to ask her, but she did not seem flighty or foolish. She clearly believed that there was some information here that was not as straightforward as a ransom being paid. She was very afraid of something. If it was just the breaking of a trust, she could have avoided that very easily by doing nothing.

"I love numbers, Mr. Monk." She was looking at him again. "That may seem to be a strange thing in a woman, but they have a beauty, when you understand them. They are utterly without emotion, and yet they have music in them, and reason, and occasionally humor. I . . ." She stopped, embarrassed by her own enthusiasm in front of a stranger.

"And they reveal something to you," he finished for her. He glimpsed what she meant and for a moment he saw something of it, too: a world where reason and beauty were the same, and quirks of pattern had wit. He liked a woman who would make a lonely adventure of the mind and find pleasure in it.

"Yes," she agreed, referring again to the papers in front of them. "The sums are nearly always right at the end of the calculation, though there have been some strange movements, things hidden. There is less money than there should be in some places, more in others. There may be an explanation I do not understand, but . . ."

"You think there is embezzlement?"

"Yes. There is something wrong. Movement that is wrong!"

"Whom do you suspect?"

She bit her lip. "It can only be Mr. Latham or . . . or Mr. Doyle."

"Which do you suspect?"

"I don't know. If it could be Mr. Exeter, I would suspect him to have done it to raise the money for the ransom. But these figures predate the kidnap of Mrs. Exeter by a long time. There are small amounts over the years, and they are very carefully hidden. I found them only because I noticed one error, and then I looked for more. Also, of course, Mr. Exeter has not access to these accounts, and . . .

and, taken individually, they are trifling compared with the sum of the ransom."

"You know how much that was? How?"

"The money appeared in Mr. Exeter's account, and then disappeared, in the space of a few hours—on the day of the . . . the attempt to pay." Her face was pale, as if she were weighing the tragedy of the event as she said the words.

Monk knew he would not have blamed Exeter if he had embezzled the money to save Kate's life. He himself would have taken it if he thought of Hester and the nightmares she lived through on the battlefield, the scores, maybe even hundreds, of men she had seen die. She had helped those she could. He knew at times she had been overwhelmed. He had held her in his arms on those rare occasions she still had nightmares. She was worth that.

He returned to the bank papers and the reason the bookkeeper had come. "Miss Franken, you know about what money you moved. You have done what you can, and it must have taken some courage. Please take care not to reveal that you have given me this information, and do not look for any more. Keep your own counsel. I will take care of this, and find out if it helps us. Please . . ."

She rose to her feet. "I will, Commander."

"I will walk with you to the main street and see you get a hansom," he replied. "And thank you."

MONK DID NOT KNOW an expert in fraud or embezzlement in the River Police, at least not one capable of distinguishing the complexity of the bank's papers. But Rathbone would know someone. And he owed Rathbone a call anyway. It was something he had been putting off, because he dreaded it. Bella Franken's visit gave him the impetus he needed.

He arrived at Rathbone's home at a quarter to eight. It was an inappropriate hour, and he was aware of it. But since Rathbone's marriage to Beata, he had gone out far less often. His ideal evening was spent at home with her. He was fortunate that it seemed to please her just as much. Perhaps she had had her fill of social events when she had been married to the arrogant and, in the end, also violent judge, most of whose friends had been in high society. Any evening out had been preferable to an evening at home with his uncertain temper. When he had finally driven himself into a paroxysm of rage and had an apoplectic fit, he had been incapacitated for over a year before he died. He was brutal and determined to live as long as possible, to deny her the freedom to marry Rathbone. During that long and difficult time, Rathbone had refused to compromise her reputation or his own. There must have been several people who knew of his love for her, and he was not without enemies either. He had appeared in many controversial trials and defeated most of the leading lawyers on both sides of the court, not all of whom took it well. He had made mistakes, for which he had paid dearly. He had been a friend to Monk when few others had.

Monk would have said no others, until he realized that he had had more friends than he had at first thought. His former superior, Runcorn, in his own way had been a friend, and then an enemy, and then a friend again. The enmity had been at the very least as much Monk's fault as Runcorn's. Orme had been a friend, and Hooper, too—a far more complex man than Monk had originally given him credit for.

And there were others, people who had come into his life with a brief, bright light, and then gone again for their own reasons.

And there was Hester. No truer friend existed. Had Harry Exeter lost a friend like that in Kate?

At Rathbone's home he was welcomed in. Within five minutes he was sitting beside the fire with a glass of brandy. Beata was in the kitchen preparing a dish of pork sausages, with some apple and mashed potatoes, and later possibly a dish of hot sponge pudding with syrup.

Rathbone had read what the newspapers reported about the death of Lister, which was very little. They had said nothing about his possible involvement with Kate Exeter's death.

"Well?" Rathbone asked, sitting back and crossing his legs, attentive, interested, but supremely comfortable. He was home in all senses, possibly for the first time in his life.

"Lister was the man who actually took her," Monk told him. "At least we think so. The cousin who was with her at the time, Miss Darwin, identified him."

"Do you doubt her?" Rathbone raised his eyebrows.

"Not her honesty," Monk answered. "But she may wish to help so much that she sees more than is there. It's easy to do."

"But if she's right?" Rathbone asked, searching Monk's face. "Does it help?"

"I don't know. Some satisfaction, I suppose. Ironic, if he had the money, or most of it, he was so careless that he gave himself away. Or he was just killed by a couple of thieves, unrelated to the kidnap. Then we'll probably never find them, unless by chance."

"Not entirely satisfactory," Rathbone agreed. Then there was a softness in his voice, an awareness of pain: "What about the man among your own that you suspect gave away your plan?"

Monk froze. He stared at Rathbone as if he had suddenly turned into a monster. Nausea washed over him like a wave, suffocating, stopping his breath.

"Monk!" Rathbone's voice came from far away. "Monk! Are you all right?"

He felt Rathbone's hand gripping his wrist, hard enough to hurt. He concentrated his mind again. "I never even thought of that," he said in a hushed voice. "God help us."

"Thought of what?" Rathbone demanded. He was leaning forward now, his face showing unmistakable fear. "What? You know it was one of your own men who betrayed you! You told me."

"That one of my own men killed Lister to keep him from naming the betrayer." Monk's voice was so choked he did not recognize it as his own.

"Right," Rathbone said firmly. "You know when Lister was killed? It was a very narrow frame of time. Find out where all of your men were, and you'll exclude some of them, if not all. And pull yourself together! You've been through worse than this."

"I'd never suspected my own men of betrayal before Kate Exeter's murder," Monk said steadily now. "And I realize now how little I really know them—and perhaps they know me as little."

"You don't have the right to know everything about anyone, Monk. You have to take the bits you do know and judge by them. You don't know all of me, or even of Hester. You don't even know all of yourself. Live with it, man. You have no acceptable alternative. Now, are those bank papers for me, or are you just carrying them around? Beata will be here with your supper any moment."

Monk pulled the papers out of his pocket. "A young woman brought them to me this evening. They're exact copies, she tells me, of papers from Nicholson's Bank. They have to do with Kate Exeter's trust account, which she had yet to come into. The woman says there is something wrong with them, small amounts taken, but over a long period of time. The bit I've underlined is the exact amount of the ransom. Have you got a financial expert who can tell me if there really is something wrong?"

"I'll find out." Rathbone took them from him just as Beata came in carrying a tray with his dinner on it. Since it was informal, perhaps he should call it supper. He could not remember if he had had lunch or not.

"Thank you," he said with deep gratitude.

CHAPTER

11

Hᴇꜱᴛᴇʀ ᴡᴀꜱ ɴᴏᴛ ᴀᴛ home when Will came to see her, but at the clinic in Portpool Lane. She was standing in the store cupboard where the medicines were kept, taking stock of what they had and what they needed more of. As usual, it was more bandages, surgical spirits for sterilization of instruments, wounds, and so on, and decent wine when a sip was all people could take. Some of the knives and scissors needed sharpening, but that was easily seen to.

She turned when she felt Will's presence behind her. She was pleased to see him, but the fact that he had sought her out here, rather than at home, caused her a quick flicker of anxiety. What was it that he did not wish Monk to overhear?

Will smiled at her. He was so much a man now, but his smile still held something of the child he had been.

"It's not Bathurst," he said immediately. "He disappears so often and he's tight with money because he's the eldest of a big family, and they're always broke. Father's dead, and Bathurst's is the only regular money they get. One sister works, but women, girls, don't get paid that much. He's always scared she'll get sucked into making it on the street because they need it so bad. I guess that's why he's nice to street women, too. He can understand how they got there." His face reflected the pity he felt. A few years ago it might have held envy, too, for being part of a large family, even if a poor one. He was too sure of where he belonged to feel that now.

Hester smiled at him. "Thank you." She could not help wondering how vulnerable that constant need made young Bathurst. What emergency, no matter how slight, might rock that precarious survival.

"I know," Will said quickly.

"Do you?" She thought of covering her doubt, but she had done that once and he had seen through it, and been not only hurt, but angry.

"Yeah. Crow has treated some of his family. You've got no ground for thinking ill of him."

Hester did not want to argue, but he was waiting for it, his eyes steady. When had he grown up so much? The answer to that she knew. Helping Crow, especially dealing with her friend from the Crimean War, who was so terribly wounded, both in mind and body. Will had had a violent dose of the reality of war and loss, and he had borne it well.

This time she smiled at him without the shadow. "Thank you very much."

"I couldn't find much about Laker, except he was in the army for a while. You might know someone who knew him then. He left . . . under a shadow. Don't know what it was."

So that was why Will had sought her out at the clinic, instead of at home. He would not say so, but he was afraid of what she might find. Was he afraid for Monk? Had he seen the vulnerability and known that Monk cared so much more than he pretended to?

Their eyes met for a moment. Will smiled and then looked away. He wasn't prepared to share the extent of his loyalty to Monk, just in case she didn't know. She felt the sudden sting of tears in her eyes.

"Thank you," she said softly, and hoped Will had no idea what she meant.

She finished up her list of supplies needed and put it in her pocket, then excused herself, saying she would make the purchases the next day. This afternoon she had another errand to perform.

SHE HAD ALREADY DECIDED exactly who to ask for help regarding Laker and whatever his tragedy might have been. Major Carlton knew, or had known of, almost everyone who had served in the regular army since the beginning of the Crimean War, especially if they were from the counties around London—the Home Counties, as they were known.

She found him where she had expected, sitting in his small front room by the fire, reading regimental histories from his vast collection of books. She had nursed him through a particularly painful injury, and he had not forgotten her patience or, more particularly, her discretion. A man's moment of weakness or indignity was never referred to again, or spoken of to others.

His manservant let her in and then disappeared to make fresh tea and, if there were any left, a few jam tarts. It was not four in the afternoon, but exceptions could be made. A man should not be a prisoner of convention.

Carlton stood with difficulty to greet her. She did not tell him it was unnecessary. He disliked above all things being reminded that he was an exception to the general rules of courtesy. He did not wish to be an exception. Everyone knew it. No one spoke of it.

"How are you?" she said warmly. "You look well." It was not a nurse speaking, but a woman. The nurse saw the strain in his face, the pain, the added stiffness, the loss of a little more weight, and could guess the reasons. The woman did not.

She sat quickly so he might follow suit.

"I want your help." She came straight to the point. There had never been pretense between them.

He tried not to look surprised. "With what?"

She had thought very hard how to address this. Even with complete honesty, there were several sides to it.

He was waiting, interested, keen to be of use again, in anything.

"My husband is commander of the Thames River Police."

"I know."

"Do you?"

"I keep up with you . . . and anyone who matters to you." His expression darkened. "I know the terrible crime he is investigating."

This made it more difficult, and at the same time, she was touched that he should still be interested in her life. Perhaps he had no one of his own. She could not remember his having mentioned anyone. Perhaps she should have come more often.

"One of the young men who works for him served in the army before joining the police. He is under a certain degree of suspicion, and I . . . I would very much like to clear him. He seldom speaks of his past, or his family. He will not say why. It may be something unhappy, rather than wrong. And it may be nothing to do with this current investigation."

Carlton looked at her, also without pretense at belief. "Suspicion of what? Surely not of being involved in this . . . atrocity?"

"Of having to conceal something, maybe for privacy's sake, his own or somebody else's," she answered. "If I knew what it was, it may well clear him of all suspicion."

"And if not?"

"Then it might clear all the others who are also suspect."

"Yes, I see. Who is this young man?"

She gave him Laker's full name and date of birth.

She saw from his face that he did not need to think about it. "Yes, of course. A bit rash. A bit emotional. But a good man. I think he will do better in the River Police than in the army. More room for . . . individuality."

"What did he do? I believe your judgment, but the commander will need more."

"Long story, but I'll make it brief."

He was interrupted by the arrival of tea and a plate of raspberry jam tarts.

He resumed as soon as it was served.

"This is the truth . . ." he began, and told her all he had learned.

"Thank you. That . . . that sounds like the Laker I know. Arrogant, impertinent, brave . . . and vulnerable. Thank you, Major Carlton. These are most excellent tarts." She looked at the huge bookcase. "Learned many good secrets recently?"

"Oh, yes! Yes . . . I can't tell you . . ."

SHE TOLD MONK ABOUT her visit that evening. As it was late and he was weary, she related only the least of it, starting with what Will had told her of Bathurst and his family, then what Major Carlton had said. ". . . So you have no reason to doubt Laker," she finished.

"Thank you," he said quietly, too tired to go through the emotions of surprise, pretense, doubt, questioning.

She touched him gently. "You're welcome. I rather like Laker."

"I'LL FOLLOW UP ON the accounts," Monk told Hooper the next morning. "Laker can handle looking into whatever is known about Lister. We ought to find something useful. There's been a break-in at Johnson's Warehouse, down on the south bank. Got to send Marbury and Walcott that way. I want you to find out all you can about the bank manager, Doyle. But be discreet, make up some story that won't get back to him." He stopped, his face gray. "He could be behind this, and on the other hand, he could be another potential victim, or one already!"

"Yes, sir."

"Everything you can find out. Where does he live? Has he any income other than his salary? Does he own the house? Married or not, and has he a mistress on the side, or a more serious affair? If he's married, what is she like? Extravagant? What children has he? Are there commitments to family, or past debts? Does he gamble? Drink? Anything? Has he spent money lately, or does he appear to have skimped? Debts? Who are his friends? What color socks does he wear?"

"What?"

"I want to know the man. Bella Franken is right. It looks as if he fiddled with the books for the exact amount of the ransom money for Kate Exeter's life. That can't be a coincidence. He's involved somehow, knowingly or not, and willingly or not. We need to know."

"Yes, sir." Hooper was glad he had something definite to do, something that could possibly lead to progress. Everyone was on edge. No one spoke of the actual kidnap or murder openly, but the undercurrent of it was always there, the tiny instances of mistrust, the remarks that might have been all right but were taken the wrong way. There was no teasing, no irreverent humor, in fact very little humor at all. No one was overtly suspicious. In fact, if anything, they were overcareful, but it was in the air. Whoever was responsible, Hooper hated him for that. These men were as close as he had to a family, and it made him more aware of loneliness than he had been in years. He found he was self-conscious of even the smallest acts of kindness, and thought perhaps people were unnaturally guarded with him, as if he were trying to conceal a reality, when the reality was friendship, the need to touch another person in thought at least.

Everything about investigating Doyle was easy to begin with. It was simple to discover where he lived. It was a pleasant house, larger than Hooper expected, but there had been several children, all grown up and gone. It would have been a good place for them to grow up, perhaps a little ambitious at the time. Doyle might have incurred some debt to own it. From the outside, it looked a comfortable and prosperous man's home.

Inquiries of the neighbors and the local tradesmen took him until the early afternoon. Doyle sounded bland, a man with nothing exceptional about him, other than diligence in his work. He was ambitious and had risen to become manager of the bank, attracting many clients of great means, largely through his discretion and reliability, desirable qualities in a banker. An unremarkable man, easily lost in a crowd: in fact, boring.

Hooper caught himself with surprise that he should, in a way, condemn a man delineated by other people's words. If someone were to make such inquiries of him, would they come up with the same answers: good at his job, but boring? No remarkable achievements, nothing to make him interesting or different, looked pretty much like what he was: a merchant seaman. Indeed, he might have risen in the ranks, but didn't. They would not know why. No extravagances, no obvious weaknesses, no unusual relationships, all very ordinary. How facile to describe anyone like that! He knew how complicated he was himself, how full of dreams, regrets, wishes that he could not share, hopes that perhaps he would never realize. And loneliness.

Maybe Doyle was just as complicated if he could ever share those parts most men keep hidden, the soft inner core that so easily could be hurt.

He should look at Doyle again, with more imagination this time! Do the job properly, not merely fill in the blanks on a police record that could fit ten thousand men and touch the reality of none of them. He should look at him as if he liked him, as he had looked at the men he worked with and been afraid of what he might find, in case any of them were the one who had betrayed Exeter, and Kate, and all of them.

He worked into the evening, looking more carefully, listening to what was said, and even more to what was not said. He found a barmaid at the local public house where Doyle sometimes stopped for a drink on the way home, especially if he was tired and knew he had missed supper.

"Always came at the same time," Betsy said, leaning on the bar and smiling patiently at Hooper.

He looked back at her. "Habit can be comfortable," he observed, hoping she would understand what he meant. They had already established a certain rapport, because they had discovered that they both liked walking down the beach when the rare opportunity offered itself. Hooper had recognized Betsy's Essex accent, which had quickly led to finding they loved the same parts of the east coast.

"Bless you, luv," she said. "Not for me. Sounds too much like house rules, if you know what I mean? Bit like having the same thing to eat, depending on what day of the week, like. Hot roast on Sunday, cold meat and leftovers on Monday, shepherd's pie on Tuesday, sausages on Wednesday—and like that."

Hooper gave a little groan, which he knew she would understand.

"Exactly," she agreed. "Sometimes it looks safe, like you lock the door at night so nobody can break in."

"Or out?" he suggested.

She sighed. "You're a wise one, you are!"

"Did Mr. Doyle want to break out?" Hooper asked.

"I think at times maybe he did. Or leastways, he daydreamed about it."

Hooper wondered more exactly what Doyle daydreamed about. "Going to faraway places? Having adventures?"

"More like some of them fancy clubs up in the city. For gentlemen, like." She rolled her eyes. "You've got to be special to belong to them."

Hooper imagined the very ordinary Doyle thinking of such a place. Perhaps Harry Exeter had described one—or, better still, taken Doyle to one as his guest. "I expect he's heard about them from his customers. Been there, even."

"Should've seen his face when he told me about it." She smiled, but there was a certain pity in it, a gentleness, because in her mind he would never belong, and she was probably right.

"I can imagine," Hooper said quietly. "Never been to one myself. More comfortable here!"

She smiled and blushed very slightly, offered him another drink and, when he accepted, busied herself with pouring it.

Hooper spent the next morning following up on the various things he'd learned about Doyle. He seemed to have few friends, and they were largely within the banking business, people he had met because of his position. He dined with them occasionally, and at predictable places, such as local sporting clubs, a historical appreciation society, although he seemed uninterested in their journeys to local battlefields.

He liked good food but seldom tried anything new. He had made one journey across the Channel to France, several years ago, and never repeated it.

He went to the theater, but to Shakespeare, never anything modern. It substantiated the nature of a lonely man, trapped in progress in a job he did well, but always an outsider to the life his major clients enjoyed, which he could view only from a distance; see, but never taste.

Was he vulnerable enough to temptation to fall for it? Had it somehow gone beyond his grasp, out of his control, into a violence he never intended?

Hooper considered attempting to meet him without saying who he was but realized how difficult that would be, and how awkward. He could not pass himself off as a man who earned the kind of money to bank at Nicholson's. And if Doyle were involved in the embezzlement, either by mischance of being drawn in or by inattention, then he was guilty from the beginning. If Hooper made the slightest error, it would warn him. Possibly Doyle even knew Monk's men by sight. If one of them had betrayed the rest to him, he certainly would.

Instead, he decided to go speak with Harry Exeter himself, to see if he could reveal a side that he did not show when Monk was there. Monk understood the adventurer in him, and the man who had adored his wife. Perhaps Hooper would see something different.

To go at lunchtime would be clumsy. In the middle of the afternoon was more appropriate, and if Exeter was not in, Hooper would wait until he was.

That proved not to be necessary. Exeter was at home and seemed quite happy to see Hooper. He ushered him in and offered him a drink.

"No, thank you, sir," Hooper declined as he thought he was meant to. It was a gesture of hospitality, not intended to be taken up.

"So, what can I do for you, Mr. Hooper? Have you any further news?" Exeter frowned slightly. He expected Monk himself to bring any, if there were, and his tone implied as much.

"No, sir, just a few further inquiries."

Exeter could not conceal his interest. "What about?"

Hooper had the feeling he was stepping into dead water. Exeter had an air of power. He did not want to show it, except by casually exposing the things he had earned, his possession of more money than he needed to count. He asked for things as if he were accustomed to people being eager to please him, and he accepted them with grace, but no surprise. He still looked tired, as if his emotions were further beneath the surface but still just as consuming as the evening of Kate's death.

How could it be anything else? He must still forget at times, and then remember again with all the weight of new grief. How long did it take a man to realize his wife was gone for the rest of his life? Did Exeter have any religious faith? Did most people, when it was tested to the breaking point? Probably, in some form or other. But in the dark, alone, in the middle of the night, when perhaps he would have turned to her, and there was only an emptiness there, a cold sheet.

Hooper had always slept alone or with other ship's crew. But it was not by choice. He could not involve a woman with the ghosts of his life and the probability that they would return. He could not ask anyone he loved to share that.

Exeter was waiting.

"We think the bank manager, Mr. Doyle, may have more information than he is aware of." He watched Exeter's face intently. He saw the tightening of the muscles, minutely, and the slow intake of breath.

"Really?" Exeter raised his eyebrows. "In what way?"

"Quite unintentionally," Hooper said, choosing his words carefully. "I believe."

Exeter sat quite still, not moving at all except for the slow intake of breath, and then the exhalation. "Unintentionally? Are you sure?"

"I have no reason to suspect otherwise. It is only a possibility to follow up. I am assuming this case is about money, sir. You have assured us that Mrs. Exeter had no personal enemies. Nothing more than perhaps the odd bit of envy because she was beautiful, charming, rich, and married to one of the . . . best catches in London, if I may put it so bluntly." Again, he used exactly the words he meant and watched Exeter's expression pass through awareness, amusement, apprehension, and then a moment of thoughtfulness.

"I believe that to be true, yes," he said. "I . . . I hate the thought, but I have to face it, that my wife might have been murdered to get at me. I have enemies." He waited, as if to see what Hooper would make of that.

Hooper must keep it impersonal, always with the proper respect, the little bit of distance that showed he never presumed to be equal. "Of course, sir," he said gravely. "Many men must envy you, and envy is sometimes the beginning of hatred."

"What are you suspecting Doyle of, exactly?" Exeter asked.

"I hope nothing. But he is your banker. He could be the person you might turn to in order to raise such a large sum quickly, in treasury notes rather than something less negotiable, such as deeds."

Exeter appeared to consider it for some time. "Of course," he said at last. "You are quite right. I went to Doyle. I've known him for years. Always found him . . . reliable. But I suppose the poor man has never faced a situation like this before. Thank God, there are not many kidnappings in London. At least not for that kind of sum." He nodded with a shadow of a smile. "He raised it for me. He liquidated certain assets immediately. Used his influence, and his word, to get the money very quickly. I . . . I thought we had met their demands . . ." He blinked quickly and turned away, avoiding Hooper's eyes. His voice was thick with emotion as he continued. "We did exactly what they said! And still . . ."

"I know, sir. You were not at fault," Hooper said quickly, to save Exeter from having to repeat again the dreadful events. "If something went wrong, then it was at their end."

"Good God, man!" Exeter said furiously. "If . . . if something went wrong?"

Hooper stayed perfectly steady. "It is possible, sir, that they never intended to give her back to you."

Exeter looked as if Hooper had struck him.

"I'm sorry, sir, but that is a possibility. The other possibility, perhaps more likely, is that Mrs. Exeter recognized one of the men, and either he killed her to save himself, or one of the others killed her to save all of them. The person she knew could have implicated all of them, sooner or later."

Exeter stared at him as if seeing the depth of his character for the first time. This very ordinary-looking ex-seaman had arrived at the possibility before him. "Maybe you are right," he said slowly, only just loud enough for Hooper to hear him. "Of course you are. And if Doyle was involved, Kate had met him. She was good at speaking to ordinary people—tradesmen and so on, and never forgetting their names. It's a skill."

Hooper thought it was hardly a skill; it was a decency. And Doyle was hardly a tradesman, but that was not the point now. If she thought of him as such, that would only add to Doyle's sense of exclusion.

"Do you really think Doyle could have done this?" Exeter was frowning now. "How would he know people such as the . . . creature that you found in the boat, with his throat cut? And are you sure he—Lister, wasn't he called?—was involved? That is only a deduction, isn't it?"

"It seems very likely, sir. Lister had been spending what were for him huge amounts of money. He was known to be violent on occasion, and when we followed him he was keeping company with other violent men."

"Not a lot to go on," Exeter pointed out. "Doyle had the connection. He knew about the kidnapping. God! When I recall his sympathy and apparent shock when I told him about it! He looked . . . shattered . . . but it makes sense. Have you any connection between Doyle and this fellow . . . Lister?"

"We followed Lister and know he met up with Mr. Doyle. And Miss Darwin recognized him, sir."

"What!"

"Miss Darwin recognized him, sir," Hooper repeated.

"What do you mean, recognized him? When in hell's name did she ever see him?"

Hooper felt the blood rush up his face. Had he made a mistake in telling Exeter this? "She was with Mrs. Exeter when the man took her on the—"

"I know she was!" Exeter cut across him. "But when did she see him again, to recognize him?"

Hooper's mind raced. "She did not name him, sir." He had to admit to taking Celia to the morgue and showing her the corpse. Exeter would be furious with him. He could understand it. In his place, he would have felt the same. "She identified his body as the man she had seen on the riverbank," he finished.

Exeter's face paled. "God Almighty, man. You took Celia to look at the corpse, with his throat cut, of the man who kidnapped her cousin in front of her and then hacked her to death? Are you insane? You . . . you . . . Words fail me!" His face was flushed with rage.

"He was cleaned up, sir, and his throat was not visible. She saw only his face."

"And that makes it all right? What kind of a man are you? Maybe the women in your society are used to that kind of thing, but Miss Darwin is a lady! She might be poor and from the least successful side of the family, in all respects, but she is . . ."

Hooper kept his temper with difficulty, but his anger was evident in the timbre of his voice, if not in his actual words. "Miss Darwin behaved herself with perfect composure, Mr. Exeter, as a lady would, in my experience. Mr. Monk's wife, whom I have the privilege of knowing, was a nurse in the Crimea, with Florence Nightingale, and has seen more bloody corpses than all the police force put together, and certainly than you or I have. Neither she, nor the ladies with her, many of them from noble families, screamed or fainted or generally got in the way. Birth and death are both bloody, and frequently intimate and painful, and women usually do the attending to both."

Exeter drew in his breath sharply, then his face eased into blankness. "You are perfectly correct," he said with amazement. "I had never thought of Celia being any use at all, but perhaps she has at least that quality. Either that, or insufficient imagination to be horrified. I hope she did not identify this wretched man simply to please you."

Hooper had had that thought as well, and had dismissed it. Now he was angry with Exeter for suggesting it, and yet he had no right to be. "So do I, sir. I hope it every time someone identifies a potential criminal. She did not see him for very long on the riverbank, but I believe her. She is observant."

"You hardly know her well enough for such a judgment, Mr. Hooper." Exeter's face was slack with surprise as another thought came to him. "Unless, of course, that was not the first time she had seen him? Is that what you were suggesting?"

For an instant Hooper had no idea what Exeter meant. Then it came to him in a rush of profound anger. It took him a moment to hide it. Exeter must not know the regard Hooper had for this woman he had met only three times, and so briefly. He breathed in and out slowly, as if pensive rather than controlling his emotions. "I was not suggesting such a thing, sir. I have no reason to suppose any of you met Lister before, except perhaps Mr. Doyle. And I am sure you would tell me if you had any evidence of that."

"How could I have?" Exeter demanded. "I have never seen this . . . Lister!"

"No, sir. I forgot that. If you think of anything else that might be of use in tracing the money through Mr. Doyle's hands, his foreknowledge of the ransom and its amount, anything at all—"

"Yes, yes. I'll tell you," Exeter assured him. "Thank you. I'm sorry if I was short with you. This is all terribly hard for me. Nothing is as I thought it was . . . as I believed. It is all . . ." He shook his head.

Hooper rose to his feet. "Appalling, sir. I can hardly imagine," he said quietly.

12

Monk listened closely as Hooper told him about his visit to Harry Exeter. They were sitting in Monk's office with the door closed. The kidnapping was still at the forefront of everyone's minds although it was a week and a half since the event. It was a failure that ached like a deep wound. They were becoming used to it, and there were always other cases to deal with: robberies, smuggling, stolen goods moved from place to place, in and out of their jurisdiction, and violence here and there, usually bar brawls that got out of hand, occasionally a knifing or a body thrown into the water. But the murder of Kate Exeter was deliberate and unnecessary, and a failure of which they were forewarned and yet had still succumbed.

"But you think Miss Darwin's identification was good?" Monk asked a second time, studying Hooper's face. He was not a handsome man in a traditional way, but he had a good face. The strength in it was gentle; there was nothing coarse in him. Monk was overwhelmed with a sudden wave of hatred toward whoever had betrayed them and sown the seed of this darkness. Good men were unfairly doubted, robbed of a trust they had earned—more than earned—through danger, boredom, physical hardship, and pain. Yesterday he had followed up on young Bathurst's paperwork on the arrest of a thief, and Marbury had seen him do it. Would he tell Bathurst? Or simply think that Bathurst needed more guidance?

One of his men had let him down, but in a sense he himself had let them all down. He repeated his question to Hooper in slightly different words. "You think she is right, not just trying to help, to do something for Kate, without thinking it through?"

"She is very . . . sensible," Hooper said slowly. "If you met her, you would know what I mean. She understands that truth is the only thing that helps."

"Are you sure?"

Hooper thought for a moment and then answered, "Yes, I am."

Hooper was a good judge of character. Monk had come to rely on him more and more. He thought of the trust he had placed in Orme, when he was alive. That was a loss they all still felt. Sometimes Monk remembered a familiar phrase that Orme had used or passed a place on the river he had loved, and a shadow would pass over his face.

"Who betrayed us, Hooper?" he said suddenly. "Could Lister have told us, and that was why he was killed?"

Hooper's eyes widened a fraction. Perhaps because it had not occurred to him? Or because he realized Monk must trust him to ask him that?

"I don't know," Hooper replied. "I knew it wasn't you or me. And I trust Laker. He's a cheeky devil, and ambitious, but I trust him. He wants to be like you," he smiled. "Or even better. And that means being straight with everybody, whether they like it or not."

Monk winced and felt the heat climb up his face. He had not done much to deserve that kind of praise lately, and he realized with surprise how valuable it was to him. "What about Bathurst?" he asked. "Are you satisfied about him?"

"Yes," Hooper replied. "That leaves Marbury and Walcott. But so much about this case isn't how it looks, and everything is to be questioned. Exeter even tried to make me doubt Miss Darwin's identification."

Monk waited. He could see that Hooper was fighting some emotion. Whatever Exeter had said, it disturbed and also angered him. Was that because he felt something for the woman? It looked like that, from his expression.

Hooper lifted his head. "He half suggested that she wasn't a reliable witness, that she was likely to be overcome with horror or emotion, and her judgment affected."

"Isn't that fair?" Monk asked, surprised that Hooper should not see that himself.

"Because she's a woman?" Hooper said with disbelief. "What, and confused, overemotional? Like Hester?" He used her first name quite naturally, as if this was how he thought of her. "Or the other women who work with her at the clinic, or did in the Crimea?"

Again, Monk felt the heat rise up in his face. "So, Exeter views women as weak and suggestible? I wonder if that was how he saw Kate." He found that hard to believe when he remembered Exeter's face when he spoke of her, or the few incidents he had recalled in Monk's company. Did he have conflicting ideas? Kate, and then other women? Did he even know other women, apart from Celia Darwin, who was family and of little more interest to him than a servant? He had spoken of her dismissively before.

"He tried to make me doubt Miss Darwin's identification of Lister," Hooper repeated.

"Perhaps he wants to believe the kidnapper is still alive, either to get information or to feel the pain of punishment," Monk suggested.

"I think Doyle's part of it." Hooper picked up the other thread of the conversation. "He wants to be something he can't be without a lot more money than he'll ever earn at the bank. Exeter took him to a gentlemen's club, according to the woman at the public house where he drinks."

"Exeter or Doyle?"

"Doyle, although I gather Exeter's been in there a couple of times.

Slumming, showing he's one of the men!" The expression on Hooper's face was a mixture of derision, disgust, and pity. "Fool," he said under his breath.

They stayed and turned over every possibility again, but no new thought arose. Eventually Hooper left, and a few moments later Monk took the ferry home across the river.

He was pleased to see Hester and glad of the warmth of the sitting room, but he wished he had progress to tell her, or at least that someone had proved conclusively that he could not have been the one to betray them to the kidnappers. But with Hester, Monk could not even try to pretend. It was not for her sake, but mainly for his own. He had to have one relationship without even the smallest lies, no shifting of position to make himself look better, no wondering if she would find out this or that. Everything would be different, shallower, without the shadows that made it real.

He went to bed early, too tired to think of anything to say. Sleep might repair some of the frayed edges of his temper.

But he did not sleep. He lay stiff and awkward, listening to Hester's breathing become deeper, softer, as she drifted off. Somewhere outside and far away a church clock chimed midnight, then one, then two. The wind rose a little and whined round the ridges of the roof. It would be freezing out there, a few yards away, above the slates. It seemed all the warmer in here. He wanted to wake Hester and hold her in his arms, have her tell him none of his men had betrayed him. That good things in the world were still as he had believed. How infinitely childish! He turned over and put his back to her, to stop himself from doing anything so self-absorbed.

"William?" she said quietly.

Damn! He had woken her anyway. Should he pretend to be asleep?

"William?" she repeated.

He did not answer. He felt her moving beside him, pushing the covers back and climbing out of bed. She walked across the floor and took her robe off the peg on the back of the door. She put it on and, hugging it around herself, went outside onto the landing.

He waited, but she seemed gone for ages. He would not go to sleep until she returned.

When she did, the light was on on the landing. She came in and put the bedroom light on, too. She was carrying a small tray with two mugs of tea.

"We'll talk it through," she said, as if picking up a conversation they had left in the middle.

He thought of arguing, but it was ridiculous to deny it now, when really what he wanted was truth. Tousled, he sat up, pushed his hair off his face, and accepted the hot mug of tea. He sipped it very carefully. He was surprised how good it tasted.

She put her own mug down, climbed into bed beside him, and then sipped hers, too. "Are you still worrying about who betrayed you?" she asked after a moment or two.

"I wish I could find another answer, but we were the only ones who knew exactly where we were going in, and there were several possible ways. They were waiting for us and took us by surprise, one by one."

"Could there have been a lot of them? One for every possible way in?" she asked.

He thought for a moment. "The more there were of them, the more to split the money. And the more risk of one of them turning informer. They could have been more . . . I suppose."

"Could it have been Exeter himself, unintentionally? Someone had to help him get the money. You said it was a very great deal. He wouldn't have had it in the house!"

"Bank manager, Doyle."

"Did he know what it was for?"

"Yes, Exeter told him. He had little choice, to raise that much so quickly. If he sold everything, he'd have had to do it at a loss, and in a hell of a hurry."

"Does he trust this Doyle?"

"I think he did. Not that there was a lot of choice in that either." He stared at her. "Are you thinking that whoever took her would know he'd go to Doyle?"

"Well, it's not a great feat of the imagination, is it?" she said reasonably.

"No . . ." The more the idea settled in his mind, the more it seemed to fit in with all the facts they knew.

"Could he have told Doyle what the arrangements were, perhaps without realizing how much he was giving away?" Hester went on. "He'd be desperate to get the full amount of money by the time they demanded it. Time was against them all."

"All?" He took another sip of his tea. He found it oddly relaxing, the heat of it, although it was not cold in the bedroom.

"The kidnappers as well," she answered. "The longer they had her, the more chance of something going wrong. Perhaps it did."

"They murdered her, Hester. Slashed her . . ."

"I know. But perhaps she tried to escape? Or maybe she knew one of them. They might not all have been pirates, or smugglers, or whatever they were. We don't know who they were, do we? Apart from the man in the boat, who spent his money too openly?"

"Are you thinking it was someone she knew? They both knew? An enemy of Exeter's, of his own social class?"

"It's possible, isn't it?"

"Not likely. Not to know Jacob's Island the way these men did."

"I suppose not. But couldn't one of them have known it, and have hired the others? Do you know Exeter's background?"

"Not in river pirates and kidnappers!"

"Isn't he very rich, indeed?"

"Yes."

"Do you know how he made his money? All of it?"

"You're letting your imagination run away with you; he makes it in business: building, draining land, and trading. He's thoroughly respectable. I did check that!"

"William," she said patiently, "respectability can be bought, and quite a lot of it at a reasonable rate! Put money in the right places and you'd be amazed how it opens doors. A lot of them anyway, though some aren't for sale."

He suddenly realized again the gulf between his past and hers.

Her parents had been gentry—not nobility, but well acquainted with the aristocracy and their beliefs and manners, from the inside—not looking on from beyond a circle of familiarity. She had occasionally entertained uncles and aunts, cousins with titles. And in her work with Miss Nightingale she had met many titled and privileged people, perhaps nursed their sons in the desolation of battle, when all men are equally vulnerable, wounded and sharing the commonality of death.

He had no idea who his family had been. Fishermen, from the snatches he could remember. His own patterns of speech did not give him away, because he had schooled himself to speak like a gentleman. That much he had discovered about himself in some of the time when he had been obliged to find out, to learn from others who he had been, the mistakes and the enemies he had made. His were never complete memories, just flashes and things other people had told him. Perhaps his judgment of Harry Exeter had been based too much on who he was now, not considering that he might once have been very different. But Exeter himself would know! "Do you think Doyle could have been bribed by someone with an old score to settle?" he asked.

"It's a brutal thing to do," Hester replied. "If it was just for money, why didn't they take the money and give her back? There's more than money behind it, William."

"I've asked him, but he doesn't seem to know."

"Have you considered that he might have a very good idea, but intends to get his own vengeance? It wouldn't be unnatural. Or possibly that it is something he can't afford to have the police know? Please, when you do find out who it is, be careful! Be very careful that Exeter doesn't use you to lead him to the man behind it, and take his revenge before you can stop him." Her face was tired and frightened in the lamplight, and, with her hair lying loose over her shoulders, she looked vulnerable.

Suddenly Monk could imagine very easily that if anyone hurt her, let alone did to her what they had done to Kate Exeter, he would want to kill them himself, with his own hands, tear them apart like the carcass of an animal.

"William!"

"I'm listening," he answered. "Yes, I'll be careful. But I owe him a debt, Hester. I made a promise to him, and I failed appallingly to keep it."

She drew in her breath to argue; he knew what she was going to say. He put the tea down, leaned forward and kissed her, gently at first, and then more deeply.

THE NEXT DAY, HE woke late and went straight to see Exeter again.

Exeter was in the hallway with his coat on and a heavy walking stick in his hand, about to go out. A look of intense relief filled his face. "I was coming to see you. I thought a lot about what you said. It's a hard thing to face, Monk—and God knows, I have—but you were perfectly right." He winced looking into Monk's eyes in the clear light of the hall. "If you're decisive, if you take life by the neck and fight, sometimes you win, and sometimes you lose. But always there will be other men who long to do the same and haven't the courage. They're too afraid of pain and humiliation to take a chance. So they don't win either . . . at least, never enough. You know what I mean, don't you." It was a statement of fact. "A man doesn't hate your win, he hates himself because he could have done it, but can't admit that. Didn't you find that, on the Barbary Coast? You did . . . I can see it in your face. God help me, I never thought it would cost me this!" For a moment he turned away, and Monk stood still, knowing exactly what he meant and that he needed his moment of grief.

Exeter turned back to face Monk. "Kate was different. No one hated her—not anyone who would even think of something like this, let alone know how to go ahead and do it." He gave a bleak smile and put the cane back in the stand. He took his coat off and hung it up. "Come inside, please."

Monk took his own coat off and followed Exeter into the withdrawing room, where a maid was clearing the ashes out of the hearth.

"I'm sorry, sir. I'll just be a few minutes. But the fire's lit in the morning room."

Monk went to the morning room as directed and was standing in front of the fire a few minutes later when Exeter returned. Without his coat on, he looked thinner, even stooped a little. He had aged visibly in the days since the murder. The vitality seemed to have drained out of him. Without asking Monk to be seated, he slumped into the chair on the opposite side of the fire.

Monk felt the guilt rising inside him, and tightness seized his chest.

"What is it?" Exeter asked. "You know something, or you wouldn't have come again so soon. You are not responsible for me, you know." He gave a ghost of a smile. "Perhaps one of your men did betray us, but we all put trust where we shouldn't, at one time or another. You have to give a man the benefit of the doubt, until you have proof. I daresay he was not greedy so much as frightened. It is a terrible thing to fear for your own life." His voice sank a little. "Worse to fear for the life of someone you love, who trusts you. Child? A mother or sister? You can blame them in the heat of your own loss, but when you think about it afterward, you understand, at least most of the time, your heart may be another thing." He sat silent for a moment, watching while Monk struggled to find an answer that did not sound trite yet conveyed his understanding, even his respect for such a compassionate and forgiving view. He was not sure in similar circumstances he could have risen above the torment of his own grief.

Exeter was still looking at him when the ease left his face, his body stiffening, and he gradually leaned forward. "You have something to tell me, haven't you?" he asked hoarsely. "You know that it was not just the money, or Kate; it was hatred for me. The money was to disguise that! So I wouldn't start racking my mind to think of all the people who blamed me at one time or another, because I succeeded where they failed. Someone's hate has grown monstrous, hideous, consumed everything in them that used to be good."

"No . . . I . . ." Monk began.

"Don't evade it," Exeter said, a sudden gentleness in his voice. "It isn't a kindness. I have to accept some . . . some creature from my past has let jealousy devour what was good in him, and . . . and destroyed any happiness and even his own sanity. I've been feeling it lately . . . not just thinking about it, although I've done that—of course I have. I've been followed sometimes, felt as if I've been watched. I suppose that makes sense. If I hated someone to that depth and saw their loss but left them living, hurting, aware of it, I would come to witness what I had done. Simply imagining it would not be enough. Eventually, I would have to see him, taste the pain in him, perhaps even let him know that it was I who brought it all on him." He gave his head a little shake, as if it would rid him of something. "Maybe even make him physically afraid, wonder what I was going to do next."

Monk was startled and worried. Was Exeter losing his grip on reality? Or was he possibly right? It made a certain sense. Monk had come here to ask him if he might have told Doyle any details of the plan to rescue Kate and hand over the ransom money. The demand for money had been their way into the case. It had made Exeter believe it was greed, and that he could buy his wife back again. It was an additional piece of cruelty.

Monk looked at Exeter again now and saw the fear in his face, in his body, the desperation in his eyes. What could he do? He had no men that Exeter would trust, and even if he did, he could hardly guard him night and day, indefinitely. The only answer was to find the truth, the man behind Lister, which was probably the man who had killed him, or the man behind that!

"Doyle is the answer," he said. "I'm convinced of it and we'll prove it. In the meantime, trust no one and avoid being alone wherever you can.

"And I would advise you not to go out unnecessarily, especially after dark. That's a miserable restriction, I know, but please, God, it won't be for long."

Exeter sighed. "Thank you, Monk, you're a decent man."

13

Monk left Exeter with a new determination to follow the course of the money, and then Doyle. The only way to do that was to go and see him. He had obtained a letter from Exeter's solicitor granting him access to certain of his accounts, so that Doyle would not be in a position to deny him.

He went in the middle of the afternoon and was told that Mr. Doyle was occupied at the moment, but if he cared to wait, Mr. Doyle would see him in half an hour or so.

He was given a rather bare room to sit in. He had the feeling it was not so much for his comfort as to keep customers of the bank from seeing him. He was certainly respectable enough in appearance, even rather elegant, which was a harder thing to be in the River Police than when he was a detective in the regular Metropolitan Police. He had always favored good tailors. He remembered with a twisted smile going to his rooms when he first recovered from the accident, knowing nothing of his previous life, to find the tailor's bills. Thank heaven they were all marked as paid!

Working on the river was different. It was far more physical and frequently dirtier, because docks, by their nature, were places of salt, dust, dubious old timber, and packing materials. He was dressed in a better suit than he would normally wear. With his strong-boned face, slate-gray eyes, and grace of movement, he was a dangerous-looking man.

He did not blend in with the city-clothed businessmen who had come to the bank on financial affairs in their frock coats and pin-striped trousers.

Eventually a clerk came to fetch him to Doyle's office and opened the door for him to enter. Doyle was sitting at his desk. He did not rise. Monk was in his domain, and he was not a potential client.

"Good afternoon, Mr. Monk." Doyle inclined his head politely but did not use Monk's professional title. "What may I do for you?"

Monk sat down uninvited. "Good afternoon, Mr. Doyle. I'm afraid I'm here regarding the tragic kidnap and murder of Mrs. Exeter."

A shadow passed over Doyle's face. His back stiffened a little. "I am afraid I can tell you nothing, Mr. Monk."

Monk felt his body tighten. The man was clearly being obstructive, and the reason for it was becoming clearer every moment. "I have Mr. Exeter's permission to see all his records that you have, Mr. Doyle. I am aware of your assistance to him in getting hold of a very large ransom amount. It was a very good service you rendered him. Although I cannot imagine him leaving his considerable amount of money in your bank, had you declined."

"That is a disgraceful suggestion!" Doyle said furiously. "And totally without foundation. I cannot think of any honorable reason why you would make such a suggestion."

"And since I have Mr. Exeter's permission, I cannot think of any honorable reason why you would refuse to show me the accounts."

"Because they would show not Mr. Exeter's money, but amounts he paid to others that have nothing to do with this matter, and of course payments made to him. They concern other people who have not given you their permission, Mr. Monk!" Doyle snapped back.

"Do you not think it probable, Mr. Doyle, that all demands for so huge a ransom were made by someone who had knowledge of Mr. Exeter's financial position? And that such money was lodged all in one place with you? And then, with a little maneuvering, you were able to lay your hands on it, at short notice? That is not public knowledge. In fact, if it were widely shared, it would hardly be worth your taking so much risk in keeping it from the police."

Doyle's face, which had been red with temper a few moments ago, now was drained of all color. "Are you accusing me of something, sir?"

"Nothing more than being pompous and obstructive," Monk replied. "So far!"

Doyle pushed his chair back from the desk and stood up, banging his knee on the high side of the drawer and wincing with pain. "I shall have to get them from the safe and choose those that will serve your purpose, without revealing other men's private affairs."

"I'll wait." Monk sat back in his chair.

"Indeed, sir," Doyle agreed. "But you will not do it in my private office!" Walking with a slight limp to the door, he held it open for Monk to leave.

Monk went out; he had no reasonable alternative. He would not have looked at any of Doyle's other papers, but another man might have. And perhaps, if he thought that the key to Kate's murder lay there, he might have also. But he would not have the time or the financial skill to have known that at a glance. It was Doyle's job to keep them safe, and he would have thought less of him if he had not done so.

He waited on a seat in a hallway outside Doyle's office. It was comfortable enough. He had been there only a few moments when Bella Franken walked past him, dressed in black and carrying a pile of ledgers. One slipped from her grasp and landed on the floor, almost at his feet.

He bent to pick it up for her.

She looked a little flustered. "Thank you, sir. I'm so sorry." She lowered her voice even more. "Please meet me at the south side of the river, by the Greenwich Stairs, at half-past seven this evening. I'll

have the true papers for you then." And before he could ask her anything further, she straightened up the files in her arms and hurried on.
She disappeared around the corner without looking back.

Doyle returned with a few sheets of paper and opened his office
door. "Please," he said sharply, ushering Monk inside. "These are the
papers you will need in order to see how the money was obtained so
rapidly. They are exact copies. We cannot let the originals out of our
keeping. Anyway, if you do bring a case against someone, you may
need them. I don't see why or how, but I presume you know your job.
Or you employ someone who does!"

He gave the papers to Monk, who took them with an expression
of thanks. Five minutes later he was outside in the street again, the
papers tucked in his inside pocket, his head down against the rising
wind.

AT THE POLICE STATION Monk studied the figures Doyle had given
him, but he had to admit they meant little to him. He was familiar
with ordinary accounting, but some of these on one sheet of paper
and some on another did not mean anything to him but simple arithmetic and sums. All of them, as far as he could see, were correct.

Of course, Katherine's inheritance was not included among these
papers. It was a quite separate matter, and Exeter had no access to it.
That had been a very specific part of the bequest. He imagined Exeter
had found that insulting but not of any financial consequence to him.
The amounts he dealt with were huge, and he was more than com-
fortably off. That, at least, was obvious.

BY LATE AFTERNOON MONK was tired and felt he had accomplished
little. He went home early, so that he could eat something before
going down to the Greenwich stairs to meet Bella Franken at half-
past seven.

At quarter-past he set out, closing the front door behind him and
walking in the crisp evening air. The wind had fallen a bit, and it was

really quite pleasant. Still, it would be cold on the pier and he would not allow her to get chilled waiting for him.

It took him ten minutes going down the hill, and it was twenty-five past when he reached the stairs to the water. There were a couple of people waiting for the next ferry, a man with his coat collar turned up, pacing back and forth, and a woman with a shawl around her head, which hid most of her face. They acknowledged each other with a nod, but no one spoke.

Seven or eight minutes later, a ferry arrived. A man in work clothes got off, but there was no sign of Bella Franken. The man and the woman who had been waiting got on board. The ferryman looked at Monk.

"No, thank you," Monk declined. "I'm waiting for someone."

"Right you are, sir." He gave a salute, then took up the oars and pulled away. For a few yards, the pier lights lit the water off his oars and made the slight ripple of his passage bright; then he was gone, beyond the pool of light. And it fell silent again, except for the flutter of the wind moving a piece of rubbish across the open boards of the wharf and the whisper of the tide past the edges of the pier.

Quarter to eight. Where was Bella?

He wondered what she wished to tell him, or to show him. Was it more pages from a ledger that read differently from the one he had seen, or would she just explain the figures he already had? Doyle was deceiving him about something, he felt sure about that.

He was growing cold standing still. He began to pace back and forth, from one end of the pier to the other.

Was Doyle a go-between or an arranger for the kidnappers, a man who knew who was vulnerable? Did he know who had the ability, with his help, to lay his hands on the greatest amount of money? And who loved his wife enough not to put up a fight, to just pay it, without a struggle, to get her back? There would not be so many men in that category. For a start, few men ever had the wealth of Harry Exeter, and of those who had, much of it lay in property and investment that could not be liquidated immediately, whatever the need.

Was Doyle a willing participant? Or was he blackmailed in some way to do that? He gambled. Was it a far deeper problem than Hooper had been able to discover? If he slept with women of the street, who cared? So did many others. It was not a big enough matter to blackmail him to betray a client in such a way.

For a moment, Monk thought of other past cases, where people had done appalling things under pressure of blackmail. He and Oliver Rathbone had fought some of the worst imaginable.

Eight o'clock! Where was Bella Franken? Had something prevented her from coming? Even if she had found it difficult to catch a ferry, she should have been here by now! He would give her another fifteen minutes, then leave.

Without fully realizing it, he was watching the water, seeing the light reflected from riding lights on the ships at anchor, seeing the small boats moving, coming to the south bank or going back toward the north. Where was she?

He walked back toward the step again and looked down. The tide had risen, one step fewer visible from the water line to the top. There was more flotsam drifting by, bumping the stones. It looked like cloth, a bag of something thrown away.

Suddenly his stomach knotted, and for a moment he thought he was going to be sick. He saw the rest of it as it turned in the water. It was a body—a woman's body, fully clothed in dark fabric, a boot on the one foot he could see. Her face was only a pale blur, just beneath the water.

He scrambled down the steps, heedless of slipping or getting himself soaked, and reached the water line just as the current carried her almost out of his reach. It was strong and, beyond the steps, deep. He lunged forward for her, as if she might still be alive, although everything in him knew she was not.

He felt the bottom of her skirt and pulled. She swung around, held on to by him and carried by the current. There was no point in calling for help; there was no one else on the pier. Clinging on to her, he was carried off the steps into the deep water himself. His coat hampered his movement, and he felt the stakes of the pier scrape against his shoulder and bruise his arm. He had no footing at all. The water was deep under him.

Where were the next steps, where he could hope to get a foothold, or a handhold? The river was strong and ice cold, and he was soaked through already. What an immensely stupid thing to do. He didn't even know for sure that it was Bella! But he did know. He was certain, even as he clung on to her, winding his hands into the fabric of her dress so the strength of the water would not rip her away from him. Why? He couldn't help her now.

Suddenly he was aware of a darkness beside him, and then something wooden hitting his shoulders.

"'Ere! Grab that, mate!" a voice shouted at him.

The wood hit him on the shoulder again. It was an oar. A ferry-man was offering him an oar to hold on to. He grabbed it hard with one hand, keeping the other on Bella's body in case the river took her away again. He pulled and felt the oar drawing him toward the side of the boat.

"Hold on, mate!" the voice called out again. "I'll take the girl first. You hang on to the gunwale."

He felt Bella move as the man struggled to lift her out. It seemed to take him forever. Monk's hands were growing colder and weaker; he could not hold on to Bella any longer, and he felt her slip away.

Then an arm came and gripped him. He used what strength he had left to heave himself over the gunnel and roll onto the hard boards of the floor inside the ferry boat, gasping.

The ferryman let him be and put his shoulder into getting the boat to the nearest steps and then moored.

Monk was dazed. He sat up slowly, taking a moment or two to make his arms and legs work. He was shaking with cold.

The ferryman was shouting, bellowing for help. "'Ere, mate. Stand yourself up and get onto the dry, will yer? Else you'll get froze to death. I'm sorry, the lady's gone. Reckon there was nothing you could ever 'ave done anyway." He looked at someone beyond Monk. "Come on, yer great nelly! Come and get her up the steps, then! I'm not letting him die of cold, after I took that much trouble to get him out o' the water!"

Monk was hardly aware of the arms helping him up. There seemed to be at least two others, apart from the ferryman.

"Thank you," he said with intense gratitude.

The man's voice was filled with pity. "I'm sorry, mate, there ain't nothin' you can do now."

"I know," Monk answered him. "I saw her in the water. I couldn't just let her be . . . washed away with the tide, like rubbish."

"Do you know who she is?" He put his hand on Monk's arm, strong and steady, as if he feared Monk might collapse.

"Yes. Bella Franken. I think she was murdered."

"Then we'd better get the police. And you'd better stay here, like. Right?"

"Right." Monk gave a twisted smile. He could feel the emotion well up inside him, close to hysteria. "Get Runcorn. I think this is his patch."

"Do you know Mr. Runcorn, then?"

"Yes. Tell him it's Monk."

"Jeez! You're Monk of the River Police? Never thought you'd be such a fool as to get in the water after a corpse. 'Ere—she isn't . . . ?" He stopped, his voice choked with emotion now.

"No," Monk told him more gently. "She isn't anybody I really know."

"Thank the Lord for that!" The ferryman's voice cracked for a moment.

"Send someone for Runcorn," Monk repeated. "And thaw me out before I'm bloody dead as well!"

"Right! Right, sir. Just you 'ang on."

Monk shrank into himself, trying to find a little heart of warmth within his body.

The ferryman moved back, and for a moment or two, Monk did not know where he had gone. Only moments later, there were more men about, regular police. He was helped to his feet, shuddering with the almost living cold of his wet coat clinging to him. He could hardly feel his feet, although he could just manage to find them enough to stand up. The men made him walk. He had no idea how far. He became dizzy, needing their strength not to buckle and fall.

Eventually, he was aware of being inside a room and someone taking his coat, then his jacket and trousers. Someone was handing him a rough towel, and then a kind of shirt and dry trousers. There was a mug of hot tea in his hands, and somebody helped him to drink, holding it steady for him.

He heard the voice, and the moment after he saw Runcorn's bulk in the doorway and then beside him.

"What the hell are you doing, Monk? You look absolutely god-awful. Who is she? And who killed her?"

"She's Bella Franken, bookkeeper at Nicholson's Bank, who worked for the manager, Mr. Doyle. She was coming to meet me. She had something to give me, but it's gone somewhere down the river. I think it was some important figures."

"But they got to her first," Runcorn said quietly. "You better tell me more about it. You're in no fit state to manage this—and don't argue with me. She was washed up on my patch, and so were you!"

"But . . ." Monk said, then tried to sip the tea in his mug.

Runcorn took it from him and held it to his lips so he could drink. "You're in no condition to investigate this," he said when Monk had his mouth full of tea. "You'll catch your death if you don't go home, have a hot bath, and put on dry clothes. This needs following up now. Fresh witnesses, if we can find them. Either way, the ferryman who pulled you out and people on the last ferries that crossed. Many people are regulars. Anyone who was around here in the last hour or two."

He gave Monk another sip or two of the tea. For a large, usually clumsy man, he was surprisingly gentle. His quick, unexpected marriage had changed him. He believed in all the best in himself. Before that, Monk had believed in the worst in him and let him know that, something he now regretted. But perhaps they had both changed since then.

"Why were you going to meet this woman?" Runcorn asked.

"She found some discrepancies in some figures and was bringing them to show me."

Runcorn screwed up his face in clear disbelief. "At the Greenwich Pier, in the dark? For heaven's sake, Monk, if you're going to lie, at least make it credible. And you need help, whether you want it or not. This Exeter case has got you down. Don't blame you. It's horrible. But you're not chasing young bookkeepers in the dark, on the dockside, over some petty fraud in a bank. You don't know the first thing about bookkeeping. Anyway, the bank is miles from the river."

Monk was too tired and too cold to argue. In spite of all their vast differences, it was pleasant to be able to rely on Runcorn. The man was not always as quick in thinking as Monk, as he had proved, but the fact no longer irritated Monk. Runcorn had other qualities, including common sense, and Monk trusted him.

"It's to do with the kidnapping case," he said, without prevaricating. "Doyle was Exeter's banker, and I think he may have helped the kidnappers."

"What a filthy thing to do! What makes you think that?" Runcorn's voice reflected his disgust.

"If you think about it, there aren't so many men, however wealthy, that could come up with that sort of money in ready cash, at short notice." He looked up and saw the understanding in Runcorn's face.

"Selected out of enmity, but access to the cash," Runcorn summed it up. "And this girl knew it?"

"Looks like it." Suddenly Monk was overwhelmed again with the thought of Bella's death. The coldness of the river ached in his bones, and he could see her dead face in the water, whether his eyes were open or closed. "I have made a hell of a mess of it so far. I should at the very least have met her somewhere safer!"

"Who suggested Greenwich Pier?" Runcorn asked.

"She did, but I could have said somewhere different!" Monk was sharp. Guilt and sorrow cut deeply; she'd been a young woman full of character.

"How did she tell you where and when?" Runcorn asked.

"When I was at the bank seeing Doyle. Damn him! Why had I

not insisted she meet me somewhere safe, with people around?" He could have found a way to send her a note, if he had tried.

"Like where?" Runcorn asked, the corners of his mouth pulled down.

"I don't know! Any main street near wherever she lives! A public house. Even my house. It's not far from the pier."

"She didn't even make it to the pier," Runcorn pointed out. "Monk, Doyle or whoever has done this was going to get her somewhere. He's desperate. If she really has proof of embezzlement, or straight-out theft, he couldn't afford to let her give it to you. Kate Exeter's was one of the worst murders in London in ages. Whoever did it will swing for it. No mercy, no excuses. And precious little gentleness on the way."

"Double murder," Monk pointed out. "Kate Exeter, then one of the kidnappers. He's not such a great loss, but he was still a human being."

"And now three, with that poor girl," Runcorn added. "Does it matter who gets him, as long as we do? And I hate to remind you, but it's the truth, and one we can't ignore: I've been following this case with interest and I'm aware somebody betrayed you and took the money at Jacob's Island. You won't be all right until you've found him, too."

"I know." Monk said it in a tight, husky voice. "Here, give me my mug of tea. You don't have to hold it for me, I'm steady now."

"You're not," Runcorn argued, but he let Monk have the mug. "Then you're going home. You're only a damn nuisance here, and we need you alive—and not with pneumonia or croup tomorrow morning. Sanders will walk with you up the hill to be sure you make it."

"The ferryman—" Monk began.

"Yes, I'll question him, see if he saw her or anything else. And I'll thank him for fishing you out. Do you take me for a barbarian?"

Monk did not bother to answer that. In the past, he had made exactly that hasty and mistaken judgment. "I've got to see if she had any papers," he said quietly. "That's what she said she was bringing."

"I'll go look," Runcorn stood up slowly. "I didn't know her. It won't be so hard for me. You stay here."

Monk wanted to argue with him, but it was a kindness, another healing of an old wound, and he didn't want to reject it. And he didn't want to look at Bella's dead face. He nodded and watched Runcorn go out the door.

Runcorn came back in about fifteen minutes. He had a package in his hand. "Wrapped in oiled silk," he said. "Still wet, but it's India ink. Waterproof . . . enough to read, anyway. Clever girl . . . it's . . ." He gave up looking for the right thing to say. "I'll hold on to these and get an accountant to look at them properly. This murder is on my patch and I think maybe you need a helping hand with finding how it all fits together."

Monk could only agree.

Hooper looked up from the desk he shared with Laker and saw Monk standing in front of him. In the hard morning light, he looked terrible. He was wearing his standby coat, not his good one, and he had a gray muffler round his neck, up to his chin. He had not shaved with his usual punctiliousness and his skin appeared colorless. It would be foolish to ask him if there was anything wrong; clearly there was.

"I went to Greenwich to meet Bella Franken last night," Monk said before Hooper could ask. "She had more to say about Doyle."

Hooper's first thought was that she had told Monk which of his men had betrayed them. Of course, they had to find out, but as long as they did not, they could hold each man independently innocent. Hooper felt the misery grip hard inside him. For the moment, he could not think of anything in the world more painful than betrayal. "What did she say?" He heard his own voice as if it were someone else's, unconnected with his thoughts.

"Nothing," Monk answered. "She was dead. In the river. I tried to pull her out, but it was too late . . . far too late." Monk looked as if he was apologizing. His face was filled with sorrow and a degree of guilt. "A ferryman helped pull us both out of the river."

"Us?" Hooper demanded. Already he was beginning to feel the coldness that Monk carried with him.

"I saw the body there," Monk was saying, "floating. I had nothing to pull her out with except my arms. Otherwise, she'd have gone with the tide, maybe got caught up in rubbish, and eventually mangled to bits, unrecognizable, even gone out to sea."

Hooper did not argue with that. He knew it was true. The Thames yielded up many bodies, but no one knew how many it kept.

"They called the police," Monk went on, still standing in the same spot. "Runcorn. He's going to help us with the case. I told him she was connected with the bank that Doyle works in, and she was bringing me some papers. Of course, they'll be sodden now, but perhaps still legible. Runcorn has them, as he's taken on investigating Bella's death."

"You think they might prove Doyle has the money?" Hooper said doubtfully. "Surely he wouldn't put it in his own bank? And why kill Kate in the first place?" But the answer was obvious. "You think she saw him, and of course she'd recognize him immediately. That was stupid of him. If she hadn't, they would have given her back and got clear away." It made no sense to him. "Something happened . . ."

Monk moved at last. He walked over to the pot of tea sitting on the hob and poured himself a mug, then came back to Hooper, carrying it in his hand. "I don't think Doyle took all the money. Maybe some. Payment for his part in it," he went on.

"What? As extra muscle for the fight on Jacob's Island?" Hooper said with open disbelief. "A local bank manager?"

Monk was too tired for sarcasm. He sat down in the second chair and sipped at his tea, not even noticing how stewed it was. "No, and the risk of being seen was obvious. I think he found the ideal victim for the kidnappers—that's what he was paid for—and of course maybe by Exeter, too, for help with the ransom . . ." His voice trailed off, heavy with disgust.

"Kate Exeter? Why?" Although Hooper thought he knew.

"Harry Exeter. A man who had a lot of money in liquid assets that he could lay his hands on in a matter of days, without having to sell anything, which takes time and draws attention. And Exeter is a man who loved his wife to the degree that he wouldn't try to bargain or trap them. He'd just do it, no questions asked," Monk explained.

Hooper weighed this in his mind. "Then it was Doyle who knew Bella Franken had seen the books and worked out how he fiddled them, and he who followed her and killed her. Have you told Exeter yet?"

"No, but I think he won't be surprised. He lost his wife, a friendship he trusted, and his money, all in one night." Pity appeared naked in Monk's eyes for a moment. "And we still don't know who betrayed us. That can't have been Doyle. We were the only ones that knew exactly what we were going to do, where we were going in, what route. He's probably never been to that part of the river in his life. How many men have? Most avoid the place like a plague pit!"

Hooper did not reply immediately. What they had deduced made sense, but it was very far from being enough to arrest anyone. There were pieces missing that could be any shape, any size, and alter the meaning in almost any way at all. The papers Runcorn had taken from Bella's drowned body were now in the hands of an accountant.

"We're going over to Greenwich to see Runcorn," Monk interrupted Hooper's thoughts. "See if he's got anything at all."

IT WAS A SHORT trip over the river and then a quick walk up from the pier to the Greenwich Police Station. It took them well over half an hour, even at a brisk speed, and the watery sun was rising in pale colors across the river as they arrived at the door. Runcorn was waiting for them, as were several other men. Greenwich was on the river, so the River Police and the regular police quite often cooperated with each other; only occasionally was there a clash of jurisdiction. Today was going to be one of the better collaborations. Everyone knew of the Jacob's Island kidnap case, and of the critical things the newspa-

pers had said of the River Police's failure to capture the men responsible. Everyone received such blame at one time or another, but it
never got any easier, particularly when you felt the fault yourself most
clearly of all.

Hot tea was handed round, and thick slices of bread were toasted
at the open door of the stove.

"Right," Runcorn began. "Police surgeon doesn't have a lot to tell
us. Healthy young woman, poor soul." His voice caught for a moment
and he swallowed and moved on. "Neck was broken. No water in her
lungs. I assume that was a mercy. No other damage that he could see,
so it looks as though she never put up a fight. Caught unawares,
like—"

"Or it was somebody she trusted," Monk cut in.

"That's interesting, sir," Hooper replied. "'Cos if she was bringing
the papers she said she was, she couldn't have trusted Mr. Doyle."

Most of the half-dozen men in the room twisted round to look at
him. He had spoken out of turn, but he was right.

"Took her from behind?" one of the men suggested. He looked at
Monk. "Was he the sort of person to trust someone else to do his dirty
work—hands-on stuff? Got to trust a man a lot to give him that kind
of knowledge over you."

Hooper stared at him. Something of the inflection in his voice
started a memory, but he could not place it. He looked at the man's
face and could recall nothing. He was blunt-featured, with sandy-
colored hair and deep-set eyes. His nose was crooked, as if it had been
broken and not properly set.

"I wouldn't have thought so," Monk replied. "But then, I didn't
think he had anything to do with it at all, until a few days ago."

"What happened to change your mind?" Runcorn asked.

Monk answered immediately. "I realized how ideally Doyle was
placed to know exactly who could pay such a ransom. He could handle it himself, so he would know precisely how the deal was to be
done. And I think Exeter saw that for the first time also. The whole
case is riddled with betrayals."

No one argued with him.

"All to do with money, or do you think there were emotional is-
sues as well?" The man looked first at Monk, then at Hooper. He was
the same man who had caught Hooper's eye before, the man with the
crooked nose. Had he worked with him at some time?

Hooper waited to see if Monk would answer. Meanwhile his mind
raced. He thought of what Celia Darwin had implied about Kate's
feelings.

They were waiting for Monk to answer, the man with the crooked
nose in particular.

"Are you asking if there can be a failure like that—money stolen,
a beloved wife hacked to pieces, the only kidnapper we could identify
murdered, and now, too, the young woman who might have known
some secret about that money—and there are not profound emotions
involved?" Monk could not keep the bitterness from his voice.

"Not to mention whoever in your team told the kidnappers the
details of your plan on Jacob's Island," Runcorn said. "But was that in
the name of money, fear, or the hunger for some old revenge?"

Hooper had a sudden flash of memory. It was a windy deck, sunlight bounced off the water, and the sound of sails cracked in the
wind as a ship came about with the rush of water and fear. Then it was
gone again. Sometime in the past he had deliberately driven it from
his memory. He knew that. It was the one certainty.

He concentrated, forcing his mind to clear and answer the man.
Monk must not see this in him, the confusion and fear.

"No," he said abruptly. "We are narrowing it . . ."

"Hard thing to do, narrow down suspicion like that," the man
with the crooked nose replied. "Not nice to suspect the men you've
worked with, trusted your life to, of betraying you. Big thing for a man
to live with." He never took his eyes from Hooper's face.

For Hooper, it was as if they were the only men in the room—or
on the deck! Was it him? Was it Twist? It had been twenty years since
the mutiny on the *Mary Grace*.

There was silence around him. Was everyone staring at him,
wondering why he did not answer? "Yes," he said slowly. "And a terrible thing to suspect a man of, if he isn't guilty. You might learn that

and trust him again. But he knows you thought it of him. Will he ever trust you?"

Now all the men in the room were definitely staring at him. He was conscious of Monk above all, but of Runcorn, too.

"I guess you're still looking," the crooked-nosed man said. "Still, if you catch this banker fellow, perhaps he can tell you."

"Maybe," Runcorn said briskly. "But that's Commander Monk's job. It's ours to find out who killed this poor woman and get hold of him."

"With enough evidence to hang the bastard," one of the other men added. "She was only a slip of a thing. Could practically lift her with one hand, when she wasn't soaking wet. Clothes carry a woman down even faster than a man." He had been one of those who carried her body, and his voice was choked with pity.

No one answered. This close to the river, everyone had their recollections of people drowning. The fact that she had been dead before she went in was beside the point.

"Right!" Runcorn recalled their attention. "Question, everyone: Did she go in this side of the river or the other? Speak to ferrymen, anyone else on the river around dusk. You know the regular passengers crossing that sort of time. Find them and see if anyone saw anything at all. Bargees, lighter-men—bit late for them to be out, but try. Ask and see what they can tell you. She was supposed to keep her appointment at half-past seven. She probably left the north bank about seven, if she came that way. Cabdrivers? Peddlers? Dockworkers? Ferrymen, whether they carried her or saw her when someone else did. Get started!"

"Yes, sir," half a dozen men replied, and they left, some of them giving orders as they went.

Runcorn turned to Monk, his face suddenly gentle with pity. "I'm going to see what else the police surgeon can tell me. There may be something about the way she died that will tell us more about who killed her. Bruises come up after death—that kind of thing. You need to follow Doyle and find whatever kind of a man you need to tell you what money he took, and how. This kidnap seems to be more of a bloody mess than any other I've seen. Believe me, Exeter might be a decent enough man, and I daresay you like him—"

"That's got nothing to do with it!" Monk said a little irritably. "What happened to him shouldn't happen to anybody! I don't need to ask you how you'd feel if it was your wife! You'd be as gutted as I would be if it was Hester."

Runcorn went pale, as if even the thought was a blow so hard he did not know what to do with it.

Hooper wondered if that was what was gnawing at Monk: the knowledge of how fragile happiness was. One sharp cut with a knife, one slip of a foot on wet stones, and it could be gone. It almost took your courage away to grasp at it at all. Much safer not to care so much. But that was not a choice for some. Not for Monk. Hooper thought it was not for him either. To be afraid to care was to deny life itself.

"Hooper!"

Hooper straightened up. "Yes, sir?"

"Go and see what you can find out about Doyle," Monk told him. "Where was he last night? Where does—did—Bella Franken live? Could he have gone there yesterday evening and followed her to the ferry? Anyone see him today? What time did he get in to the bank this morning, if he was there? Any sign that he was out last night? Anything at all?"

"Yes, sir." Hooper was glad to accept any duty that took him away from the Greenwich Police Station and Runcorn's men. And he wanted to find whoever had killed Bella Franken every bit as much as Monk himself. Even though he had not met her, he felt her courage and her vulnerability.

HOOPER'S FIRST DUTY WAS to go to the bank and inform Doyle of Bella's death. Possibly she had family outside the city. He would have to find that out, because they would need to be told as well. That was always the worst part of any death, worse even than finding the body.

One could find ways of dealing with horror or grief of one's own; it was other people's grief for which there was no answer.

He took the ferry back across the river again and then a hansom cab to Nicholson's Bank. He walked in at the rear door. They were not busy yet, and he approached a young clerk who was carrying a pile of ledgers. "My name is Sergeant Hooper, and I require to speak to Mr. Doyle," he said quietly. "It is regarding a matter of tragedy, and I need to see him immediately. Will you please take me to him? I'm sure he is busy with clients' affairs, but this will not wait."

The young clerk drew breath to argue, but looking at Hooper's face, the words died on his lips. "Yes, sir. If you will come this way . . ." He led him to the manager's office. He knocked on the door, and as soon as it was answered, rather peremptorily, the clerk went in.

"There is a policeman here to see you, sir, and he says it's regarding a tragedy that cannot wait." He opened the door wider for Hooper to pass him.

Doyle looked annoyed but calm enough. "Good morning. What may I do for you?" He looked beyond Hooper and told the clerk, in peril of his job, not to repeat what he had heard, and to close the door behind him. "Now, tell me, Mr. . . . ?"

"Sergeant Hooper, sir."

"All right, Sergeant Hooper, what is this tragedy you have to tell me?"

Hooper had weighed his approach in his mind on the way here. He had decided not to conceal his own reactions. He wished Doyle, innocent or guilty, to feel the full import of the facts. If he was innocent, he would be horrified. If he was not, he would be afraid. The heat of emotion often betrays the would-be liar.

"I'm very sorry to tell you, sir, but one of your employees was attacked and murdered last night."

Doyle made one or two attempts to speak, but the color drained out of his face so completely that Hooper feared the man might have an attack of some sort. He half rose to his feet, in case Doyle lost consciousness and slipped to the floor.

"Miss . . . Miss . . . Franken is not in yet this morning," Doyle gasped.

So, he knew who it was! Deduction? Or more than that? "She's usually here by this time?" Hooper asked.

"What? Oh, yes. She is very . . . punctual . . . diligent . . . reliable . . ." Doyle seemed to want to add more, but he was gasping. He looked everywhere but at Hooper. "Very . . . For God's sake, what happened? Where was she found? Not in . . . anywhere . . . where?"

"Where were you thinking she might be found, Mr. Doyle?" Hooper asked.

"What? What do you mean?"

"Did you think her death had something to do with Mrs. Exeter's murder?"

"No!" Doyle was appalled. "She . . . she was a pleasant young woman, a bit opinionated . . . but for the love of heaven, man, she's dead!"

"And if she were not dead, would you think her connected to Mrs. Exeter's kidnap in some way?"

"No . . . of course not. She was an employee!"

"So where did you expect her to be found?" Hooper pressed.

"I don't care to . . ." Doyle colored with embarrassment. It was clear to Hooper that his assumption had been that the circumstances of Bella Franken's death were in some way compromising.

"Say?" Hooper finished for him. "Why not? Are you seeking to protect her reputation rather than help us find who killed her? She was killed, Mr. Doyle. Murdered—with a man's hands around her neck . . . her throat . . ."

"Stop it! If she was found with some wretched man's hands around her neck, then you know the answer, don't you!" Doyle protested. "There is no need to exercise your cruelty on me. I had nothing to do with it. I knew absolutely nothing of her private life. If she had a lover, or whatever, I knew nothing. I always thought her rather bookish, not a particularly attractive quality in a young woman. I think the ability to add and subtract with accuracy excellent in a ledger clerk, not a . . . a companion." He straightened his collar and cravat and sat a little more upright in his chair. "So, you have the matter settled, and you have informed me. Thank you. I will tell the staff about it a good deal less brutally than you have told me. I suppose the newspapers will get hold of this? They love scandal. I shall have to think of how to deal with this. I appreciate your telling me. That is all I have to say."

Hooper smiled very slightly. "I have not come merely as a courtesy to inform you, Mr. Doyle. I need to ask you a good many questions. And it seems you have taken too much meaning from what I said as to the manner of her death. She was strangled and her neck broken, but whoever did it was not there when we found her. She was thrown into the river, like rubbish. It was Commander Monk who saw her and, with a ferryman's help, pulled her out." He watched Doyle's face intently, saw the newly returned color ebb out again, and anger mixed with fear.

"What . . . what was she doing in the river?" Doyle demanded. "And what was Monk doing? How did he come to be there? I think I have a right to know."

Hooper made a decision. "Yes, sir, perhaps you do. If Miss Franken has no family in the area, then as her employer, you are, in a sense, her guardian. She was quite young, and seemingly alone. You appear to assume some moral turpitude on her part . . ."

"No! No, not at all!" Doyle protested, shifting his position in the chair uncomfortably. "But you said she was alone in the street at night, and she had been murdered."

"Yes," Hooper agreed. "She had made an appointment to see Mr. Monk early yesterday evening, and he was at the right place at the right time, but she was not. He saw her body in the water and pulled her out, at some risk to his own life. But she was far beyond help, poor soul." He waited.

Doyle could not resist. "What . . . what was she going to see Monk about? Did she tell him?"

"Yes, some irregularity in the bookkeeping, I believe. She thought it might help us find out who was behind Mrs. Exeter's kidnap and murder."

Doyle swallowed. "How on earth could the words of a ledger clerk like Miss Franken be taken seriously on such a subject? You seem to be suggesting that Mr. Exeter himself was doing something other than paying an exorbitant amount to save his wife's life. The young woman is . . . was . . . light-minded, hysterical, if you like."

"Was she?" Hooper felt his body stiffen in anger at Doyle's attitude to someone who had risked her life, and lost it, seeking the truth. "It seems to me as if she was highly perceptive. Still, when we see the books, we will be able to tell. I merely wanted to let you know that, unfortunately, she gave her life to find the proof and could only hand it over in her death. Thank goodness it was Monk who pulled her out of the water, not someone who did not appreciate what the papers meant. I'm sorry to be the bringer of such news." He looked rather critically at Doyle. "Should I ask your clerk to bring you a cup of tea, perhaps? Or maybe you have a little brandy somewhere available."

"Get out!" Doyle said between his teeth.

HOOPER SPENT THE AFTERNOON tracing Doyle's movements. He was a widower who still lived in the house he had shared with his wife. He had two adult children, both of whom lived in other parts of the country. He kept a full household staff and occasionally entertained those men and their wives that he had befriended when his own wife was alive.

He dined at his club at least twice a week. It was a pleasant gentlemen's club; not aristocratic, but a place to display one's respectability and increasing wealth. The chief steward could swear to Doyle's presence at the time the kidnapper, Lister, had been killed. He had been involved in a game of cards that had lasted several hours. Doyle had not been there on the night of the kidnap, nor the night following the attempted ransom that had ended in murder. He had not been there on the previous night when Bella Franken had been killed, either.

Doyle's butler was loyal and discreet, but he could hardly rely on the rest of the staff lying effectively. They were too confused, contradicting each other without realizing it. In the end, Hooper did not know who to believe. They were partly motivated by loyalty, but partly also by the fear of losing jobs they needed, without letters of recommendation and character, as a result of being disloyal.

Hooper told Monk this before he left for the evening, too tired to think about it clearly.

He was about halfway home before he remembered Celia Darwin implying, rather obliquely, that Kate was not as happy as one might suppose. What did she mean by that? Did she know something personal and was only being discreet in not mentioning it? He remembered her face very clearly as she said it. He could see it in his mind, as if they had only just parted. She had an expression almost of embarrassment. There was the faintest possible flush in her cheeks. She had fair skin, a little too colorless for some tastes. Hooper found it pure, like a canvas upon which anything could be painted.

Was there something more about Kate that would explain, at least in part, the circumstances around her death?

He wished he could go and ask Celia what she had meant. He even hesitated in his step. Could she really tell him anything? And would she? He thought—in fact he was certain—that she would keep other people's secrets even more fervently than she would keep her own.

Would she judge the weight of it in hindsight, now that Kate was dead?

Secrets brought Twist's face back to his mind, bright as if in direct sunlight, just as he had seen it, for an instant, in Runcorn's police station. Except now that person called himself Fisk. Surely that kind of glittering sunlight happened only at sea, where the mirror surface of the water magnified it and repeated it a thousand times? Tropical sea. The answer was there in his mind.

The only question was, was it him at the station, or was it only someone who was reminiscent of him? He quickened his step again. He did not want to see Celia Darwin right now. She woke ideas in him of things he could not have, and they were better untouched.

Even so, he went. It was late, an unsuitable time to call. He knew all that, but he went anyway.

The maid must have been off duty, perhaps in her own bedroom, because it was Celia herself who answered the door, opening it guardedly, then almost with relief when she saw it was Hooper.

"Come in, Mr. Hooper." She stood back to allow him to pass her before closing the door again and slipping the bolt home. It was habit rather than forethought; she seemed scarcely aware of doing it. She stood in the hallway, facing him. "What has happened? You look very grave."

"I am afraid there has been another death." How could he explain why he had come to see her, this late in the evening? "I . . . we have to—"

"I understand," she cut across him, perhaps seeing his difficulty. "Come in by the fire." Without waiting for him, she led the way into the parlor. The fire was low. She had obviously let it die down for the night. She had probably been intending to go to bed very shortly. Now she bent down and picked more coal out of the scuttle.

"Let me," he said, kneeling beside her and taking the tongs from her hands. He was aware of her closeness, of the faint smell of something warm, like vanilla, or some kind of flower. It was clean rather than sweet.

She hesitated a moment, almost as if she did not mind his being so close to her. Then she stood up and murmured her thanks.

He fueled the fire, mindful not to use the last of the coal, then rose and sat in the chair opposite her. There was no point in putting off telling her. It might look as if he had no urgent reason to have come.

"It was the bank ledger clerk," he said quietly. "A Miss Bella Franken . . ."

He was not prepared for the shock with which Celia recognized the name: shock and unconcealed grief.

"You knew her?" he asked.

"Yes, not well, but . . ." She took several deep breaths and tried to compose herself. "How did it happen? Please . . . be honest, Mr. Hooper. This is too horrible to trivialize for the sake of mercy. Poor Bella, she was so . . . alive!" For a moment she could not mask her distress. She put her hands up to her face and bent forward, struggling to keep from weeping openly.

Hooper felt profoundly for her. It was not the time to berate himself for his stupidity in not having thought Celia might know Bella Franken. All he could think of was what he could say to ease the misery. He wanted to touch her, to put his hand over hers at least, but that would be an inexcusable intrusion when she was so very vulnerable.

"She did not suffer," he said softly. "She knew nothing. One blow . . ." He thought of what she would read or hear tomorrow. "She was found in the river, but she did not drown."

She looked up slowly. "Found?"

"She went to meet Mr. Monk, to tell him something. They were to meet at the Greenwich Pier. Her choice of place. But she never got there."

"Tell him something? You mean from the bank?"

"Yes."

She searched in her pocket for a handkerchief. He handed her his. It gave him a ridiculous feeling of pleasure that she might keep it.

"Thank you," she whispered. "I . . . I have some idea of what that might be."

He felt a sharp stab of interest. "What?"

"She knew there was something wrong with the inheritance money."

"What inheritance?" He had no idea what she was referring to.

"Kate's inheritance. It is a very great amount. She would have received it in a year and a half, approximately."

"And where is it now?"

"In a trust, in Mr. Doyle's bank. The trustee is our cousin, Kate's and mine, Mr. Maurice Latham. He manages it. But it is not there now. Naturally both he and I were willing to use it to pay the ransom. It was Kate's money anyhow. It is only a technicality, a temporary one, that Maurice has charge of it."

Hooper was stunned. Seeing the house, Celia's obvious restrictions in the spending of money, he had never considered the possibility of her being an heiress. It was vaguely troubling. The past lay over him like an iron cage. He would never have asked her to marry him. But he realized that, but for his own emotional imprisonment, he would have. But if she were an heiress, that would be absurd. She would not even imagine him in such a way.

. He looked down, avoiding her eyes. He forced his mind to consider the case.

"It would have been Kate's very soon," she interrupted his thoughts.

"And who inherits it, now that she is . . . dead?" he asked, although he thought he had already guessed the answer.

"No one," she said a little briskly. "The kidnappers have it. Maurice came to ask me only as a matter of courtesy. Of course, I gladly agreed to give it to Harry to pay them. As I say, it was Kate's money anyway." There was an edge of anger in her tone that he even had to question it.

Suddenly the pieces fell into a pattern in Hooper's head. So that was where the ransom had come from—Kate's own money. "Why would Doyle hate that?" he asked. "I can see why pride might make Exeter hate it, but what reason could there be for Doyle, or anyone, to prevent the police from knowing that? It is what any decent person would do."

"I don't know," Celia said quietly. "But one thought comes to mind—and may God pardon me if I am wrong—but perhaps it was the accounts of the trust that Bella Franken was bringing, and . . . and they were not in order."

"You mean sums were embezzled from it?" he asked very quietly.

Her face was flushed with shame. "Perhaps. I am so sorry. It is a terrible thought. I do not like Maurice, but I would not wish that guilt upon anyone at all."

"I am sorry, too. But I must tell Monk tomorrow. Perhaps from the papers that were saved from the river, he will be able to tell if that is so. I'm sorry to ask, but could Exeter have taken anything from the trust?"

"No. Maurice is the sole trustee. I believed the money had been invested through Mr. Doyle's bank, on their advice. I was not told the details. It is not really my concern."

He stood up. "I'm sorry . . . Miss Darwin."

She smiled. "Please . . . do not feel uncomfortable. You had to tell me. Just find . . . find some sort of peace for Kate. No, I don't mean that. Of course there is peace for Kate. To deny that would be to deny God. Find some ease of heart for the rest of us. Then at least we can stop suspecting the wrong people."

"I will," he promised. "I will."

She stood up and went with him to the door, but they did not speak again. He waited for a moment, seeing her standing in the light, tears brimming in her eyes. Then he turned and walked out into the chill of the night.

15

Monk began the day hearing from Hooper the news that Katherine Exeter's inheritance, held in trust until her thirty-third birthday, was to be passed to her cousins, Maurice Latham and Celia Darwin, should Kate die before inheriting. However, they had both willingly granted access to it to Exeter, for the purpose of paying the ransom for her life.

"Does that mean the kidnapper has to be someone who knew of the legacy?" Hooper asked miserably. "That could be Doyle."

"Yes, it could," Monk agreed. "Or someone who had no idea about it, but knew that Exeter was a very rich man."

Hooper said nothing.

Monk worked for the rest of that day with Runcorn. He found it both a pleasure and, at times, a strain. Runcorn did not mention it directly again, but his remark about finding out which of Monk's men had betrayed them stayed with Monk. He recognized that he had been avoiding the issue, always putting it off for something more urgent. The murder of Bella Franken had distressed him deeply. If he had stopped at her desk and insisted they meet at some safer place, she might have been alive now. He had liked her and admired her courage. He could not get the sight of her wet, bruised face out of his mind.

Should he? Should he have enough self-control to be able to dismiss it and get on with the job? Kate Exeter had been slashed to pieces! Although it didn't haunt him constantly as Bella's death did, that did not leave his mind for long either. The sound of dripping water took him straight back to Jacob's Island and the darkness, the bone-chilling cold.

Did it affect all the men like that? Even whoever had caused it to happen? Did the betrayer mean to do that? Or had he intended something else, something that ended only in the kidnappers escaping? Well, they had escaped, all but Lister. Why not him? Had he been greedy and wanted more than his share?

Or was he destined for death anyway, as soon as his purpose was served? Whoever had done that, it was not Hooper. It could not be. They had been together at the time Lister must have been killed.

He had checked on the other men. None of them was accounted for beyond doubt. Laker had said he was with Bathurst, but that was a lie. Bathurst said he had met with his sister and had supper with her, but he was supposed to be on duty. His sister was in some kind of difficulty and needed his help.

He knew Laker's secret because Hester had told him, and he no longer suspected Laker or, honestly, Bathurst either.

"Don't blame Laker, sir," Bathurst had said urgently. "I took too much time off. He did that to cover for me."

"Why did your sister need you so urgently?"

Bathurst blushed. "She's only fifteen, sir, but she's very pretty. She doesn't know how to say no to her boss like she means it. And she can't afford to lose her job. There's too many to feed . . ." His voice trailed off. He did not want to tell Monk about his family's poverty. It seemed a private thing, so telling would be like breaking a confidence, like looking at someone when they did not realize they were naked.

Monk was angry with himself for being so clumsy. "I'm sorry," he said immediately. "Would an inquiry from the River Police trim his ambitions a bit?"

Bathurst's eyes widened. "Please don't, sir. She'll learn. She'll have to. My older sister, Edith, she's pretty good at making people . . . cool off. Only Lizzie doesn't like to admit she can't do it herself. Laker was looking out for me."

"Someone told the kidnappers which way we were coming."

Bathurst's expression reminded Monk how young he was. He looked like a schoolboy at the age when loyalty was everything. "Then it must be Walcott or Marbury, sir," he said. "It isn't any of the rest of us." He looked straight at Monk, his eyes unwavering.

Monk did not argue. That was his own feeling. He needed to trust the men he knew. It was the safety of the familiar. That was why it was so hard to be a stranger too many times, the person unknown, the first to be suspected. It had nothing to do with your behavior or your inner self. It hurt to remake the ties, try all over again to adopt new patterns with people: new things to understand, to laugh at, to feel comfortable with.

"I believe you," Monk said. It was at least partially true, but he said it because he knew Bathurst needed to hear it. Something inside you dies, some source of courage, when you know you are not trusted. It is a loneliness of the soul. "Be careful," he said then. "Don't let anybody think you don't trust them. That would—"

"I know," Bathurst had agreed, before Monk could finish. "That could make them turn on me. I just find it hard to go into anything first, trusting them to watch my back, if you know what I mean."

"You've got to get it over with," Runcorn said, when Monk confided he was still looking for the traitor among his men. "You owe it to the rest of them to find the one that's bad. It's not fair to—"

"I know!" Monk said sharply. "You don't need to tell me again. I'm protecting one at the price of the others. Who's Fisk? What did he do before he joined you?"

"Fisk?" Runcorn's eyes widened. "What's he got to do with it?"

"What was he? Merchant seaman?"

Surprise rippled across Runcorn's face. "Yes. How did you know? It was twenty years ago. And what has it to do with this?"

Monk clenched his teeth. He hated having to explain this to Runcorn. "I've seen him looking at Hooper as if he's trying to remember something."

"You suspect Hooper? I thought he was your best man?" There was surprise and sadness in Runcorn's face.

"He is. One of the best men I've ever known. He should be the first one I clear." He hated saying the words, especially to Runcorn. They had been such enemies and, he thought now, that had been more his own fault than Runcorn's. His upbringing had made him cautious, not quick or naturally able to explain himself in words. He understood rules and was confident with them. They were like armor: restricting, but also protective. Monk had been a natural renegade, mercurial, easy with words, and with a wry humor. Runcorn hid his insecurity by clinging to the rules. Monk hid his by carving his own path and trying to be right every time. He had not even looked for the best in Runcorn, until circumstances had forced him to.

"Do you want me to ask?" Runcorn said with surprising gentleness. "Or would you rather speak to Hooper and let him tell you himself? It probably has nothing to do with this."

"Anything could have something to do with this," Monk replied miserably. "Whatever a man can be pressured over, blackmailed for, or have taken from him makes him a hostage to fortune, in the right hands."

"And whose hands are the right ones, Monk? Who's behind this? The bank manager, Doyle? He's a master blackmailer? How on earth would he know something about Hooper from twenty years ago? You think Fisk told him something?"

"I've no idea. Maybe people who knew about other men's debts and fortunes hear a lot of things." He sounded bitter, and he knew it. One touch in the right place and so much could unravel: things he had taken for granted. He felt as if he had looked down at his feet for the first time in years and found that he was walking along the edge of a precipice. Perhaps a degree of blindness was the only bearable way to live.

He was stunned by how much it all mattered. Friendship was a common cause that was truly worth fighting for. There were so many people who mattered: Hester, Will (now no longer Scuff in his mind), Rathbone, Hooper, even the peripheral ones on the edges of his life, like Squeaky Robinson, the bookkeeper at Hester's clinic who had kept a brothel there until Rathbone had tricked him into deeding the property and staying on to run it as a refuge for the sick. They were all parts of a whole that was immeasurably precious to him. Was the price of it finding who had betrayed them? And even as he asked, he knew the answer.

"So, you think it could be this bank manager, Doyle?" Runcorn broke into his thoughts.

"Yes. Hooper's gone to see where he was at the times of the murders—"

Runcorn winced.

"What?" Monk asked. "They're tied together: Kate Exeter; Lister, the one kidnapper we know; and Bella Franken."

"Other suspects?" Runcorn asked.

"No one, except possibly Maurice Latham. Unless it's one of us."

"Who the hell is Maurice Latham?"

Briefly Monk told him.

"Or else what? Lister was working for one of your own? Come on, Monk! You don't believe that any more than I do. There's somebody behind this with a real power and intelligence, using the others. If you were thinking straight, you'd know it, too. If you get no other ideas, then either it's Doyle, or you've got to find your own man who's in debt or being pressured by someone, maybe got an old grudge against you," Runcorn said. "Is that what you're afraid of? Some issue dug up from the past?"

For once, Monk had not even thought of his own past in this.

"No, I hadn't thought it had anything to do with me."

Runcorn stared at Monk steadily, and it was as if a parade of ghosts had walked between them. "If it is," Runcorn said, "I'll help you catch the bastard. I'm not afraid."

From another man, it might have seemed pompous, self-praising. From Runcorn it was simply a statement of fact, and of friendship.

Monk found himself absurdly choked with emotion. He looked away in order to shield himself. "Thank you. I'm going to work on my own men. See what they're each afraid of. I've got to get rid of this . . . doubt."

MONK TOOK LAKER WITH him to try to learn more about Bella Franken's death. He went by boat to begin with, because it gave him the chance to be alone with Laker and not be overheard. He hated this, but Runcorn was right. Until it was resolved, they would have suspicion like an unwelcome guest between them all the time.

It was a cold, damp day on the river, but the fog was holding off and there was no wind. It was an excellent day for rowing and they were going downriver with the ebb tide.

"Do you think we'll really learn anything about Bella Franken, sir?" Laker asked. "Wasn't she killed by Doyle because she found where he fiddled the books, probably because he was stealing, along with getting the money for Exeter to pay the ransom?"

"You think he took the chance to take something for himself while he was at it?" Monk asked. Actually, it was what he thought himself. Either him or Latham. It was what the figures suggested, as much as he could understand the bookkeeping. It certainly made sense, and although she had not said so, he was almost certain that was what Bella had thought. "And Doyle knew he'd been found out, so he killed her?"

"Wasn't that what she said?" Laker's voice was sharp with disgust.

"More or less," Monk agreed. "She explained something of the ledgers to me. It wasn't obvious. He'd been very careful about it. Lots of small discrepancies, as if someone had been bad at arithmetic, or done it late at night, with quite a lot of corrections. Once you knew what to look for, it seemed clear enough."

They rowed in silence for a minute or two.

"What do we expect to find out downriver, then?" Laker asked.

"How do you suppose Doyle got in touch with Lister, or any of the kidnappers?"

"Did he? You think he actually had a hand in it, rather than just . . . I don't know . . ." Laker stopped, sounding uncertain.

"You don't?" Monk affected surprise. He hated this game of cat and mouse, but he had to go through with it. If Laker knew something he did not, then this long time alone with him, when conversation came naturally, was the only way to find out. "The kidnappers got in touch with Exeter," he went on. "And someone who betrayed him—and us. Someone knew our plans exactly. Knew which way we were going in, which buildings we'd go through, which passages we'd use, what time."

Laker did not answer immediately.

Monk waited.

"You're back to which one of us did it, aren't you?" Laker said at last. "If you think that I did, you're wrong. I don't know. I've learned a lot about the men, but it's none of my business. Things I don't want to know. Bathurst's hard up because he gives everything he can to his mother. But I'd put my life in Bathurst's hands any day. And Mr. Hooper. I'd be ashamed to think ill of him. He's one of the best men I've ever known. He'd be killed himself before he'd betray the rest of us. Mr. Marbury's got a bit of temper if you hurt an animal, but he's decent enough. Share his food, or a mug of beer. A dry coat."

Laker threw his weight against the oar and Monk had to dig deep to stop the boat from swinging off course.

"So, what are you saying?" Monk asked after a moment or two. "That it has to be Walcott? Just because he doesn't fit in so easily with the rest of us? Everybody's got secrets, Laker, vulnerable places, things they value too much to lose."

"You . . . you thinking of anything in particular, sir?" The tone of Laker's voice had changed. There was fear in it. Monk did not know exactly which words had caused it. Was Laker thinking he meant him? Or did he somehow know Monk's own secret? It was too late to pull back now.

"I know what it's like to have to face your worst fears, the ones you won't name, even in the middle of the night," Monk began again.

Laker pulled steadily on the oars, in silence but for the creak of the boat and the sound of the water.

"There's one sort," Monk went on. "Like when Hester was kidnapped, and I thought they would kill her. I know what Exeter was suffering." The guilt chilled him again. He remembered Kate's body. How would he have reacted if it had been Hester? He had nightmares even now, dreadful images of Kate's body turning into Hester's, of a loss that was far worse than being killed himself.

This could so easily have been him instead of Harry Exeter. Why had the woman Monk loved survived, and Exeter's wife died horribly? Was it Exeter's fault somehow, or just his hideously bad luck? Surely it could happen to anyone with money, power of some kind, knowledge that could be used?

When he looked into Exeter's face he saw himself, the loneliness that robbed the meaning from everything. He felt guilty that he had not been able to save this man who had trusted him.

Laker dug his oar in and pulled at it so savagely it took all of Monk's strength to keep them steady.

"And I know what it's like to have your own past threatened, things you know you did and want to hide, dug up and displayed for everyone to see. It's bad enough your errors show, but the thing you are afraid of the most is how your friends will feel. I know about your cashiering from the army, but nobody else needs to."

"Thank you, sir."

They rowed in silence for a space. Finally, it was Laker who broke it. "Are we going to find out who killed that poor girl?" he asked.

"We're going to prove that Doyle did," Monk replied. "We need to find who was in it with Lister. I don't know how many men there are. What do you think?"

They discussed the subject most of the way back. Going over

what each of them knew from their experience, there appeared to have been at least four.

"Do you think she was killed before we got there, or sometime after?" Laker asked.

"I don't know," Monk said quietly. He had been thinking about that on and off since the night it had happened. "Did they always intend to, or did something happen that made it necessary? What could that be? Other than that she recognized somebody?"

"She knew one of the kidnappers?" Laker said incredulously. "She's acquainted with that kind of person?"

"If it's Doyle, perhaps."

Laker did not answer but dug the oar in deeply again and matched his stroke to Monk's.

16

Monk was whittling it down, one by one, all the time fighting against every thought that the traitor could be Hooper. And yet that fear was always at the edge of his mind—the unknown in Hooper, a man he realized he cared for as a friend more than anyone else he knew, apart from Rathbone, perhaps. But there was an unknown in everyone, even himself—especially himself. There had to be another answer, and yet what if there was not? How would he live with it? Hooper had not turned his back on him! Without knowing the details, he had accepted. Not even forgiven. Not judged.

He went over everything he knew about Marbury. He even went to see his previous commanding officer in the police, who expressed a profound regard for him.

"Why did you let him go?" Monk felt compelled to ask. They were sitting quietly in a public house in Shoreditch, well to the north of the river.

"Had to," Reilly said with a sad smile. "He'd have had my job, else. I'm not ready to retire yet. Few more years before I can afford that."

"So, he's after mine!" Monk said with surprise.

"Doubt it. But he was due for a promotion, and I'd no place to put him. Couple of men ahead of him, and I'd find myself nudged into oblivion if I didn't get rid of one of them. Marbury, I could do it fairly. Knew he'd be in the right place with you. Bit more active. Doesn't sit behind a desk and tell other men what to do." He gave a sharp little laugh. "Never got over losing his son. Wife took it even harder."

That explained the loneliness Monk saw in Marbury, and perhaps his love of dogs. A man could touch a dog with affection, talk to it often, and not be thought odd.

"Why are you asking?" Reilly asked. "He giving you any trouble?"

Monk had already made up his mind to be honest. It was past the time when he could afford to be making elaborate evasions. "Not with him. Don't know who it is. Got to learn a bit more about all of them."

Reilly drew in his breath and then let it out again. He waited a few moments before he spoke. "If it's a question of dishonesty, it's not Marbury. He's straight. If it's drink, it's not him either. If it's goods or money missing, it's definitely not him. I trust him with everything I have—not that that's so much."

"But . . . ?" Monk prompted him after he had been silent too long.

Reilly sighed. "It's his temper I'm not so sure about. If someone hurt a woman or an animal, Marbury could have forgot himself and beaten the hell out of them."

Monk couldn't keep the smile of relief off his face. It wasn't only that he instinctively liked Marbury, but he was relieved to have his own judgment vindicated. It hadn't happened often enough lately, and self-doubt was crippling him. He could feel it like an increasing ache inside him.

"I've seen flashes of it," he said to Reilly. "It's not that, it's . . . a betrayal."

"Then it's not Marbury. I'll swear to that," Reilly answered him.

Monk smiled again. He believed Reilly—as much as he had believed his own instincts, until that night on Jacob's Island. He would have sworn he knew his own men, all of them, in one way or another, but Hooper in particular.

Then it had to be Walcott! There was no one else left.

It was easier to ask questions about Walcott. Of all the men involved in the Jacob's Island rescue, Walcott was the one he liked least. But when he set out the next day, it was with a sense of guilt, nonetheless. There was nothing to point to Walcott, only that there was no one else left.

Once Monk knew it was Walcott, even before he knew why, it would at least remove the suspicion from everyone else. But would anything blot out the fact that they had suspected each other?

He spent all day at it, speaking to men who had worked with Walcott, to a few Walcott had arrested. He spoke to the landlord at his regular pub and found that Walcott was notorious for his ability at street fighting. He was a small, neat man, swift-moving with a hard left punch, which some said was vicious. But he never showed anger or seemed to lose his temper. It all came out of nowhere, often without warning. So far as anyone knew, he had never killed anybody, although in really nasty brawls he had once or twice come close, usually when someone had attacked with a knife. He did not like knife fighters. Monk shared that feeling with him. There was something primitively vicious about a knife.

Walcott's love of music hall songs, especially sentimental or funny ones, was already known to Monk. An ordinary ballad did not interest him. However, all of this was incidental. It proved nothing, except that there was more depth to him than Monk had known. Had the other men been aware of, perhaps even shared some of his taste in songs?

What did matter was that on every occasion when he was unaccounted for by Monk's own men, he was entertaining people at a beer hall, and every second of his time was vouched for.

It was not Walcott.

Tired and with very mixed feelings, Monk went to the Green-wich Police Station looking for Runcorn.

Monk had been there only fifteen minutes when Runcorn came in, looking tired but smiling widely.

"Glad you're here," he said, looking at Monk. "I think we've al-most got it. A few details to fill in, but got the core of it all right." He sat down heavily in the chair behind his desk, sighing as he did so. "Horrible, but inevitable. I will never understand some men."

"Doyle." Monk said. "I didn't know for sure but he seemed central to the whole Kate Exeter business. And whatever he did, I can't for-give him for having Kate Exeter killed. What in hell's name did he have to do that for? I suppose she saw him and worked it out, and so he had Lister kill her. Have you told Exeter himself yet? Can I do that . . . I'd like to."

Runcorn looked unhappy, even a little confused. "Sorry . . ."

"What? You've told him already? You don't need to look so guilty. You're the one who solved it. You've a right to tell him." Monk tried to sound generous about it, as if he didn't mind. He had wanted to keep his word, or at least be the one to tell Exeter that this part of it was over. But that was small-minded. Runcorn deserved this. Any-way, it was not over. He still had to face Hooper. That was going to be the very worst.

Runcorn was staring at him now. "You can see Exeter if you want," he began.

"What do you mean, see him?" Monk asked. "Is he ill?" Another thought struck him. "Did he beat the truth out of Doyle? I can hardly blame him."

"No. Monk, it was Exeter who did it . . . all!"

Monk was stunned. "What are you talking about? That makes no sense! Besides, he couldn't have. He was with us when Kate was killed!"

"Was he? Right with you, where you could see him?"

"Couldn't see anybody in that gloom," Monk responded tartly. "But he was there. I know he didn't pass me."

"Couldn't he have gone round you, down another side passage?"

"You'd have to know that place damn well to do that. He didn't know it at all!"

"How do you know that?"

"He said so. That was why he needed us . . ."

"That's as may be, but he was behind it," Runcorn insisted. "The money was the thing. He may very well have meant them to get her back—heroically rescued by him—and the money passed over. They double-crossed him and killed her. Perhaps she saw Doyle and knew it was—"

"No!"

"Fisk was the man who got it tied up," Runcorn went on, speaking over Monk, insisting on saying what he meant and finishing it. "Lister knew it was Exeter, which is probably why he had to be killed. He would have blackmailed Exeter; perhaps he even tried it."

"No!" Monk insisted. "Why? What for?"

"The money—"

"That's rubbish! It was his money."

"No, it wasn't," Runcorn insisted. "It was Katherine's inheritance. A lot of his money is only on paper. You need a clever accountant to see it, but the bank's books are thoroughly fiddled. Doyle was probably in on it, and Miss Franken discovered it. That was why she had to be killed."

"By Doyle, for heaven's sake. Not by Exeter!"

"Yes, by Exeter. Doyle hadn't the stomach for it. He's greedy and quite capable of fiddling the books, but he's essentially a coward."

Monk was bewildered. He remembered Exeter's grief, his horror and utter misery afterward as sharply as if it were a thing that could be inhaled, filling his own body. "I don't believe it. Who got this evidence? You?"

"Mostly Fisk. He's a good man, reliable and honest."

"Which is he?"

"You remember him. You said he was staring at Hooper . . ."

It came back to Monk in a flood of memory. Now it was like a dark tide, drowning everything. If he had been wrong about Exeter, that was an unusual error of judgment on his part. But if he was wrong about Hooper, too, that was more than a crack in the surface; it was a flaw through the heart of all his decisions, his trust, everything he thought he knew.

"Monk," Runcorn spoke softly, "Fisk's a good man. He's not wrong in this. I gave him the books to look at and he took them to a fellow he knows, a first-class cheat and embezzler. There isn't a trick he doesn't know. Fisk showed him this, and then Fisk showed me. Once you see it, it's as plain as day. Exeter came out of this a rich man."

"Or Doyle did!" Monk insisted, refusing to believe that the man whose suffering he had seen so instinctively was a sham.

"Granted, he came out richer than he went in, but the big gain was Exeter's," Runcorn insisted.

"I don't believe he did it, certainly not that he had any part in Kate's death. Fisk's wrong." Monk stood up. "I'll go and see Exeter tomorrow. I'll get Rathbone to defend him. Tonight, I want to see Hooper."

Runcorn stood up as well. "If you have unfinished business with him, you'd better. I'm sorry, I know you trusted him." There was intense pity in his face. "It's the worst thing I can think of, to have trusted someone and been betrayed. That's what you're thinking, isn't it?"

"It was one of my men," Monk could hardly get the words through his aching throat. "And we've excluded all the others." He had to face it at last. There would be an explanation: someone else's life, maybe, a price Hooper could not pay. Monk refused to think what it could be.

"There's something he's not telling me. It's in the air like a fog between us. Someone must have blackmailed him. That's what's been crushing him all this time. I need to know what it is. Good God, Runcorn, do you think I don't know what it's like to have the past weighing on you till you can hardly breathe? Does he think I don't know that? Why didn't he tell me? I would have helped. He doesn't trust me. He knows all about me . . . everything I know—not that that's much, but the emptiness still weighs like a lead coat. Couldn't he have trusted me?"

"You trusted him because you had no choice," Runcorn pointed out. There was no flinching or evasion in his eyes, but no blame either.

"Well, he's got no choice now!" Monk said. He was so torn with emotion that he almost stumbled out the door, and went into the street without speaking again.

HE FOUND HOOPER IN Wapping Street, looking cold and white-faced. "Come to my office," Monk ordered. "And close the door."

Hooper followed him in and did as he was told. He did not sit. Monk chose to stand as well.

"Runcorn has arrested Exeter," Monk stated simply.

"For what?" Hooper asked. "Why?"

"Apparently Fisk took the bookkeeping pages to an embezzler he knew, who said that Doyle snatched up some of the ransom, but Exeter took the bulk of it, by a long way."

"That doesn't make any sense." Hooper looked totally bewildered. He must have known from Monk's face to expect something hard and ugly, but this took him completely by surprise. "Why on earth steal your wife's inheritance, which will be yours anyway, and then give your bank manager part of it? Whatever for?"

"You don't know?" Monk said.

"Me? Of course I don't know!" Hooper's voice was fraying audibly. "Do you?"

"No, I don't. But Runcorn said Exeter came out of it very well. Richer than he went in."

Hooper was silent.

"That's one thing I intend to ask Fisk, when I see him," Monk went on. "Is he somehow framing Exeter for this?"

"Who? Fisk?"

"Yes, Fisk. What do you know about him, Hooper? And don't tell me you don't know anything. Fisk knows you, anyway."

Hooper stood still. He seemed incredibly familiar to Monk, as if he had known him as long as he could remember. They had faced all sorts of victories and defeats together, hardships and pleasures. He remembered sharing a single ham sandwich after a long night on the river. He had first seen the real beauty of wild birds when Hooper had pointed to a pair of swans flying high over the estuary in a stainless sky. Monk thought of them as lonely. Hooper had seen the certainty in them, the knowledge of where they were going.

And yet he was also a stranger, a stranger in pain. But there was no way to avoid it now. He had come this far. He must go all the way.

Monk waited.

Hooper faced him. "I used to be a seaman."

"I know." Monk sat down.

Hooper sat slowly in the other chair, awkwardly, as if he were too stiff to bend easily. "I came ashore about twenty years ago."

"Does this have to do with Fisk?"

"Yes. Though not a great deal. He was a seaman also."

"On the same ship, I presume?"

"Yes."

"Go on . . ."

"I was the first mate then." Hooper spoke quietly, more as if he were avoiding an old wound than to keep him from being overheard.

Monk was unsurprised. He himself had been to sea, but he knew it only in second-long flashes. However, he did remember that first mate was next after the captain in a merchant ship.

"Ledburn, the captain," Hooper continued, "was a big, fair-haired man, quite young. His father had seen to it he got the place. Big-moneyed family. He wasn't bad, but he wasn't as good as he thought he was. Changed his mind when he should've stood firm, then stood firm when he should've changed. Not an uncommon fault. Lots of us do that, one time or another."

Monk listened, waiting. The pain in Hooper's face told him something very bad was coming.

"He kept the log, of course," Hooper went on. "I warned him about writing ones and sevens. Put a cross on the seven, I told him, and watch your threes and eights."

Monk could not push him to get to the point. But he could see that Hooper was working up to it. He needed time.

"He made a mistake," Hooper continued. His voice was getting quieter and a little rougher, as if his throat hurt. "Read a seven as a one. Found that out afterward. Got us off course into a strong current, and the wind changed and we were in trouble."

Monk could imagine it. A ship at sea, probably quite a small one, off course. No land in sight. Wind rising and sea getting choppy, captain sure they were on course, first mate sure they were not, emotions high. "Where were you?" he asked.

Hooper's eyes were fixed on something only he could see. "I said we were off the Azores. Atlantic coast, west of Africa. Ledburn was sure we were north of that."

"Who was right?"

Hooper moved uncomfortably in his chair. "That doesn't matter . . ."

Monk took a breath to argue and realized at that moment it didn't. It was Hooper's story, and the pain was very deep. Monk waited in silence.

Finally, Hooper began again. "The wind was rising and it was getting cloudy. Hard to get a position from the stars. I wanted to go further out to sea, until we could be sure. Ledburn said he was sure.

"The ship was beginning to pitch," Hooper went on. "Climbing the peaks and hitting the troughs hard, sails bellied out, too much canvas up. Racing before the wind. If she went over that, broke a mast, there'd be nothing and no one to help us. Nothing on God's earth as lonely as a ship out of sight of land. And Ledburn was the sort of man who couldn't admit a mistake. There was still time then to put it right, but he insisted he was right in the first place."

"Was it such a big error that it mattered, in the face of a storm?" Monk asked, when Hooper remained silent.

"It wasn't the original mistake," Hooper said slowly. "We would have found her back on course when the weather cleared. It isn't the latitude that's difficult; it's the longitude, how far we were from the coast. He altered other figures to make them tally with the error."

Monk began to see a glimpse of something much uglier.

"When the storm blew out," Hooper said, "he corrected for the error. But we were at least fifty miles further east, and after running before the wind for a day and a half, we were well to the south, too."

"What happened?" Monk asked.

"One lie to cover another," Hooper said. "I could see he was afraid. The original error wasn't so bad, but he compounded it. No one dared tell him. He made it a question of obedience and loyalty. He couldn't admit he had ever been wrong. One man questioned him in front of others, and he had the man put in the brig for a night. That was it for the crew. They couldn't take it anymore. It . . . it frightened him, and he became belligerent. I tried to reason with him. Fisk tried. He was an ordinary seaman, but he knew his job. The crew started to divide between being for the captain and . . . and for me." He stopped again, still not looking at Monk, as if to do so would require a response he was not yet ready to face.

"Which side was Fisk on?" Monk said quietly.

"He knew the captain was wrong," Hooper replied. "But there was one man, the second mate, Chester, who was in Ledburn's father's pocket, and he backed the captain all the way. I spoke to him, quietly, aside on deck at night. Told him how far off course we were, and that if we went on this way, we'd be too close to the coast of Africa. He said that to go against the captain was mutiny. And that's a hanging offense. I told him that if we drowned, it would hardly matter."

Monk's fingernails were digging into the palms of his hands, but this time he did not interrupt. He saw Hooper sitting forward, his shoulders hunched so tight his muscles must ache.

"I don't know if he thought it would all sort out, or if he wanted a fight," Hooper said. "He told Ledburn, and like a fool, Ledburn didn't look at it again and recalculate our position. We would all have been relieved and let him pretend what he wanted, just to get back on course now. But he accused us of trying to start a mutiny. Said I should apologize, admit he was correct, and take orders accordingly." Hooper closed his eyes. "I stood there on deck. It was dawn, sun coming up, light on the waves, bright and sharp. I could see the coast of Africa on the eastern skyline. My sight was something special then, although some of the other men could, too. Fisk could, I knew. They were all waiting to see what I would do—see if I had the guts to speak the truth or not. I had to. Ledburn put his telescope to his eye. 'Non-sense,' he said. 'Cloud bank, man. Nothing more. There's no land there.' 'Yes, there is, sir,' I said. 'We're off course about a hundred miles too far east. Get any further and the current will carry us in.' That was the truth."

Monk held his breath.

"He ordered me flogged," Hooper said in just above a whisper, "in front of all the men."

"And . . . ?" Monk prompted in the silence. He knew that a naval flogging was brutal, even fatal at times.

"They hesitated to take up the lash. It was Fisk who stepped up and refused. Then another, and another . . . and . . ."

Monk could feel the sweat break out on his skin. Hooper was here; he had survived. So had Fisk. But who had not? He was terrified Hooper was going to say they had killed the captain somehow. "Go on!" he said sharply.

It was hard; the memory of it still had the ability to scour deep with pain. This was visible in Hooper's eyes, the pallor of his face, the tension in his whole body. Monk was making him relive the worst memory of his life. Like Monk's own memory, always just out of sight, beyond all but nightmare's reach, there was something terrible lying there, waiting to come back when you least expected it.

"Hooper . . ." he said more gently.

"There was a fight," Hooper resumed the story. "First it was the captain and Fisk, then others joined in. I tried to stop them before someone got killed or we were so busy fighting we lost control of the ship. The wind was rising, not a lot, but there was a storm on the horizon and closing on us fast.

"The captain was driven backward by the men, up onto the poop deck. I went after him, facing back to the men, trying to stop them from attacking again, but they were frightened. They had started a mutiny, and there's only one way that could end: hanging from the yardarm, kicking the air as the noose tightened around your neck. The captain was terrified, lashing out at the men closest to him. Some of them hung back, undecided still. He had tried to cover his lies, and nobody knew what to believe. It was all so . . . stupid! If he had just admitted his first mistake, the rest would never have happened . . ." Hooper's voice broke and he had to struggle to control himself.

Monk waited. He wanted to reach out and touch him, express his understanding, because no words would do. But it was too intimate a gesture.

"He didn't trust me either," Hooper went on suddenly. "He lunged at me and we struggled together for several moments. I was shouting at him. But I don't think he could hear me above the other men or the wind in the ropes. He wouldn't let go of me, punching me. I had to hit him back or he'd have decked me. He was strong. Then the other men would have swarmed up onto the poop deck, and God knows what would have happened. They would have killed him, and we'd all have been hanged."

He took a deep breath and closed his eyes. "He slipped and went down over the rail. His own weight behind the blow carried him over. I went to grab him. I caught one of his arms and managed to lean over and catch the other. He was flailing around, terrified. He thought I was going to drop him deliberately. I wasn't." Suddenly Hooper opened his eyes and stared straight at Monk. "I did everything I could! But he slipped out of my grasp and went into the sea. There was nothing I could do . . . any of us could do. We were running before the wind and it would have taken us fifteen minutes, with most of the men up the masts, to shorten sail and come about. We tried, but it was too late, far too late. There was no sign of him. We waited as long as we could, but the storm was coming in, and we had to reef in and run before it. We reported him lost at sea in the storm."

"That was the truth," Monk pointed out. "Even if not the whole truth. I imagine his family would far rather know only that much of it than the rest."

"It was still a mutiny," Hooper argued, "and I sided with the men."

"The men were right." Monk was perfectly aware of the enormity of what he was saying. There was no proof of that. It was only Hooper's word that the captain had made the first error, then lie after lie to cover it, but Monk believed it absolutely. "Wouldn't Fisk back you up?"

"I don't know. I never asked him. If we were not believed, it would be his neck for the rope as well."

"In Runcorn's office, he recognized you."

"I think so."

"And the other men of the crew?"

"I don't know. It was twenty years ago; they could be anywhere."

"Your name?"

Hooper hesitated.

"Your name?" Monk insisted.

"Jacob Abbott."

"Maybe if I had a memory, it would mean something," Monk said wryly. "But I don't. You're John Hooper to me. What about Fisk?"

"Twist. Joe Twist."

Monk wondered if that was why Hooper had never married. He would not risk visiting that disgrace on any woman he loved. Possibly his family had had to be abandoned the same way.

"It's a high price," he said. "Don't pay any more for it." He held out his hand. "You did the only thing you could, given the circumstances."

Monk looked at Hooper steadily. His eyes were such a clear blue, Monk felt as if he could look into his head.

"Thank you, sir."

"We're off duty," Monk said slowly and distinctly. "Commander Monk knows nothing about this and will continue to know nothing. William Monk, whoever he is or was, is proud to know you."

Hooper clasped Monk's hand and held it so hard he all but crushed his fingers.

Monk slept better that night than he had done for some time. He believed Hooper's account of the incident. Apart from the honesty that Monk had known in Hooper the entire time they had served in the Thames River Police together, it fitted in with the facts he knew of maritime discipline, and with Fisk's apparent recognition of Hooper. And clearly he had not told Runcorn anything about it. It seemed he had no intention of betraying Hooper.

Had anyone else known? The enemy of Exeter who might be behind all this, whether it was Doyle or someone else? Monk did not believe so. Hooper had not been blackmailed into betrayal. That person they had yet to find.

Monk went the following morning to see Exeter in Newgate Prison, near the Old Bailey, where he was being held. He walked along the stone floor with the heat of rage inside him. It was almost enough for him to ignore the icy chill in the air and the occasional clang of iron on stone as a door slammed.

"There you are, sir. I can only give you a few minutes, like, since you're not his lawyer," the warder said. He knew Monk and held the River Police in some regard.

"Thank you. I'll contact his lawyer and let him know." Monk stood back for the door to be unlocked.

Inside the cell, Harry Exeter was standing. He must have heard the footsteps in the passage stopping outside, so he was expecting someone. His face lit with relief when he saw Monk. Some of the tension knotted inside him seemed to relax a little. "Thank God you've come," he said immediately. "This is a nightmare! You've got to help me!"

The door closed behind Monk, and he was aware of a lock turning and the steel flanges going home.

Monk looked at Exeter. He was wearing an old pair of trousers and a comfortable shirt. It was made of flannel but hardly enough to keep him warm in this unheated stone room. Exeter was wretched, and it showed in every line of his body. Monk made a mental note to bring him fresh clothes—warmer ones. But Monk knew nothing would banish the ice inside him, except practical help. He might already have asked someone to bring him extra clothes himself, but he looked stunned by shock and horror. The grief of his wife's death was only two weeks behind him.

"I'll get you some fresh clothes," Monk said straightaway. "Have you been in touch with Rathbone?"

Exeter looked puzzled. "Rathbone?"

"You'll need a good lawyer. Well, maybe they can sort this out quickly without one, but you're better off having somebody to speak for you, someone experienced. Do you have a regular man you would prefer? Give me his name and I'll make sure—"

"No. No," Exeter cut across him. "Rathbone is the best there is. My regular chap has been here, of course, but he deals with real estate and wills, civil law, that kind of thing. I need Rathbone, you're quite right." He frowned. "But do you think he'll do this? Will you ask him for me? God, this is a nightmare! I still can't believe it's real. Why would they think such a . . . terrible, hellish thing? It makes no sense." He shook his head, as if in doing it hard enough the horror would detach from him.

"I don't know." Monk kept his voice steady, trying to concentrate now on Exeter and the nightmare he must be going through and not let his own mind race ahead to who had made this decision, and why. What had Monk missed? Was Runcorn involved in it? Or had Doyle said something to remove the blame from himself and place it on Exeter? Was it some lie in the ledger that pointed to Exeter, of all people?

"Probably whoever did kill her has implicated you," Monk answered Exeter's question. "I'm afraid it may be someone you know well enough to have trusted. I'm sorry."

Exeter stared at him. "I suppose it must," he agreed very quietly. "Will you go to Rathbone for me? Tell him all you know and all you can find out. Please? I feel as if the whole world has suddenly turned into a bottomless pit beneath my feet. I take a step and where there was earth, suddenly there's nothing! I can't see the bottom of this! Help me, Monk! I didn't do it! Maybe Rathbone can prove it— maybe . . ."

"Yes, of course, I can get him," Monk promised. "He's been in this almost from the beginning. He'll have his own questions to ask you, but so that it doesn't take up the precious time he has with you, and so I can find out anything I can, what ideas have you? Rivals? Jealousies? People who owe you money and won't have to pay if you're in jail?"

Exeter was shaken. He looked close to hysteria. "Not if I'm hanged anyway!" His voice was too high-pitched.

Monk put out his arm without thinking and took Exeter by the shoulder. "You won't hang. We'll find out who really did this. Think of a list of all the people who might benefit from your death, emotionally or financially, or because of personal life. It doesn't matter who they are, we can go as high as you like, or as low. Note all of them, and tell Rathbone. He needs to know everything there is. We can't tell where it will lead or afford to be caught on the blind side by any information we don't have." He tightened his hold on Exeter. "We don't know who did it, do we? Is there something you know and haven't told me? To protect someone's feelings? Or reputation?"

"Good God, don't you think I'd tell you?" Exeter said, his voice rising almost uncontrollably, close to panic. "I've been over and over everything I said to anyone and . . . it always comes back to the money and Doyle. I've known him for years." He looked steadily at Monk, searching his face for understanding. "Of course, he's a bit of a social climber. He's ambitious for far more than I think he'll ever achieve. But most of people's dreams are beyond them. Ambition is good. Dreams are what drive us to try. So often we don't get what we want, but we get something else, and that can be good, too. At least Doyle understood other men's dreams. He understood work and disappointment, what it takes to succeed and . . . and how badly you can want it." He looked down. "I know people laughed at him now and then. I did myself. He was gauche, at times." He looked up. "But I trusted him, and as far as I know, he never let me down."

"He helped you get the money together for the ransom from Kate's inheritance."

Exeter colored faintly. "Yes. I had to. I don't have that much money myself. I asked Latham's permission, of course. And Celia's. She gave it willingly. She loved Kate—and it was Kate's money, and Doyle facilitated it because he understood." Exeter swallowed hard. "Are you really wishing me to consider that Doyle could be behind this . . . this most terrible thing that happened in my life . . . really?"

"Who else?" Monk asked. "Someone did. Was it you?"

"Of course not! What do you think I am? For God's sake, Monk . . ."

"I know," Monk said quickly. "Then face the fact that it must be somebody else. It happened. You know that. And not only to Kate, but to Lister, the one actual kidnapper we know, and to poor Bella Franken. If it's not you, I accept that, but if you don't think about who it is and fight it, you will be the next victim."

Exeter shut his eyes as if it would be easier to answer Monk if he could not see him. "I know," he said very softly. His voice had a crack in it; he was close to losing control. "I do know, and I'm terri-fied."

Monk could hear the humiliation in him, a man unused to admit-ting any weakness in front of someone else. Perhaps he was ashamed to admit it even to himself. He had fought hard for all he possessed, fought to own it and to keep it. And now suddenly, in less than a month, he faced losing it all, even his life.

"You can't give in," Monk insisted. He searched his mind for some real hope to offer, something that was not patronizing and meaningless. He had faced the same thoughts himself once, and only Hester's belief in him had given him the will to continue.

But Exeter had not even that. Kate was gone, broken, and almost torn apart. Exeter had been betrayed, but he had met all the demands the kidnappers had made, and still he had lost her.

"We'll find the truth," Monk said rashly. "There are only so many people it could be. We must reason. Think clearly. We can't let them get away with it, for justice's sake! And, in harsher reality, because they will do it again."

Exeter stiffened, then slowly lifted his head. "You're right. I should stop being so . . . cowardly. I can't let them win. Help me, Monk, please."

Monk could only imagine what it had cost him to say that. He spoke before he could beg again. "Of course I will. I want the bastard caught almost as much as you do."

Right now, he must save Exeter. There had been some grave error in his arrest. It was understandable, perhaps. Runcorn was as different from Monk as could be, but Monk understood him. If circumstances had been different, without the accident that had robbed him of memory, he could have been very like Runcorn. He had the same passion for life, and the courage and appetite to take chances and win. His flashes of the Barbary Coast, the gold rush, the open ocean and the life of the deck beneath his feet, the open sea before all, testi-fied to that.

He had lost immediate control of the case because he had taken that quixotic plunge to try to rescue Bella Franken; he had at least saved the papers she was bringing him, but he could not continue that night. He had yielded the case to Runcorn, and Runcorn had made the arrest.

"We must get all the information we can for Rathbone," he said, with his self-control back again. "Tell me everything you know, as far as money is concerned. For a start, exactly how much did you tell Doyle about the kidnapping? Details?"

"Does it matter now?" Exeter asked without hope. "He obviously knew it all anyway."

"Yes, it matters," Monk replied. "What he knew that he didn't get from you, he learned another way. If we can prove that, we are half-way to demonstrating his guilt! The other half we must work on, but it will come far more easily. Now concentrate!"

Exeter made a deliberate effort to muster his thoughts, and then slowly, carefully, he relived some of the arrangements he had made with Doyle. As he spoke, he clearly felt again the near panic of reviewing his assets, what they would fetch if sold in such urgency, and what, as far as he could remember, he had told Doyle to do on his behalf.

Monk wrote it down, even though he did not fully understand it.

"You mentioned evasions," he said gravely. "Who did you beat in business deals, or anything else: social achievements, positions they wanted, or whose wives admired you—anything, whether the hatred was justified or not? Especially if they might have known Doyle, banked with him—anything at all." He waited with his pencil in the air, watching Exeter's face.

Exeter was silent for several moments. Then he looked up. "Do you think you'll find them?" he asked huskily. "Before the trial? Is it possible?" The hope in his eyes was painful to see.

"Doesn't have to be before the beginning." Monk fought for something to say. "All you can think of. It doesn't matter how trivial it is: a social humiliation, a financial loss more than they could absorb. You don't know what they might have lost by it. Anything you think of, give it to Rathbone. Anyone you threatened, even unintentionally. There isn't time for us to do it without your help."

Slowly the total fear faded from Exeter's face and he breathed deeply, an attempt at a smile returning to his face. "I'll do it. I trust you, Monk."

RATHBONE WAS IN COURT all day, and Monk needed to speak to him more than the brief moments he could snatch in the middle of a case. He spent the day collecting all the paperwork he had that might be useful to Rathbone in the defense. He even found proof of the success of Exeter's career and the envy it might have engendered. There were deals that showed great skill, high risks taken, and some resounding defeats of powerful men.

It was late in the evening by the time Monk reached Rathbone's house, but at least he knew Rathbone would be there. Few dinner parties lasted this long, so even if he had been out, he would be home by now. Monk felt no compunction at all in getting him out of bed if necessary. Tomorrow morning would be late to start, and anyway, Monk felt the rage and compassion burning a hole in him now, and all his thoughts were clear in his mind.

It was several minutes before Monk heard the bolt withdraw. The butler, clearly hastily dressed, opened the door cautiously.

"Yes, sir?" he asked, and then recognized Monk. "Is everything all right, sir? Are you hurt?" He pulled the door wide and ushered Monk inside from the darkness and the freezing drizzle.

"No, thank you," Monk replied, pushing the door closed behind him. "I'm sorry to get you up at this hour. Is Sir Oliver in bed yet?"

"I imagine so, sir. There are no lights on upstairs."

"Oh. I suppose it is later than I thought. I apologize. Is it possible to wake him? Mr. Exeter has been arrested and charged with the murder of his wife—the woman who was kidnapped and . . . knifed to death on Jacob's Island."

"Oh, my . . . I beg your pardon, sir. I was about to take the Lord's name in vain! This is terrible. I'll . . . I'll call Sir Oliver, sir. If you would like to take a seat in the withdrawing room, the fire will still be warm. I'll come in and stoke it for you when I've woken Sir Oliver."

"I'll stoke it myself, thank you," Monk replied. He did not want to usurp the man's job, but at this time of night it was bad enough he had woken him at all.

The butler was correct. The fire was very low, but with a little poking and putting small pieces of coal on it carefully with the tongs, it soon burned up. He had just finished when Rathbone came in, wearing a thick dressing robe and obviously fully awake. He closed the door behind him.

"The butler will bring some hot tea and a drop of brandy in a minute. God, this is awful!" He sat down and gestured to the chair opposite for Monk to do the same. "You didn't arrest him, I suppose? Who did?"

"Runcorn. He took over the Bella Franken case. It was more on his territory. Even though she was washed up by the river, she was almost certainly killed on land, and I was in no shape to act immediately." He saw the confusion in Rathbone's face and realized he did not know of the case in any detail, if he knew at all. "Sorry," Monk said. "Bella Franken was Doyle's bookkeeper at the bank. She was the one with some figures that struck her as wrong. When I went to keep an appointment with her I saw a body in the Greenwich dock, and it was her. I nearly caught my death pulling her out."

Rathbone looked stricken. "Good God! That's terrible! And Runcorn thinks Exeter did that? Why, for the love of heaven? Doyle was the one who helped him get the money together in time to pay the kidnappers . . . for . . . Kate." His voice trailed off, memory of the tragedy of it all overwhelming him. "I presume you came to ask me to represent him. Of course I will, unless he has someone he prefers?"

"No, of course not! Whoever could he possibly prefer? There's no better lawyer in England, and you know him and the beginning of this hideous affair already. The poor man's distracted with grief, and now fear. He's almost ready to give up. And who could blame him?"

There was a knock on the door, and the butler brought in a tray of tea with a small decanter of whisky on the side.

"Thank you," Rathbone said quietly. "Now go back to bed. We

can manage. I'll let Mr. Monk out when we've finished. And yes, I'll
be sure to lock the bolts on the front door. Good night."

"Yes, sir, if you are sure?"

"I am."

"Thank you. Good night, sir."

Rathbone poured the tea and the whisky, and as soon as the butler closed the drawing-room door behind him, he began. "What is he
charged with? The murder of Doyle's unfortunate bank clerk, or
bookkeeper, or whatever? Why, for heaven's sake? What could she
know that could be any danger to him? If she was embezzling, or
whatever, that's nothing to do with him!"

"It looks as if Doyle was fiddling the books to some extent, not
exactly sure how, but we have an expert on it. Bella Franken was
murdered bringing those papers to me. Possibly he or Maurice Latham,
Katherine's cousin, was embezzling from Katherine's trust. Maybe
both of them. It would have come to light sooner or later, when she
inherited. Doyle had to protect himself. And he took a bit of it on the
side as well," Monk replied. "We'll need to look at Latham, but I
don't know if he has the stomach for violence."

Rathbone was watching him intensely. "That makes sense. Then
surely Doyle is the one most threatened by that, and Doyle either
killed the girl himself or hired someone else to. Perhaps he was the
one who contacted Lister?"

"Lister was already dead by the time Bella Franken was killed,"
Monk pointed out.

"But we already knew this whole affair involved more than one
person," Rathbone said patiently. "Don't dismiss Latham so easily.
Who did you work out must have known Jacob's Island for the kidnapping?"

"Four of them, at least. And that is if they came by land and
didn't need to have someone in a boat for their escape," Monk replied. "And we knew Doyle wasn't one of them."

"He doesn't sound like a man for violent adventures," Rathbone
said. "He's a bank manager! But he could well be the brains behind it.
Sounds like a very careful planner, good with figures and access to

money to move it, and at least four ruffians to carry it out. One of them, Lister, is already dead. The other three we seem to have no lead on . . . yet . . . but one of them killed this poor girl. Are we any closer to finding the others?" Rathbone's voice dropped a little, as if he feared a negative answer.

"No," Monk said flatly. "Not at all. I haven't spoken to Runcorn about them yet. I went straight to Exeter. We've got to prove his innocence, whether we ever get the guilty ones or not. What that man has endured . . ."

Rathbone's face softened. "I know. We'll get him out of this. I just haven't thought how yet. Getting the right person is the best way, but it's not the only way. Do you know which of your men betrayed you yet? I'm sorry to put it so bluntly, but there isn't time for delicacy."

"No." Monk realized what a weight it had been on him when he feared it was Hooper. And yet it would still hurt, whoever it was. "It looks as if it might have been Walcott. I can't even narrow it down to when it can have happened. He must have told the kidnappers on that day, because we didn't finalize the plans until then. But how he got the information to them, I have no idea. Unless he did it somehow after we arrived? We were all alone then, at least for a few minutes. It was getting dark, and it's like a maze in those old rooms. Passages where one can walk have collapsed, physically. Anyone could have been anywhere."

"Then we have to find the answer another way." Rathbone was silent for a few moments.

"I'm trying to find Exeter's enemies," Monk digressed. "I've got a list, and I'll put my men on it and ask if Runcorn can spare any of his. If there's another client at Doyle's bank, someone Exeter outbid on a big building or anything else, it would help to know who."

"Good," Rathbone acknowledged. "Reasonable doubt doesn't save a man's reputation, but it will save his life. That may be the best we can do—in the meantime."

Monk sipped his tea. It was hot and tasted rich because of the whisky, but it certainly made him feel warmer, and more awake.

"Exeter was with you in the original attempt to pay the ransom and get Kate back," Rathbone said slowly. "He was at home, though we've no proof of this, when Lister was killed, but we could presume Lister definitely was the man who originally snatched her? Yes? One thing proved, more or less. Presumably he was killed by his fellow kidnappers, and you saw him before and after, so you can pin down that time? And anyway, why would Exeter kill him? Revenge? Without catching the rest of the killers or getting his money back?"

"He's not charged with killing Lister. But if he was, there would certainly be mitigating circumstances. And he could always put up an argument for self-defense," Monk pointed out. "Tie all the murders together, and guilty of one has to be guilty of all! Or innocent?"

Rathbone's face was very somber. "Not if he hired Lister in the first place."

"To take his money and kill his wife!" Monk took a deep breath. "What happened to the money? Anyway, that's not what they're charging him with."

"What are they charging him with?" Rathbone asked.

"Exeter said with the murder of Kate."

"Well, surely you and your men can prove where he was, between all of you? Put your evidence together."

"Difficult," Monk pointed out bitterly, "if one of my men was actually betraying us! And for God's sake, don't say that one of my men actually killed her!"

Rathbone's jaw dropped. "I . . . I hadn't even thought of that! But I suppose it's not impossible."

Monk gulped, his mind filled with horror.

"Damn it, Monk! I don't mean one of them did!" Rathbone exploded. "I mean they might charge one of them! That wasn't up to Runcorn. Once the prosecutor gets hold of it—and feelings are running pretty high over this—if they think of it, they could do it!"

Monk said nothing. His mind was whirling, as if he were in the center of a storm, buffeted from every direction, almost off his feet.

Rathbone's voice reached him from far away. "We had better start working on this straightaway. Put down all the evidence we are certain of, and why and how we are certain. Then all the stuff that's ambiguous. And start clarifying what we need to know, what all the possibilities are, however remote or unpleasant, and see what we have left. Who killed Kate? Who has the money, if it even existed? Who killed Lister? Who killed that poor girl Bella Franken? And who's trying to kill Exeter, through judicial execution!"

"And if one of my men is involved, what man—and why?" Monk finished.

"It's going to be a long night and an early morning," Rathbone said, taking a sip of his tea and adding more whisky.

18

"I DON'T KNOW," RUNCORN SAID, his voice rising in exasperation as he sat late the following evening in his office, Monk in the chair opposite him. "I don't know why Exeter did it. I don't even know for certain, in my own mind, that he did. But I can't ignore the evidence."

"What evidence?" Monk demanded. "He certainly didn't kill Kate. He was with us. He was attacked, too, and he doesn't know Jacob's Island any better than any ordinary, well-to-do man in London would."

"He didn't kill his wife himself," Runcorn agreed. "He paid Lister to do it for him. First to take her from the riverbank, where she was walking with her cousin, and Celia Darwin was the only one who knew that they were."

"You're not suggesting she was in it with Lister, are you?"

"No, of course not. Although she would be . . ."

Monk was aware of the unlikelihood of that, even as Runcorn said it. But all sorts of people had the strangest weaknesses, doubts, fears. He should have looked further into her life, and maybe even her envy of her wealthier, more fortunate, more beautiful cousin. Hooper had expressed great regard for her honesty. But not inquiring closely about Celia Darwin was an oversight he should remedy while there was still time.

"I should look into that," he admitted. "It's an ugly thought, but I can't ignore it."

"It's all ugly," Runcorn pointed out. "I haven't found out anything about her."

"I'll have Rathbone ask Exeter." Monk was reluctant. "All trage-dies are ugly. Someone is hurt more than they can bear. All secrets laid open hurt far more than just one person."

"You'll have to. I can't get anything out of Exeter. Rathbone seems to have told him to keep quiet, and he's doing it. So would I, if I were trying to defend him."

"What else have you got against him?" Monk asked. "Anything more than suspicion?"

"Far more than suspicion, Monk! Do you think I arrested him just to say I closed the case?"

"No. I know his butler said that Exeter was out the day Lister was killed and the afternoon Bella Franken was killed. It sounds like a disgruntled servant. He can't prove it."

"None of the other servants saw him during those hours. His boots and the cuffs of his trousers were wet."

"He went to post a letter and get a breath of air," Monk said quickly. "He'd been cooped up in the house with his grief for days! He went out when no one would see him. He didn't want to make polite conversation with neighbors and answer questions. 'How are you?' and other damn silly things. He's feeling like hell. I wouldn't want to answer questions either, in his place."

"I've got two witnesses who say they saw him with Lister."

"Who?"

"On a building site."

"For God's sake, Runcorn, he owns building sites! That's what he does. Maybe Lister was doing a day or two of manual labor? Ever thought of that?"

"If Exeter didn't murder Kate, who did?" Runcorn asked innocently.

"Doyle, of course! He's the one changing around the money, taking a good bit for himself! There could be someone else involved. I've got some of my men looking into it, and I've got a list for you to try. Exeter is a very successful man. He's bound to have enemies."

"Doyle got the money together for the ransom. It was in his bank, and he made it available immediately. Cut all the red tape." Runcorn ticked off the points on his fingers. "He took a part as payment—maybe not admirable, but understandable."

Monk had no argument, at least not one that would count in court. "Reasonable doubt . . . ? Did you look into this trustee Maurice Latham?"

"Maybe Rathbone will go with that. Unless he has a rabbit to pull out of his hat?"

"Not that I know of. Did you check Latham's account of his time?"

"Yes. He can account for it." Runcorn's face tightened in unhappiness. "Do you know yet which of your men tipped off Lister and his crew?"

"No."

"You'll have to find out. You can't go on knowing one of them did and not knowing who, for whatever reason, even if you understand it and might have done the same."

Monk jerked his head up.

"Hostage to fortune," Runcorn went on. "A man will do most things to save his family. It may not be greed or resentment, envy, revenge, any of those things. Just someone you have destroyed, someone you have a duty to protect. Or just someone to whom you owe an unpayable debt—guilt as a payment. You have to know."

"All right! Yes, I do," Monk said quietly. "I wish . . . no, of course what I wish is irrelevant. We all . . . wish."

———

Monk spent the next days still working every angle he could think of to prove both Exeter's innocence and, in its place, Doyle's guilt. He even tested Latham's account of his time, but he could not find a weakness. The first day of the trial dawned without any new evidence of value.

"I'm coming," Hester said. She was not asking him or making a gesture of support. It was simply a statement of something she took to be unarguable. She was dressed in a blue jacket and skirt, very plain but well cut. Monk looked at her with appreciation, although she had never been traditionally beautiful. Her face was too strong for that. The only really tender thing in it was the curve of her mouth, and for him, the gentleness and the passion in it made her all the more lovely.

"Thank you," he said simply. He was the first witness. Rathbone had warned him that the prosecutor was a clever man, but far more than that, he was a decent man who would not be carried away by emotion or vanity. This made him more difficult to trip up than a man more interested in his own reputation. Rathbone regarded him as a friend outside of the courtroom.

Monk looked at Hester for a moment, hesitating inside the front door. She was smiling at him, but her look was guarded, as if she were trying not to let her emotion come through. She was afraid for him; he knew her well enough to see it. She was afraid he was going to lose and be hurt by it. He was glad she did not say so aloud.

She was not in any way a witness to the case, so she was allowed to be in the court the whole time, and she had promised, unless there was some crisis in the clinic, that she would be there every day. He was not sure he was pleased by that. It was not the savagery of the crime that he would protect her from; she had seen war, dozens of deaths, perhaps even scores of them, injuries worse than any normal man or woman's most terrible nightmares. But there was something impersonal about war. You were a soldier on one side or the other. This was intimate, one to one. This had happened unexpectedly, to people who knew each other.

But she was outside already, waiting for the carriage that would take them to the Old Bailey. The wind was pulling at her skirts, and behind her the Thames was gray, dotted with breaking whitecaps on the rough water. He must go.

ALL THE USUAL PRELIMINARIES were over by the time Monk was called and went into the packed courtroom. He walked across the open space to the steep, twisting steps up to the witness stand. The stand itself stood well above the level of the floor, and he looked slightly down on Rathbone, who was dressed very formally in his black robes and barrister's wig.

Across from him in the dock, also above the body of the court, he could see Harry Exeter. He looked the way he had the day after Kate's death: gray-faced, the life drained out of him. Monk wanted to smile at him, but it would be ill-advised. It might give the jury the idea that he knew the man, even liked him. He must appear neutral. Exeter's life might hang on Monk's testimony. Who knew what word or gesture, what fleeting expression of the face, made a man believe or disbelieve what you said?

After Monk had taken the oath to speak the truth, and nothing but, and testified to his name and occupation, the crown prosecutor, Peter Ravenswood, rose to question him. He was a mild-looking man, one a person might not have taken seriously had they not noticed the expression in his eyes and the marks of a sense of humor in the lines of his face. And Monk had the feeling already that that would have been a mistake.

"Commander Monk," Ravenswood began calmly, "would you tell the court how you came to be involved in this terrible case? It has to be harrowing for you, but we need to know, and justice is not always easy for any of us." There was no overt emotion in his voice. It might have been easier if there had been. There was nothing for Monk to fight against. And yet this was the man who was going to get it all so tragically wrong and hang Exeter for the crime that had cost him all that was most dear to him already. Now it threatened to take his life as well.

Monk drew in a deep breath and began. He did not even attempt to be impartial. He remembered the depth of his feelings that night.

"Sir Oliver Rathbone, whom I have known for years, came to my house and said that he had a client who needed my help, or more specifically, the help of the Thames River Police. He was waiting at Sir Oliver's house and would I go there immediately. I went. There I met with Mr. Exeter for the first time."

Ravenswood interrupted him. "What was his manner? His appearance?"

"He was extremely distressed. Much as he looks now. He told me that his wife had been kidnapped. He was willing to pay the ransom. Enormous as it was, he had managed to get the money together. It was to be handed over the following day. All he wanted from me was to accompany him to Jacob's Island, a place he was afraid to go alone. Very particular instructions had been given him, which he was unable to follow, since he did not know the area. Few people do. It is one of the worst Thames-side slums, slowly sinking beneath the mud. The place specified was below the high tide mark, and the appointment was at dusk." He let the image hang in the air, sink into the jurors' imaginations.

"I have heard of it," Ravenswood remarked. "Indeed: vile. I can see why he would not want to go alone, and possibly not even be able to find it. Nor, perhaps, take a boat there by himself. How far did you go?" He looked interested.

Monk tried to remember exactly what Exeter had said. The memory of the journey came unbidden to his mind. The cold, the evening light, the sound of the water at slack tide, everything dripping. "All the way," he answered.

"With a lot of men?" Ravenswood asked. "Were you not afraid the kidnappers would see you?"

"The boats are all large, but easily managed by two men," Monk answered. "And they are not an unusual sight on the river. More usual than a boat with one man."

"Although a fisherman might go alone." Ravenswood lifted his eyebrows.

"In the Pool of London?" Monk looked even more amazed. "Nothing lives in that water. The estuary, perhaps."

Ravenswood gave a slight, acknowledging smile. "How many men did you take?"

"There were six of us altogether. Two to remain in the boats, four to go with Mr. Exeter. He had already decided that he would not come alone."

"Did you not think that strange?"

"No. He did not intend to fight with them, only to give them the money and get his wife back unharmed. That was all he cared about." Monk looked at Ravenswood's smooth, artless face and realized he had believed Exeter was innocent, but he wanted Monk to prove it. "I saw the money myself," he added. "It was real, and it was all there. If he had meant to fight, he could have hired men. Easy enough to find on the dockside. I think he took police to assure it was a smooth exchange."

"Is that what he said?"

"More or less. I don't remember his exact words."

"It's what you understood?"

"Yes."

"Is that what you did, when your own wife was kidnapped?" Ravenswood asked quietly, even gently.

For a moment, Monk was speechless. How on earth did Ravenswood know that? Runcorn, of course. Suddenly, Monk felt vulnerable, as if the man had caught him unexpectedly naked—not different, just without the camouflage for emotions that one habitually wore.

Ravenswood was waiting for an answer. Should Monk say that he had not even thought of it? Whether it was a lie or not, it would sound like one. He would not get another chance to create a good first impression.

"If I had the money, yes, of course I would pay it," he answered.

"Of course," Ravenswood agreed. "Most of us would. It is the only thing a civilized man could do."

Monk was about to reply. Then he realized how oblique the second remark was, how double-edged. Of course, any man would say that was what he would do! Whatever his feelings were. "He raised the money," he pointed out to the court. "All he wanted from the police was guidance in a strange and dangerous place."

"Very natural," Ravenswood smiled slightly. There was no sneer hidden in it. "So, you agreed to go with him, either for his sake or for Sir Oliver's."

"And for Mrs. Exeter's," Monk added.

"Quite. Who knew of your plans?"

"The men I took with me." Already they were approaching the wound that still hurt, still bled. Monk could see Ravenswood's awareness of it in his face, in the care with which he chose his words. He might not like to poke it, but he would.

"I imagine you told the men to tell no one else?"

"Yes."

"So before you went, it was only you, Mr. Exeter, and your own men who knew?"

"Yes. And before you say so, I will admit we made one or two last-minute adjustments, so when it came to the point, even if someone else had known of the original plan, they would not have known the changes."

"So, Mr. Exeter could not have told anyone?"

"No."

"What happened, Commander Monk? Tell me how events transpired, to the best of your knowledge."

Monk had been rehearsing this over and over in his mind ever since it had occurred, and he still hated it. He could smell the stench of the river water in enclosed spaces as he spoke of it.

"We went downriver just before slack tide. It was the only time the lowest point was accessible. We took two boats, one for each entrance, to comply with the instructions. Left a man in each boat—Bathurst and Walcott. Laker, Exeter, and I went in the south way. It was already early dusk." He could remember it vividly, the sour odor of the water, the drips off the sodden beams, the movement that could have been tide, or rats, or just rubbish bumping against a fallen beam.

"We went into the first tunnel, really just a room whose walls were collapsed on two sides. We had an exact map, and we followed it. It was slow. If you dislodge something it could collapse on you. We were moving inland and upward—"

"You know the place well, Commander?" Ravenswood interrupted him.

"Only as well as I have to. It seems to change with every tide. A timber here and then gone, shifting mud and small stones," he replied.

"A dangerous place?"

"Very."

"Was that why Mr. Exeter needed someone of your experience to go with him?"

"Possibly. And also to make sure that he did not get lost in it, unable to find the place where the kidnappers had arranged they meet." He could remember it as sharply as if it had been yesterday. The fear, the confusion in Exeter's face, his eyes. And he could barely have imagined it would end in this tragedy, and that he would find himself blamed for it. Had any man enough courage to face that? If it had been Hester taken, he didn't think he would have cared if he had been blamed or not. He would have been numb with grief. Of course, he would've had to stay sane, for Scuff and all the other people who cared for her. Exeter did not seem to have anyone who really supported him, needed him. Not even Celia Darwin! Was he so private a man he had refused all help? And refused also to give way, to Celia or to anyone else? He did not seem to think very highly of her.

Ravenswood was talking to him but he had not heard.

"I beg your pardon?"

"Did you separate during this journey into Jacob's Island?" Ravenswood repeated.

"Yes. But I stayed with Mr. Exeter. That was the purpose of going with him, to see that he did not get lost."

"He kept hold of the money?"

"Yes. Then we were attacked. I don't know by whom, because it was getting darker and the only light inside the place came from

bull's-eye lanterns we carried. We both managed to fight our assail-
ants off, keep the money, and make our way to the place where we
were to meet the kidnappers."

"Together?"

"Yes."

"You could see Mr. Exeter at all times?"

Monk tried to visualize it in his mind: the rising tide, the thicken-
ing darkness, what he had actually seen, rather than heard or imagined. "Yes. Right until he went alone the last few yards to meet the
kidnappers."

"Yes. The last few yards. He was out of your sight then?"

"It was getting darker, and I was attacked myself. From behind. I
had no idea who it was, but I wasn't badly injured . . . just . . . out of
it for a few moments." It was a humiliating memory.

"Was Mr. Exeter also attacked, do you know?"

It sounded a harmless question, but Monk was beginning to see
that Ravenswood was not as innocent as he seemed, merely well
mannered.

"When I saw him again, he was filthy and badly bruised."

"He was gone a long time?"

"No. It was getting dusk and very difficult to see anyone clearly,
unless one of the lanterns was close to him. He went to give the
money to the kidnappers and—and get his wife back. He was willing
to part with the money! All he wanted was to get her back—safe . . ."

"That is what he told you? And you believed him, because you
put yourself in his place, and remembered how you felt when your
own wife was taken." Ravenswood made it a conclusion, not a question.

"Any decent man . . ." Monk began. Then he checked himself
and made his voice softer. "He had given me no reason at all to believe it was not exactly as he said, then or since. He had acquired the
money, I believe, with some difficulty. It was an extraordinary amount.
He took it to hand over, but they had already killed her. They took it
and fled. I believed at the time that that was what had happened, and
I have had no reason since then to change my opinion."

"If they had the money and were in no danger of imminent arrest, why would they kill her?" Ravenswood looked sad and puzzled.

Monk had wondered that himself. But he knew that Exeter's defense relied on there being some credible answer. "I assume she recognized one of them," he said.

"Kidnappers? Really?" Ravenswood looked mildly puzzled. "You think she had acquaintance with such people? Where would she have been likely to encounter them? Hardly in her social circle." He shook his head very slightly. "I imagine you did look into this, as a matter of course."

"Yes. There was no one who was sufficiently in debt or otherwise vulnerable, and we looked carefully. We also asked Mr. Exeter, and he knew of no one at all."

"You'll forgive me if I do not find him as believable as you do," Ravenswood said drily.

"We narrowed it down to the bank manager, Roger Doyle," Monk carried on. "He knew about the situation, and he knew Mr. Exeter's financial circumstances: that he had the means to raise exactly that amount of money, at the highest end of possibilities. He also knew Mrs. Exeter by sight and could be certain that Mr. Exeter would turn to him for help, so he would always be aware of exactly how the case was proceeding."

"And yet you did not arrest Mr. Doyle?"

"I would have, within the next couple of days." That sounded like an excuse, and Monk could hear it in his own voice.

"What persuaded you, Mr. Monk?" Ravenswood sounded interested more than critical.

"The desire to have sufficient evidence to charge him also with the murder of Bella Franken, his ledger clerk, whose body—"

He was interrupted by a swelling murmur of horror and general disturbance in the gallery. For the first time, Monk looked across at the dock and saw an instant of surprise in Exeter's white face. Then it was gone again.

"Yes?" Ravenswood asked.

Where was Rathbone in all of this? He had not said a word yet.

"Whose body I found floating in the river," Monk said. "She had already approached me about errors in the ledger and made a second appointment to speak with me, which she did not keep because she was dead."

"And you are suggesting a connection?" Ravenswood asked.

Monk realized he had been led into springing Rathbone's trap too early.

"You are looking for me to do your job for you," Monk said a little tartly. "You ask me why I had not arrested Roger Doyle. Perhaps I should say only that Superintendent Runcorn arrested Mr. Exeter instead."

"Indeed. And I shall be asking him, in due course, to testify. Let us for now go back to the evening of the tragedy on Jacob's Island, if you please." It was not a request, however much it might have sounded like one. Ravenswood was very much in control of events. "You say you were attacked?"

"Yes."

"And Mr. Exeter was also attacked, as far as you could tell?"

"He was. There were marks on his face, his clothes were filthy as if he had fallen in the mud several times, and there was blood on his head and hands."

"Were any other of your men attacked?"

"Yes, all of them were, except the two left to mind the boats." Monk could hear the anger in his own voice. The whole affair still hurt: the pain of failure, the grief of Kate's death, and through it all the corroding misery of betrayal.

"So, the kidnappers took the money and killed the woman they had held hostage? A tragic outcome all around."

"Yes. And how the devil you think Exeter himself caused this, or ever had any part of it except in misjudgment, I cannot imagine."

"And you, too, Commander Monk. Did you not perhaps trust a man you should not have? How did it happen? How did the kidnappers know exactly where you would be, how you would come to the place they specified, how you would position your men, so they could overpower them one by one, unless someone told them that information?"

Monk forced out the words, and for an instant he hated Ravenswood for his smooth, gentle face as he spoke of such horror. "I don't know. I've searched the past, the family, and the circumstances of every man who was there, and I don't know!"

"You appear certain that Mr. Exeter is not guilty, and yet there is still a key element of this case that escapes you, is there not?" Ravenswood shook his head. He looked at the judge. "My lord, I have no more questions for this witness. After the luncheon adjournment I wish to call the police surgeon to give evidence as to the manner of Katherine Exeter's death."

The judge adjourned the court accordingly. Monk left the stand feeling miserable, as if he had somehow failed again, although he could not think of any answer he could have given differently.

THE AFTERNOON WENT QUICKLY. The police surgeon's testimony was clinical, and yet the matter-of-fact way he described Kate Exeter's wounds somehow made them more terrible. There was no horror in his voice, only an intense pity. In the rigidity of his body, he clearly felt a rage that any of this should happen to a living person, a sentient being capable of laughter, tenderness, and fear. He made her special as he described her wounds, and yet universal in the terror and destruction—the blood, the flesh, and the pain that could have been anyone's.

Monk walked out into the cold, already darkening afternoon beside Hester. He had not seen Hooper. He was not here because he was to testify the next day, and so was not allowed to attend in case anything he heard might influence him.

And he had not seen Rathbone, because he would no doubt be weighing the evidence of the day and preparing for tomorrow. He had not challenged anything so far, but what was there to contend? All the evidence had been only a matter of fact. He would not have wished the surgeon's testimony to be any longer than absolutely necessary. Monk had looked at the faces of the jurors and seen indelible horror. They were helpless to relieve any of it. It was fact, already passed into history. To have made light of it would be an offense against life itself. But justice was their domain, and they would want someone to pay. If they acquitted Exeter, then who would it be? Doyle?

But the police had charge of Exeter. Would actions, the need for someone to balance the scales for Kate, outweigh judgment or mercy for the husband who mourned her?

Monk and Hester went home by hansom, over Blackfriars Bridge. It was too cold to take a ferry over the water. They rode, both lost in their own silence, until they were at the door, and Monk brought in more coal and built up the fire. Hester had left a stew on at the back of the stove, and she brought it to the front, heated it up a little more, and served it in big bowls. They ate, and finally they spoke.

"I didn't expect Ravenswood to be . . . so gentle," Monk said at last. "I expected to be attacked more."

"He attacked, William," she said quietly. "You just didn't recognize it, until it was a little too late to alter your response." She hesitated a moment. "Not that there was anything you should have said differently."

"Oliver didn't do anything!"

"There really wasn't anything he could do, without seeming desperate," she pointed out. "If you attack every little thing, it looks as if you don't know where you're really going."

That was true, and yet he felt as if they weren't really fighting. He wondered if Exeter felt the same, that Rathbone had let him down and wasn't as clever as his reputation suggested. Monk looked at Hester. Were the same thoughts going through her mind? "Does he believe him?" he asked.

"You mean, does Oliver believe Exeter? Oh, I think so. He told me he did," she said with certainty. "Why? Are you wondering about Exeter now?" There was no avoiding the candor in her eyes.

"No, I'm wondering how we can pin Doyle down. I would never

have judged him to be so clever. I thought of him as a dull, local bank manager with ambitions to be socially acceptable, to go to the gentlemen's clubs as a member in his own right, not dependent on being a guest of his clients. I imagine managing all their money must be hard enough on his pride without being condescended to socially."

"If he wanted money and perhaps to feel superior for once," she asked, "then why kill Kate?"

"Because she recognized him," he said. "He couldn't afford to let her live."

"And Bella Franken?"

"Because she knew there was something wrong with the ledgers."

"And Lister, the real kidnapper?"

"He didn't want to share the money. And perhaps he tried a little blackmail."

"And the other men? There were far more than just Lister there. There had to be. Or did Doyle kill Lister alone? Does he look like a man who could take on a wiry, fighting sort of man like Lister?"

"Not at all. He must have taken him by surprise."

"I thought you said he was on the run, in an open boat?"

"He was," he agreed.

"So there must have been two of them, at least. You can't leave a boat to drift while you stop off and cut someone's throat!"

A coldness crept into Monk, as if they had inadvertently left the back door open. "You don't think we'll get him off, do you?"

"I don't know. I don't know that we're there yet. I'm sorry."

She had said "we." That was a kind of warmth, a comfort.

"Do you think Hooper betrayed me?" He was afraid of her answer, and yet that mattered to him so much he could not leave it unasked any longer.

"Hooper? Of course not! What makes you even ask, William?"

Because I know things that you don't, he thought. *Painful things that might cost everything one has. And I care more than I ever thought I would, or wanted to. But you won't hear that, without tearing yourself apart.*

"William?" she asked very quietly.

He could not answer honestly, so he said nothing at all.

19

The following day, Hooper was the first to testify. It was years since he had been so nervous about anything. He had nothing to say that was untrue, or was in any way his fault. He had done exactly as ordered. He did not know of anything that could have been done differently. Ravenswood was prosecuting Exeter and doing it, so far, without accusing the River Police of any kind of incompetence, except for one of them having betrayed them all to the kidnappers. And that had been hanging over them since the night they went home weary and so bitterly defeated.

Still, he climbed the steps to the top of the stand with a dry mouth. He swore to his identity and to tell the truth, the whole truth, and nothing but the truth, in a hoarse voice. Twice he had to clear his throat. The truth, yes—but the whole truth? Even his identity? The mutiny was always there in his mind, because he knew that others knew it. Fisk, for certain.

And Monk knew. At least, he knew what Hooper had told him, but did he believe it? Behind Hooper's gravity, even his gentleness, did he now doubt his loyalty? Was he disappointed even if his reason told him not to be, reminding him of his own vulnerability? The renegade that Runcorn had described Monk to have been would have understood it, and he would have agreed with it. But what about Monk now, the commander of the Thames River Police?

Sharp in Hooper's mind, with a cutting edge that hurt more than he would have believed, he also cared what Celia Darwin thought of him. He wanted her to see him as an honest and loyal man, a man to be respected, above all trusted, even with the possibility of the charge of mutiny over his head for the rest of his life. He could not court her—and he wanted to very much. But he could at least keep her good opinion of him, the belief that he was a man she could have loved, not someone she would never knowingly have associated with.

"Mr. Hooper . . ." Ravenswood's voice broke through his thoughts.

"Yes, sir," he replied, standing a little straighter.

"Under Commander Monk's directions, did you and the rest of the men on that fateful trip attempt to find the kidnappers and murderers of Mrs. Exeter?"

"Yes, sir."

"That would be yourself, Laker, Marbury, Bathurst, and Walcott? Is that right?"

"Yes, sir. And Mr. Monk himself."

"Even though one of you had informed the kidnappers of your plan?"

"It seems that way, but we did not know who, and we were reluctant to believe it."

"Did you have any suspicions yourself?"

How honest should he be? Suspicions were only thoughts. But it wasn't about truth or facts, not yet. It was about impressions. The jurors were watching him, listening to his tone of voice. They were judging him, not his exact words.

"I didn't think it was any of the men I knew well. I couldn't believe it of them. So, my attention went first to the new men, Marbury and Walcott," he answered.

Ravenswood smiled bleakly. "Had you said otherwise, I would not have believed you, unless, of course, you knew none of them was guilty, because it was yourself who betrayed them."

So soon! Hooper had thought that at some time the question would be put to him, but not yet and not without any warning. He must measure his words exactly, but he could not help the heat rising up his face. Would they take it as guilt? Or recognize it as fear? Would they even see that there was a difference?

"I did not betray them," he replied. "And I find it difficult and very painful to accept that anyone did."

"But you do accept it?" Ravenswood pressed. His voice was quite gentle.

"I think I have no choice," Hooper answered.

"I will see if I can offer you one, in due course." Ravenswood's smile was grim. "But for now, let us explore your investigations and see how they led you unwittingly to the only one of the kidnappers whose guilt seems to be unquestioned. Please describe for the court what you and Commander Monk did, and the order in which you did it, so that we may understand."

Detail by detail, Hooper recounted it. It sounded simpler than it had been because, worked backward from memory, it all made sense. He told them the reasoning behind each inquiry, and what they had heard of Lister spending money too freely, his appearance, what was known or believed of him.

"Did you arrest him, Mr. Hooper?"

"No, sir. We hoped that he would lead us to the others."

"And did he?"

"No, sir." Hooper wondered whether to mention the two men who had escaped after he and Monk pursued them from the roof, but since he did not know their names, and they had not done anything in Hooper's sight, it would sound like evasion.

"And Lister?" Ravenswood asked.

"We found him in a rowing boat, sir. I'm afraid he was dead. His throat had been cut."

"I see. Did you ever find out by whom?"

"No, sir."

"Did you ever find any other of the kidnappers? I assume you are satisfied Lister was one of them?"

"Yes, we are, and no, we didn't find any others." It sounded pathetic. Was it better to labor the fact of how hard they had tried, and still failed? Did that make them seem even more incompetent? "We decided it would be more profitable to follow the trail of the money. Lister's spending it too freely is what led us to him."

"So you told us. Did it help?"

"A young lady came to Commander Monk, secretly. She told him she was from the bank."

"That would be Bella Franken, from Nicholson's Bank?"

"Yes, sir."

"Where Mr. Doyle is the manager?"

"Yes, sir."

"Did you see her yourself?"

"No. But her information led us to examine the bank's records more closely, and to make inquiries about the manager, Mr. Doyle." He half expected Rathbone to object, but perhaps he was going to make more of this in his cross-questioning, or leave it until his defense. He would use it when he believed it would make the strongest impression on the jury. Was not Monk even now desperately searching for some thread that would lead him finally to Doyle, and possibly Doyle to some other enemy of Exeter's? "It was the only other reasonable line of suspicion we had."

"Yes, Mr. Doyle," Ravenswood agreed. "Miss Franken worked closely with him, I believe?"

"Yes, apparently."

"And what else was she able to show you?"

"Nothing. Commander Monk went to keep a second appointment with her and discovered her body in the river. Washed up, close to the Greenwich Pier."

"Did you see it, Mr. Hooper?" Ravenswood did not express any pity in words, but it filled his face.

"No, sir. Commander Monk called the local police."

"That would be Superintendent Runcorn?"

"Yes, sir."

"Have you continued to pursue the case since then?"

"Yes, sir."

"And found anything of value?"

"No, sir."

"Thank you, Mr. Hooper. Please remain there. Sir Oliver may have questions for you."

Rathbone stood, walked out in front of the witness stand, and looked up at Hooper. "Just a few questions about your observations, Mr. Hooper. The facts seem to be remarkably few. You have worked closely with Commander Monk for several years, have you not?"

"Yes, sir."

"And do you have a high respect for him?"

"The best officer I've ever worked with, sir." He could say that honestly. Monk was not perfect, but then a perfect man would not have understood the frailties of other men's natures, the foibles of their judgments, nor would he have understood those who through carelessness or greed fell into evil ways. He would not have been much good as a detective, or as a friend.

"Does he often make mistakes in judgment, either of men or of events?"

"Very seldom. Sometimes the evidence looks the other way, and it takes us a long time to understand it."

"You sound very certain of that."

"Yes, sir."

"Where is Mr. Monk now? I've not seen him in court."

"No, sir. He's still out hunting for the facts that will prove Mr. Exeter's innocence."

"He still believes Mr. Exeter is innocent?" Rathbone affected surprise. "Do you?"

"Yes, sir. We both do."

"Without naming anyone, is there someone else you suspect?"

"Yes, sir, there is."

"With cause, even if you cannot yet tell us what that cause is?"

"Yes, sir."

Rathbone smiled. "Thank you for having been most helpful. That is all." He did not even glance at the jurors. If he had, he would have been well satisfied by the smiles on their faces, the sudden sharpening of interest.

Hooper was excused as he went and sat in the gallery of the court. It was infinitely preferable to being skewered, flapping like a moth, in the stand. He sat down on the end of one of the benches. There was no space for him beside Hester, and he preferred not to sit there anyway. He did not know what Monk may have told her of the mutiny, or of anything else. Thinking of her and her judgment of him was more than he could cope with at the moment. It would too easily make him think of Celia and how she'd be affected if she knew. Her smile would leave, the steadiness of her eyes, the gratitude for his understanding, the friendship.

He forced the thoughts out of his mind as Doyle took the stand and was sworn in. He looked every inch what he was, at least professionally: a small-town bank manager dwarfed by the affairs of a very large city. In fact, the largest city in the world.

Had Doyle ever imagined this, when he set out to kidnap Kate Exeter? Had he meant just to gain her inheritance for himself, without violence, without murder after murder? Had he even meant to slash Lister's throat, to drown Bella Franken? He was standing in the witness box now, in the Old Bailey. He should be in the dock. And if Exeter was hanged, then Doyle was guilty of his death, too. In a way, that was the most horrific aspect of the situation.

Doyle looked miserable and frightened. He kept moving his neck and jaw, as if his collar were too tight. Was he imagining what a rope would feel like?

He swore to his name, address, and occupation, and to tell the entire truth. Perhaps Ravenswood would go lightly with him. Rathbone certainly would not. Please heaven Monk was finding something— anything—to cause a reasonable doubt! A connection to an enemy that one of Exeter's deals had ruined, a poisonous enemy.

Ravenswood led Doyle softly through his career at the bank and the years he had handled Exeter's accounts. He touched lightly on the profits and expenses, the enormous chances Exeter had taken, and the money he had made, and occasionally lost. Yes, he was indeed a client who had earned the bank a great deal of money. And yes, Doyle's own fortune had risen with Exeter's. Not to the same degree, of course, but more than most men's. A lot more.

"So, you owe much of your success to the fact that he is one of your clients?" Ravenswood asked.

"Yes, sir." Doyle shifted his weight as if his back pained him.

"Did he come to you when his wife was kidnapped and a very large ransom was demanded of him?"

"Yes, sir. He was very distressed."

"Did you help him realize his assets in order to have the money to hand over?"

Doyle looked uncomfortable. He answered slightly aggressively. "Yes, sir. He did not have the amount readily available in cash. Hardly anyone would. Selling property, even if you are prepared to take an immense loss, can still not be accomplished in so short a time." He cleared his throat. "And even if the kidnappers were prepared for urgent negotiations, say a week, what man would leave his wife in the captivity of such men even an hour longer than he could help? God alone knows what they might have done to her . . ." He trailed off, leaving it to the imagination. A glance at the jurors' faces made it nightmare-clear what they thought.

"Indeed." Ravenswood nodded gravely. "So, what did you do, Mr. Doyle?"

Doyle cleared his throat again. "Mrs. Exeter had a very large trust, which she would inherit on her thirty-third birthday, which was over a year away. Mr. Exeter asked the trustee, Mr. Maurice Latham, if he would consider using it to save her life. Of course, he agreed. It was lodged in my bank. With Mr. Latham's agreement, I had instant access to it. I gave it to Mr. Exeter, for the ransom of his wife, the saving of her life. I could hardly do less."

"Quite so," Ravenswood agreed. "And did Miss Franken assist you in these . . . preparations of yours, Mr. Doyle?"

Doyle's face froze for a moment, as if he had not expected this question. Surely, he had been prepared by Ravenswood? A good lawyer—never mind a brilliant one—does not ask questions to which he does not already know the answers.

"I . . . I do not wish to speak ill of the poor young woman," Doyle began. "But she was not as skilled or as experienced in banking as she thought. She is dead, poor creature. Can I say that she was diligent, a good student, but she had a tendency to leap to conclusions that were not justified. She had met Mrs. Exeter on a few occasions, and Mrs. Exeter had been very gracious to her. I'm afraid poor Bella took her death, and the manner of it, very hard."

"So, she could have read into the papers things that were not there?"

Doyle looked relieved. "Yes. Indeed, looking back on her remarks, I think she did. She did not fully comprehend the situation."

"And Miss Franken knew nothing that would harm your reputation in the bank, were she to confide in Mr. Monk?"

"If he found something amiss in it, it would be his lack of understanding of banking or figures. They can be confusing when you are not accustomed to dealing with them," Doyle replied. "There are fees to be paid for urgent transactions, which might look to someone unfamiliar with the process like miscalculations. And when one adds up columns of figures several times, one tends to make the same error each time. A person more experienced would do it upward one time, and downward the next. Books have to be balanced every day. Errors are quickly found." He seemed satisfied with the answer.

"And you did not confide in Miss Franken at all?"

"About the private accounts of a client? Certainly not."

"Because you did not trust her?"

"No. I would have dispensed with her services had I not trusted her. Simply because such accounts are private, and even more so at a time like that, when a woman's life hung in the balance. I think, sir, that much is obvious." Doyle sounded eminently reasonable, but there was a distinct discomfort in the way he stood, altering the balance of his weight every now and then.

"Did you have any idea of Miss Franken's personal life, Mr. Doyle?"

Doyle's eyebrows shot up. "Good heavens, no! As far as I know, and of course I inquired, her reputation was as a very respectable young woman. A little . . . bookish . . . to attract the attention of most men, if you know what I mean?"

"She lacked the opportunity to misbehave?" Ravenswood's face was difficult to read, but Hooper thought he disapproved of the un-kindness of the remark.

"I . . . I meant the temptation did not easily come her way," Doyle recovered himself. "Perhaps she preferred books." Then he must have realized that a perfect excuse to explain her death had been offered him, and he had refused it. He drew breath quickly. "I really did not take much notice of her personal affairs. Perhaps I should have done. The honest answer is that I don't know."

"But she was clever with figures?"

"Yes. Very."

"Is it possible she was better acquainted with Mr. Exeter than you were aware?"

This time, Doyle did not miss the opportunity. "I suppose it is."

Hooper listened as the afternoon wore on, but he could see noth-ing deeper than the lawyers moving cautiously, testing each other. The only drama lay in the minds of the audience in the gallery, pos-sibly in the tense and watchful jurors, and of course in the minds of the witnesses and of Harry Exeter, sitting white-faced and haggard in the dock.

The day finished with the forensic accountant that Runcorn had employed, who gave details no one understood of the figures in the bank's ledgers. He was able to show that there had been both licit and illicit movement of funds, and that a good deal of money had disap-peared from Katherine's trust over the years. It could have been in-vested, but badly, because there had been no yield. Mr. Doyle's own account had also grown considerably since the week after Kate Ex-eter's death. Mr. Latham's records were unavailable to be checked, but that was about to be rectified.

Mr. Doyle's personal accounts were also examined. Rathbone pushed this but could only make Doyle look greedy, and certainly opportunistic, if not worse. It raised the first natural doubt of Exeter's guilt.

Hooper was able to report this to Monk when he saw him in the early evening at the Wapping Police Station.

"Haven't you found anything?" he asked when he had finished.

Monk looked exhausted, and there was no energy coming from him to indicate he had a new idea to work on. The question was a matter of form.

"No. I've been looking further into Lister's associates. Someone must know who killed him, but they're very quiet indeed. Some people suggested they've gone to sea, to one of the big European ports. There's always labor needed there."

"Not many where strangers are welcome," Hooper pointed out. "More likely to stay at sea. That is, if they're seamen in the first place. Any idea at least of their names?"

Monk shook his head.

"And enemies who might be behind it all?" Hooper asked. "With Doyle or not?"

"No," Monk said flatly. "I've got men on it; so has Runcorn. We found a certain amount of dislike, envy, grievances over shared investments gone wrong, but they all seem to have taken it as the fortunes of business. Sometimes you win, sometimes you lose. Either Exeter is not hated as much as he fears, or his enemies have been better at hiding it than I can uncover."

They spoke a little longer and moved to memories of past times: of Orme and the house he had been going to build by the riverside, down the estuary a bit. They had both been thinking of the old loyalties, people who had been part of their lives. They were grieving not only for Orme, but for all the old memories and safeties that he represented. It gave some comfort; there were things that, for a moment at least, could not be tarnished by the present and what was going on at the Old Bailey.

HOOPER RETURNED TO THE trial the next day. Ravenswood had not finished presenting his case for the prosecution. Hooper knew from the focus of the jurors that Rathbone was going to have an uphill battle to win them over. But if any man on earth could do it, he could. Hooper had watched him win seemingly impossible cases before. So far, he had questioned hardly any of the evidence. Hooper looked at him sitting quietly in his seat at the front of the court, in his lawyer's white wig and black gown. He looked comfortable, biding his time. Please heaven, he was!

Ravenswood called Runcorn.

Runcorn crossed the floor and went up the steps to the witness stand. He was big, solid, heavy. He was quite a good-looking man in a long-nosed and solemn sort of way. He looked humorless, but Hooper knew he was not, only because he had seen him with the wife he adored—who was socially immeasurably above him, but also wise enough to recognize his worth—and with the baby daughter he could still hardly believe was real.

Runcorn swore to his identity and rank in the police.

Ravenswood asked about his being called to where the body of Bella Franken had been pulled out of the river. Runcorn replied with very little detail, but in spite of his best efforts to keep his feelings to himself, his deep sense of both pity and outrage marked his features and rang through his voice. Anyone listening might have imagined he saw, for a moment, his own wife or daughter used in such a way, and he could not bear it.

"You saw her pulled out of the river?" Ravenswood questioned.

"No, sir. Her body was already out of the water when I arrived."

"And you said Commander Monk pulled her out?"

"Yes, sir. At least, rightly put, I suppose he had to go in after her. She was beyond his reach from the dockside, which is where he was. I mean, he went in a boat in the water."

"So, he went in after her?"

"I didn't see, sir. But I have been told by numerous witnesses that that's more or less what happened. He was waiting for her. Had a meeting with her, to get more papers or something. And he saw her, did the only thing he could . . ."

"Oh?"

"Well, he couldn't leave her there," Runcorn's face showed clearly his opinion of anyone who would do that. "She might have been still alive! It's . . . possible . . . at least it could be. For heaven's sake, man, you wouldn't leave a woman in the water, would you?"

"I hope I wouldn't, Mr. Runcorn," Ravenswood said gently. "But it still takes a brave man to go willingly into that dark, swift-running water after a body that is almost certainly already dead."

"Well, Monk's that sort of a man," Runcorn said flatly. "And I've known him near on thirty years." His glare defied Ravenswood to question it.

"Then why did you take the case from him? She was found in the water. He knew her as a witness in a case he was handling, and he pulled her out. Why hand the solving of her death over to you? If ever a case belonged to the Thames River Police, this one does."

"As he was half-drowned and freezing cold," Runcorn said with a tone that made it sound as if the answer was obvious, "he was in no state to follow up. Just about caught his death in the river. Whoever did it could have still been around."

"I see. Did he identify her for you?"

"Yes. Told me briefly about her then, and more the next day."

"He was willing for you to keep the case, even when he had recovered from his near drowning himself?"

"Yes, sir. Glad of the help. Needed to get started straightaway."

Ravenswood drew out of Runcorn how he had questioned Doyle again, gone over all the evidence from the kidnapping itself, the finding of Lister, and then his death. Lastly, he spoke of the pursuit of the killer of Bella Franken, and the way it tied in with raising the ransom money.

"Lister had much of it, didn't he?" Ravenswood asked. "That was how Monk found him in the first place."

"Lot of money, sir, for a man like Lister. Not much for a man like Harry Exeter," Runcorn replied.

"Quite so," Ravenswood agreed.

"But why would a man steal money from his wife's trust, when in a matter of a year or so it would to all intents be his? That's what we have to understand," Runcorn said. "But the papers that Miss Franken brought to show Mr. Monk, they were wrapped up inside a piece of oiled silk, and you could still make out the figures. India ink. It's waterproof, sir. They explained it. If you're clever enough with ledger sheets and that kind of thing, you can move money and make it appear on the pages twice, when it's only one lot of money."

"I find that hard to believe, Mr. Runcorn. Are you saying that there was not as much money passed to Lister? Then where did he get it from?"

"There was more money passed to him, then only a bit. At least on paper. Same as Mr. Doyle got a bit for doing it. Quite a big bit. But Mr. Exeter got the main portion . . . or that's how it looked."

"It was his wife's money in the first place!" Ravenswood protested. "It would have been in his charge in a year!"

"Yes, sir. But he needed it before that. Mr. Exeter hadn't enough liquidity to build that large development on the south bank, and he needed the money up front, and urgently."

"Ah," Ravenswood said quietly. "That sounds very clear. I think we can all understand that. And you are quite satisfied, Mr. Runcorn, that Mr. Exeter hired Lister to play kidnapper? Mr. Exeter was observed by Monk and his crew during the exchange that went so disastrously wrong, and then Lister was killed to keep him quiet, and finally so was poor Miss Franken, when she disentangled the books and realized what he had done?"

"Yes, sir, I am."

"Just for the record, did Mr. Monk agree with your conclusions?"

"No, sir, he did not."

"And also there is, of course, the matter of embezzling from Mrs. Exeter's trust fund, which will be completely investigated, and to which Mr. Exeter had no access. But it would, no doubt, have come to light at the time of her inheritance? There is much to be looked into yet. Please remain in the witness box, Mr. Runcorn. Sir Oliver may want to question you."

But there was nothing left for Rathbone to ask. Ravenswood had drawn the story already from Runcorn's disagreement with Monk. There was little point in challenging any of the identifications of witnesses. Who can tell one man from another in the wind and rain of a November dusk?

Rathbone declined, and the judge adjourned for the day.

Hooper left the Old Bailey and walked down the slope of the street toward the river, wondering what on earth Rathbone would do the next day to begin the defense of Harry Exeter. He could pursue the embezzlement as much as he liked. Latham could account for his whereabouts at all the relevant times. He was a thief, but not a killer.

He could think of nothing that did not have the unmistakable air of desperation, and the jury would know it.

20

Rathbone began straightaway by calling Celia Darwin to the stand. Hooper was in his place again, in order to carry any message to Monk that might alter the course of the case, and to return to Rathbone with any last desperate evidence they might have found.

Hooper watched Celia walk across the floor and climb up to the stand, holding on to the rail. She looked a little clumsy, and she actually tripped on one of the steps, only just catching herself in time before she lost her balance completely. Hooper rose from his seat and then sank back again. He had no right to go to her assistance. He would make a fool of himself and only draw more attention to her. Clearly, she hated having to relive Kate's abduction, which she had tried futilely to prevent. It must haunt her every waking hour, whether she admitted it or not. Kate had been not only her cousin but her dearest friend, the one family member who remained close.

Celia turned when she reached the top of the steps and faced the room. As she took the oath her voice wavered, and once she actually stopped, as if she had lost the words. The usher prompted her, and she completed the ritual. Never once did she glance across at Harry Exeter in the dock.

Hooper looked up at him. He was staring at Celia fixedly, but Hooper could not read his expression. It could have been hope he was trying not to show, or perhaps he was endeavoring not to betray his fear or his vulnerability to the jury. He must hate being so exposed! Nothing of his old wealth, dignity, wit, and swagger was left to him.

Rathbone treated Celia with respect, at least in his manner. But he was acting for the defense, and Hooper knew now how much Celia disliked Exeter and had guessed how much he disliked her. Kate had remained her friend only because of her own insistence. Exeter had tried to wean her away from all her family, but especially Celia, who was from the branch that had missed out on the wealth, the social success, and all the general popularity. But Kate had found her one true friend and confidante in Celia, and she refused to set her aside.

What could Rathbone ask Celia, other than about the actual abduction, which she had seen? She had identified Lister once he was dead. Could he be going to challenge that? To what end? There must be some attack, or why would he bother?

Rathbone had already established Celia's friendship with Kate. In her account she reached the day of the abduction and the fact that they were walking along the riverbank in the sun, talking together of personal matters.

"And you turned away briefly?" Rathbone asked.

"Yes. I . . . wished to blow my nose," Celia answered. Such a personal digression seemed to embarrass her. "The sound . . ."

"Very natural," Rathbone responded. "What happened while your attention was diverted, Miss Darwin?"

"A young man came up the bank, from the direction of the river."

"If you did not see him come, how do you know from which direction?" Rathbone interrupted.

"Because I could see around us. If he had been anywhere near, on the path or on the grass, I would have seen him approaching." Her voice came levelly, perfectly polite.

Hooper, who knew her—at moments he felt he knew her very

well—noticed the tension in her. She was afraid. Of what? It troubled
Hooper because he did not understand. Actually, he did not understand why Rathbone had called her at all. That Lister had kidnapped
Kate from the river walk was not disputed by anyone. What else could
she know? He was for Exeter's defense. Hooper found his hands rigid
in his lap, his shoulders hunched.

"Quite so," Rathbone agreed. "What did you do when you saw
Mrs. Exeter was engaged in conversation? Were you alarmed?"

"No, not in the least. The man was quite well dressed, and she did
not seem frightened. I wondered if perhaps she knew him, or he just
found her attractive and hoped to make her acquaintance."

"You judged him to be a man of roughly her own social class?
Perhaps an acquaintance or a friend of one?"

"Yes."

"And then what happened?"

"They were walking, and so as not to seem to be eavesdropping, I
moved some distance from them. I lost sight of them when a group of
people passed between us. Then quite suddenly they were no longer
there."

"Did you recognize the man at all?"

"Not then."

"We will come to that later, in due course. But as of then, he was
not known to you?"

"That is correct."

"What did you do? Did you scream for help?"

"In the November wind, on a deserted riverbank?" she said a trifle
sharply. "I went for help, to find a policeman if I could, or anyone else
with the power to do something. I passed a nursemaid with children,
but she could hardly help me. Eventually I found a policeman and
repeated the whole incident to him. He was helpful, but by then
there was little he could do. By the evening, Harry—Mr. Exeter—
had received the ransom demand."

"Just so. Did you have any reason to suspect, any reason at all,
that he already knew of the kidnap, or that he had any part in it, Miss
Darwin?"

Her voice was very quiet. "None at all."

"Then, or at any other time?"

She was silent for several moments. What was she waiting for? Hooper stiffened.

"No," she said finally.

"Did the police take you to see if you could identify the man we now know as Lister, when he was dead?"

"Yes. It was the man I saw talking with Kate."

"You're quite sure?"

"Yes."

Rathbone hesitated a moment, then continued. "Did you see Mr. Exeter after Kate's death, Miss Darwin? I mean anytime after? To express your condolences, to show your grief, to be of any assistance that you might?"

"Of course. I saw him several times. I was most concerned for him." She took a deep breath, as if saying something that was difficult for her. "I saw his grief and I . . . I wished to offer any comfort I could. To . . . share my own grief. He visited me and was quite devastated."

Hooper sat forward in his seat. That was not what Celia had said to him. She had said Exeter had largely shut her out of his feelings altogether. Had she deliberately protected his moment of complete vulnerability, out of character for him, because she had been aware that Kate's friendship with her had irritated him? Celia had not been specific about it to Hooper. She would consider that indelicate to discuss, even a betrayal of Kate in some way. Could he have misunderstood her so completely? Her sensitivity in a way pleased him, but was it honest? Was she saying this to protect Exeter, now that he was charged with murder?

That would mean she did not believe he was guilty. But to lie about it? That was not the woman Hooper had thought he knew, even in so short an acquaintance. But how long does it take to fall in love?

Rathbone was speaking to her again.

"Miss Darwin, I realize it must be difficult for you. There has been more than enough tragedy in your family over the last months, but I need to ask you in some detail, you understand? To dispel the notion of Harry Exeter that my learned friend for the prosecution has presented, and replace it in the minds of the men who are to judge him with the picture you see. You have known him for years. You saw him during the time of the greatest grief and trial in his life. Perhaps you will begin with his reaction to his wife's death, if you please?"

It was several seconds before Celia started her reply. Hooper ached for her. She was being asked to relive her own pain and her observation of Exeter's distress, which should have been exquisitely private, a man at the extreme of his emotional agony. It seemed like a total betrayal, and yet it was necessary to save his life.

Hooper glanced for a moment up at the dock and saw the tension in Exeter. To look at him seemed intensely intrusive, even prurient, at such a time, and he turned away.

There was not a sound in the entire court. Not a person even shifted position.

Celia began in a low voice, making a visible effort to speak clearly and loudly enough to be heard, perhaps dreading having to do it again if she failed.

"At first he was totally distraught. He wouldn't see anyone. I think he could not face the reality of it, could not bear . . . what he saw . . . what had to be in his mind. The recollection of it was . . . awful, unspeakable. It takes time to face reality. I did not see her body . . ." she gulped, "slashed and . . ." She shivered and took a moment to get her voice under control.

Hooper longed to be able to help her, even to tell her she did not have to do this. But he knew that she did. In her mind, she was telling the truth, regardless of her own feelings and whether she liked Exeter or not. Hooper had felt certain that she did not, but she would not let him hang for a crime she profoundly believed he had not committed. Did she believe it was Doyle behind Kate's kidnap and murder? How she must loathe him! But she would not let fear of him or the pain of reliving that time make her keep silent.

"I did not want to disturb him, and I knew sight of me would distress him," she continued. "I was deeply, terribly grieved myself. Kate was . . ." She struggled against tears for a moment or two, then mastered herself. "Kate was my only close relative and my dearest friend. She was like a younger sister to me. I think that was . . ." She took a deep breath. "That was what made Harry come to see me at all. He understood my grief. He looked terrible. He looked twenty years older, and ill . . . terribly ill. I think we just sat silently that first time. Later, we talked . . . about Kate, how she was. What she enjoyed, what made her laugh, the flowers she cared for, wildflowers . . ." She could not stop the tears now, and she did not try. "Hawthorne in bloom, the smell of it, the bees. And bluebells in the spring, the beech woods full of them till there was nowhere to put your feet. So much birdsong!"

Rathbone interrupted her. "Thank you, Miss Darwin. You have explained to us very clearly, so that we feel as if we knew Kate as well. So, you sat together and shared your happy memories of the woman you both had loved."

It was a moment or two before Celia overcame her emotions. Finally, she lifted up her head. "Yes."

"Did it ever occur to you that Harry Exeter himself might be responsible for her death?"

"What?" She took a deep breath. Her whole body was shaking. "Of course not! The idea is . . . preposterous and repulsive."

"Were you acquainted with Miss Bella Franken?"

"Who?" She looked totally confused.

"The bank clerk whom Commander Monk found dead in the river," Rathbone explained.

"Yes. I had met her once. In a matter of . . . of Kate's trust."

"Bella Franken died sometime between six and eight o'clock on the evening of the twenty-ninth of November. Do you recall what you were doing at that time? On that day?"

In the gallery, everyone, men and women alike, sat motionless, as if they were paintings rather than people.

Hooper felt his own breath suffocate him.

"Yes," Celia said at last. "I was visiting Harry. We had supper . . ."

Her voice trailed off. "And we spoke of Kate." She finished in almost a whisper.

"So, he was at home at that time?" Rathbone pressed.

She fought for control of herself. "Yes."

"Thank you, Miss Darwin." Rathbone resumed his seat, nodding to Ravenswood.

Ravenswood hesitated, looking confused. It was obvious to Hooper, and must have been to the rest of the court, that he had not expected this testimony. If he had spoken to her before, she cannot have given it to him then. Was he going to try to shake her? Hooper felt hot at the thought, and then freezing. Would she be able to with-stand him? Was it the truth? She had mentioned none of it to Hooper. But then, it was her private life, her extended family. Why on earth should she have told Hooper anything about it? He realized with a wave of misery just how much he had presumed she had liked him, trusted him, when in truth it was possible that she was merely being polite. She was a courteous woman. She was probably polite to every-one. How foolish of him, how very vulnerable and naïve! It could be excused a nineteen-year-old, but not a man in his early fifties.

Ravenswood stood up at last. "Miss Darwin, you mentioned none of this before when we spoke. Why was that?"

She looked surprised. "Did I not? I . . . I'm sorry . . . I must have forgotten. Or perhaps I did not understand your question. I was very distressed by Kate's death and the manner of it. And I was so . . . so grieved for myself, and for Harry. I did not mean to mislead you." She looked very miserable, as if she had a pain deep within that was tear-ing her apart, something so deep she was barely in control of herself.

"Did Mr. Exeter ask you to say that you were at his house for sup-per the night Bella Franken was killed?" Ravenswood's voice was soft, but his expression offered no forgiveness for evasion. "Think care-fully, please."

She breathed in and out, trying to keep command of herself. Then she opened her eyes, tears running down her cheeks. "No, Mr. Ravenswood, I am quite sure."

Ravenswood hesitated, doubt, pity, and finally defeat all reflected in his face. "Then I have no further questions. Thank you."

The judge offered Rathbone the opportunity to speak to Celia again, but he had won, and he knew it.

The judge adjourned the court for the day and told Rathbone to call his final witness when they reconvened tomorrow.

Hooper should go and find Monk and tell him that they had won—or very nearly. Exeter would tell his own story. He must feel safe to do so now. If he made no major error, he would be found not guilty. Probably Doyle would be arrested, and Maurice Latham, too, regarding the embezzlement. But the edge was gone; they could not convict Harry Exeter now. It was victory snatched from the jaws of defeat. Why did Hooper feel so terrible?

Everyone was leaving the court. Hooper stood up and followed the stream of people going out into the bleak winter air. Celia would probably be going home. He spotted her in the crowd easily by her walk and her isolation. She looked as if she'd been leaving the funeral of all she loved. Her step was even slower than usual, her shoulders bowed. She was probably making for the river and the ferry home again. Or perhaps she would take a hansom all the way and go across one of the many bridges.

Hooper was walking swiftly to catch up with her. Why? What could he say to her? He had no right to say anything at all. Still, he walked as fast as he could, until he was level with her. The emotion was so choking inside him that he did not even stop to think of the inappropriateness of it. If she was not furious with him, he had nothing else to lose now. He caught her arm, not hard, but enough to cause her to stop abruptly and swing round to face him. Her eyes were angry and full of tears.

"I'm sorry," he said immediately. "I . . ." Then he did not know what to say. She had lied, and he knew it, but he had no idea why. What on earth would make a woman like her tell a lie, and under oath? It was against everything he thought he knew of her. Was he so wrong? It was not her face that attracted him, although it pleased him; it was her voice a little, but it was really her purity. What a funny choice of word! It was the inner honesty and gentleness in her that pleased him so intensely. He had to speak. He had spent far too much time thinking of her, imagining what it would be like to know her.

"Please leave me alone, Mr. Hooper," she said quietly. "I did what I had to. There really isn't anything to say."

"You have to protect him? Why? For Kate's sake? Do you really think that's what she would want you to do? Is he going to say something of her that's . . . ?" He began to see what the reason could be. "Are you protecting her memory? What could he say? Nothing could justify what was done to her."

She pulled her arm away from him, looking not at him but straight ahead of her. "No. It was nothing to do with Kate. You . . . you don't understand at all. Please leave me alone."

He moved to block her way. He was not thinking, just reacting to his own emotions, the beliefs he had of her. "He'll get away with it! Is that what you think is right?"

"Maybe Doyle did it." Still she did not look at him. He had believed because he thought he knew how she disliked Exeter, far too much to have shared her grief for Kate with him. He had guessed she was lying because she seemed almost ashamed of what she was saying. Now he was convinced she was lying, but why?

"Who are you protecting?" he asked, letting his hand fall from her arm. "Why? Do you really think it was Doyle who killed her?"

"There's no way out of it. Please, John, leave it alone." It was the first time she had used his name. It mattered. It was an expression of instinct, as if she had touched him.

"Do you know how serious it is to lie?" he said more gently.

She swung round to look at him again, her eyes filled with tears. "Yes, of course I do. Just . . . leave it alone! You don't know Harry! He will do what he says. He'll have nothing to lose, and he won't go alone. He'll see everyone else suffers, too!" She was crying now, and terrified.

The two of them stood in the street, in the wind and the rain, as if there was no one else around.

"He did it, didn't he? And you know it. How can he hurt you? Tell me. Perhaps I can stop it." He spoke gently now. He wanted to protect her more than he could remember ever having wanted anything else. "Celia! What will he do if they find him guilty?"

"Leave it alone!" she said again.

"Will he do something to you? If he's hanged, he can't hurt you physically. Is it your house, your means? Are you dependent on him for something?"

"Oh, for heaven's sake! Do you think I'd let him get away with it for that?" She was angry now. "Just leave it be. Isn't there anything you're afraid of? Really afraid?" She was looking directly at him now, her eyes blazing.

"Not enough to save a man who would do that to a woman," he replied. "You didn't see her body." The minute the words were out, he would have given anything to take them back. Her face was ashen, and she was shaking. But it was too late.

"Hanging is not a nice death." Tears almost choked her voice.

"I know. And I wouldn't choose to have him hanged," Hooper answered quietly. He touched her gently, hardly feeling her flesh through the thick coat. "But it isn't up to me. They'll hang whoever it was. Doyle, if it's him."

"It's got nothing to do with Doyle," she said in exasperation. "He's a silly, greedy man, but he hasn't killed anyone. Harry's as near evil as a man can be. He killed Kate and Lister and that poor girl in the bank. And he'll kill you just as easily."

"Me? He can't touch me from jail!"

"Oh, for goodness's sake! Fisk can, and Ledburn."

Hooper felt as if he had suddenly been stripped naked to the icy wind. He was cold to the bone. That was why she had mentioned hanging. They hanged mutineers. She had lied under oath, not to save Harry Exeter, but to save him, John Hooper.

"How . . . ?" he stammered. Then his throat seemed to close as he gasped for breath.

Now she was looking at him clearly, without pretense, not caring that he knew her feelings. "He was looking for which of Commander

Monk's men he could blame for betraying you. Looking for weaknesses."

"We . . . we didn't . . ."

"Of course you didn't. He did it himself. But he couldn't have you know that. He read about the mutiny. He found the Ledburn family. They're still alive. Captain Ledburn had a younger brother. At least that's what Harry told me. And he made it very clear: if he hangs, so will you. Now just leave it alone, please. The only thing is that if they don't hang Harry, you have to make sure they don't hang Doyle for it—if he had no part, except to take a bit of money."

"Why? Why did Harry kill Kate?" He was bewildered.

"Because she was beginning to realize what he was," she answered. "How he made some of his money. She would have left him and taken her trust money with her. Now leave me. Please."

"I can't." He could hardly believe he was saying the words, but there was no choice. It had caught up with him at last, and there was nothing good left but to act with honor. He realized just how much he cared for her. That she was prepared to do this to save him was reward for anything. "We must tell Monk, and I'll face the charge. I've been running away too long. I didn't kill Captain Ledburn. I tried to save him. If you believe that, I'll take my chance with the court. Fisk knows it's true." He must say that quickly, before the reality of what he was doing sank in.

She looked at him very steadily. Twice she nearly spoke and then changed her mind. What was there to say?

Slowly he bent and kissed her. He held on to her for as long as he could, as long as he dared. This kiss might have to last forever. Then he took her arm and they walked to find the nearest hansom to the Wapping Police Station.

21

"WHAT?" MONK COULD HARDLY believe it. And yet, standing in the Wapping Police Station looking at Hooper and the white-faced and determined figure of Celia Darwin, his struggle against acceptance was over before it began. There was no question in his mind that she was speaking the truth. The cost to her would be immense. She had lied under oath, yet her reasons were so blindingly clear.

Piece by piece it all fell into place. Exeter was guilty. From the very beginning he had chosen Monk to play his part. He was ideal for it! Brave, clever, but not clever enough. His own wife, whom he loved even more deeply than perhaps he had ever acknowledged, had been kidnapped. Monk identified with Exeter from the start, because he understood exactly the emotions that Exeter had affected to feel. All the fears were magnified, the guilt because Hester was saved but Kate had been lost. Monk had put himself in Exeter's place, exactly as Exeter had intended.

It wasn't about love, or even about the men who had envied Exeter's success and perhaps blamed him for their own losses. It was about money and the wounded vanity of a man whose wife intended to leave him, for all the world to see.

Monk must make sure Exeter was convicted somehow, without lying, without sacrificing Hooper or Celia Darwin. He had one night to find a way to do that.

He must go home—think! All night if necessary.

He opened the front door of his house and saw the lights on in the kitchen. Never could he remember feeling so glad to know that Hester was home. His spirits lifted and the warm air wrapped around him. She called out from the kitchen, and when he did not go to her, she came out to find him.

"What is it?" She hurried forward. "William? What's happened?"

Wordlessly, he drew her toward him and put his arms around her, holding her tightly.

She stayed with him for several moments, then pulled away. "What is it?" she said again. "Are you going to lose the case? Is it worse than that? You know which of your men betrayed you?" She searched his face, his eyes. "Not Hooper. I don't believe that."

"No." He spoke at last, his voice sounding husky. "Nobody betrayed us. I should have known all along. I'm sorry. I was wrong. Wrong about the whole case."

She frowned and pulled away a little, looking into his eyes. "Wrong about what? Who?"

"Just about everything," he said. "And unless I can work out how to do it, tomorrow the case is going to close. Exeter will be found not guilty. You know he can never be tried again for any of these murders? Not Kate, not Lister, nor Bella Franken—and if they convict Doyle, not for his death either."

"William . . ." Her voice froze. There was horror and the beginning of realization in her eyes, but she did not yet see clearly what it was she feared; only that he feared it, too.

"He will have got away with it. He killed them all, even Kate," he said.

"But he was with you! And there were other men there."

"No, there weren't. We thought about it hard, Hooper and I. Wrote down a plan of Jacob's Island and worked it out."

She could not see it.

"If Laker and I have a fight," he explained, "rough each other up quite a bit, and then tell you we were attacked by two men, already you have four in the fight, when in fact there were only two," he explained. "Exeter was fairly thoroughly beaten. He said it was kidnappers. It could as easily have been like the fight Laker had, where he thought I was a kidnapper. And I thought he was. Multiply that. It only took two of them, and it would seem to be at least four—if Exeter knew exactly where each of us was. And he did: he actually drew it up."

"Exeter and Lister?" she asked.

"Yes."

"Did Lister kill Kate, then, and Exeter took his revenge on him later?"

"No. I believe Exeter killed her himself, while Lister kept us busy. Exeter killed Lister later on, to keep him quiet."

"That's . . . terrible. But why?" She was fighting herself whether to believe him and the horror of it. There had to be some other explanation.

He could see it so clearly in her eyes, because he had felt that himself as Hooper was telling him. "Because he's corrupt, and she knew it and was on the verge of leaving him. And of course taking her own money with her. This way, she is dead, the picture of the perfect marriage is preserved, and he gets her money as ransom. Nobody is pushing him to pay his debts because they all know, or think they know, that he hasn't got the money now. He has, instead, a most public sympathy."

"And Bella Franken was beginning to see that?"

"Yes."

"So he killed her and threw her body in the river? But William, Celia Darwin, who is Kate's cousin and closest friend, testified that she was with Exeter at his house at the exact moment Bella was found. And she can't have been killed more than a few minutes before that, or the river would have swept her—"

He did not let her finish. "I know. Celia lied."

"Why?" she demanded. "It was clear she absolutely hated saying it, but honesty compelled her. Anyone could see that."

"No. Love compelled her."

"Love! William, she loathes him. She's hiding it well because she's been brought up not to feel such things, and above all, not to own that you do. But I could see it, and so could any other woman in that court who wasn't asleep!"

"You saw a woman forced to lie or see the man she loves hanged!" he corrected her.

Hester was incredulous. "She loves Exeter? I don't believe it. You've got something terribly wrong."

"No!" He dismissed the idea as almost blasphemous. "She hates him as much as few hate at all! She loves Hooper."

"Hooper?" Hester took a deep breath and let herself smile. "Of course! They are perfect for each other, but—"

"I have to tell you something else," he cut across her. "An old story, which Exeter will expose if she tells the truth."

"Come into the kitchen. It's warm. I've got soup on the stove. You're freezing. And I'm not going to stand here in the hall any longer." She pulled away from him, and he felt the separation like a jarring break.

He followed her and accepted the soup while he told her the full story of the mutiny and Hooper's part in it, and Captain Ledburn's death.

She sat white-faced, her own soup untouched. "What can we do? They'll hang Hooper. Mutiny is a very serious crime, and they can't afford to let it go. You can't let that happen, not to Hooper. He's . . . one of the best—"

"I know," he cut across her. "That's why Celia Darwin lied. And Exeter will have been tried and found not guilty, so afterward it doesn't matter what we learn, or what we can prove. He cannot be tried again. And I brought that about, Hester. It's my fault. And the worst of it is, he still knows about Hooper and could turn him in. He'll have that over our heads as long as he lives."

"But then we . . ." The breath went out of her. "It doesn't matter, does it? Once he's been found not guilty . . . the bastard! The utter . . . I haven't got a word vile enough!" She said it helplessly, as if not putting a name to it were the final defeat.

"Hooper won't let her," Monk said quietly. "He'll tell them himself, if she won't withdraw it, but better for her if she does. She'll pay a heavy price if he confesses it instead. But he will. He can see that once Exeter is cleared, he's untouchable, and the law will want someone to pay for these deaths—four, if they hang Doyle. He'll not let that happen." The look on Hooper's face as he had said that would haunt Monk's mind for the rest of his life.

"What can we do?" Hester looked as if she were going to add something, but fell silent.

"First thing is, I'm going to tell Rathbone. He has to know the truth."

Very slowly she shook her head. "You can't. You'd put him in an impossible position. Exeter is his client, and he's guilty. You know that, but Oliver doesn't. He still has to represent him to the best of his ability."

"I know—but I can't let this happen."

"Oliver will know Exeter lied to him, but only because you say so, not from any facts anyone has told him," she pointed out. "And Celia has lied, too, under oath. Hooper lied by omission. I know that in a way it's no one else's concern, but do you think the jury will see it that way? You believe him because you know him."

"Stop!" he said abruptly. "I believe Hooper, and I believe Celia Darwin. I've got to find a way to save them . . . I don't mean from the law! I mean from the guilt of knowing they let a triple murderer go free and an innocent man hang in his place." He gritted his teeth. "And if all this is true, and I believe it is, I can't think how I could have been so gullible."

"Because you saw yourself in him," she said quietly. "He played on that. You imagined his pain and his grief as if it had been yours. What kind of a man would you be if you had not?"

"It's little excuse," he said impatiently. "I still need to put it right. Do you think Exeter will let them live indefinitely, knowing what they do? He killed Lister. He killed Bella Franken. He killed Kate. Do you think he wouldn't kill Celia? She hates him, and she knows him through and through."

Hester's face was white. She had not even considered that, but she saw it immediately now. "All right! I see. We must put this right ourselves, though. We can't do it by putting Oliver in a position that will ruin him. His job is to defend Exeter to the best of his ability— not to be his judge—and by failing to do his job to the fullest of his skills, he will be his executioner. All the witnesses have already testified. We have to do something with what's left."

"That's only Exeter," he pointed out.

"Then that's what we must use."

"How? Exeter is his own witness. And it's Oliver's job to help him clear himself. He's not going to lead him into giving himself away."

She looked consumed by the desperation she felt. "Then Ravenswood will have to do it. That's all there is left. You're sure about Hooper, William? They will—" She stopped. They both knew the words, but she could not bring herself to say them.

"Hang him," he finished, his voice choking in his throat as he said it. "I know. So does he. This is his decision. He will not let Celia Darwin carry this for the rest of her life. And I daresay he also thought of the fact that Exeter will hold it over her, until he can find a way to kill her and get away with it. He would also, in a sense, own Hooper . . ." He did not need to finish the sentence.

"And you," she pointed out. "You knew who Hooper was, and you didn't turn him in."

"Turn him in!" He was horrified until he realized that, strictly, under the law, perhaps he should have, and have left it to the courts to decide whether Hooper was speaking the truth. "No. You're right. We must go and see Ravenswood."

"Now," she agreed. "There is no time to waste. Please heaven he's at home. Where does he live?"

"Oliver will know. We'll ask him on the way. This can't wait. If we have to hunt him down at dinner or the theater, we'll do it."

"He'll be at home, going over his case," she said with certainty. "He's losing."

THEY FOUND RAVENSWOOD WITH no difficulty and, an hour later, were shown into his quiet study.

"I cannot spare you very long, Mr. Monk." He glanced at Hester to include her in the apology. "I have to close tomorrow. And I have no idea what I'm going to say. Miss Darwin's testimony caught me completely off balance. When I spoke to her a few days ago, she gave me no inkling whatsoever of this."

Monk had been considering how much to tell Ravenswood of the truth and now felt that, as much as he wished to protect Hooper, he must tell all.

"She didn't know then any reason not to speak as she did," he said. "I can't tell you how to proceed, but she was lying and will now, I think, tell you everything."

Ravenswood looked dubious.

Monk spoke without hesitation. He told Ravenswood the whole story of the mutiny, as Hooper had told him, and then about the pressure put upon Celia with the threat. Then he explained how he believed the murder of Kate Exeter had happened, with no more than Exeter and Lister on Jacob's Island. There had been no betrayer among Monk's men. He knew that now with certainty. It was all Exeter's deliberate creation. The relief was wonderful, like a dawn light spreading through everything. But it showed many things unseen before. The distrust and misery that had been sown by the suggestion had made everything seem different. That was how Monk had heard of the mutiny.

"This man, Fisk," Ravenswood interrupted, "he would say the same?"

"Yes."

"And Ledburn was the captain's name?"

"Yes."

"I remember the affair, vaguely. Hooper realizes he may hang, in spite of all we can do?" The pain in his face was acute in the lamplight, and his voice carried it as well.

"Yes," Monk said huskily. "But he won't live with the lie. Nor will he allow Miss Darwin to."

"There must be something you can do," Hester interrupted. "Once the verdict comes in that Exeter is not guilty, he'll be free for the rest of his life! And he may well kill Celia after a little while, just in case she changes her mind. To . . . tidy up, as it were."

"Yes, I see that, Mrs. Monk." Ravenswood did not argue.

"Exeter's going to testify. He's cocksure," she went on. "Can't you get him to say something that will open up a . . . chance to trip him? Then another . . . and another?" She leaned forward a little. "He thinks he's got away with it. Three murders, four if they hang Doyle for it. And they'll have to hang someone! Public opinion won't let it go. And he'll have got away with it all!" The anger made her voice sharp, desperate.

Ravenswood was thinking.

"He's vain," Hester went on, leaning forward a little further. "He thinks he's cleverer than all of us—you," she amended quickly. "He thinks Celia is stupid. Inferior. And he wants the world to think he and Kate were idyllically happy, that she adored him. You've got to be able to make something of that. Trip him up. Once will be enough. If you don't, not only will he get away with it, but the good people—and Hooper is good, really good—will suffer. Celia may even get killed, too," she reiterated. "You—"

Ravenswood held up his hand. "I understand, Mrs. Monk." There was a very faint smile on his lips. He turned to Monk. "Are you prepared to work all night?"

"Yes," Monk said immediately.

"Of course," Hester agreed.

Ravenswood looked slightly taken aback. He started to speak, but she cut across him.

"I was with Miss Nightingale in the Crimea," she said simply. She saw in his face that it was enough. She did not ask whether he had lost anybody he loved in that senseless and bloody war. Everyone knew Florence Nightingale's name.

"Very well," he said with a new respect in his voice. "We need to find this man Fisk, which should not be difficult if he works for Runcorn. And if we are to save Hooper, then we need to find the survivors of the Ledburn family. If possible, one of them may tell the truth about the captain, or at least enough of it to substantiate what Fisk and Hooper say of events. And we must persuade Miss Darwin to amend her testimony, regardless of what it costs her. That may not be easy. She will be admitting she lied to protect a man she loves, who has made no such commitment to her. Rathbone will not like doing it, and he will have to attempt to destroy her credibility. And that will involve embarrassing her profoundly, humiliating her even." He looked from one to the other of them.

Monk turned to Hester. "Would she do that?"

"We must give her that choice," Hester replied. "We have no right to make it for her."

"She may not realize—" Ravenswood began.

"It is very gracious of men to protect us," Hester snapped. "It is also extremely condescending. We would like the dignity of making our own decisions."

"Even if they are wrong?" Ravenswood said quite gently.

She gave a tiny shrug. "I am tempted to say that we are never wrong. Which would be ridiculous. All of us are wrong at times. Even men! But you never grow up if you are treated like a child and someone else makes all your big decisions for you."

"She may pay very . . ." Monk started to argue, then saw the expression in her eyes and decided it would be time wasted. Time they could not afford.

"We will work all night," she said firmly. "Where do you wish to begin?"

WHEN MONK AND HESTER arrived in the court the following morning, Ravenswood was already in his seat, but he looked haggard, with deep circles under his eyes. Monk knew that he could not have had more than an hour and a half of sleep, if that.

Rathbone looked his usual self, except with extra energy, because he was on the brink of victory in a case he had expected to lose.

Monk felt a stab of guilt so deep it was almost physical. But to have warned Rathbone would have compromised him in a way that lasted far longer than the brief pain of losing this battle—if that could be brought about!

Exeter was on the witness stand. He looked pale, but more intensely alive than he had in the dock. He had taken an immense gamble, and he could smell victory. Now he was answering some question Rathbone had asked him.

"It was the most terrible day of my life," he said quietly.

The atmosphere in the room had altered palpably. In the past, the jurors and the people in the gallery had looked on him as a monster. They had stared with loathing, fear, even hatred as he sat in the dock. Since Celia's testimony, he was a hero, wrongly persecuted, deserving of all the admiration and support they could give him. Perhaps because they had made no secret of their feelings before, they were plagued by guilt now and the hunger to make amends.

Monk felt Hester's hand creep into his and clasp it firmly.

Rathbone led Exeter through the succeeding days of grief, the mounting suspicion of the police, and his eventual arrest.

"Yes," said Exeter. "But it wasn't Commander Monk who arrested me."

"Oh?" Rathbone feigned surprise. "Who was it?"

"Superintendent Runcorn. I . . ." Exeter smiled, a charming, slightly lopsided gesture. "I don't think Monk honestly ever thought I was guilty. And much as he hated it, he knew it was one of his own men who betrayed us to the kidnappers."

There it was! Ravenswood's chance. Did he see it? Monk gripped Hester's hand so hard he crushed her fingers without meaning to.

"A painful experience for him," Rathbone agreed. "Did he visit you in jail?"

"Yes. He came to see me immediately and promised to get me all the assistance he could. It was he who informed you, I believe?"

"Indeed, it was," Rathbone agreed.

He then led Exeter into more details of his financial affairs, ending up by referring again to Celia's testimony that she had been with Exeter at the time of Bella Franken's death.

"Did it surprise you that Miss Darwin came forward?"

"A little. We had not been close, but she certainly has been loyal all through this. She is a very quiet, retiring woman, but perhaps Kate's . . ." He appeared to be fighting his emotions, which threatened to run out of control. "Kate's closest friend."

"Why did you not tell the police this at the beginning?" Rathbone asked.

"I should have. I . . . was still so distressed, I did not know it was the same time. I mean . . . I knew what time Celia came, but I did not realize what time Miss Franken had died. Kate's death . . . losing her like that . . . I was not able to master my feelings, my pain. I find that there are gaps in my recollection of things, of ordinary things. It was Celia herself, even in her grief, who brought it to my mind."

"Thank you," Rathbone said seriously. "Will you wait there in case my learned friend has some questions for you?"

"Of course."

Rathbone walked back to his seat. Ravenswood stood up. He walked slowly out onto the center of the floor and looked up at Exeter.

"You said, Mr. Exeter, that Commander Monk knew it was one of his men who betrayed you to the kidnappers? You mean, who told them the way you were going to come into the meeting place in the slums of Jacob's Island?"

"Yes."

"Did that make a great difference, really? I know it was described for the court, but I am a little lost. Would you not pass each other regardless? I didn't know of betrayals." Ravenswood looked confused.

Exeter leaned forward a little in the witness stand. "There are at least three ways in, two by sea and one or two by land. They all could lead in several different directions. Imagine a large house, joined to another, with certain walls at least partially washed away and beams rotted."

"Sounds appalling!" Ravenswood shuddered. "But you describe it very well. In fact, rather better than Mr. Monk does."

Exeter smiled. Did he not realize how well he had described a place he purported not to know?

Ravenswood smiled back. "And one of Monk's men betrayed to the waiting kidnappers which way you were going to come in, so you could be ambushed?"

"Yes . . ." Exeter's face showed that he sensed there was something wrong, without knowing exactly what it was.

Ravenswood did not strike yet.

"Did he ever find out which of his men it was?"

Exeter was surprised. "Not that he told me."

"And you did not know?"

Again, Exeter hesitated. He glanced sideways at Rathbone and then back at Ravenswood. "I . . . suspected."

"Whom did you suspect? Mr. Exeter, you must have hated this man very much indeed. You would hardly be human if you did not hold him accountable for the terrible death of your wife and all the grief that has followed." He waited with his eyebrows slightly raised, as if it were a question.

Rathbone started to object and then changed his mind. It was clear from his face that this was not going according to his plan or foresight. The trial was over. What was Ravenswood doing?

Monk averted his eyes and kept them from meeting Rathbone's.

"And why did you suspect whichever one of Monk's men that you did, Mr. Exeter? Did you tell Monk? Challenge him to clear the man? It is a very serious charge. In a way, it is akin to murder. If he was guilty, then he is directly responsible for your wife's appalling death, is he not?"

Monk felt Hester's grip tighten on his hand again. Ravenswood was playing a dangerous game, but he was playing it to win. Monk felt a certain warmth toward the man.

"Yes," Exeter agreed. "He was." He let the emotions show again.

Monk hated him with a sudden fury. He had taken them all in, Monk included. Now he was getting ready to throw Hooper to the wolves. There was a dreadful inevitability to this. Please God they had made the right choice!

"Don't play this for drama, Mr. Exeter," Ravenswood said with dignified disapproval. "This is a court of law, not a theater."

A tide of color washed up Exeter's face, which was surprisingly unflattering.

Rathbone looked confused. He had been in complete control until a few minutes ago. Acquittal was within his grasp. Now something had radically changed, and he did not yet understand what it was.

Exeter started to speak, leaning forward over the railing, then abruptly changed his mind.

"If you did not want to tell Monk before," Ravenswood went on, "tell him now. Doesn't he need to know? Don't we all? Whether it is you, or Doyle, or whoever else, that man is responsible for your wife's death! Who betrayed her? Why? How do you know?"

"It was Hooper!" Exeter's voice was shrill. "John Hooper." All the ease, the charm, vanished out of his face.

"Indeed. How do you know this?"

"Because I know what sort of a man he is, and maybe Doyle, or whoever it was who killed Kate, knew it, too. Blackmail is a powerful weapon when you know a secret that will send a man to the gallows."

"Indeed, it is," Ravenswood said, his voice touched by sadness. He hesitated, clearly making a major decision. He looked down for a moment and then looked up again, directly at Exeter. "And is that secret that he was a merchant seaman before he joined the police? In fact, first mate on the *Mary Grace* when she hit a gale off the coast of Africa and very nearly ran aground because the captain had misread, or miscalculated, their position? All the men knew and tried to persuade him to alter course, further out to sea, to ride out the storm. But it was Hooper, the second in command, who faced him down. The captain attacked him, was struck by a boom as the ship veered, and was knocked to the side rail. Hooper dived after him, hung on to him for agonizing seconds, but the captain was a big man, heavy, and he slipped from Hooper's grasp."

There was a silence so tense each man could hear his own breath.

"You wonder how I knew that?" Ravenswood asked calmly. "My dear man, it is my job. I heard it from Captain Ledburn's family, just as you did. And the basis of what actually happened from another member of the crew, who works for Superintendent Runcorn. I shall call him as a witness, if his lordship will permit me. A rebuttal witness, you understand, because regrettably I need to prove that Miss Celia Darwin's testimony was given under duress by you, on the threat of sending Mr. Hooper to the gallows." He was interrupted by a gasp from the gallery, a wave of shock like the first murmur of a breaking storm.

In the stand Exeter was rigid, his face mottled with purple.

Rathbone looked one way and then the other. Then his dismay melted into a dazed realization.

The crowd subsided, utterly silent now, waiting.

Ravenswood continued, "As Mr. Doyle would have been, if convicted of the crime with which he would be charged."

Monk felt poised on the edge of victory, appallingly guilty of what he had done to Rathbone, and yet he could see no way out of it. In the stand, Exeter was almost frozen in disbelief.

The judge looked at Rathbone. "Sir Oliver, do you need time to consult with your client? Do you wish to call Mr. . . . er . . . Fisk, is it?"

Rathbone rose to his feet. "Yes, my lord. Thank you. I think perhaps it is best we leave no doubt in the jury's mind as to who is telling the truth. Mr. Fisk may say something entirely different under oath. Either way, my client has the right to face his accuser and rebut his accusations." He did not look up at Exeter in the stand.

Monk had known Rathbone well for years. They had won all sorts of cases together. Rathbone would not give up, whatever vortex whirled around his mind at this moment. Could he possibly still believe Exeter innocent? He had to fight anyway. He was sworn to take part on Exeter's side, whatever his private opinion of the man—unless he knew something both certain and provable to the contrary. He would take care not to put himself in that position.

Exeter was temporarily excused. Stiffly fumbling his way down the steps, his face contorted with rage, he was escorted back to the dock.

Fisk was duly called. As Ravenswood had said, he was in court, and it took only a few moments for the usher to find him outside.

He walked down the aisle of the gallery in such silence that one could hear the creak of corsets as a woman turned to look at him. He took the witness stand and swore to his identity and present occupation in the Metropolitan Police, stationed at Greenwich.

"Thank you, Mr. Fisk," Ravenswood addressed him. "Were you previously in the Merchant Navy?"

"Yes, sir."

"And some twenty years ago, you were on board the *Mary Grace*, off the coast of Africa, under the command of Captain Ledburn?"

"Yes, sir."

"Will you please give this court a brief account of the events, as you know them from your own observations, leading up to the storm and the death of Captain Ledburn? Friendship and loyalty are both important to any decent man, Mr. Fisk, but without integrity, you have little to give anyone."

"Yes, sir." Fisk stood straight-backed and faced Ravenswood without any apparent awe. He did not waste words. "Captain Ledburn made a wrong reading, or calculation, as to our position. Mr. Hooper told him he was incorrect, but the captain wouldn't listen."

"Do you know for yourself it was incorrect?" Ravenswood interrupted him. "Or are you taking Mr. Hooper's word for it?"

"At the time, I took Mr. Hooper's word for it, but later events proved him right. By then, we were much too close to the coast, and when the storm came, we were in danger of being driven onto the reefs, and—"

"How do you know that?" Again, Ravenswood interrupted him.

"Most of us here are landsmen. On the open sea, we would have no idea of where we were."

"You can see the white water, sir. And if the wind is offshore, you can hear the roar of it."

"I see. I can only imagine the fear that must cause a man. Would you survive such a wreck?"

"I never knew anyone as did."

"What happened?"

"The captain realized what he'd done and gave the order to shorten sail. But you couldn't send a man up the mast in weather like that. Mr. Hooper gave the order to come about and go before the wind. It was the only chance we had."

"Clearly, you survived."

"Yes, sir. But the captain was angry because he was scared, and confused. There was no time for an argument. Rain and wind and water . . . there was little chance of hearing what anyone said, any-how. She came about hard, and one of the sheets snapped loose and—"

"Sheets?"

"Ropes, sir. One of them snapped under the strain, the weight of the ship against the wind, and the end of it caught the captain. Swept him over to the side, but he clung on. Mr. Hooper went to haul him back, but Captain Ledburn was a heavy man, and Hooper couldn't hold on to him long enough to prevent him going over."

"Into the sea," Ravenswood confirmed.

"Yes, sir. We reported him lost at sea when we came back to Lon-don. For his family's sake, we didn't tell everyone it was his own mis-calculation that near lost us all our lives. The ship's owners wrote it as a mutiny, sir, but it wasn't. We went against a wrong order that would have killed the captain and lost the ship, too."

"Why would anyone report it as a mutiny?" Ravenswood asked, shaking his head in incredulity.

"Insurance, sir. That's a crime, so the ship owners are not to blame for it. Captain's miscalculations are their fault. They picked him for the captain."

"You sure of that?"

"You asked me why anyone would do it. I told you the only reason I know of. Captain Ledburn wasn't a bad man, sir, just didn't believe in himself enough to be able to admit when he was wrong."

There was a moment's silence, then Ravenswood nodded slowly. "Yes, indeed, Mr. Fisk. That may be the core of more tragedies than this. Who else knows of these events, so far as you are aware?"

"Most of us that were on the ship, and Captain Ledburn's family."

"Are you sure they know?"

"Yes, sir. I told them, sir. I took along with me other witnesses, but I wanted them to know the truth."

"When was that?"

"Just a few days ago, sir. I kept quiet before, as the captain wasn't a bad man, just weak. It was hard enough for them that they lost him. Didn't need to know the rest."

"What changed a few days ago?"

"Mr. Exeter found out about the incident and used it to make Miss Darwin lie, in order not to have Mr. Hooper hanged, sir. I suppose he looked it up. Anyone could have, if they knew the right people and wanted it bad enough."

"And would you lie in order to save Mr. Hooper from being hanged, Mr. Fisk?"

"I don't know, sir. I think nobody knows what he'll do if he's not been tested. But I don't have to. I was there and I told you the truth. Miss Darwin wasn't. And I suppose she would rather see a guilty man go free, like Mr. Exeter, than an innocent one be hanged, like Mr. Hooper. Doesn't the law say something like that?"

"Yes, Mr. Fisk, it does." Ravenswood agreed quietly. "In fact, it goes further. It says a dozen guilty men should go free rather than one innocent man be hanged. But in this case, we have only one guilty man, even though three people are dead, and it would have been four, if Mr. Doyle had taken the blame for the crime being tried. I have nothing further to ask you. Please remain where you are, in case Sir Oliver has questions for you."

Rathbone stood up slowly. He looked dazed. "My lord, I have

nothing to ask of this witness. Nor do I have any wish to recall Miss Darwin. I understand why she misled us. She was on the horns of an impossible dilemma. I, too, might have preferred to see a guilty man go free rather than an innocent man hanged, whether I loved him or not. I hope I believe sufficiently in myself and the ideals I hold to admit when I am wrong."

"Indeed, Sir Oliver, you have made it manifest that you do," the judge replied. "I also see no reason to recall Miss Darwin."

Exeter turned in the dock, leaning forward, his face contorted with rage and disbelief. "Liar!" he screamed. "Liars! All of you . . ."

The warders beside him yanked him back so sharply he cried out in pain, but they silenced him.

In the gallery, Hooper tentatively put his arm around Celia, and then—when she did not move away—a little more firmly.

Hester slid her hand into Monk's, and he held on to her as if she were a lifeline. He felt the light, smooth strength of it as she put her other hand over his as well.

ABOUT THE AUTHOR

ANNE PERRY is the bestselling author of two acclaimed series set in Victorian England: the William Monk novels, including *An Echo of Murder* and *Revenge in a Cold River*, and the Charlotte and Thomas Pitt novels, including *Murder on the Serpentine* and *Treachery at Lancaster Gate*. Her most recent series, set in Edwardian England, begins with *Twenty-one Days*. She is also the author of a series of five World War I novels, as well as sixteen holiday novels, most recently *A Christmas Revelation*, and a historical novel, *The Sheen on the Silk*, set in the Ottoman Empire. Anne Perry lives in Los Angeles.

anneperry.co.uk

To inquire about booking Anne Perry for a speaking engagement, please contact the Penguin Random House Speakers Bureau at speakers@penguinrandomhouse.com.

ABOUT THE TYPE

This book was set in Goudy Old Style, a typeface designed by Frederic William Goudy (1865–1947). Goudy began his career as a bookkeeper, but devoted the rest of his life to the pursuit of "recognized quality" in a printing type.

Goudy Old Style was produced in 1914 and was an instant bestseller for the foundry. It has generous curves and smooth, even color. It is regarded as one of Goudy's finest achievements.